CARVED FROM WOOD

BOOK TWO OF
CRAFTING HUMANITY

For Nonnie and Mar.

PART I

CHAPTER 1

James's HOLO bounced in his lap. He gripped the side of his seat to steady himself from the constant motion.

"Could you try to drive in a straight line?" Deck shouted weakly from the back of the bus. James glanced to look at his friend whose head hung limp in the aisle. "I don't have anything left in me," he added, clutching the garbage pail he adopted as a puke bucket. It emitted a revolting background odor counteracting the rust and aging paint permeating the air. Throw in eight unwashed bodies and James was sure a guest on their bus would not last long without their own vomit receptacle.

"Don't worry, Deck. Almost out of these mountains," Clint called back cheerfully. "These people drive like freaking maniacs huh?"

He finished his sentence swerving into oncoming traffic to avoid a mule cart and narrowly missed the ledge on the side of the road. He then careened back into the right lane almost colliding with a pickup truck overflowing with wooden crates.

James took a deep breath, concentrating on his HOLO screen, preferring it to the death-defying stunts. He was not used to the intense driving on the mountain roads and although queasy was glad his lunch remained in his stomach.

"I hate this," Deck mumbled, dry heaving into his bucket and collapsing in a jumble with his head in his arms.

"Suck it up, Deck. You'll be fine." Stacie clapped him on the thigh getting a tortured sigh from Deck as she gripped the faux leather seats and made her way to the front of the bus.

"How much longer? Seriously, this time, Clint, none of this *almost there* bullshit," she asked.

"Ten more minutes, honestly. Gotta stop for gas soon anyway," he replied, nodding at the dashboard.

"Sounds good."

Stacie pinballed her way down the aisle to James, flopping next to him as the bus went airborne, leaving them suspended for a second and crashing back to their depleted cushions the next. James rubbed his lower back grimacing. He didn't blame Deck for his misgivings about the bus.

"Find anything on there?" Stacie asked, pointing at James's HOLO.

"I think so," he said, pulling up the map and displaying his work from the morning.

"The majority of the Federation's military has pulled out south of this line," he said, pointing at an invisible boundary not far south of the former Panamanian border. "This is the choke point they're using. Shouldn't be a problem getting near there, but crossing could be trouble. Troops will be swarming the area, not to mention there's the distinct possibility the BZ has set up its own defensive positions. Add to it that we're technically AWOL while potentially being pursued by military police and we have an uphill battle on our hands."

"We've found our way through worse," Stacie said, taking control of the map and zooming in on the border. "I think we can make it. Just need to improvise."

"No doubt about that," James agreed, nodding.

Stacie dove back to her seat while James delved further into the 3D images searching for the easiest route.

This is going to be tricky, he thought scanning the dense rainforest separating them from their destination. *We don't want to go through there.* James shivered imagining an unchartered rainforest after dark and zoomed in again tracing routes around the park's edges while comparing them to suspected Federation troop positions.

South was always the destination. James knew that the second he decided to leave the Federation military. It was the best way to aid the war effort while maintaining independence from the central command… or at least that was James's opinion. During the first attack in the Northern Federation, James and the team had the added benefit of Brandt to advise, protect, and eventually sacrifice himself for them. The cities in the Southern Federation were not so lucky. The BZ did exactly as James and Brandt had imagined. They had decimated two cities on the East Coast and used them as doorways to flood the rest of the continent.

It was remarkable how simple the BZ's game plan was and more impressive how well it worked. Within a week of the cities' fall, reports were coming in about mass swaths of land on the southern continent succumbing to further attacks by the BZ army. The motherships, as James called them, moved along the coast fulfilling more of James's predictions, attacking major assets actively protected by the Federation's military. Power structures, harbors, inland mines, factories, energy production centers, and food depots were overrun by the BZ army. A combination of sheer numbers and an unprecedented amount of firepower, reduced cities to rubble while leaving their targets unscathed.

The unnecessary towns or cities were razed and, from what James witnessed over satellite images, adapted for use by the BZ army. At the tip of the continent lay sprawling operations centers, aircraft fields, barracks, training facilities, military hospitals, and structures too numerous to quantify erected at breakneck speed.

They were efficient, lethal, and destructive. The Federation was enough in the dark about their enemy that James was unable to tell how they would ever be able to fight back. He needed to learn more about them and the way to do that was to go to the source. So south it was.

He scanned the mountain pass routes, guessing as to whether some of the smaller paths would have Federation checkpoints. The whole experience was a crapshoot, but it was their new way of life. It was still crazy for James to think Jon had been here visiting family under two months ago. Now the roads leading north were never-ending chains of cars fleeing the coming invasion.

"Heading down, folks. Out of this in five more minutes, tops!" Clint yelled back to the team.

"So soon?" Kyle asked, perking up with a yawn.

"All right everyone, you know the drill. Keep your eyes peeled for Federation soldiers or activity. If we see them, we keep driving until… I guess we run out of fuel," Stacie said, giving Clint a stink eye.

"Those mountains burn gas faster than anything," Clint replied. "The Roaring Chameleon eats a lot."

"Goddamn death trap," Deck murmured, holding his head between his legs in the aisle, his height adding to the perpetual discomfort.

"Don't worry, buddy. I'll find something to help you once we stop," Bob said, sympathetically patting his shoulder. "You're gonna need fluids, man."

"I won't be able to pee for a month. I've got nothing left."

"That's a positive, huh?" Bob replied, sitting back in his seat, "Sit tight. Not much longer."

"Bullshit."

Their trip had started with a bang. They arrived at the base's airfield to find all the planes waiting to refuel. Clint selected the best option available, but it would only get them so far. The initial plan to lift another plane from an unsuspecting base and continue to trade planes the entire way to the Southern Federation had to be scrapped. Their starting fuel gauge was low enough that they were forced to perform an emergency landing. They bailed out an hour after leaving the compound in the middle of the desert.

Knowing the Federation would chase them with as many resources as it could muster, the team took off on foot due south straight through former Mexico. There, they made it to the coast and shacked up in a small town on the Pacific.

Over the course of two weeks, the team begged, borrowed, and stole anything they could to get them to where the BZ border started somewhere in Columbia.

They traded Federation gear to get a couple of old HOLOs and discovered a rusting minibus in a landfill. Clint spent five days and nights fixing the bus, sending the team on missions back into the dump looking for pieces until he restored the decaying piece of machinery. James regretted not looking harder for a better vehicle to get them through the mountainous terrain, but it did the trick and Kevin made the good point that no one would be looking for them in "this piece of crap".

Clint originally took Kevin's description of Stella, the name of his bus, to heart until Kevin explained it was because it looked like a heap of junk but worked, and that's what was important. To James' surprise, the explanation worked, and Clint changed the name from Stella to the Roaring Chameleon.

For the last three weeks and a day, they had been driving south following the coastline until they decided to head inland to avoid run-ins with Federation troops amassing along the oceanfront.

James turned his attention to the HOLO in his lap.

The map showed a village splayed out at the bottom of the mountains. A sparse town was split down the middle by the highway with a smattering of houses, a gas station, and a couple of food stands. More of a roadside attraction than an actual location, but it would work.

James needed to turn on the network drive they obtained in their HOLO trade, but he was nervous to try any long-term connection. Their activity on HOLOs could be tracked and even though they traded for newer models, the Federation would know the kinds of searches James and the team needed to perform. Searching was their easiest way to get found. It was especially dangerous when connected to the Federation's centralized systems, so he tried to minimize the time spent connected to any network. Until Jon could figure out a way to securely connect to the Federation drive and hack in unseen, they were forced to limit their connections to under a half hour at a time, once a day.

James shut his HOLO. He preferred to wait until he could think clearly about their next searches rather than use his connection for the day careening down the side of a mountain.

They had already compiled a series of maps for the Federation and plug-ins to overlay recent satellite images for updates. Once they stopped, James would work with Jon and Stacie to establish troop movements in the area. It was guesswork for now, but better than making stabs in the dark by himself.

James shoved the emitter into his bag and walked to the front of the bus, gripping the seats for balance, and took a seat behind Clint across from Jon and Kevin.

The road was leveling out by the second and the sticky humidity returned with the flattened landscape.

"You came here every summer?" Kevin asked Jon, staring out the window at a sprawling banana field.

"Yep, we lived in the capital but would visit during breaks from school to spend time with my abuela," Jon said. He was the only one unfazed by Clint's driving. His years traveling through the mountains with his family numbed him to the experience. They were all jealous, especially Deck.

"Did she live in one of these towns?" Clint asked, checking his rearview mirror.

"No, she was on the coast. She had too many fruit trees to count, a cow she adored, and chickens outnumbered people, ten to one. There were snakes, lizards, anteaters, monkeys, sloths, and more. You name the jungle animal, and it probably lived on her land."

"Sounds cool, man," Kevin said. He frowned and added, "Except for the snakes. Those are gross."

"Get used to it. You're in la tierra de serpientes," Jon said grinning.

Kevin gave him the finger, turning to examine their new homeland through the window.

"Three minutes out," Clint yelled to no one in particular.

James tapped Jon's arm. "Let's turn on the network, and make sure we're okay to stop."

Jon pulled out his HOLO emitter summoning the screen with a swipe. His fingers flitted about until he pulled up a map and, with a final flourish, populated it with their latest satellite feed.

James stood over his seat to get a closer look, zooming in on the town.

"Looks safe," he said, rotating the screen to check every angle. "When's this from?"

"Four days ago," Jon said, splitting his screen into a second monitor to examine the file details.

"Could you do a sweep of the neighboring towns?

"Will do."

"Good. While we're in town, download an updated sat file and keep working on the ghost program."

Jon sighed.

"What?"

"We can keep it up longer. We don't *need* the program to be built out first. I mean the Federation—" Jon started to explain as James cut him off.

"I know, I know. Humor me for now. We've made it this far sticking to our rules about the network. Once you've got the cloak around our connection, we can do what we want. Sound good?"

"You got it, boss."

"All right, good." James switched lanes, turning his attention to the front of the bus. "Clint, go straight to the gas station. Kevin, Stacie, you two come with me. Let's see if there's a place to stay. Bob, Kyle, check for network hubs and while you're at it, see if you can find some supplies."

A round of affirmative responses came from the team. James turned his attention to the back of the bus where Deck sat with his arms propped on his knees, his head bobbing up and down.

"Deck… you stay put, buddy," James said, giving Deck a less than encouraging thumbs-up, to which Deck replied with a weak wave proceeding to lean face-first against the windowpane.

The humidity smacked James in the face when he stepped off the bus. He could feel the stinging itch of his sweat glands flying open and moisture penetrated his shirt's fabric in seconds.

This is miserable, James thought, pulling at his shirt to unglue it from his torso. Beads of sweat gathered along his chin, and he wiped his jawline with the back of his hand scraping his skin on the five o'clock shadow condensing on his cheeks.

He followed Kevin and Stacie across the highway into the collection of buildings. The locals watched them, not hiding their open stares.

The residents of the area were old, very old with most of them sporting gray hair and sitting on porches in decaying furniture. The town looked as if it was fed from the residents' yards or supplied by the pulperia in the center of the building cluster. James approached one of the street vendors asking in broken Spanish if there was a place to stay for the night.

"Hola, señor. ¿Tiene un hotel aquí?" James knew his Spanish was close to unintelligible, even for the entry-level class he took in school, but the man understood and shook his head avoiding eye contact while backing away.

"Gracias," James said, waving politely. He turned back around to find Kyle and Bob had rejoined them.

"Not a lot here, huh?" James said with his hands on his hips, peering around their dead end.

"Not exactly," Bob replied. "We can buy a few bags of plantains for the trip. Better than going hungry."

James nodded his assent, sending Bob back to the pulperia for the plantains while the rest of the team made their way to the bus, dejected by their failure and not looking forward to another night on the dank, sweaty bus.

"This sucks," Kevin said, his stomach grumbling audibly. They leaned against the Chameleon's hood in a line and Kevin ticked off a summary of their situation on his fingers. "No food, no place to sleep, no way to connect to a network safely. Just a rusty tin can filled with the aroma of puke. Stupid fucking rainforest."

James glanced at his friends. The collective group had their hair grown out to an impressive level. Kevin's, whose hair was fashioned in a perpetual buzz cut, puffed out on top with the sides matted with lines of sweat while Kyle's normally flowing locks fell in greasy clumps along the sides of his face.

We look like we've been through it, James thought, waving a hand in front of his face to cool himself while the sun continued to heat the area like a soup can.

"So, what's the deal with this place?" Clint asked, walking from the back of the bus while wiping his hands on a rag. "We staying the night?"

"No good," Kyle replied. "Bob's getting some chips for dinner."

"So, the usual. Sounds great," Clint said, sitting heavily next to James on the bumper.

"How much was gas?" asked Stacie, taking a notebook and a pencil out of her pocket.

"About fifty dollars."

"Okay, not bad, but we're going to need more money if we want to make it all the way to the top of the southern continent."

"How much do we have left?" asked James.

"About a hundred fifty," Stacie replied.

"So that gets us…?" James said, trying to do the math in his head while hoping Stacie would bail him out.

"Nowhere close to the BlankZone is all I know," Clint said staring at the ground, "We're out of the mountains for now, but they'll pop up again. The Chameleon's not cheap to feed, man."

James saw Jon emerge from the bus with his HOLO pulled up.

"I've got the sat files updated. We're getting closer to the rest of the Federation's troops. Splitting them in half from the looks of it," he said, rotating the image to show the Federation's most recent positions.

"Goddammit, they're right on us," Kyle said, shaking his head.

"They don't know we're here, but we're going to need a more consistent connection. Every few days isn't enough," Jon said, looking at James.

"All right, let's take an hour here, then we'll hit the road."

"I'm gonna try to take a quick nap. Those mountains are exhausting!" Clint said, heading back into the bus.

"Where the hell is Bob? I am starving," Kevin said, grabbing his stomach.

"Relax, big man. He's crossing the street," Kyle said, playfully jabbing him in the shoulder.

"About fucking time," grumbled Kevin.

"I'm going to check on Deck," James said, following Clint through the folding doors ignoring Kevin's sour mood.

He walked to the back of the bus where he found Deck sprawled out on his seat with a forearm covering his eyes.

"How you doin', bud?" James asked, sitting on the bench across from him and slapping Deck's knee.

"I'm fading, James," Deck said in a weak voice.

"Bob's getting some plantains for dinner now. You think you can stomach some of those?"

"I'll try. I'll probably die first, but I'll try." He reached out his hand and gave James a weak thumbs-up before collapsing back on the seat.

"Dramatic much?" James mumbled, standing up.

He heard a muffled "fuck you" float from Deck while he walked to the door.

He stepped outside, pulling a cigarette from the pack stuffed in his pocket. He walked to the edge of the gas station and stared into the dense greenery through tendrils of smoke, listening to a stream of cars driving in the opposite direction from their destination.

Not for the first time, James wondered if he had made a wise decision. Was he leading his team to utter failure at the end of a path marred by an unpredictable future?

I guess that's the game we're playing here, he thought, *rolling the dice on unpredictable futures. This is the best way we can help right now. Nothing else to do, but throw ourselves into the middle of the action.* The decision, although morally correct, weighed on him every day.

He could see the goal in his mind—the BlankZone camps. They were headed in the right direction. That much James knew. Once they arrived though, he had no idea what to do first. The cities the BlankZone army erected were filled with enemy soldiers from end to end and grew exponentially every day. Reports he read emphasized the lack of details from the Federation's military heads, but James expected that.

Live satellite images, once shared with the civilian population were cut off. When they did release any images, large pieces of the satellite feeds were redacted with the Federation citing military necessity. James surmised the truth was more about limiting fear in the population. The team needed to figure out how they could learn more about their enemy while the Federation was no doubt losing more and more access to views of the BZ from the same satellite jammers they used overseas.

First things first though. The team needed supplies. This was the problem tormenting him as he lay awake at night sliding on his bus bench in a pool of sweat. They needed everything from new HOLO devices to bug nets. The closer they got to their destination, the worse their prospects to fill those needs became. There was no legal market to shop for military-grade equipment and the underground markets were too expensive. They needed some other way to get their gear or this trip was useless.

He finished his cigarette, flicking off the ember into a puddle. He turned around and headed back to the bus where he tossed the butt in an old coffee can they kept as an ashtray taped to the back of the bus.

Low snores greeted him as he walked down the side of the bus.

Glad someone's sleeping, James thought jealous of Clint. He waved to the rest of the team standing outside eating chips and kicking a pipa on the ground like a soccer ball.

"Let's hit the road. I'll drive tonight," James yelled.

He climbed the steps of the bus and flopped into the driver's seat, turning the engine on while he waited for everyone to join. At least on the road at night he'd be able to think through their scenario in quiet as long as Deck wasn't throwing up everywhere. James grimaced at the thought, leaning back in his seat watching the shadows lengthen in the equatorial dusk.

CHAPTER 2

James made up his mind. After driving eight hours in pitch-black, stopping once for a coffee, half a cigarette, and a long pee, James knew their best option was also the riskiest.

It's the only way, James thought, chewing his lip, the raw skin brushing against his tongue.

He knew he would get an earful from Stacie, but eventually, she'd realize it was their only hope. *Maybe she'll come up with something better,* he reasoned. James desperately hoped she would.

The darkness was beating the Chameleon's lights, at least that's how it appeared to James. He was happy to be on the road alone for once. Ever since starting their trip on the coastline, cars flowed in an unbreakable line headed north. Vehicles of all sizes filled with families, packed to the brim with everything they could carry, fled their homeland for the promise of safety.

Every day James pulled up new reports from survivors farther south. Their stories were all the same—fire, explosions, absolute destruction. The pictures were heartbreaking and steeled James's decision more. However, it was the soldiers he was most interested in learning about. The descriptions of the enemy, by those lucky enough to escape with their lives, were vague but matched his own experiences. Inhuman, taking orders at face value and carrying them out with a ruthless devotion to their mission. James remembered the soldiers coming off the ships from the BZ's transports, so intent on carrying out their destruction that they walked into flying bullets. The memories were unsettling, but their similarities to the survivors' reports meant he had not imagined their behavior. He needed answers.

James's eyelids drooped for the sixth time in as many minutes, and he looked for somewhere to pull over. He needed to rest. A clear-cut field opened to the right. He parked the ancient bus alongside a few trees lining the border of the property and turned off the ignition. He leaned back in the driver's seat pulling his hat over his eyes and breathed in the humid air seeping through the cracked driver's window.

BANG! BANG! BANG!

James awoke with a start and his hat fell off his face. Sun peeked over the tree line, and he rubbed his eyes regaining his senses.

BANG! BANG! BANG!

A hazy figure waved at James through the foggy glass, trying to get his attention. James swung the door open, and a man yelled at him in rapid Spanish James could not understand.

"¡Tienes que moverte! ¡Tienes que moverte! ¡Esta es mi granja! ¡Lárguense de mi tierra!
¡Vaya! ¡Vaya!" he shouted waving at James and pointing back at the road.

James held up his hands to apologize, "Sorry… siento. ¡Lo siento! I don't speak Spanish! Sorry!" James fumbled with the keys while the man continued to yell.

I need to learn the language down here, he thought as the engine roared to life.

"The hell is going on?" Deck shouted from the back. His sleep-lined face hung like a wet mop in the aisle with his hair drooping over his forehead. "What are you doing?"

"I think I parked on this guy's lawn. Or house? Or something? I don't know but he is pissed," James said, checking his mirrors, putting the bus in reverse and backing up, eliciting more frantic shouts from the man outside.

James stopped short, causing most of the team to fall off their seats.

A chorus of swears erupted when James put the bus into gear and sped forward, pulling around in a circle through the middle of the empty field and flying with a jolt back onto the road.

James glanced at the mirror and caught sight of the farmer waving a machete above his head and shaking his fist at the back of the bus.

Making friends everywhere, James thought.

"That was a new way to wake up," Kyle said, cracking his neck side to side. "What happened back there? Villagers chasing you off?"

"I've gotta learn the goddamn language is what happened," James said, his heartbeat steadying. "How'd you sleep?"

"About as well as you can on a bus in eighty-degree heat and 90% humidity," Kyle replied, wiping the sheen of sweat from his brow.

Jon joined them at the front, opening the last of the plantains. He offered the bag to Kyle while addressing James. "Pissing everyone off, huh?"

"I didn't know!" James said, looking over his shoulder accusingly. "Besides, where the hell were you? You're the only one that speaks Spanish fluently."

Jon waved him off while he finished a mouthful of plantains. "You were fine. Relax. How far did you make it last night?"

"Eight hours," James replied, reaching his hand out for breakfast. "No one else on the road. We must be on a route away from the migration."

"It sounded quieter," Kyle said, pulling up a downloaded

map on his HOLO. "We need gas again?" he asked scrolling along the road going south.

"We will. Besides I need a break from driving. Came up with a plan for how we can get supplies last night, but not sure if it's sane. Sleep will let me know."

"Oh, really?" Kyle said, arching his eyebrows. "In another twenty miles there should be a town where we can switch drivers."

"Sounds good. Get Clint ready to dr—" James was interrupted by a shout from the back.

"Fuck no! No, I do *not* want Clint driving yet," Deck yelled, his face, adamant at first, dropped to a pathetic expression. "James, please. I mean… have a heart."

James looked at him in the rearview mirror. "All right, buddy. Someone else will drive."

Deck nodded slumping in his seat.

James heard Clint grumble to himself, "Can't handle a little adventurous driving. Suit yourself…"

Four hours later, James was rested and ready to talk. Stacie had parked on the side of the road across the street from another highway town in the middle of nowhere.

James sat on the front bumper of the bus while the team rested among the grove of trees they had parked under. They passed a knife around to cut holes in the pipas they had picked that hung from the grove's branches.

"What'd you have for us James?" Stacie asked, bending to light her cigarette off the tip of Jon's, "What's the plan?"

"I don't think it's good," James said.

"That's not a promising start."

"I mean, it's risky."

"Go on."

James took a deep breath and started, "The Federation has shut down almost every public avenue necessary to learn about the BZ or their own troop movements. From satellite imaging to news reports, the Federation has blocked information. We're almost to the tip of the Southern Federation's primary landmass and it looks as if the black markets have dried up as everyone flees north, and anything worth a damn is going to cost an arm and a leg. We have zero intel on what's happening near the cities initially taken by the BZ and we're almost out of money."

"Are you trying to tell us why we're screwed?" Jon asked, looking up from where he sat with his elbows draped across his knees.

James ignored him, continuing his preamble. "We've seen Federation transports making their way south, too. Leadership is at least making the appearance of bolstering defenses."

A smattering of snorts interrupted him.

He held up his hands. "Regardless of whether that's true or not, we may be able to use them to our advantage."

James paused to scan the emotionless faces.

"It's well-established Jon can hack into anything. I think we should hack into the Federation's control center and get as many images as we can of the BZ's setup. We need a lay of the land and it seems like the only real way to do it." James paused again, searching the faces around him for signs of disagreement.

"James, I hate to say this, and you know I've got your back and all, but we've been saying we should do that for weeks now, pal," Deck said, his eyes narrowed, confused. "I mean it's great you agree but…"

James took a deep breath, "Right, and I still believe we should not hack them in any regular circumstance, but we need supplies. Desperately. If we're going to do anything about the BZ and their army, we need equipment. So, while we're inside their system we locate the nearest Federation troop camp. Find them. Steal as much gear as we can and hightail it to the BZ border."

The group did not speak. James leaned against the bumper and shoved his hands in his pockets. He expected some initial silent reflection time, but the quiet was stretching longer than anticipated.

"Okay…soooo you weren't okay with us hacking the Federation servers, buuuut you *are* fine committing highway robbery and becoming felons on top of AWOL soldiers." Deck stopped and looked around at the rest of the group for confirmation. "I mean, that's what I heard. Anyone else have comments or questions?"

"It's the only thing we can do," Kevin said, nodding.

"Agreed. It sucks, but we don't have another choice," Stacie said, making eye contact with James from across the circle. "In any other scenario, I'd say this is the stupidest idea I've ever heard."

"But?" James waited for Stacie to finish her statement.

"Just what I said. Any other circumstance, stupidest idea I've ever heard."

James breathed a sigh of relief. Confirmation from Stacie and Kevin was all he needed.

"So are we agreed?" he asked. "Riskiest plan we've ever made?"

A series of nods confirmed their acceptance. They had a plan.

"What now?" asked Kyle, pushing off the ground and pulling his leg behind him in a stretch.

"We need a strategy. Jon, how long will it take you to hack in and download those images from the Federation's servers?" Stacie asked. James watched while the wheels in her head moved, arranging the details in her mind.

"Depends on a lot of things—file size, connection stability, image resolution. I mean, I won't know until I get in there," Jon replied, counting off the items as he said them.

"How about a tenuous connection in the back of a bus, pulling the highest quality images possible, likely measured in terabytes?"

"In that case, about ten minutes to get into the server, five for some sleight of hand, an hour to download, and five more to leave with some pizazz."

"Pizazz?" Kevin asked.

"Yeah, pizazz, keep 'em guessing a little bit," Jon said, winking. When he noticed the concern etched on James and Stacie's faces he held up his hands defensively. "Relax. I'm going to set up a couple of false trails. Don't want them finding everything out immediately."

"That solves the first step," James said while he envisioned the next stages. "Now for the tricky part. Stealing everything."

"The fun part you mean," Deck said, his face interested in more than breaks from driving for the first time in weeks.

"Right, the fun part. We've got four major phases: infiltration, intel grab, supply grab, and extraction. Deck, you're going to run the infiltration and extraction with Bob. Kyle, Kevin, and Clint, locate the supplies and get them to a single spot for an easy exit. Stacie, we'll look for physical intel. Maps, hard drives, HOLO files, whatever we can find. We won't be able to get details together until Jon gives us a layout of the camp. Get in your teams and come up with what you need. We move out in a half hour. Any questions?"

"Rules of engagement?" Kevin asked.

"Friendlies, we surrender if we get caught, but maintain silence. If one of us gets caught, it doesn't mean we all did, so expect to be broken out." James looked around at the rest of the group who bobbed their heads accepting the fact that they may be military prisoners in the next twenty-four hours. "Jon, how long until you find a Federation camp?"

"Twelve minutes," Jon said, pulling out his HOLO emitter, the glowing screen springing to life.

"Right. Kevin, Kyle, anything you two need to prepare?" James asked, turning to the broad-shouldered men.

"Not that I can think of," Kyle said, glancing at Kevin and shrugging, "Just for Deck to get us in the door."

"Once we have a location, we need to move fast. After we connect, it's a slippery slope to ending up in a military prison."

Murmurs of agreement chorused around the circle. James became lost in his thoughts about how they might pull this whole thing off when Clint spoke.

"Listen, you get me a location within a hundred miles of here and I can get us there in under seventy minutes," he said casually.

"Fuck no! No. No. No." Deck stood up, about to stomp his feet. "I know for a goddamn fact you need me to pull all this shit off so absolutely fucking not will we let Clint take us on another thrill ride. I will not do it. I won't be able to do it. I mean it. No." Deck stopped, his chest heaving from yelling so much, but James could tell Deck knew he was against the lot. "Please, guys, I can't. I'll throw up everywhere. Again! I mean, I can't take this shit." His shoulders slumped and Bob clapped him on the back.

"There, there, buddy. I'll give you some of the weed I took from the compound. Should help with that little tummy of yours." Bob patted his stomach and Deck's face drooped further.

"Great, not only will I have motion sickness, but my doctor is going to send me spiraling down a paranoid anxiety tunnel for the trip. This gets worse and worse."

"Relax, Deck. It'll be fine and you're right. We will need you, but let's work on getting those coordinates up. Jon, it's your play." James stood and anticipatory adrenaline kicked into low gear humming through his limbs.

Fifteen minutes later, Jon located a Federation camp. The clock started.

Clint sped them in the direction of their supply target while the rest of the team crowded around Jon's seat to get their first glimpse of Federation intel in months. Within minutes they had a laundry list of items in the camp ripe for the picking. HOLO emitters, combat suits, skeleton shelters, water purifiers, mechanic's tools, prefab IEDs, MREs, and weapons galore. It was all there. Even new vehicles to swap with the Chameleon. James's stomach tightened. They would need to do everything perfectly or their lives would be spent in Federation holding cells.

The sun had set by the time they neared their target. Taking extra precautions, they disembarked from the bus five miles away and walked to the Federation encampment. They cut a hole in the vegetation and started into the forest.

James padded behind Deck who, after enduring most of the trip with his eyes closed, was in a zone. The jungle was anything but quiet. Birds, insects, reptiles, and even the plants themselves covered their approach with noisy bedtime routines. James brushed against the edge of a banana leaf and felt a long tubular object fall across his arm. It took all the inner calm he possessed not to scream only to realize it was a vine hanging from a tree branch above.

Keep going, James thought gritting his teeth.

Sweat was soaking through in spots on James's chest when Deck held up a hand for everyone to stop. They were in a clearing and the moon provided light through the interwoven treetops circling their position.

"We're about a kilometer from the camp," Deck said to James in a subdued voice, showing him their location on the map from their intel download. "This looks like as good a headquarters as any."

James nodded and motioned for the rest of the group to rest. It had been decided that he and Deck would scope out the base. They headed out again into the pitch-black night smacking mosquitos off their arms.

After what seemed like another interminable trek through a bug-filled sauna, light filtered through the jungle wall and Deck held up a hand to stop. He walked to the edge of the shrubbery and motioned for James to join him. They crouched and peeled back the oversized palm fronds obscuring the camp from view.

"Hot damn," Deck whispered under his breath. "This is more than I expected."

An impeccably well-established, portable military headquarters lay in front of them. Floodlights stood in a wide circle around the camp at what James guessed to be fifty yard increments bathing the scene in light. Soldiers were interspersed along the edge of the base on guard duty covering every inch of the encampment with a pair of eyes. Inside the defensive ring were ribbed canvas buildings and lines of various military vehicles. The remaining soldiers not actively watching the perimeter milled about or performed their assigned duties under the flood lights.

"How are we supposed to get in there?" Deck asked, searching around the circle.

"It's early. Things will quiet in a couple of hours," James replied. "Let's get back to the others and have them come in pairs to check out the scene. The more eyes we have on this the better."

James started to head back when Deck spoke up behind him.

"Well, let me just…"

James turned around in time to see Deck break through the foliage and sprint into the shadows.

What the hell is he doing? James's heart pounded as he walked back to the edge of the forest and pushed his face through the leaves.

Deck stayed inside the shadow line, crouched low to the ground while he moved to one of the buildings throwing himself against the rear of the tent. He stood with his back to the wall inching to the side and peering into the center of the camp. His head remained tucked around the side of the building for what felt like an eternity before he turned back to face James. He motioned to James with the sign language they had used during their time in Croyton's training compound:

Undetected. Active campsite, multiple teams, mixed Federation troops. Coming back.

James held his breath while Deck checked around the corner again and disappeared into the shadows. He broke through the edge of the foliage moments later without disturbing a leaf.

How does he do that? James thought, shaking his head and waving for Deck to follow him back to the team.

They waded through the underbrush slapping at real and imagined bugs until they came upon the clearing where the rest of the team waited.

"We've got a bunch of time, folks," Deck said, leaning against a palm tree and sliding to the ground. "The whole damn camp's awake."

"He's right. Good time for everyone to scout the area. We need to be ready once our moment comes," James said, fanning his face with his shirt and wishing he had brought more water.

"They have as many as it said? Two hundred or more?" Jon asked.

"I'd err on the more side. From what I saw, they've got tanks, Humvees, a couple of choppers, transport trucks, the works. Close to dinner time though. Everyone's going in and out of one tent together," Deck responded, grabbing a banana leaf from a nearby bush to use as a fan. "Hot work doing recon in the jungle."

"How close were you?" Stacie asked, squinting her eyes.

"Got right in there. Those guards ain't worth shit. I made it through the light's blind spots and posted up behind one of their tents. It's an impressive setup."

"You are one risky motherfucker," Clint said, shaking his head and pointing at Kyle and Kevin. "You two want to go check it out? Might take a little bit of time to get our bearings in there."

"Let's do it," Kyle said, standing and shaking out his arms.

Kevin nodded in reply and cracked his neck.

"Be careful and stay behind the brush line. Only need one of us stupid enough to put an ear against a hornet's nest," James said, glancing in Deck's direction.

"Geez, try to do something for the good of the group and get smacked in the mouth for it. Next time you go. I'm gonna get some shut-eye before this dance kicks off." With that, Deck put his head back and closed his eyes.

"Not a bad idea," James said, looking at the rest of the group. "Those not on recon duty, get some sleep. I'll take first watch."

It didn't take long for the rest of the group to drift off. James sat in the middle of the woods, the stillness and noise a paradox he could not wrap his mind around. Night intensified the sounds. Everything hummed, rattled, or chirped, but nothing moved. The eeriness of it kept James on high alert.

Aromas were more intense in the dark than in the daylight hours. The sun evaporated the scent of the flora and his nasal passages filled with the liquid floating in the air. At night those smells came alive. The water sitting on leaf pedals and tree branches brought the darkness to life and it was as if James could find his way through the lush greenery following his nose.

An hour later the first recon team returned.

"They're packing in for the night, we'll be able to make our move soon," Kyle said surrounded by Clint and Kevin.

James nodded. "Sounds good. Kevin, can you take watch while I grab some sleep? Kyle, wake up Stacie, Bob, and Jon. They can do their recon and keep an eye on the camp. When they're done, we make our move."

Silent agreement answered James, and Kyle went to wake the others.

"Night, man, at least for a little while. Before the fun begins," Clint said with a wink, slumping at the foot of a tree close to Deck's.

James shut his eyes. It took a second for his body to fully relax, but he fell hard into sleep to be woken a moment later by a sharp jab in the side.

"They're asleep. Let's go."

Bob's lean face and side-swept hair were outlined in the moonlight.

"How long was I out?" James asked, holding out a hand to Bob.

Bob grasped his hand and pulled him to his feet. James brushed his shirt and pants off with his hands, hoping no insects had burrowed in his clothes.

"Couple of hours, but the camp's quiet. Deck's already there. Said it's time to move."

James nodded. "Lead the way."

They trekked through the woods until the familiar glow of dimmed floodlights seeped through the foliage. The rest of the team was crouched around Deck who sat in the middle of them.

"You ready?" he asked James.

"Good to go. Everyone has their targets?" James saw the heads bob around him. They were prepared.

"Stacie, I'm following your lead. Deck, you have point and command. Once we get into camp, gather supplies and get the hell out of there as fast as possible. Remember rules of engagement—we surrender before we attack. Got it?"

More nods greeted the end of the command.

"Follow exactly in my footsteps," Deck said, eyeing everyone in the circle. "This isn't hard, but we need to be precise. Once we're in, things only get harder so start slow."

Without hesitation, Deck turned to the wall of plant life, peeled back the first overgrown leaf, and stepped into the opening between the forest and the campsite.

James and the team watched Deck in a crouched run hovering in the dark spaces between the light areas to the back of the first tent. When he arrived, he turned and signed to the rest of the group:

Next up.

Stacie did not give anyone else the chance to go ahead of her and within seconds her back was against the wall next to Deck. Another sign from Deck signaled it was James's turn to go.

Why the hell did I have to follow Stacie, he thought tensing his stomach muscles, crouching as low as his body would allow, and sprinting to the edge of the camp. His heartbeat remained taut while he walked the tightrope of slim shadows under the glare of the floodlights until he stood shoulder-to-shoulder with Stacie. Deck signed to them:

You two get the intel. I'll handle the rest of the team.

Stacie and James nodded in unison and walked to the edge of the tent. Stacie held up her hand to stop and in one swift motion brought it down. Time to move.

James followed her, sticking close to the shadows. They reached the front of the tent.

No sentry, thank God, James thought, and Stacie guided them farther into camp. They discovered a natural hiding place behind racks of ion shield emitters where they could regroup to locate intel. James scanned the tents. Deck wasn't kidding about erring on the more side. Four barracks stood side by side on one half of the camp while the outer ring housed functional buildings indicated by their standard Federation insignias etched into the front flaps. Vehicles were lined up in an orderly fashion, their headlights gleaming in the dimmed lighting. Beyond the barracks lay a long flat strip of asphalt accompanied by a tower with a beacon alternating white and green flashes.

Do they have a runway? James thought, wondering how temporary this camp actually was.

He felt a tap on his arm and Stacie pointed at one of the tents. It looked like nothing at first, but when James looked closer, he saw the telltale generators stacked outside its doors likely there to fuel HOLO emitters. The front flap bore a compass rose with swords as the directional points indicating intelligence in Federation icons.

That's where we need to start, James thought, scanning the area around the tent and evaluating their options to move closer.

Stacie placed her hand on top of one of the shield emitters and James knelt next to her ready to sprint when he was blinded by light accompanied by a loud *CRACK*.

James reacted, dropping flat behind the emitters. He reached out, finding Stacie's shoulder, rolling her behind the shield with him. He regained his vision while purple and blue dots popped up in his sight line. He shifted another one of the emitters in front of him while Stacie grabbed the other, penning them inside the bunch. Overhead sirens blared and the shouts of a military camp coming to life roared around them.

Someone must have tripped an alarm. They woke up the entire camp.

His hands curled into fists and his leg muscles tensed ready to spring.

Stacie leaned over and whispered in his ear above the cacophony and chaos surrounding them, "We're fucked."

CHAPTER 3

It was over.

That was the thought streaming through James's mind as the camp blew up into a well-organized monster. All they worked for, the pools of sweat he slept in on the Chameleon, the hordes of mosquitoes they battled, the dusty towns, empty stores, and hours of endless highway punctuated by an odor of dried vomit in the background. For what? For nothing. It was over.

James inched nearer to Stacie pulling the shield packs closer to his body to block them from the buzz of activity surrounding their hiding place. It would be of no use though.

The loudspeaker's wail let out one last shriek then shut off, leaving an eerie silence in its wake. The camp was awake. Troop movements were everywhere, no doubt directed by silent instructions through HOLOs telling soldiers the best way to imprison the forces caught breaking into their HQ.

I wonder who it was, James thought, looking at the sky to see the perimeter floodlights turn on in the distance, their bursts of light complemented by more cracking noises. *Independent solar generators, I bet,* James thought idly, impressed by the level of tech they were carrying down here. *Maybe the Federation cares after all.*

His positive impression of the Federation was interrupted by a rumble underfoot as a mammoth winged shape passed over the top of the camp, whipping dust into his eyes.

"Sonofabitch," snarled a passing voice. "Why the hell can't they land that thing from the other side?!"

"Quit bitchin', Arnold."

"Yes, ma'am."

"Perez, Calcetto, run final checks on the barracks. Thomas, you're with me."

A chorus of affirmative responses followed the orders.

What the hell is going on? James thought questioning his initial belief that the team had been found.

He glanced at Stacie who shrugged, looking perplexed. She put a finger to her lips and her other hand to her ear.

James listened for context to the sudden troop movement, but the only sounds in the camp were the shuffling of feet.

"How're we looking, Perez?" The commander's voice broke through the monotony.

"Barracks A and B are cleared, ma'am."

"Good. Calcetto?"

"C and D cleared, too."

"Excellent. Thomas, where are we with loading the planes?"

"All ground troops are lined up for the transport ships. Should be on in the next ten minutes. We have five escort fighters circling above with two HOLO drones on top. We're good to go."

"Great. Let's get outta here."

"Are we going to leave all this behind, ma'am?" Perez asked.

"You bet. No time to pack up. Orders are to abandon posts and head north immediately. We need to get ready for when they mobilize. This… this is energy we can't afford to spend."

"But Captain Armstrong, isn't this leaving them extra gear and intel?"

"Don't worry. We're not about to leave a weapons cache for them. Drones will escort us out and come back to take care of everything we leave behind. Should take us an hour until they can turn back around. The intel we have on the ground is going to be useless by the time we get North. Now, unless there's something I may be missing, can you all get the hell on one of those planes?"

Shuffling feet greeted the order and James held his breath until he was sure no one remained. What felt like an hour later, the engines from two transport ships roared overhead creating dust tornados in their enclosure. Particles of dirt stung James's eyes. He didn't care if it blinded him.

How in God's name did they get this lucky? James held his breath, not believing their fortune.

When the planes' noise dissipated, James and Stacie nodded at each other and pushed away the shields. For a second, he thought this was all a ploy when he saw two people standing in front of him next to a truck. It took him a second to recognize Deck and Bob looking into the sky and shaking their heads.

"Think, Bob, if they had been driving out of here, we would be fucked," Deck said, his voice in awe.

"This close," Bob said, holding his fingers an inch apart. "What a world."

"No time to watch the stars. We've gotta move," James broke in, startling the two would-be thieves.

"Where'd you come from?" Deck asked, confused.

"We were hiding behind the shield pods. Jumped into the back of a truck?" Stacie asked, digging through a pallet of boxes and pulled two off the top to inspect.

"Got caught in the open when the lights flipped on," Deck said, nodding and walking over to help her. "Thank God they were flying."

"No shit." Stacie flung open the top to one of the cases revealing two combat vests along with tactical glasses and earpieces. "Jackpot," she murmured.

Deck flung open another case pulling out survival kits with both hands. "Hot damn." He whistled. "Can't believe they're going to blow all this shit up."

James, still shocked by their good luck was knocked back to reality. The drones were returning in an hour.

"Let's break up and get everything together that we can. Bob, hit those med tents. Deck, gather survival equipment. Stacie, pull any intel we can find on our original target. Where are Kyle, Clint, and Kevin?"

"Over here," Kyle said, walking out from between two of the canvas tents. "Got stuck behind the buildings."

"Glad you all made it," James said, as the other three rushed off to collect supplies. "Clint, take a look at the vehicles. Pick a few that we can take. Maybe get dirt bikes to put in the back of a truck and something armored, dealer's choice."

"Roger that."

"Kyle and Kevin, you two oversee weapons and ammo. I want us to have a full armory."

"You got it, boss," Kevin said, greedily eyeing two tents with crossed rifles on their flaps next to the barracks. "I know where to start."

James glanced around his immediate area and pulled a HOLO emitter from a box outside the intel tent. He found the clock setting and blew the screen up as large as he could starting a countdown from thirty minutes.

"I'm going to grab Jon," James raised his voice to accommodate the open space and the team turned to him or poked their heads out of the door where they were working. He pointed at the glowing clock screen while searching the faces of the rest of the team. "Clint's picking out a truck. We have a half hour from this second until I want it fully stocked and ready to go. Sound good?"

A series of "yes," "you got it," and one "yes, chef" followed James while he went to retrieve their techie.

The glow from a HOLO backlighting the forest's edge was all James needed to find Jon. *He must have put the pieces together,* James thought, breaking through the foliage. Jon sat on the ground, his eyes staring intently at the hovering screen.

"Give me a sec," Jon said, not breaking eye contact with the HOLO.

James waited. He took a deep breath, the humid jungle air mingling with decaying leaves filled his mouth and was replaced by his own stale breath when he exhaled. Jon's eyes stopped flitting about the screen, and he collapsed the HOLO into its emitter and reached out a hand.

"I got it."

"Got what?" James asked, pulling Jon to his feet.

"Their battle strategy. I got my connection up before they flew off to avoid any sort of mismatched geo-location on their servers. I found their primary drives and in it their strategy," He took a breath and wiped the sweat from his brow.

"What'd you find?"

"They're pulling out. Everything, man. Anything below the Northern Federation is being abandoned. All eggs in the northern basket."

The wind left James's lungs.

"They're leaving?"

"Yep. They made the order to abandon the South and consolidate all forces in the North. They're leaving the border open for the next year, barring any major attack, and they're shutting down. James, we may not be in the Federation anymore."

James was having trouble comprehending the move. He never thought they would just leave the BZ to build whatever they wished. What the hell was going on?

"We'll talk about this more on the road. We've gotta move. Those drones are coming back in an hour."

"Already started a tracker on my HOLO. Looks like they're still escorting the planes."

"Well, let's make sure we use that time to get everything packed."

"You got it."

Jon clapped him on the shoulder and began walking to the camp when James remembered Jon's whole family was here.

"Jon, your family… what can we do? Where are they?" James asked, his mind racing, planning a detour to pull Jon's family out.

Jon turned back and put his hands up. "Tranquilo, tranquilo. I checked them out. They're already up North. We talked about what to do before I left for camp."

James's heart steadied again. "Good, good…"

"Thanks for asking though. I hid my prints, by the way, and left a little mess for them to clean up," Jon said, winking. "Serves 'em right… cowards."

James grinned as Jon broke through the leaf cover, illuminating the woods behind him with a column of light.

James stood in the crowded jungle space alone for a moment, his mind turning over what Jon had told him. Leaving the South behind? They weren't even going to try and put up an offensive attack, let the aggressor come to them… again? What were they thinking? An entire continent would be devoured.

Nothing made sense.

Stop it, James thought, shaking his head. *You have work to do*. He pushed the new information aside until he could concentrate on it later. They needed to focus on the present and get enough supplies to sustain them for as long as possible.

When James arrived back on base, the team was either loading gear into the vehicles or pulling more equipment from various tents. He scanned the group and noticed Stacie was nowhere to be found. Kevin dropped two tan duffel bags in the back of the canvas-covered truck.

"Hey, Kev, where's Stacie?" James asked.

"She's looking at intel over there," Kevin replied, pointing at the glowing blue tent set up opposite the barracks.

"Thanks. Need any help here?"

"All good. Organized camp made for easy pickings. Each vehicle has a little bit of everything, but we also broke it down by who would be where. We have med supplies, seeds, growing equipment, and one of the water purifiers in the Humvee. Bob and I will take that one. The truck has ammo, three dirt bikes, weapons, a couple of shields, and two solar generators. We gave that one to Kyle and Clint. Then we'll load the two Jeeps with tech equipment, some smaller generators, survival kits, MREs, HOLO emitters, solar battery packs, and anything else I can stuff in the top loaders. Those are for you, Stacie, Deck, and Jon."

"Nice work," James said, impressed.

"You got it," Kevin said with a thumbs-up turning back to load more into the truck. "Tell Stacie to hurry up, will ya? We're running out of space."

"Will do," James said and made his way to the intel tent.

He entered the front door and was met by the stale air associated with cooling electric parts, decidedly plastic and recycled. Stacie stood with a hovering control panel in front of six floating screens. The top three were composed of maps while the bottom three were data chunks and lines of dense code.

"Looks like we hit the lotto," James spoke up from behind. Stacie barely nodded, acknowledging his presence.

"Lotto is right. They've got everything here. Some of these HOLOs are air-gapped, too. Information Jon wouldn't be able to pull."

"Don't tell him that."

"Well, it's a fact," Stacie said, reaching out her hand and pulling one of the maps towards them. "This is from three hours ago. It's the current troop locations of the BZ. The other two screens at the top show them a week and two weeks ago. Take a look at this." Stacie swiped across the top screens. The images she had pulled of the camps shifted to a barren landscape with the BZ visible at the edge of the landmass. "This was four months ago." She flicked her wrist and pulled another series of time-stamped maps. "This was two months ago. They move fast, huh?"

James nodded numbly in response. The stark difference in the area over the span of two months let alone four was remarkable. The small towns and snaking roadways were blown away, replaced by the sprawling bases James was all too familiar with after studying them in agonizing detail under Croyton's tutelage.

How do they do this? He thought.

"They're settling in a little bit now, but that doesn't explain why the Federation would pull everything out," Stacie added with her arms across her chest.

"Covering up the fact that they don't have a plan?"

"Maybe. Seems like that's us projecting a little."

"Fair enough. What do you think the BZ's doing there?"

"Too early to tell. I've got backups of the maps. I'll study them some more and figure out what they're doing. Could be they're building forces before they go for the border, but I want to get a feel for how these changed. Get some clues on their plans."

"And what about the bottom screens? What's all that data?"

"Bizarre and damn frustrating," Stacie said in a huff.

"Care to elaborate?"

"Can't yet. It's encrypted. I want Jon to look at it."

James nodded. "Pull together everything else you need. We're out in ten."

"Already done. Everything's been copied onto three different air-gapped HOLOs, one in each Jeep, and another in the Humvee. Might be overkill, but I'm not risking anything at this point."

"Good work and smart move. Let's head out."

Stacie skimmed her fingers over the light-based controls. A dialogue box asking if she wanted to corrupt all files appeared across the screens. She tapped it without hesitation and led the way out of the tent.

James joined Bob and Kevin carrying crates from the armory tents to the back of the truck where Kyle and Jon organized the content. After three of four trips, the truck was loaded to capacity and James had to stop Clint from wheeling on an ATV he had found near the dirt bikes.

The team met in a circle next to the assembled vehicles.

"Driving teams are Kevin and Bob in the Humvee, Stacie and Jon in one of the Jeeps, Deck and James in the other, and finally Clint and me in the truck. Any questions?" Kyle asked, looking at the group.

"Which way are we going?" Deck asked, glancing at James.

"Let's take care of the Chameleon first, then we hit the road," James answered.

"That doesn't answer my question."

"Head west, we'll hug the coast, avoid those mountains in the interior, and make our way South," James said, getting a series of nods from the rest of the team.

"All right, let's go folks." Kyle clapped his hands together and swung himself athletically into the passenger seat of the truck.

James settled into the driver's side seat of the Jeep. Deck handed him an earpiece with a wrist control.

"Pretty crazy tech they had here. Even Jon was impressed," Deck said, relaxing in the passenger seat. "They were prepping for something. Makes it weird they pulled out so quickly."

James nodded, adjusting the device in his ear, feeling it conform to the canal.

"None of this shit makes sense."

"It did before?" Deck asked in mock affront.

"Yeah, yeah, yeah," James said, following the release of Clint's brake lights.

When they reached the Chameleon, James and the team unloaded their personal rucksacks from the musty interior. When the bus was empty they stood in a line surveying the rusted-out bus.

James smelled the dried sweat and lingering aroma of Deck's puke just looking at the relic. He realized he was getting nostalgic for the bus somehow. It was strange to him how the difficult times were the moments he never knew he'd miss.

"She did well, huh?" Clint said to no one, admiring his salvaged love with a tenderness normally reserved for children.

"Sure did, pal," Kyle said, placing a supportive hand on his friend's shoulder. "Should cover her up though. Don't want to risk those drones seeing anything."

"Good call," James said. He turned to Jon. "How much time do we have left?"

"Twenty minutes," Jon replied, checking his HOLO.

"Pull the vehicles under the canopy, cut banana leaves to cover the bus's top, take off the wheels, and siphon off as much gas as possible." James gave orders while he lifted a machete from the back of the truck, throwing an extra one to Deck.

The rest of the team acted on instinct, breaking themselves into groups, picking up machetes, wrenches, and tubes, or hopping into driver seats without further instruction. Within fifteen minutes the Chameleon's tires were loaded into the back of the truck along with the siphoned gasoline and the body of the bus was covered in banana leaves, Spanish moss, and palm fronds. Some yellow poked through various spaces between the green boughs, but James was impressed with their work.

"Nice job, everyone," James said. "Care to say a few words, Clint?"

"You were a beast out there and we all owe you a lot. Thanks, man."

Clint patted the front of the bus.

"Thanks for helping me lose five pounds in water weight every day, you hell beast," Deck mumbled, receiving a swift jab in the side from Stacie's elbow.

"Thank you, Clint," James said. "Jon, can we see what's happening?"

"Sure can. We're still cloaked by the base's network. Two drones en route. Everything else is miles away."

"How far out?"

"Should be twenty seconds."

The team turned as one in the direction of the camp.

Two flashes burst above the tree line and heat washed over them. A mushrooming flame followed, capped off by a dense funnel of smoke obscuring the night sky. The smoke was silky black against the starry backdrop and the scent of burning plastic, metal, and glass wafted through the group. James glanced at Jon who held up a thumb. They were good to go.

"Let's take off," James said, patting Clint on the back.

"Yep, about that time, I guess," Deck said a bit too cheerfully, getting an eye from Clint.

"We'll take lead first," Stacie said. "What's our comms channel?"

"Stay on delta-three for now," Kyle replied tuning the display for his earpiece on his wrist control. "Jon, can you encrypt that channel for us?"

"You got it, man. Stacie, you're driving first."

"Works for me."

"We'll rotate lead car and drivers every four hours. Sound good?" James said, making his way to the driver's side of the Jeep.

"West still?" Jon asked, his fingertips tapping a HOLO keyboard.

"Until we hit the coast."

"Got it."

"Other questions?" James asked, eyeing the group.

Silence greeted him and James nodded in response.

"See you all in four hours."

James and Deck closed the doors to their assigned Jeep. James was driving first, and Deck settled himself into the passenger seat, rolling up a survival suit to use as a neck rest.

"Let's hit it, boss," Deck said, already closing his eyes.

"You're gonna sleep the whole ride?"

"You bet I am. I've been up for hours, and let's not forget I was the one running that whole raid back there. Very stressful, James. I need my rest."

"Oh, Christ, go to sleep," James said, rolling his eyes.

"Don't miss me too much," Deck said as he closed his eyes.

"I'll try not to," James said, pulling in line behind the truck, rolling through the ditch and back onto the empty road headed towards a brightening horizon.

"Here we go again," James mumbled to himself.

"Could you keep it down a bit?" Deck said, his eyes covered with one of the arms from the tactical suit. "Your comments are… distracting."

James slapped him in the chest and Deck buckled over.

"No need for that!"

James shook his head, wishing he'd been given a different driving companion.

"Maybe we should have put you with Clint?" James said, egging Deck on.

"Do not say that. Not even as a joke," Deck replied, the playfulness in his voice replaced with a new edge, sharpened by anxiety.

James grinned, realizing the quiet would be nice.

CHAPTER 4

The dinner table was still James's favorite place to visit his family in his memories.

They were crystal-clear, sitting at their seats, never quiet, always a show, sometimes loud enough that James thought the neighbors might say something in the morning. His mother and father alternated sitting at the head of the table depending on who cooked dinner that night.

His mother created sensational meals with a complex array of spices, herbs, flavors, cooking methods, and cultures filling the plate. She measured every cup, slice, and pour with a delicate sense of precision. Her kitchen was organized with definitive processes and steps to produce the perfect meal.

His father took a less careful approach, cooking as simply as he could, and nailing it each time. From measuring temperature with his palm on a charcoal grill to allowing a dish to warm while the oven pre-heated with an almost concerning lack of thought. But James was never disappointed by the outcome. Steaks cooked to rare perfection, an egg casserole that made James salivate, or a basic stack of pancakes swimming in syrup and butter, meals were always a treat.

His parents' cooking techniques could not have been more opposite, science versus art battling at their most basic forms. However, the dinner table was where they clicked. Stories flew back and forth with ease. They memorized dueling punchlines or listened with rapt attention to a story the other had not or pretended not to have heard. Those moments not only defined the unique differences between art and science but showed how much they needed each other to foster excellence. He smiled, remembering the laughing, bickering, yelling, crying, singing, and chanting throughout the years.

He and his siblings delivered their supporting roles without hesitation. James and Mar supplied sarcasm-laden comments to balance the bravado of his parents. Meanwhile, Michael and Caitlin fed off the energy of the room, soaking up the moments and spitting them back out in yells and shouts more suitable for a schoolyard fight than a dinner table.

The thoughts of noise and chaos brought back memories of the mess hall at basic training. Two hundred trainees and dozens of officers eating in a tile-covered room where sound rebounded and resounded with increasing velocity. The steam-laden atmosphere boosted the chaos in the enclosed space. Conversations, scraping chairs, crinkling plastic cups, simmering burgers, and pizza ovens slamming shut. The noises coalesced to recreate an environment filled with disorienting, hectic energy. He thought of the letter from his dad sitting in the back of his rucksack, always tugging at the back of his mind for further direction.

It'll be there when I need it, he thought, pushing it to its rightful place back in the recess of his conscious.

It was hard to relive those parts of his memory. He had been so consumed by the thought of failure leading to the downfall of the Federation and all those living there that he had not been able to focus on much else. Now, they had options, they had a plan, and they could do what they had wanted from the start—learn as much as they could about the BlankZone and find their weakness. *Hopefully more than one,* James thought, a mental wish he kept repeating.

James glanced at the clock. Half an hour to go. Deck was still asleep in the passenger's seat, his shirt over his face, occasional snores breaking the silence.

The road was empty. Jon had put them on a path along the edge of a former national park and James was fascinated by the jungle spilling onto the roadway. Monkeys hung high in the branches, weaving across the habitually wet road, the ground revealing fat snakes bathing in sunspots poking through the trees.

This is a different world, James reflected, wondering what else the foliage hid, imagining the life teeming at the edges of the trees, kept at bay by a strip of asphalt.

"Hey, coming up on a break soon. Where should we pull over?" Kevin's voice came through James's earpiece.

"There's a junction in the road forty miles from here. Let's stop there and figure out what's next," Jon replied.

"Sounds good."

James was left in silence again and he put his window down to let the humid forest atmosphere wash away the musk oozing off their bodies. The air left behind the scent of fresh leaves and wet earth.

That's a nice change, he thought. *Better than inhaling the odor of two people who haven't changed their clothes in days or washed properly since before their ride on the Chameleon.* He counted back the days since he stood under a spigot of water and realized his last shower had been more than fifty days ago.

Fifty days. That's disgusting, James thought. His skin itched thinking about it.

For fifty days he and the team were forced to splash cold water on their bodies from rivers under random bridges all while keeping an eye out for crocodiles hunting their murky territory.

A shower is number one on the list, James promised himself, and he scratched his ribcage subconsciously.

When they pulled over at the junction, Jon and Stacie were standing outside their Jeep with two HOLO screens floating in front of them. Clint lay against the truck's front tire.

Kyle stretched beside him, and Bob and Kevin were busy rummaging through the back of the Humvee.

James left behind a slow-waking Deck who had told James to get the hell away when James hit him in the chest as a wake-up.

"How's everyone feeling?" James asked, getting a few thumbs-up and distracted mumbles from Stacie and Jon. He walked over to the two standing in front of their HOLO screens and stood behind them.

They were combing through the data Stacie pulled from the camp. Large chunks of code separated into strings and paragraphs showed up on the screen.

"What is it?" Stacie mumbled, chewing her fingernail.

"I'm about to give up," Jon replied.

"What's the problem?" James asked.

"The encryption," Jon explained. "They're using a technique where each of these lines needs to get fed through multiple codices in sequence. It's incredibly complex to decode. This will take weeks, maybe months, to unlock."

"Need to create your own Enigma," Kyle said, appearing beside James.

"Exactly."

"Well keep at it. Any initial guesses?" James asked peering at their faces for clues.

"Could be anything from nuclear codes to a recipe for weed cookies. I have no idea," Jon replied.

"You got this. Don't worry," Kyle said, clapping Stacie and Jon on their shoulders. Both jumped at the physical contact, but Kyle's smiling face disarmed the two high-strung codebreakers.

"Let's get something to eat and you two should take a nap," Kyle said, walking back towards the middle of the camp where Kevin had cleared a spot for a towel where he laid out an arrangement of MREs, water bottles, protein packs, and vitamins.

"I would have been okay never seeing a spread like this again," Deck said emerging from the Jeep, "Pre-packaged meals with little to no flavor. Too reminiscent of Croyton's cooking."

"Stop whining and be glad we have more than a bag of plantains to split," Stacie said, sitting next to the towel, pulling out a protein pack and bottle of water from the pile. She shook the concoction while addressing the group. "Four hours later and here we are. About an hour from the coast and, according to the map's estimate, three hours to civilization. No idea what kind but might be a place for us to crash for the night and recharge our batteries, real and imagined. I think it's some sort of resort town judging by the beaches. Easier to determine these things now that we have the gear to check out situations ahead of time."

"I want to take a shower so bad," James said, picking up an MRE marked ROAST BEEF/POTATO STEW. He tore the top off and squeezed the dark brown goo into his mouth. He was prepared for the worst but was pleasantly surprised by the taste.

Not bad, he thought. *A little salty, but they kinda nailed it.* He squeezed some more through his lips.

"Everyone cool with an empty resort town?" James asked, swallowing the gooey meal.

"Hell yes," Deck said. "I'm a ball of grease and sweat right now."

"I bet they'll have beds, too," Kevin said, musing aloud.

"Now *that* would be miraculous," Deck said, staring dreamily into the distance.

It really would be, James thought, reveling in dreams of a shower and bed. Any temperature would do for the shower and any bed would work as long as it wasn't fashioned from a faux-leather bus bench.

The group lost themselves daydreaming of basic amenities for a few moments until Kyle broke the silence. "Good. Stacie and Jon, you two break apart. You've been burning the candle at both ends working on that code and driving."

"So have you," Stacie said, attempting a feeble argument with glazed eyes.

"He's right, Stacie. You need to sleep," James said, reviewing the driving configurations, "Kyle, can you take another leg of the drive?"

"No problem," Kyle said, standing and rolling his shoulders.

"Great, you're in the Jeep with Stacie. Jon, jump in the truck with Clint."

"Welcome to the truck, my man," Clint said giving him a fist bump.

"I always did sleep better when you were driving," Jon said.

"I knew someone appreciated my art!"

"Bob and Kevin, you two good?" James asked the Humvee duo. Kevin gave a thumbs-up in return and Bob replied with a hazy-eyed smile.

"We're killing it," Bob said, walking airily to the passenger seat of the Humvee and closing the door. He settled on the headrest and closed his eyes without another movement.

"I wish I could relax like that," Stacie said, trudging towards her Jeep where Kyle stood with the door open for her.

"Get some sleep," Kyle said, shutting the door behind her and turning to James shaking his head. "She can't turn it off!"

James grinned and hopped into the passenger seat ready to pass out for a couple of hours but was interrupted when Deck pulled up his HOLO and synced it to the Jeep's speakers.

"Any requests?" Deck asked, oblivious to James's displeasure.

Not reading the silence, Deck poked James's shoulder. "Hey. Hey, you. Any requests?"

"Whatever you want, man. I'm going to try and sleep."

"Suit yourself." A few seconds later James heard low, folky sounds come over the speakers and he took back his immediate thoughts of hatred for the driver.

Acoustic guitar played behind a deep melodic voice and James's eyes closed.

When he woke, the landscape had changed. The driver's side presented the same green wall, but James's side was covered in pockets of dense vegetation broken by wide expanses of beautiful, dark sandy beach with waves crashing against the shoreline.

James was taken by the beauty of it all, the sun sitting above the horizon, glinting off the water and casting scattered shadows across the road.

"Mornin', bud."

A water bottle appeared in front of him, and James took it to fill his mouth with the lukewarm liquid. He swished it around, put down his window, and spit it out, getting a mist of backwash from the wind blowing off the water. James took another sip, swallowing this time, and put the window back up.

"How long was I asleep?" James asked.

"Three and a half hours. We're almost to the town."

"Where is everyone?" James asked, wiping his face, realizing they were leading the pack. He turned around to see the Humvee behind them with the top of the truck visible behind it.

"We stopped when we hit the coast to regroup and review the map. No one saw any red flags and I took lead."

"I slept through all that?"

"You didn't blink, you little dickens." Deck handed James a HOLO emitter from the center console. "Look at the latest sat images coming from the town. There are a bunch of people there, but no sign of Federation. They have mansions up and down the coast where we can stop. Tell me what you think."

James swiped across the screen and a 3D image popped to life. The town was one main strip separated from the waterfront by a ribbon of buildings James assumed were bars and restaurants judging by their size and proximity to the water. The other side of the street boasted taller buildings and offshoot streets that snaked their way to residential neighborhoods identified by flat aluminum roofs on small box structures. Beyond the buildings along the waterfront sat estate-like structures. James followed the mansions and villas to a point at the end of the beach where the rock front took over and the jungle dominated again.

When he finished inspecting the model, he pulled up the latest live image of the area. Most surprising to James was the number of people there, riding bikes, walking dogs, running, and living without worry. He swiped through the photographs, timestamped from the last few weeks. There wasn't a change. With everything going on in the world, this little beach town and its inhabitants appeared to be living on a different planet.

"James." Deck hit James on the shoulder and James ignored him, continuing to scroll through the images, puzzling over why so many people were there.

"James." Deck hit him on the arm again and James brushed him off.

"Stop it, man. I'm trying to figure out what the hell this place is."

"James!"

"What?!" James yelled collapsing the screen.

"Look." Deck pointed through the windshield.

James peered through the glass and saw a group of six people dressed in bikinis and board shorts riding fat tire bikes with surfboards under their arms. The bikes veered lazily across the road and one of the women in the group waved at the Jeep to pass them.

What the hell? James thought. *Why were they here?*

"You think they live in town?" Deck asked, staring at the bikini-clad woman waving at him through the driver's side window as they drove by.

"I guess so."

"Where did they come from?" Clint asked over the intercom.

"Came out of nowhere from around the bend," Deck replied.

"They seem pretty casual," Jon chimed in.

"Very relaxed."

"You could learn something from them Stacie," Deck said.

"Shut up, Deck. Everyone keep an eye out," Stacie said, brushing off the insult.

"Agreed. Let's find a place to park outside town. We'll take things from there," James said. He was on alert, but it was different. Not danger, but a familiar feeling of anticipation James couldn't nail down in his gut.

Much to Deck's dismay, James picked Jon and Kevin to go into town with him. Deck grumbled about roller coaster buses, incarceration during raids, constant heat, humidity, and everything else he could complain about, but in the end, James thought it best to bring the most levelheaded person in the group and the only one fluent in the local language. Even Deck couldn't disagree.

They crossed a short bridge over a thin river that bled into a field of natural streams etched into the sand leading to the ocean. The buildings were empty or closed save for the grocery store and a bodega where a few older inhabitants with walkers sat watching the strangers.

The shopkeeper at the bodega was leaning back in his chair visible from the street through the service window ringed with plantain chips, sunflower seeds, and solar-powered pocket flashlights. The man eyed them for a moment but lost interest and refocused his attention on the book in his lap.

They walked through the town until they found a hostel with a vacant sign out front. They entered to find a tall, thin man with sun-bleached hair falling to his shoulders. He sat at a counter, eyes closed with his fist holding up his chin and a line of drool hanging from the corner of his lips.

James moved towards him and said, "Hello?"

No reaction.

James turned around and shrugged at Jon and Kevin. Kevin hit his palm with a fist and James followed suit hitting the counter with an open hand causing the sleeping attendant to slip off his fist and smack his head on the table.

"What the…?" the man grunted, holding a hand to his forehead and looking at James. Blue eyes and a face marked with a red spot on his chin stared sleepily at his visitors.

"¿Puedo ayudarte?" he asked.

"Ahhh…¿Tiene ingles?" James said, hoping he wouldn't need Jon to translate everything for him.

"Of course, mate. How you doing? Name's Rich," he said in a British accent, reaching a hand across the counter.

"Rich? My name's James. They're Kevin and Jon," he said, pointing back at his friends who waved approaching from the doorway.

"Nice to meet you all. What can I do for you gents?" Rich asked with an earnest face, leaning his forearms against the dented plastic countertop. "Room, house, food, drugs, booze, clothes? Say the word and I can probably help."

"A house, I guess?" James said, looking back at Kevin and Jon who nodded their approval.

"One with a shower and solar generators if you have it," Jon added.

"Right-o, boys. I can arrange that. How many rooms?" Rich said, pulling out a HOLO emitter and projecting a screen above him. He tapped the control bar and houses appeared with filter criteria running across the top of the screen.

"Eight if you can…" James replied, unsure of how much he could ask for.

"Waterfront cool?" Rich said, nodding while he pared down the results.

"Definitely."

"Make sure there's a grill," Kevin added over Jon's shoulder and Rich gave a thumbs-up. After a few seconds, he pulled up a picturesque villa with sweeping porches, views of the ocean, a private beach, and an outdoor patio with a wood fire grill wrapped around the exterior ending in a natural stone oven.

"How's this look?" Rich asked, glancing back at the three of them who stood with their jaws on their chests.

"Ummm, yes. Yes, I think that will do," said James after he composed himself. "How much?"

"How much? Ha!" Rich snorted and collapsed the emitter grabbing two sets of mag-keys from the wall behind him. "We have more houses than we know what to do with. You owe nothing. Have fun, mate." He winked and waved for them to follow him outside.

"Where are the rest of the people taking up these rooms?" Rich asked, making a right on the main street.

"They're parked outside of town," James replied, following him.

Rich stopped and handed him one of the mag-key sets talking as he walked to a bike leaned against the side of the hostel.

"Awesome. Why don't you grab the rest of your crew? Then meet me at the fifth house on the left on the other side of town. It's the one from the pictures. Tan stucco with a red tile roof and a dark wood door. The gate will be open and my bike will be out front if you need any other clues. I'll get everything ready for you and will give you a walkthrough of the property."

"Uhh, thanks," James said.

"No prob, mate," Rich replied, swinging a leg over his bike and riding down the street.

The three of them stood in the middle of the road puzzling about their interaction with Rich when Kevin spoke up. "So what are the odds we stumbled on a cult?"

"Better than zero," James replied, leading the way back to the team. "We just won't drink the Kool-Aid. Let's get everyone together and meet Rich at the house."

"He didn't seem bad. Actually, a nice guy I thought," Jon said from behind them.

"Yeah, well, this feels like the beginning of all the cult docs I've watched."

The rest of the team was spread out amongst the vehicles when they returned.

Kyle was counting items in the back of the truck as he marked them on a HOLO and Stacie sat on the front bumper of the Humvee poking at her HOLO. The other three stood by the bridge with their pants rolled up, shirts off, and feet in the water.

"So, how was it?" Deck asked, yelling from the side of the stream and wiping sand from his ankles.

"We've got a place to stay," James replied.

"Nice! Where is it this time? Another rusty bus, a murder hostel, a clearing in the middle of the jungle with pit vipers circling the camp?" Deck asked walking to the Jeep.

"Close."

"Go figure," Deck said, slamming the door shut and planting his elbow on the windowsill, "Well, let's see what fresh hell awaits us."

James shook his head and jumped into the driver's seat. He considered dropping Deck off at the hostel and leaving him there as a joke but realized it might be a bit too cruel for his dejected friend.

"You'll like it. Don't worry."

They pulled through the open gates to the villa and Deck's eyes popped, staring at the inescapable beauty of the house.

"What the…?" Deck whispered under his breath leaving the door to the Jeep open behind him.

"Welcome home, folks!" Rich said walking out the front door with his arms spread wide. "Help yourselves to all the amenities. Who's up for a tour?"

James turned to Deck, who had entered the front door and stood in the spacious front hall turning in a circle.

"Deck, want a tour?"

Deck could only nod in response and James addressed Rich. "A tour would be great."

"Follow me."

Rich took them on a full circle of the property, showing them the private beachfront, functioning pool, patio with the wrap-around grill-fireplace, and a place to park their vehicles.

They made their way inside the series of structures that in all held three kitchens, ten and a half baths, nine bedrooms, three living rooms, a private theatre, a wine cave, and a spa complete with a sauna and steam room. James was trying to get over their second stroke of good luck in as many days and, after the tour was over, claimed a bedroom on the second floor of the main house looking at the oceanfront.

He explored his room opening the bathroom door and stepping into a circular ceramic tiled stall where a rain shower head hung above with spigots poking out from the concrete walls to give an all-around shine.

This is going to be amazing, he thought, tempted to turn on the hot water, but realized he should talk plans with the team first.

He made his way down the circular staircase to the back porch where the team lounged with Rich sipping beers underneath spinning fans. Bob handed James a beer when he sat next to him on the couch, and he listened to the conversation.

"They all left and you decided to stay?" Stacie asked with a beer perched on her knee.

"That's right, and when they did, we moved in. There's no home left for me in the UK. I'm going to stay here till the end," Rich replied, sipping his beer.

"I'm sorry about your friends and family and everything. I… we…" Stacie struggled with the words, but Rich held up a hand.

"Not your problem and thank you. I've come to terms with it and have a group of great people who live here. No shortage of friends and new family."

The team was silent and nodded in response. James imagined what it would be like to have his family wiped out along with his home and everything he knew while watching smoke rise from the ocean. He shook his head to get the images out and tuned back to the conversation.

"How long have you been here?" asked Jon sitting next to Rich.

"Four years. I made it back home once a year for a month or so every Christmas to see the family and stuff. Hard though. My parents never really understood my… lifestyle."

"Lifestyle?" Kyle asked. "They didn't like their son living on a beach in paradise?"

"They didn't mind that part. More the fact that I dated men was what didn't fit with their vision of my future. It wasn't what they planned. Can't fix that, but I wasn't going to wait for them to catch up either."

"I get that. My sister and younger brother were the only ones I talked to when I came out. A religious village in the middle of the jungle isn't the easiest place to grow up," Jon added.

James nodded along with the rest of the group unable to fully relate but trying to convey a sense of support.

"Cheers to that," Rich said and clinked his bottle against Jon's. Rich drained the rest of his drink and stood removing a fistful of empties from the wicker table.

"Time for me to get back to work for another hour or two. Never know, could have more visitors. We have a town party most nights. You should join. I live in a house two doors down with some friends. Want to meet there later tonight? Say eight?"

"Sounds great!" Jon said, and the rest of the team agreed.

"Is there a place where I can buy some food? I haven't cooked a real meal in months," Kevin asked from across the room, already eyeing the grill out back.

"For sure. Want to come into town in an hour or so? I'll take you to the store."

Kevin saluted with his beer in response.

"All right. See you all later."

Goodbyes followed Rich from the room and the group was silent for a moment.

It had been ages since they had been able to sit in silence. Relax without the immediate worry of an entire military bearing down on them.

James looked around at the group. Their eyes were glazed in semi-catatonic states, the realization of their new situation settling into their collective conscience. They could rest.

James stood and held his beer in the air.

"Now, I know it's been a long time since we've gotten a little rest, but if you would all join me in a toast." The rest of the team stood and held their beers in the air over the coffee table. "To taking a fucking shower." James and the team knocked their bottles together while foam spilled onto the floor.

CHAPTER 5

Waves crashed in the background and a pesky breeze forced James farther under the mangled top sheet wrapped around his torso. He fought the sensation of waking up, but it was too late.

Still can't sleep in, I guess, he thought, taking a deep breath.

When James opened his eyes, the room was bathed in dim morning light and the drapes bordering the door to the patio fluttered in the wind. He stretched his neck to find his clothes in a crumpled line leading to his bedside. He untangled the sheets from his waist and pulled on the shorts next to the night table. He rolled off the mattress, bracing his knees when he hit the ground, and walked to the open patio. A crumpled pack of cigarettes sat on the metal table next to a beer can with ash scattered around the mouth.

He searched around his pocket then spied the lighter sitting on the rail outside. *Thank God,* he thought, glad he wouldn't need to scramble around for fire.

He sat in one of the chairs on the patio and put his feet on the balcony rail. He balanced on the back two legs of the chair while lighting his cigarette. It was beautiful outside and for the first time while in the Southern Federation, he enjoyed the morning. Tropical birds flew around the branches of tall trees, howler monkeys announced their presence in the distance, and fish popped out of the ocean at random intervals a mere fifty yards offshore, a hundred yards from his balcony.

Who could leave this? James thought. *And who knew the Federation had all this to offer?* He wondered for a second whether this was even part of the Federation anymore and suddenly his world crashed back into place. *That was nice while it lasted,* he thought, taking another drag of his cigarette and scanning the grounds for signs of life.

Chairs circled the built-in fire pit on the patio and the many side tables were filled with, James assumed, empty beer bottles and cans. He took a deep breath and exhaled, remembering the night.

Kevin had cooked a massive meal for everyone including Rich and his friends. It was simple—fish tacos, fried plantains, garlic rice, and a medley of grilled vegetables. Everything was perfect.

From there, Rich and his friends took them into town. The sleepy buildings and restaurants with the collection of elderly inhabitants had been swept away with the sunset and replaced by the night crowd—a vast array of bohemian backpackers who had decided to live out the rest of their days in a mecca of endless partying. James was envious of their freedom. They were all comfortable with their decision to live in blissful ignorance of the rest of the world. Even so, after only a few hours James couldn't rationalize staying no matter how much it appealed to him. The desire was real for James, but the team was on a different path made clear by the expressions on their faces.

Shrugging off the sudden sadness and abandoning his memories, James's attention was piqued by a pair of figures on the beach.

Jon and Rich were walking along the waterline trading a cigarette as the tide washed over their feet.

James turned away to give them some privacy. He didn't know how many more moments like that anyone on his team would get, and he didn't want to intrude. He stubbed out his cigarette and walked back into the bedroom. He picked his shirt up off the ground and headed downstairs. His tongue stuck against the roof of his mouth.

I need water, he thought.

He walked through his room glancing at the bathroom where the towels from his shower lay in a heap on the floor. The aromatic steam from the hot water floated through his memory while he trudged down the stairs running his hand along the banister.

When he arrived in the kitchen he was surprised by the lack of a mess. He remembered the intense destruction that greeted him each morning in the apartment he had shared with Kyle, Deck, and Clint in Midway and had been prepared for a similar scene.

He poured himself a glass of water and chugged the tepid liquid realizing for the first time how thirsty he was. He refilled his glass while searching the room. A pour-over coffee station idled on the counter beneath a glass cabinet filled with multi-colored coffee mugs. A trio of white ceramic jars sat next to the pour-over and James was happy to find ground coffee waiting for him with a tea kettle to top it all off.

He heated water in the kettle while selecting his coffee, tipping mounds of ground beans into the metal mesh filter. When the kettle whistled he poured the steaming water over the grounds and brown liquid trickled out the bottom into the mottled blue cup he had selected.

When the process was complete, he picked up the cup and cautiously sipped the dark substance. He was rewarded with a pleasantly bitter, hot cup of coffee. He looked out in the yard through the picture window above the sink. This reminded him of those early mornings in the compound. Not the location or the amenities, those were very different. But waking at 4 a.m., sipping his coffee outside their barracks in the freezing cold, readying himself for whatever punishment Croyton had conjured up for them that day. It felt long ago but was fresh in his mind every time he reflected on his stay in the valley.

"I thought you'd be up."

James was knocked out of his reverie by Deck slamming open a cabinet.

"How'd you sleep, big guy?" Deck asked, filling water in what James believed was a flower vase. He decided to let it go.

"Great. Little rough waking up but overall feel good." James realized he wasn't as hungover as he should be.

"I feel great! I missed this—waking with some very real anxiety." He took a deep sip from his flower vase. "Exciting…"

"I hear that," James said, nodding and feeling the same after a long night of drinking, even among friends.

"Well, the way to get over it is to own it. Is there more coffee?" Deck asked, sniffing the air.

"Kettle's hot," James said, pointing at the pour-over. "Help yourself."

"Good stuff. Patio?"

"I'll meet you there."

Deck gave him a thumbs-up as he started the brewing process.

James opened the screen to the patio where he was confronted for the first time with all the garbage from the previous night.

So this is where it happened, he thought, putting his coffee on a table under the house's awning, walking across the patio, and retrieving two chairs. He set up shop facing the beach and away from the mess, using an empty beer bottle as an ashtray while he lit another cigarette.

I need to start running again, James thought guiltily as smoke rose above his head.

"See anyone else yet?" Deck asked, bumping the screen door open with his butt. He sat in the chair next to James and helped himself to a cigarette.

"Jon," James said, handing the tip of his cigarette to Deck for a light. He could have mentioned Rich, but no reason to blow up Jon's spot.

"Where's he now?"

"Not sure. He was walking on the beach."

"Ah, gotcha. Well, I did see something this morning," Deck said, hunching his shoulders and lowering his voice. "Walked past Kyle's room this morning. Counted twenty toes if you catch my drift."

"Well, well, well. Our friend Kyle," James said, leaning back in his chair.

"It gets better. I counted no toes in Stacie's room…" Deck sat back in his chair with a self-satisfied look on his face.

"What? What are you doing looking in people's rooms?" James asked, suddenly on edge. He didn't care if two people on the team were together, but starting rumors was another thing. He had no hard evidence besides Deck's passing toe counts.

"Kyle was our roommate, man. I used to go in his room all the time after we went out. He didn't leave any sort of sign or lock his door so I went in. When I noticed he had grown a couple of extra feet I decided to leave. As for Stacie, her door was open." Deck sat back, defending himself.

"Well maybe she was going to the bathroom," James said.

"Maybe, maybe not."

"Let's keep it between us until we learn more. Cool?"

Deck waved his hand and nodded. "I know. Just interesting is all. Rich and his buddies know how to party, huh?" he said, changing the subject.

"They really do." James remembered hanging out at the bar leading to a late-night hangout back at their patio with less certainty in his memories as the night progressed.

"Morning, gents," Kevin said, opening the door to the patio.

James caught sight of shoulder-length black hair swishing out the front door as Kevin grabbed another chair.

"What a night, huh?" Kevin flopped in his chair, stretched out his arms, and cracked his shoulders in the process. "You all have a fun time?"

"For sure," Deck said. "It's been so long since we got to let loose. I don't think I'll mind the eventual crash coming this afternoon."

"That was a great time," James said. "Not sure we had as much fun as you." James winked at Kevin who grinned in response.

Deck sat up looking back and forth at the two of them. "What happened? What'd I miss? What'd you do?" Deck was on the scent, but James shook his head and stood with his coffee mug.

"Want some coffee, Kev?"

"That'd be great."

"Are you two hearing me? What happened? Why do I feel like something happened here?!" Deck's voice was reaching a feverish pitch. "Oh, come on, guys. That's not cool!"

James grinned. It was fun to make him sweat sometimes.

While more water heated on the stove top, James checked the fridge for something to eat. Their meal from last night was uncovered in the fridge and James picked a slice of avocado off the plate of veggies.

Still good, James thought, chewing the silky fruit.

"Eggs!" he exclaimed out loud, suddenly craving eggs. He decided he would head into town that morning to grab more food—eggs in particular—and would make breakfast for the team. The whistle sounded and James completed the pour-over process.

He walked back to the patio, bumping the swinging screen door with his rear end while balancing coffees in both hands, careful not to scald himself with the boiling liquid.

"I was not *that* drunk," Deck said, waving at Kevin. Rich and Jon had joined them sitting in chairs they had pulled from the patio arrangement.

"Didn't you fall down the stairs?" Jon asked, lighting a cigarette off the tip of Rich's.

"I *rolled* down the stairs. Falling would mean I injured myself," Deck said.

"Sounds like semantics," Kevin said with the slightest hint of a grin.

"It's facts," Deck said.

"You were fine, bub," Rich said.

"Thank you! I like you, Rich. You should stick around," Deck said, reaching a hand across the table to fist-bump their new friend.

"You got it mate," Rich said, enjoying the banter.

"Anyone want to come with me for eggs?" James asked.

"I'll join," Kevin said. "I want to bake something."

"Any other takers?" James asked.

"I think we're good, but the woman with the stand at the corner next to the hostel has amazing eggs and fruit," Rich chimed in.

"Good stuff," James said, giving a thumbs-up to the table while following Kevin through the door.

The path to town was short, but beautiful. The mansions and villas they had driven by the day before were even more impressive when James passed them on foot. Walking gave him time to appreciate their beauty—admiring houses with Bahama grass lawns ringed by palm trees, orchids, banana trees, and birds of paradise. The flora had lost its manicured sheen, lacking owners to keep an eye on the property, but James liked it more this way. He could hear his father's voice. "Nature looks best when its stewards don't try to over-domesticate it." As pompous as the statement was, he had to admit his dad was right.

They reached the end of the shady road sooner than James would have liked and strolled onto the building-lined street. Stray dogs scavenged the area for food, brushing against James's legs. Kevin tapped his shoulder and pointed across the road.

"There I think."

James nodded and they crossed the road coming up to the woman's stand.

The woman behind the cart was short with dark graying hair pulled back in a tight bun. Her nose was sharp and short, and her eyes were a deep brown defined by smile lines at the corners. She smiled at the two of them as they approached.

"¡Buenos días! ¿Cómo están?" Her voice was crisp and clear, "¿Quieren frutas? ¿Huevoes? ¿Carne? ¿Pollo? ¿Frijoles? ¿Arroz? ¿Plátanos? ¿Como puedo ayudarte?"

James glanced at Kevin who shrugged.

"I wish we'd brought Jon or Rich with us," James said, trying to figure out the best way to talk with her other than pointing and nodding.

"¿Ahh, podemos ver las frutas?" he attempted with caution.

"Fruit! Of course. Anything else?" The woman came around to the other side of the cart switching languages and pulling out a few buckets of strange tropical fruits James had never seen.

"Ummm, eggs? And bread, too, if you have it," James said, happy for their language luck and looking over the cart, trying to decide what else they could use.

"Sí. Sí por supuesto," she said. She loaded a loaf of bread and a dozen eggs from a wicker basket into an uncovered cardboard container. "Which fruits?" she asked waving a hand over the colorful assortment of options.

James was stumped. They all looked good, but he had no clue what any of them were besides the bananas and those seemed lame to get.

"What do you suggest?" he asked. He could feel the lost look in his eyes and she sensed it. She continued smiling as she picked a number of different fruits and dropped them in the basket.

"Here. These are the best mamones in the area, a few aguas manzanas to provide some refreshment, and finally passion fruit. You know them?"

James recognized the last one and pointed at it. "Only that one."

"Bueno, you'll love them all," she said while she added their total in a small notebook.

"Thank you. Rich sent us here, by the way. He's a big fan of yours."

"He's a good man, Rich. Very kind to the people in this area. If I lived here, I think we would spend a lot of time together. He stays up too late though." She looked up and winked with a grin at Kevin and James.

"Where do you live?" Kevin asked, examining some of the meat in a cooler next to her cart.

"Oh, I'm from the South. During the high season I work as a caretaker for some of the houses here. Normally I'd be home by now with my friends and family living off the money I make but with the war… I don't know if I'll ever get back there." Her natural cheer was replaced by a palpable sadness, but she did not let herself wallow. "Nothing I can do about it though, and not that you two don't know anything about the attacks" She winked at James, and for the first time in the South, James wasn't terrified that they had been recognized.

"I'm sorry about your people. I hope you see them again," James said, picking up his bag. It was heavier than he thought it would be.

"Thank you. But I don't think anyone will take me that close to my home. The last people that came here told me they're right on my town's doorstep. I can only pray my people are safe at this point."

"We'll pray, too, then," Kevin said, interrupting and grabbing one of the bags from James's hands.

"We will," James affirmed.

"Thank you. I appreciate that." Her kind smile graced them one last time before they waved and walked away.

When they arrived back at the house the rest of the team was awake.

James walked out to the team lounging in an expanded selection of chairs talking about the previous night.

"So he owns the bar?" Clint asked, sipping a steamy coffee.

"Yep, been here for years. Local legend," Rich replied.

"He was the drunkest guy at his own bar?"

"Emre doesn't worry about that kind of thing. Marches to the beat of his own drum, ya know? Left Turkey as a teenager running away from home. Traveled around the world prior to the Melt and when the world divided, he was here. His whole family was separated from him and he decided to stay for the rest of his life. He's been good for a lot of us. Gives us a blueprint to live off," Rich explained. "A little different now though with a destructive force waiting a few hours south."

"Do you all do this every night?" Kyle asked, peeling a banana. "I mean, that was a blast, but every night?" He took a bite and finished with a full mouth, "Id b' 'ard?"

"At least a few nights a week. Different kind of party sometimes, too. Hikes in the moonlight are common for us, and you can't exactly be drunk traipsing around the jungle at night. Way too many things that can kill you."

The team nodded solemnly. They understood more than most.

"Anyone want breakfast?" James interrupted, sensing a good moment to break in.

"James, when did you get here?" Deck asked, turning around in his chair and giving him a fist bump. "I can't speak for everyone else, but I'd love something if you're cooking. I'll even clean up. Trade?"

"For sure. Anyone else? Show of hands," James asked, surveying the crowd. "All right, I'll use all the eggs," James said, stopping his count when he realized everyone assembled had a hand raised.

"I'll help," Kevin said, turning back to the kitchen.

"Can't keep him out of there," Clint said, peering at the giant man entering the kitchen again.

"He's addicted. And good at his addiction, so I'm fine with it," Deck chimed in. He took a final slug of his coffee and stood up.

"Speaking of addictions, anyone else want some more coffee?" Deck asked.

"I do. Make it strong again. That was good," Stacie said, handing him her mug.

"You got it, girl," Deck said, and James held the door open for him to enter.

As he passed, Deck leaned over and whispered in James's ear, "Notice who's sitting next to each other out there?"

"Who, Rich and Jon? Mind your own business Deck," James said, knowing he wasn't talking about them, but attempting to focus Deck's mind elsewhere.

"Not them, dumbass. The twenty-toed and Miss Vanishing Feet." He winked at James.

"Who?" James asked, playing dumb.

"James. We talked about this. I mean…" He was getting flustered but stopped outside of the kitchen. "You're messing with me right now."

"Yes, I am," James said.

"Sometimes, man. Sometimes." Deck grabbed the kettle off the center island and Kevin backed out of the fridge with his arms full of leftover taco meat and plantains.

"What're you two talking about?"

"Nothing. Our own little inside secret. No need to tell you," Deck spoke loftily, looking at James for confirmation that they were on the same page.

"If it's about the fact that Kyle had someone else in his bed and Stacie's bed was empty, then we're all wondering the same thing."

"How did you know?!" Deck asked, incredulous.

"I had to get water this morning. I figured you saw them, too. You must have after you woke up at the top of the stairs. You had to pass them to get to your room."

"You slept at the top of the stairs?" James asked, taking the fruit out of the basket to wash in the sink.

"Well, sort of. I got up and went to bed for a little bit. That's beside the point though. What's going on with them?"

Kevin shrugged. "Don't know. Don't care as long as it doesn't affect the group."

"Ditto," James said.

"I know, I know. It's just… interesting is all," Deck said, chewing on the thought.

James sensed Deck spiraling and he put the fruit in the sink and flicked water at his friend. "Don't think about it anymore. Not really our business."

Deck finished his coffee prep, scowling at the counter. "All right, that's fair. I'll stop. Like to know about our friends' lives is all." He poured coffee into the mugs and made it halfway out the door when he stopped and turned slowly around in the kitchen.

"Was that what you two were talking about this morning over coffee?" His face was suspicious, and his blue eyes squinted shifting back and forth between the two of them.

James glanced at Kevin who shrugged.

James looked back into the sink, accidentally started laughing and felt Deck's eyes boring into the back of his head.

"I'll figure it out," Deck said, and James looked up to see him watching them as he swung the porch door open with his butt.

"No wonder he's our scout," Kevin said as he chopped an onion. "Boy's gotta know fuckin' everything."

James laughed out loud and continued washing fruit in the sink, wondering whether Deck and Kevin saw what they thought they did.

The rest of the morning passed in quiet relaxation with the team rotating through naps, dips in the ocean, and soaking in the hot tub on the rooftop. It was perfect.

Rich gave them a tour of the area with bikes they borrowed from his friends. They rode down the street taking in the beautiful oceanfront and dense jungle walls then stopped at an oceanside tiki bar for piña coladas. James could not remember a more relaxing day.

That afternoon Rich went back to the hostel to, as he put it, wait for other roving bands of northern Federation military units on the run to show up for a night of R and R.

The team took that as a signal to do whatever they pleased and James headed to the beach with Clint, Bob, Stacie, and Kyle where they relaxed with a few beers, going in the water every time they felt too warm. The rest of their friends disbanded, Kevin opted to nap while Jon and Deck went into town. Rich had told Jon earlier about a bakery in the middle of town and Deck, having overheard their conversation, was on board to explore.

James was happy he decided to stay. The wind died down for a bit, but the waves kept crashing far off the beach. He enjoyed the quiet beauty of it, listening to the echoes from rolling water reverberating across the sand.

"I don't blame Rich for wanting to stay here," Clint said, leaning back and digging his elbows into the dark sand. "This is paradise. I mean, have you felt this sand?

He held up a hand and let it fall through his fingers in a fine mist that blew down the beach into an invisible cloud. "It might as well be freakin' velvet. It's so soft."

"I agree, man," Bob said, resting his head on his forearms lying flat on his stomach with his eyes closed. "It's easy to see why people stay here."

"Not our lot in life," Stacie said, looking out at the ocean.

"I guess not," Bob responded, his words dropping the weight of the world back on their collective shoulders. "Enjoy it while we can though." He held up his bottle of beer and clinked Stacie's glass.

"We're not leaving yet. Why ruin the moment?" Kyle said.

"Yeah, seriously. I'm relaxing on a goddamn beach nestled along the Pacific Coast and you're trying to get me to think about leaving?" Clint exclaimed. "Let's talk about what we're doing for dinner. It's getting dark already. The equator's weird, huh?"

James glanced at the sky realizing he was right. "Good call," James said, standing up. "I'll go see what's in the kitchen. Anyone need anything?"

"Another beer for me," Kyle said, handing him an empty.

"Make that two."

"Three."

"How about a round?" Clint said as he finished his bottle.

James cradled the empties in his arms and tread across the spiky grass, careful to avoid the newts popping up every other step. He loved walking with bare feet while stalks of grass poked between his toes, a strange freedom he had not experienced in months.

The kitchen was empty, and the rest of the house was a maze of long shadows. *Everyone must have needed those naps,* James thought, turning on a light. He opened the fridge to a scene of wrapped leftovers and a steadily declining number of beers. *Might need to go out for food tonight,* he thought, replacing the empties in his arms with full beers from the fridge.

He was ready to head back to the beach when the door opened and Deck's distinct voice floated through from the foyer.

"That's why we came here. The way to do our job is to find out the most we can about them. So, after weeks of running out of food and supplies, we ran into a stroke of luck and now we're he—James! Hey, buddy." Deck entered the kitchen. His arms were filled with a case of beer and canvas bags were draped over his shoulders. "We're back and we bring gifts of food—not cooked yet, so hope you can wait—and more beer!" Deck put the beer on the counter then unloaded the bags into the fridge.

He was followed by Rich and Jon whose arms were equally full.

"Hola, mate. We also brought a guest chef for the evening," Rich said, nodding behind him."

The woman from the corner stand followed with a large pot in her hands. She smiled at James.

Rich continued, "I believe you two have already met, but James this is Paola, Paola meet James."

"Hola James, ¿Cómo está?"

"Bien gracias, ¿Y usted?"

"Bien, thank you," she said, placing the pot on the counter where it was picked up by Deck and placed on the stovetop. "I hope you don't mind I offered to cook dinner. Deck said you would love it."

"Deck was right, and I'm sure Kevin would be happy for someone else to cook tonight."

"I can always use help," she said. She walked over and kissed him on the cheek as she unpacked her bags.

"I was going to deliver these to everyone on the beach." James held the bottles up for them to see.

"James, I got that. Stay here and hang for a bit." Deck grabbed the bottles from his hands and walked outside in the direction of the shore.

"That takes care of that I guess. Paola, until Kevin joins us, how can I help?"

"Can you wash the rice?"

"You got it." He picked up the sack of rice Jon had dropped on the counter and put a strainer in the sink.

"We're gonna go next door to get Rich a change of clothes. Be back in a little bit," Jon said. Paola and James waved at them as they walked out the door.

"They're nice together," Paola mentioned, peeling an onion.

"They are, aren't they?" James said. He found a large pot and started the process of straining the rice.

"I like to see young people happy and in love. It gives me hope. These times are difficult… to see them… well..." She shook her head. "Que linda." She smiled at James and he grinned in response dumping another helping of clean rice into the pot.

"So why come here?" James asked, soaking another colander of rice.

"When my husband died I needed another source of income. I was online going through the available jobs in my area then looked all over the country and straying a little farther from home. Por la gracia de Dios, I found a job listing here that would allow me to keep my care center open in the low season and stay here during the high season." She explained everything with a matter-of-fact tone, peeling the skins off the onions with a deft level of ease.

"I'm sorry about your husband," James said.

"Ah, gracias, James. It was many years ago. He was the love of my life. Everything I do is because I know he would want me to do it. He would have wanted me to be happy." She paused for a second and a longing silence stretched in the room.

"I wish I could have met him. He sounds like a nice man." James felt awkward and unsure of where to go next with the conversation so he decided to go with the flow. "You mentioned a care center. What's it for?"

"Ahh, now *that* is the new love of my life." She stopped herself after she noticed James had finished cleaning the rice and went to help him get everything in place on the stovetop. They lit the burner under the pot of water and prepped the rest of the vegetables. Paola continued, "The care center is something we started for our town. My husband was given land for farming when he was a boy. His father died when he was young and his mother had to manage the house and watch the children. Hector, that was his name, took it upon himself to leave school and work the land with plans to return when he was older and become a lawyer. When I first met him he was a sad, frustrated man con un corazón de oro. He loved animals and children and was never far from his land. But his true passion was for the people in his town.

"He would wake every morning before it was light out, work until it was dark, study under a small lamp until he could not keep his eyes open, and then do it again. Six days a week, the seventh day es domingo. A day for God, ¿Entiende?"

James nodded his assent, handing her another peeled onion to slice.

"At that point, we were married and living on the finca where I would run the business. He tended to the animals, crops, and everything else that needed to be done. I would set up relationships with markets all over the country to sell our goods and he would deliver them with me. After living inside that hell for six years, he took his examinations, received his certificate, and started practicing law. Six years of hard work and extreme dedication. All that struggle came with the added stressor when we learned that we could not have children. It was a difficult thing for us to comprehend, but we discovered other ways we could provide a good life for children even if they were not our own.

Paola cleared the diced onions off her cutting board with a deft motion and sliced some jalapeños before pointing to a knife for James to join her.

"Once he got his license, we stopped working the farm," she continued. "He began taking on clients, and I contemplated my next path in life. I did not know where to go or what to do. I had always planned on becoming a wife and mother, but one of those things would have to wait for adoption papers to clear. I remembered when I would go to the markets on the weekends and see the children of the other farmers running around, often alone, getting yelled at by their parents or other adults who treated them as nuisances rather than the entertainment that I saw.

"I spoke with a few of the parents and offered to watch their children while they worked their stands at the market. They were so happy to have someone else in charge that they handed their kids off without a second thought. Those first few months were hectic. I was learning how to be a caretaker for children of many different ages and there were always new parents asking if their kids could join.

"In no time at all, I needed to bring on help and I hired two other women from town whose children were grown. The three of us pooled our resources and, with the help of my husband, applied for grants to start a center on our farm. We opened it a year before my husband passed." She paused her cutting for a second, looking at the countertop expressionless. The kind woman turned to James smiling. "I know that's a long way to explain how I found my passion in life, but his story is a big part of mine. I like to keep his memory alive so others will know about him."

James smiled. "I loved it. Thank you for telling me."

Paola nodded, wiping a quick finger under her eye. "Pues, no need to cry, huh? We're cooking! New friends in paradise, ¿verdad?"

"That's right," James said and he tipped his beer in her direction and swigged.

"What's going on in here?" Kevin said, entering the room.

"Hev Kev, this is Paola. Paola this is our primary chef, Kevin."

"Hola. ¿Como está?" Kevin said, his tall frame dwarfed hers when he bent for a hug.

"Hola, Kevin. Bien, bien, ¿Y usted?"

"Bien, gracias. ¿Puedo ayudarte?"

"¡Si, por supuesto! ¿Puede cortar el carne? Voy a cocinar carne asada con arroz y frijoles."

"¡Que bueno!" Kevin said, opening the fridge and taking out a pack of wrapped meat.

James was envious. When did Kevin's Spanish get good? And why didn't he speak up at the hostel or fruit stand? *Sneaky of him,* James thought jealously.

"I think I'll head out to the beach. You two good in here?" James asked, getting an extra beer from the fridge.

"We've got it," Kevin said and he turned to Paola again. "¿Dónde aprendió a cocinar?"

James closed the door behind him while Paola responded. *He's got a gift for languages,* James thought, walking across the grass towards the tiki torches wavering on the sand in the fast-approaching night. The scent of oil from the torches drifted into his nose filling his senses with eucalyptus. The constant breeze from the water had switched, pushing the bugs off the shoreline, and the light from the stars danced across the choppy surf. It took James a second to rationalize where he was for the hundredth time. He could have stayed there forever.

As he approached, the group was quietly watching the water lap against the sand. The mood was more somber than James anticipated.

"What's the matter?" James asked, taking a seat next to Stacie and Kyle.

"Enjoying the silence for a minute, I guess," Bob replied cleaning his glass bowl with a strand of pipe cleaner, "Anyone want to join?" he asked, holding the cleaned bowl and a bag of weed.

Murmurs of "no" echoed around the crowd. Bob shrugged and tapped ground weed into the bowl. He walked to the water line to smoke, standing as the water covered his feet.

The quiet persisted after Bob left and James was happy for the moment. He needed to think.

It was already their second night in paradise and he didn't want to leave, but he knew what they needed to do. They had all the supplies they could carry, thanks to Kevin, and the longer they stayed, the closer the BZ came to making its next move. He needed to refocus. They also required a destination, but he was pretty sure he had figured that part out. He needed someone else's take and knew Stacie was his best option.

"Hey, Stacie," he said, turning to her. "Would you do me a favor?"

"Shoot," she said, sitting up straight.

"Sit next to Paola at dinner tonight. I want to get a read on her."

"Sure. I expect this has to do with her hometown?" Stacie asked.

Always a step ahead, James thought.

"Yeah, I want another person to get a better sense of her. I've got Deck and, I would assume, Kevin who are her fans. I'm one, too, but you've got an eye for these situations."

"I'm flattered." Stacie batted her eyes at James and he gave her the finger in return.

"You know what I mean. Sit next to her, talk to her, and get back to me."

"I'll start right now." Stacie stood and wiped sand off her rear offering a hand to Kyle in the process, "Come on, ass. Let's go meet the newbie."

"You got it, Serial," Kyle said, hopping to his feet.

James grinned at their pet names for one another resurfacing and watched the two of them walk off to the house.

He turned back to the crowd catching Deck's raised eyebrows in the process. James shook his head and Deck shrugged and grabbed a beer from the bucket of ice in the center of the circle.

"Got some good vibes from Paola?" Deck asked across the group.

"I did. She's a nice woman," James said, hiding his true intentions for the time being.

"Same." Deck stood and stretched his arms pushing out his chest. "I'm gonna join Bob," He walked past James and bent murmuring to James. "You're right. We should give her a ride home."

He didn't say another word, taking a swig of his beer as he walked to find their friend in the darkness.

James grinned to himself. Kevin was right. Deck was born to be a scout.

CHAPTER 6

Paola's hands were clasped in her lap and apprehension seeped out of her pores. Even with her perpetual smile, James sensed a heightened level of anxiety, her back stuck flat against the passenger seat, her neck rigid in the air. *Not easy to do on a bumpy road,* James thought.

The view through the tinted glass bounced on the rock-strewn dirt and Paola put a hand on James's arm to indicate where he needed to turn. He pulled to the right down a narrow stretch of verdant plant walls boxing them in on the path. He glanced in the rearview mirror checking as the truck squeezed through the narrow passage. Branches bent to their limits, but James let out a shallow breath when the wide vehicle cleared the sturdy trunks on either side of the trail with a few inches to spare.

Too close, James thought, wiping sweat from his brow, relieved they wouldn't need to stop to cut another tree blocking their way.

"Que linda," Paola murmured and James squinted at the opening in front of them. Four buildings stood clumped in the middle of the jungle. They were A-frames topped with thatch roofs and protected by dark wood siding while colorful stone pathways crisscrossed the grounds. James pulled to the right and two women waited at the end of the drive. James guessed they were around Paola's age, but more gray than black colored the hair on their heads. The woman on the left was a bit taller with gloves on her hands, a blue dress hung on her lean frame. The shorter of the two was similarly dressed, but an apron patterned with bumblebees was tied around her waist.

"Mis hermanas, Rosa and Mariel," Paola said turning to James and putting a hand on his shoulder. "Friends."

"Comprendo." James nodded, shutting off the car.

She opened the door and greeted the women with long embraces. The hugs were intimate and, though no words were spoken, James sensed a different communication between the women, a language only they could understand.

The rest of the team joined James waiting for the women to finish their hellos. It was an emotional moment. James was uncomfortable and turned to Stacie and Jon. "We should get the HOLOs out to start working on the co—" He was interrupted by a pat on his shoulder and the taller of the two women stood quietly behind him.

"Hola," he said in as friendly a voice as he could muster.

"Gracias for bringing our friend home. Me llamo Rosa," Rosa said smiling. She took off her gardening gloves and placed them in hidden pockets on her dress. Without further warning, she wrapped her hands around his shoulders, kissed him on the cheek, and released him. Afterward, Mariel approached and waited until Rosa's hug was complete then greeted James in a similar manner. Meanwhile, Rosa went to Kyle, hugged him, and finished with a kiss on the cheek.

"Quite the greeting," Kyle said as Rosa released him.

Neither woman was tall enough to get near Kevin's face and they had to wave him down for the final kiss at the end of their greeting.

"This is the best hello I've ever gotten," Deck said, enjoying the attention and returning hugs with such affection James would have believed he was related to the women.

Paola's friends finished receiving their guests and the women went back into a huddle talking in rapid Spanish. Afterward, they turned and disappeared into one of the houses.

James was confused.

He looked at the rest of the group, pointing at Jon who lifted his shoulders. "Beats me. I couldn't follow anything they were saying."

"You speak the damn language," Clint said, throwing his hands in the air.

"You try understanding three women standing in a circle talking in rapid English and tell me what they're saying." Jon crossed his arms across his chest looking back at Clint defiantly.

"Standing out here won't get us anywhere," James said. "I'll find out what's going on. The rest of you hang tight for a minute, grab a bite to eat, or do whatever."

"I could eat a whole goat," Kevin said, already opening the back of the Hummer and prying off the lid to the rations bin.

"I'd pay to watch that," Deck chimed in, joining the search for food.

The rest of the conversation was muffled as James walked into the house where the women were nowhere to be found.

"Hello? Hola? Paola? Hey is there somewhere we can put our stuff? What is this place?" James walked through the dim natural lighting. The wooden walls were braced with lashed bamboo and the windows were crude holes in the wood with hinged shutters blocking the outdoors. The floors were stone slabs and dirt filled the gaps. Whiffs of bare earth and humid wood filled James's nostrils as he went deeper into the structure. The house opened into another room and James stepped carefully across the floor to avoid anything that might be lurking in the darkness.

I hope the spiders are on the ceiling, James thought, ready for tarantula pincers to sink into his skin.

He finally arrived at another doorway with a partially closed bamboo door blocking the entrance. He pushed it open, hoping there wasn't a group of BZ soldiers on the other side waiting to pounce.

Instead, he discovered a wide, open-air enclosure between a cluster of similarly styled buildings with a group of children sitting in a circle listening to a woman read a book to them in Spanish. Paola and her friends stood off to the side watching the children, all with the same pleasant smile hovering on their lips. James waved to catch Paola's eye and she ushered him over.

He followed the colored stone pathway and stood next to her on the circular patch of grass where the children sat.

She put a hand on his shoulder and motioned for him to bend to her height and she whispered in his ear, "These are the children we watch during the harvest months. I was worried some would not be here. La Guerra Blanca is very close and there was a chance they were dead." She clasped her hands together and tears gathered in her eyes, "Gracias a Dios, they're all here."

"None of them went north?" James asked, counting at least twenty children listening to the story.

"No. Never." Paola shook her head to emphasize her point. "This area is poor. They're the children of farmers or laborers. This is all they have ever known and probably ever will, even in today's world. Home and family are all they want or need. It's a beautiful simplicity, no?"

James nodded looking at the group with a pit in his stomach. The BlankZone's army was going to run over this place with ease. How did they not understand they needed to leave? He was going to say as much when Paola's small hand grasped his arm again.

"It's why we're glad you came. ¡Nuestro guerreros Nortes! The warriors from the north!"

James looked at her and smiled to hide the cold fear creeping down his spine.

Well, that's it, James thought, experiencing genuine affection for other human beings besides his team for the first time in a long time. This is why they came here. These people. This place. It meant more to them than it did to him, but it meant something to somebody and that makes it worth everything the team risked to get here. They needed to learn about, fight, and win against the BlankZone. *Whatever that takes,* James ruminated, nodding while Rosa pulled him toward the circle.

They sat on the grass and two of the children cleared a spot for him to join them. The young woman at the front gave him a wide smile. She looked around his age with hazel eyes, a nose ring, and dark black hair tied in a ponytail falling over her shoulder.

"Welcome!" she said in flawless English. "My name's Cristina. Thank you for joining us and bringing our friend Paola home." The grace and effortless gratitude layered in her voice reminded James of public appearances after the attack on Midway. The random people stopping him on the street had made him claustrophobic. However, this was different—disarming, calm, and real.

He nodded in response. "My honor."

"Well," Cristina continued, taking the attention off James, much to his relief, and addressing the children, "should we sing a song for our new friend?"

"¡Sí!" the abrupt shout jolted James, the loud noise from such a small chorus of bodies was impressive.

Cristina picked up a tambourine and played a song while the children joined one another in tune:

Los perros en la finca

Persigue los gatos

Pero...

The children continued, but James was interrupted by a tap on his shoulder. Mariel pointed at the doorway. Deck, Bob, and Kyle poked their heads through, stacked on top of one another in height order looking between James and the circle of children with questioning scowls.

James waved them in, hoping to avoid the distraction for the kids, but the singing had become a secondary activity. The children turned around mouthing words absently while they clapped to the beat. Their eyes were focused on the collection of new people in casual attire standing at the back of the area in a line looking uncomfortable in their surroundings.

Cristina sensed the point of no return and addressed the children in rapid Spanish that James could not catch. But he was able to guess her meaning when the crowd of children sprang to their feet in unison and formed a circle around his team. The braver kids would take steps forward and put a hand out to the team. In turn, one of the team would return the shake or high five and the kid would jump in the air and run back around to hide behind the group of friends whispering in excited tones with smiles spread across their faces.

James watched the exchanges continue until Paola approached him with Cristina in tow.

"James, I want you to meet my good friend Cristina," Paola said, bowing slightly when she said their names.

"We met in the circle, but thank you for the official introduction," Cristina said flashing a smile and reaching out her hand. "I understand you are guerros Nortes."

James was impressed by the seamless way in which Cristina switched between English and Spanish. *So natural,* he thought.

"Nice to meet you as well," he said, returning her shake. "That's the rest of my team. They're a little preoccupied."

A whistle pierced the air and the children's heads whipped around to Rosa who stood in a doorway to another building holding a pot.

"Venga para comida," she said. nodding her head inside.

In a rush, the collection of little bodies sprinted past James, so fast he had to stand straight with his arms in the air to avoid being hit. Paola and Cristina seemed impenetrable and the sea of kids washed around them like rocks in a river.

When the initial roar from stampeding kids died down James waved his team over. "Let me introduce you to everyone."

"I'd like that," Cristina replied. "But I'm also starving. Can we do it over dinner?"

"Yes!" Kevin said suddenly from behind James. "I mean if we're invited."

Cristina laughed. "Of course. I hope we have enough for you."

"I'll take whatever you've got," Kevin said, bending to fit through the doorway.

The shouts from the kids echoed out into the courtyard and James followed them inside.

They were set up in a rectangular room with wood tables and benches in rows. James looked around the room and, realizing they would not all be able to sit next to one another turned to the rest of the team, but found they had already figured out the situation.

Bob remained and James nodded at two open seats at the head of a table with a group of girls whispering.

"Wanna sit together?" James asked.

"Lead the way, my man," Bob replied, and they approached the end of the table where the girls sat. Curious eyes looked at them expectantly and James pointed at the two empty spots on either side of the table.

"Do you all mind?" he asked, peering at each of the faces in turn.

The blank stares reminded him of the language barrier, and he tried to translate everything in his head when Bob broke in. "¿Podemos sentarnos?"

Bobbing heads responded and James took his place at the end of the table, wondering when everyone else in the group but him had become fluent in Spanish.

I need to practice more, I guess, he thought as Paola placed plates in front of him and Bob, filled with rice, beans, and chopped chorizo.

"Here you go. The specialty of the house," she said, continuing to the next table, trailed by Cristina with a tray of plates to deposit.

James took a bite and was taken aback by the sudden onset of spice from the chorizo. He bit into a forkful of rice, cooling his boiling tongue as he tried to speak to the girls at the table.

"¿Este es su escuela?" he asked, cringing at his broken accent.

"This is where we go in the summer when we don't have school," the little girl closest to him spoke in crisp English. She had two long ponytails draped down her back tied with bright red ribbons at the top. Her thin face was placid and mature for her age defined by expressive eyebrows.

"Oh," James said, taken aback by the sudden change in languages. "So this is like camp?"

"What's camp?" the girl asked, munching on a forkful of rice.

"It's a place where parents drop their kids in the summer when they go to work," Bob said, munching on his chorizo.

"Then yes, like camp." The girl shrugged. "Who are you?"

"I'm James and this is Bob." James replied, pointing at his friend across the table who waved at the group. "What's your name?"

"Layla," she said, and pointed to her friends one by one introducing them. "That's Sophia, Mercedes, and Dina."

"Nice to meet you girls." James looked the girls over. They were all around the same age, probably between five and eight years old, and relied on Layla to be the speaker of the group.

"What are you doing here?" Layla asked.

"We're here to check out the BlankZone," James said and noticing the look of confusion on her face, translated, "La Guerro Blanco."

Layla's eyes widened and she shook her head. "They're bad. That's what my abuela says. Some people think they might be here to help us, but not what my grandparents said. All bad."

"Yeah, we think so, too," James said, searching for a way to change the topic when he noticed a stack of palm fronds on the table surrounding a group of figures tied to resemble monkeys. He picked one off the table and admired it handing it to Bob to inspect.

"Did you make these?" James asked, picking another off the pile.

"Sophia made that one," she responded, picking another and handing it to James, "This one's mine."

"So cool," Bob said, holding it to the side where he could use the window light to get a better look.

"Could you show us how?" James asked, and the little girls smiled and looked at each other speaking in another secret language of silence James did not and would never know.

"Of course!" Layla said, receiving an unspoken okay from her friends. She pushed her half-eaten plate aside and picked one of the unbent fronds off the table.

They spent the rest of the mealtime tying the palms into different animals, a talent James did not know he would be good at, but he caught on quickly. The girls loved the attempts Bob made at manipulating the plants into dogs, cats, and birds, but each one of his creations was more and more debauched than the last until he eventually gave up, telling the girls they would need more palms if he was ever going to learn.

James didn't even notice the time that had passed until a bell rang and the girls sprang from the table. He looked to the front of the room and saw Paola, Rosa, and Mariel wishing the children a good day on their way out the door. He glanced outside and saw the sun dipping in the sky.

We need to figure out where we're staying for the night, he thought. He stood to ask Paola about where they could set up camp when Stacie caught his eye from across the room and motioned him outside.

He said goodbye to the girls and clapped Bob on the shoulder as he followed Stacie out the door to the center of the clearing where they met Cristina and Deck chatting.

"What?! You have a beautiful voice. Or at least what I heard of it," Deck said, thick charm laid on every word.

"Thank you," Cristina said, not taken by the obvious flattery. "I enjoy singing to kids now. It's my new calling, I guess."

"I think you should give it another shot," Deck replied with his hands on his hips. "Really, I mean we were all impressed. Right, James?"

"Certainly. You have a talent," James said, grinning and trying not to laugh at Stacie's eye roll.

"I appreciate it, but enough about my singing. Paola wanted me to give you a quick tour of the land. Then we'll take you to town. Follow me." She started into one of the other buildings they had not entered and James pointed for Stacie to follow, grabbing Deck's shoulder as he dove ahead. "Ladies first."

Deck mumbled under his breath, "Yeah, yeah, yeah. Ladies first, I guess."

The structure they entered this time had its windows open and circular tables spread throughout the room. Art supplies of all kinds and bins with musical instruments were overflowing in the corners. Like the cafeteria, it was all one big room, and was also completely constructed of wood boards with lashed bamboo holding it together. They walked through to the other door where a trail appeared with all manner of orchids, birds of paradise, and dense greenery edging the path.

"This was all the land Paola and Hector gave to the care center. It was built as a place where the children could roam freely and safely around the school while still interacting with nature. None of the children are permitted on the trails alone, but it allows us to show them the world they live in." Cristina guided them down the pathways, identifying all the flora James would never remember and pointing out birds and the odd sloth they came across.

They were in Eden. A gorgeous strip of untouched jungle rife with fruit, towering trees, and vines draped across the path like bedroom curtains. Of all the rainforests James had experienced, this was the one time he enjoyed it and he reveled in the idea of appreciating the moment. After walking for twenty minutes, they came to a clearing ensconced in more vines and hidden from the world by a wall of vegetation.

"And here," Cristina said, sheathing the machete she had used to cut a door in the shrubbery, "is where you can stay."

James stepped through the hole to inspect their quarters. Sunlight reached the ground and it looked as if they could climb trees to install whatever solar panels they would need to get electricity.

"Can we get the truck back here?" Stacie asked, sizing the space and placing a hand on a moss-covered tree.

"There's a river on the other side of this. We can ask one of the men in town to help us with a raft to bring the vehicles back here. You can take down the vegetation necessary to get everything else."

"Looks solid to me," Deck said, grabbing a branch and pulling himself up the nearest tree with ease. He stepped onto a thick limb hanging over the encampment and sat looking back at the three on the ground. "It's secluded enough in here to do what we need and if we get the truck back here installing those solar panels shouldn't be a problem. Also, living next to a river could be a good entry or exit way."

James had to agree. Paola had thought of everything. He was impressed by the way her mind managed to fit the location to their needs.

"This is perfect. Onto town?"

"¡Por supuesto, James!" Cristina said, clapping her hands. "Let's get the rest of your people and head there now. I'm sure your arrival has not gone unnoticed. With all the children back home by now you'll see many people trying to get a glimpse at the guerros Nortes." Cristina finished her sentence with a wink and pulled the vegetation back for them to duck through. They followed her to the care center where the rest of the team stood chatting in broken Spanglish with Mariel, Rosa, and Paola. When they were all assembled the team followed Paola and Cristina to town while the other two women stayed behind.

Stacie and James walked next to each other following the rest of the team.

"What do you think?" Stacie asked, peering at him with a thoughtful expression.

"Seems like they think we're saviors or something," James replied, looking up to spot a macaw fly overhead and land on the branch of a long tree.

"I know. That makes me nervous."

"Same," James said remembering the sickening lurch in his stomach when Paola mentioned no one would leave the village. "But we're their only hope. It's so isolated, I feel like we have to help."

"I want to see the BlankZone."

"We will. That's what I want to do, too, but let's be gracious to our hosts. They've earned that much." Stacie nodded.

James was in full agreement with her. The BlankZone was why they were here and the best way for them to help these people and the Federation was to learn as much as they could about the enemy while they were so close. "When we finish with our tour of town, I'll bring it up to Paola."

"I trust you. I want to get going is all." Stacie stepped over a line of ants crossing the trail while she continued. "I'm stuck on that stupid code and could use some fresh anger and inspiration by getting a look at the enemy."

James grinned and patted her shoulder. "We'll get you that creative spark soon. Don't worry."

Stacie grunted and they walked the rest of the way in silence admiring the spectacle of the nature all around. The group ahead stopped and turned around to face them. James and Stacie caught up in no time.

"What's up?" Kyle asked Paola, holding an arm above his head in a stretch.

"We're about to enter town. Many of these people have never been outside the village and they'll be suspicious of you at first, but they're muy amable."

The group nodded and Jon looked behind him. He already knew James's unspoken request and whispered "nice" over his shoulder, translating on the fly.

"That works for us, Paola. Anything else we should know?" James asked, interested to see what everything looked like.

Paola looked at the air, thinking, and James sensed discomfort in her stance. After a moment or two she looked back at James, "Not yet, but let's go meet the people and we can talk afterward. Okay?"

James was unsure of how to respond other than returning a thumbs-up and a smile. "Let's go!"

He knew he sounded falsely cheery to the rest of the team, but it was good enough to fool Paola who relaxed her stance and recouped her smile. She led the way off the trail onto a hardened dirt road.

"That was odd," Stacie said under her breath.

"Keep an eye out. There's something Paola doesn't trust here," James said back to her. "I have a feeling there's a reason they run the care center two miles away from town."

"I'm on it."

James's stomach twisted with all the unknowns building in his mind, but he brushed it aside. Focus on the now. He repeated the mantra concentrating his attention. They emerged from the foliage onto a wide roadway with hedged walls of green surrounding them on either side providing a corridor to the end of the road where bare bulbed streetlights stood to either side announcing the entrance to town.

CHAPTER 7

Town is an overstatement, James thought. He walked past the flickering lights on either side of the planks that made the bridge marking the entrance to town.

Old thick wood boards spanned the width of the lazy river as water swirled in ebbs and flows underneath their feet. Center of town was a square pavilion with a few picnic tables standing under sparsely canopied trees. Hard-packed dirt was covered by more dust than grass and a few chickens wandered the ground pecking at unseen bugs. Directly to his left and creating two sides of the pavilion were rows of squat cement houses with aluminum roofs. They cut off at the end of the far row, but James noticed the road snaked back into what he presumed was a more condensed neighborhood set up inside the fringes of the river. To his right along the river front was an open field with faint chalk lines, rusting goalposts set up on both sides, and a stand of old metal bleachers. Finally, on the far side of the pavilion stood a brightly colored mansion. James couldn't tell what it was for, but it was an important place to someone in town. Cement outer walls topped with wrought iron fencing wrapped in razor wire let off the odd glint of color from the edges of broken glass stuck in the cement. As a final deterrent, an array of cameras the Federation's military command would be impressed by captured every angle imaginable.

Why would someone need all that here? James thought looking around the center of town, confused.

People huddled on their porches watching the strangers, waving back at Paola's cheerful hellos with caution.

"Not the parade we hoped for, huh?" Deck said, dropping back to walk by James and Stacie.

"You expected a parade?" Stacie asked. She attempted a wave at one of the porches but received no response from the young family watching them.

"I expected a banner at least."

"What's that?" James asked. He nodded towards the enormous building across the pavilion towering above the trees.

"Looks like a goddamn castle," Deck said, shading his eyes from the sun's glare.

"Or a fortress," Stacie added, pointing at the cameras. "Someone's worried about their safety."

"Here?" Deck asked.

"I'm guessing that has something to do with Paola's concern," James replied. "Let's wait, Paola will tell us." *What is this place?* James's thought thrown off by the inconsistent world they had discovered when he heard someone calling his name.

"James! James!" Paola shouted from one of the porches. She waved her hands to get his attention.

He walked to the house where Paola stood talking with an older couple sitting on a bench against a blue cement wall. The house was well-kept. A garden lay across the front of the porch with plump multi-colored peppers hanging from the stalks and an intricate system of strings and wooden stakes scattered amongst the greenery to keep the plants from toppling under their own weight.

"James, these are my good friends Jose and Selma," Paola said turning to the couple on the porch. "Este es James. El es el capitàn de los guerros del Norte."

"Mucho gusto, James," Selma said in a calming voice. She smiled when she stood to greet him with an outstretched palm, "Welcome to Río Negro."

"Mucho gusto," James replied, shaking Jose's hand after letting go of Selma's. Jose smiled at him and sat back down, but Selma remained standing, leaning against a wooden post holding up the porch's awning.

"Your town is beautiful," James said, trying to find something to say.

Selma chuckled. "That's nice of you to say, but it's… not."

James didn't know how to respond and struggled to form words, but Selma held her hand up, "I love the sentiment, James, but this"—she held her hand up and waved at the dilapidated town center behind him—"es muy feo. It's sad really." Her face dropped and her eyes held back words James knew he wanted to hear. *I'll have to figure out what that's about*, he thought, noting the moment.

"Either way, we're happy to be here."

"Bueno y bienvenidos," Selma said, sitting back in her chair guided by her husband.

"Come on, let's get the rest of the team. Cristina and I—" Paola was cut off by the arrival of a black SUV pulling into the town square.

Billows of dust surrounded the mystery vehicle when it stopped. James glanced at the mansion beyond the trees, noticing that the cameras had moved to train themselves in their direction. James looked at Stacie, receiving a slight nod in response. She had seen it, too. Someone was watching.

Two men in dark suits exited the SUV and set themselves up around the vehicle, one at the back and the other at the front. The driver got out and opened the back door for a short fat man in a well-tailored tan suit. James took a long look at the man standing next to the SUV. He sported a well-trimmed black goatee and short-cropped hair. Each of his fingers donned a different ring. He dabbed sweat from his brow with a pristine white kerchief and tucked it back into his lapel. The way he examined his surroundings was not normal. He ingested the sight, feeding on what was around him, analyzing everything, looking for something. James didn't know what it was. The familiar feeling of iron braced James's stomach.

The man pretended to catch sight of Paola and walked over to her with his arms spread wide.

"¡Paola, mi profesora favorita! ¿Como está? ¿Dónde están los niños?" He kissed Paola on both cheeks. Her body language was clear. Paola was disgusted. She pulled away from the second kiss and folded her arms across her chest, staring at him with tightly pressed lips.

Paola's features contrasted sharply with the false smile painted on the man's face. The tension was obvious. James caught Stacie's eye again during the exchange. The team had fanned out and everyone stood within striking distance of the vehicle. Kyle walked across the circle, pretending to inspect the top of a tree so he could stand next to the man at the front of the SUV. The atmosphere was stiff and the eyes of the men darted at the casual warriors who had them surrounded. James worried their trigger fingers were getting jumpy.

"Goddammit," he swore under his breath, realizing he needed to do something.

"¿Hola, còmo està?" he said to the man staring down Paola. He stuck his hand out in front of them, half expecting one of the bodyguards to make a move, but he kept himself steady, not showing the rigidity of his muscles ready to launch at the first sign of trouble.

"Me llamo James. ¿Y usted?" He held his breath, glad his Spanish skills went far enough to ask the man's name. He would have a rough time if things changed.

The man eyed James, the smile increased in intensity as he shook James's hand, pumping his arm.

"¿Hola, còmo està? Your accent? Are you from the North?" he asked. James took a deep breath, thankful the conversation had switched to a language he was comfortable with but noticed the condescension in the man's voice when making the change.

"We are. We came to get some needed rest and picked up Paola a little farther north. She was excited to get back here."

"Well, we're glad to have our Paola back," he said. He turned to Paola and beamed the same false smile. "How is your land?" He waited for her to respond, but she held her blank focused stare without offering a reply.

"Anyway, it is a pleasure to meet you, and welcome to my town! I'm the mayor, Juan Carlos Morenos Salvades. Come, let me give you a tour."

James glanced at the rest of the team and saw a shrug from Stacie before replying. "That would be wonderful, but I think Paola and Cristina were going to show us around."

"Are you sure? I am the keys to the city," Juan Carlos said, pushing out his chest, boasting. "I came here ten years ago. Since then, it's been nothing but success, largest pineapple producers in the territory and on the way to the largest in the Federation."

"Thanks, but maybe another time. The ladies were kind enough to offer their services."

"Let me accompany you. I'd love to join," he replied. He clapped his hands and his driver opened the door for them. Air conditioning washed over James and the skin on his arms prickled when the cool air made contact.

"That's a fine offer, but I think we'd rather walk."

Juan Carlos's smile wavered for a second, but James kept his grin fixed and firm. Kyle moved behind the man at the front of the vehicle and James caught sight of the knife concealed on his friend's waist sliding from its sheath discretely hiding it behind his forearm. James was glad no one noticed and he returned his host's intense eye contact.

Juan Carlos's eyes flashed as he read the situation. James interpreted the machinations behind his eyes analyzing their options while his bodyguards appeared ready to spring, but Juan Carlos put up his arms.

"Of course, how rude of me." He turned to Paola.

"Whenever you can, please bring our new guests back. I'd love to learn more about them and tell them the story of Black River."

James took a breath, unwilling to break his mask of carefree tourist yet. "That would be great."

Paola maintained her placid observation of them while James shook hands with Juan Carlos. The driver opened the door, and Juan Carlos stepped onto the runner of the SUV but paused.

"I do have one question," he said with his back to James. He turned in place and stood on the runner with an arm draped over the open door, his other hand clenching the top of it. "How did you end up here?" His persona changed to a more calculated guise than he had originally shown during their introductions.

James decided to keep the details light. "As I said, we're from the North and gave Paola a ride home. That's it."

"Ahh. And how about the military vehicles you drove?" Juan Carlos's smile had dropped and he gazed at James, mocking him with feigned curiosity.

James chose to remain aloof. "Need something to drive and they're leaving them all over the place."

This response caught Juan Carlos by surprise and rather than waiting for him to continue asking questions he didn't want to answer, James cut off the conversation. "As much as we'd like to talk more with the town's mayor, we need to get some food and sleep. It's been a long journey." He held out his hand again and Juan Carlos accepted defeat for the moment.

He held James's hand for a second too long. "Whenever you want, come to the mayor's residence. I'd love to show you around."

James nodded as they watched the bodyguards re-enter the vehicle. James motioned for the rest of the team to follow him toward the path. A cloud of dust rushed over their shoulders as the SUV drove away and the team walked to the trail heading back to Paola's care center.

He waited until they were far enough away from the head of the trail to turn toward Stacie. "What'd you think?"

"I want to cut that guy's balls off."

"We all do," Kyle said, walking up and standing next to them.

James said, "If that's the case, who knows, Stace, maybe you'll get to one day."

"It's on my bucket list."

James grinned, but internally he was flipping through his conversation with the so called mayor of Río Negro. Juan Carlos was an issue. He would have to confirm it, but he was pretty sure the man was Selma and Paola's reason for sadness and hesitation when showing off the town. *I need to ask Paola*, James thought glancing up at their host in front of the team.

They finished their walk to the huts with Paola and Cristina leading the way in silence. When they arrived, Mariel and Rosa were busy preparing a table with bowls of fruit and taco mixings.

"Back so soon?" Rosa asked with a grin.

"Couldn't have come back fast enough," Deck said, picking a slice of orange out of one of the bowls. "Who the hell is that guy anyway?" he asked. A mouthful of citrus, juice poured down his chin and he mumbled under his breath, "Oh my God, this is the best orange I've ever had."

"Juan Carlos is a dangerous man," Paola said, sitting at the table making eye contact with the wood surface.

"You never mentioned him," James said, sitting and taking a piece of fruit from the bowl. "There a reason for that?" He popped the unidentified ball of sweetness into his mouth and was blown away by the crisp, honey-layered sensation.

This is the best fruit I've ever had, he thought. He was distracted for a second by the intense flavor coating his tongue when he realized he had asked Paola a question and he reconcentrated on their guide.

Silence flooded the room while Paola wiped her hands, front and back, on her dress in a nervous tick, looking at the ground deep in thought.

Paola, finished with her thoughts, placed her hands on the table and stared at James. "If I had told you about him, you might not have come here. It's as simple as that, James. Necesitamos ustedes. We need you, and I hope you can forgive me for not mentioning him to get you here."

Regret and shame were painted on her face and rang through her words. James knew he would have done the same in her position. He decided to save it for another time. There were more important things to talk about right then.

"I understand. I do want to learn more though," he said, putting a hand on Paola's. "For now, when can we go see the BZ?"

"¿Como?" she asked, not following his question.

"La Guerra Blanca," James said, pointing in the direction where he thought they were.

"Ahhh. Sí, in the morning. We'll leave at daylight."

CHAPTER 8

Humid air clung to James, soaking his shirt while they walked. He shifted the rifle slung across his back to alleviate the sweat drenching his arm as droplets tickled his bicep.

I hope this is almost over, James thought, smacking a mosquito against his head.

As promised, Paola had roused them at daybreak to see the BlankZone's camp. They had been walking for an hour with Paola telling them a little further every ten minutes. James had stopped believing her and Deck grumbled under his breath about the difference between a little further and six miles. Even so, the excitement kept the team moving fast. The first part of a long journey was coming to a close. Adrenaline coursed through James, and he wasn't sure if he was ready for the next step.

"What do you think it'll look like?" Deck asked.

"Similar to the satellite images we saw of Africa, but less built up. They would have to clear a massive swath of rainforest to do anything on that scale, but given their previous accomplishments, it wouldn't surprise me."

"Yeesh, football fields of planes set up hours south of the northern border. Scary shit."

"You're telling me," James replied. He recalled the BZ's base in Africa. An entire continent transformed to house the vast BZ army. Whatever they were doing here, James knew it would be something he never expected.

Paola held a hand up and the team stopped. She put one finger to her lips and motioned for James to join her next to a towering tree with vines hanging down its trunk in pendulous loops.

"Climb and look. They're two miles to the south, but I don't dare go closer." She handed him one of the vines and pointed at the grooves in the tree that appeared as footholds.

"I've got it, James," Deck said reaching for the vine. "Figure this is what a scout's for."

"Not this time. I've got it," James said. He took the scope off his rifle and handed the long gun to Deck. "Signal me if anything pops up."

"You got it, boss," Deck said, disappointed but respecting the decision. "Watch your step, might be snakes," Deck quipped with a wink.

James flipped him off and turned around, planning his first steps.

He picked out the footholds he would use, pulled on the vine to test its strength, and started his climb.

He went slowly, ensuring the vine was holding until he reached the first branch twenty feet off the ground. The supersized flora was fed by the rich soil and misty rainforest, creating the arboreal monsters looming about the forest. The first limb was as thick as a tree trunk and its branches were proportionally as large. James kicked off the smooth bark up to the set of branches another ten feet above his head. He reached his second mount and did the same thing, pulling himself up the gigantic structure and kicking off to climb the thick natural cords swinging against their host. He was in awe of the tree's size, but even more taken by the ecosystem it supported. As he ventured farther into the canopy he found branches growing closer together, but capable of supporting his weight.

He decided to climb by hand the rest of the way. James searched for a thick vine that vanished in the leafy clouds marking his path. He yanked to test its strength and, satisfied, tied the end of the thick plant material around his waist before restarting his journey.

The birds in the treetops eyed him from afar. James imagined himself in their minds, watching him encroach on their world.

Don't worry, James thought, willing the words in his brain to the birds, *I'm not gonna do anything to your nests. Just relax. And don't knock me off this branch,* he thought, realizing his position of weakness.

He looked down. Between the dense leaf cover and height, the ground was nonexistent. He took a deep breath, pushing higher, past the height of his safety line until he pulled a branch aside and a deep blue sky appeared.

He shimmied along the thinning tree trunk until its branches were too sparse to continue.

James decided this was a good stopping point. He pulled up enough of his plant rope, untied the vine, lashed it around the tree, and back around his waist. He tugged, testing his safety belt. Ready. James leaned back against the tree trunk and examined the world around him. He was over two hundred yards off the ground and trees of similar sizes stood challenging one another for height supremacy.

Whisps of cloud grazed the treetops and birds floated across the sky dipping to land on branches before continuing their travels. A hundred yards away James spotted monkeys eating fruit. Insects buzzed around his ears, and multicolored butterflies and beetles intersected in the air. It was an awesome sparkling kaleidoscope of silver, gold, orange, and blue in the high-noon sun. A deep breath of pure air renewed James's sense of the unique world perched atop this behemoth of a trunk, centuries in the making.

"This is incredible," James said under his breath, gazing at the beauty.

Forgetting himself for a second, James snapped back to reality. James held the rifle scope up but put it down a second later realizing he wouldn't need it.

He gritted his teeth and stared in wonder at the world they had created. The base melded perfectly with the forest creating the illusion that everything, including the steel structures, grew naturally in the surrounding jungle. Fleets of vehicles glinted in the sunlight underneath bio-manipulated canopies of trees acting as both shelter and shade for the vehicles. The world they built was synchronous with the jungle, and ant-like soldiers moved fluidly in the distance.

Large cement structures interspersed the grounds appearing as natural pyramids in the landscape. James puzzled over their appearance, rectangular blobs rising at random from the dark soil, but brushed past them quickly.

James put the scope to his eye for a closer look, in awe at the incredible feats the BZ had conjured from nothing in the Amazonian rainforest. Solar receivers were spread throughout the compound and James heard the hum of their nature-driven generators buzzing from his perch in the sky a whole two miles away. The buildings consisted of sheets of aluminum and dense walls of thin tree limbs hanging from their hosts. The only hangar James could see housed a few helicopters under an intertwined canopy of branches while Spanish moss created a watertight shelter for the hulking machinery.

Drainage systems were erected as long hollowed open-top pipes ending in a myriad of cisterns dotting the camp. Their creation had no end, stretching as far back and to the sides as James's scope would allow him to search. It was miraculous. James had climbed the tree expecting to find a paved-over rainforest with glinting metal replacing the natural perfection of the jungle. Instead, he discovered a world built into an ecosystem, reliant on and designed to give as much as it took from the space it occupied.

What is this? James thought, blown away by the sheer size and creativity of the mecca the BZ had created for themselves.

How could the Federation compete with them?

He knew he was taking too long, but he couldn't take his eyes off the sight.

We need to learn as much as they could about that tech, James thought, trying to figure out how to get close enough to understand their enemy.

He put the scope back to his eye, focusing his attention on people this time. Soldiers walked with a purpose, entering and exiting buildings with choreographed ease crisscrossing open spaces in purposeful lines. Much like those exiting the boats on the shores of Midway months ago, these men and women were inhuman in their movement. No motion wasted, no step out of place. Communication was non-existent between the paths of steadily intersecting bodies.

What am I watching? James thought, scanning the camp to get a sense of their defenses.

A glint of sunlight caught James's eye and he focused on a wide flat metal disc fixed to a tree. *Sensors or cameras?* James wondered, spotting a similar device buried higher in the canopy. They were hidden in the treetops extending from the edge of the camp. James stopped counting after he had reached two dozen devices. He turned his attention closer to the camp searching for other preventative measures when he spotted another one of the sensors. But this one was different. It hovered in the air as if it were hanging off a wire. Then, without warning, the disc floated and stopped a few yards away, refocusing its attention on its new location.

"It's a Sentinel," James murmured under his breath, surprised the BZ had brought the devices used to guard its borders overseas to defend their new camp in the Federation.

Confused and overwhelmed by everything he had seen, James decided it was time for someone else to look and he started his descent to the forest floor.

He plucked his way down the tree, lost in his thoughts of the BlankZone. Who were these people? And what are they doing right now? The soldiers walking with no interaction, shoulder to shoulder along the unseen pathways of the camp spooked James as did the existence of their Sentinels floating on the edge of the camp ready to decimate any threat. How were they supposed to combat something like that?

A poorly placed handhold on the slick bark sent James's elbow crashing into the branch beneath his shoulder. Sparks of pain erupted up and down James's arm and he instinctively reached out to a vine hanging in front of him to regain his balance more than fifty yards above the ground. He took a deep breath, steadying himself on the branch, and moved his arm to relieve the aching pain. He looked to the ground from his dizzying height and refocused his attention on the remaining descent. *The last thing I need is a broken back,* he reasoned, grasping the next branch and testing its strength.

He made it another twenty yards and glimpsed through the mesh of branches and leaves revealing the dark forest floor. He stopped himself, found a wide branch, and sat against the trunk to think for a moment.

The world seemed small from his perch in the rainforest. Living things ran along the branches searching for pieces of life to digest. James wished he could talk to the animals that lived there. Maybe they'd be able to tell him all he needed to know about the layout and goings on of the BlankZone camp. Who was their leader? How did the camp's order break down? What kinds of resources were moving in and out of the camp?

James let himself slip into the fantasy of wild sentient monkeys answering all his questions when he stopped himself. There were people who knew this information. There were hundreds of individuals who could give them everything they needed to know about the BZ and its population. The answer was right in front of James, but he had not put the equation together. It was too simple to be true.

"We're going to kidnap someone from the BZ camp."

He said it aloud trying to make eye contact with one of the monkeys a few trees over so he couldn't take it back. That was their option. They were going to kidnap a member of the BZ, and they were going to get their answers directly from the source. They were about to embark on the most dangerous mission ever taken in Federation history.

PART II

CHAPTER 9

Ragged breath shook James's chest while he leaped over the moss-covered mound blocking his path. His eyes searched the forest floor, glancing up intermittently to check the trail, but he focused most of his attention on the jungle's myriad of hidden roots. A low roar trembled the ground, growing in intensity as James came to the edge of the river. A wide swath of swiftly moving water opened in front of him and James gazed at the point where the world dropped off the edge of the earth. Hazy vapor rose from the waterfall and James splashed cool water on his face letting the slow-moving cloud wash over him.

"All right, let's go," he said under his breath, imploring his aching legs to move. He hit his thighs with his fists and before he could second-guess himself dove back into the jungle foliage.

On the path, leaves and trees created a sound barrier dulling the deafening roar of the waterfall to a muffled crash in the background. Rays of sun poked through the canopy creating golden shafts of light that revealed layers of mist in the early morning. Toucans and macaws cackled in the forest and James breezed through the tropical setting, controlling his breathing as he ran.

This was the time he could run. He couldn't go out for a jog at noon. It was too hot and the paths were crammed with workers traveling between fields. His afternoons and mornings were always busy whether he was analyzing imagery from BZ reconnaissance, helping the school, or teaching English classes in town. James was needed in a million places at once. Then, when the day was over, the sun was too low for him to go ten miles before he was running alone in the pitch-black. A dangerous proposition for more than hidden roots.

So, here he was, 6:30 a.m. on a Wednesday in the middle of a rainforest, running full tilt into his eighth mile of ten. Tomorrow was a rest day and he needed it. Well, a rest day from this kind of exercise, an hour of lifting followed by a ten-mile run, five days a week. It kept him sane and focused on the day. Even on his rest days in their HQ he stretched or did a light yoga session. However, when he traveled to the BZ border, it was different. He eased up on the last mile, jogging slower every quarter mile until he was walking, getting his heart rate under control.

James took the HOLO emitter from his pocket and its screen appeared in front of him. He normally wouldn't let himself look at any tech during his workout, but James needed to be prepared today. He was on recon for the next week with Kyle and wanted to make sure they had their plan airtight. After ten months of careful watching and intel gathering, they were ready to finalize their plans.

A team of ants distracted James for a second, crossing the dirt path carrying shards of green leaves on their backs, no doubt returning to a queen hidden in her underground castle. James stepped over the line of workers, leaving them to finish their job in peace while he finished his exercise, and replaced the emitter in his pocket.

James refocused on the day and week ahead, mentally steeling himself for what was sure to be mind-numbing boredom mixed with the real possibility that this could be the last recon the team needed until they carried out their plan to kidnap a BZ leader. All the pieces were there. For ten months the team had analyzed the BZ from the outside in. They started off learning how the sensors worked by sending in miniature drones, the size of hummingbirds, to distract the devices and discover coverage gaps. They even figured out how to move the Sentinels to where the team wanted them to open paths into the BZ's camp. It took a lot of coordination from the unmanned drones, but Jon and Clint had perfected their flight patterns. Not to mention, Kevin had a few tricks of his own to keep the camp busy.

After the boundary research was complete, James and the team focused on the internal machinations of the camp. How many people were stationed there? What was their social order? How did the hierarchy manifest itself? Who were the leaders? What was their routine? How did they communicate? The questions were endless, and James became frustrated, coming up with a new one every time they thought they had made a breakthrough. But it was time. Two weeks ago, Jon and Clint had been stationed on the border and officially confirmed leadership ranks. James remembered the moment vividly.

It was dark, as always, when they switched team members for recon. Sending two people at a time was the best way to complete research. They followed a strict sleep and wake schedule and had to spend a certain amount of time together and apart. The first few missions had not been easy and included a lot of bitter, angry fighting that once even devolved into an intense wrestling match leaving someone unconscious in a sleeper hold. James had felt awful, but Deck eventually forgave him. Clearly, they had needed a system and Stacie was the best person to develop a routine.

The pair who came back from the line normally spent their first few days in a slight stupor, breaking out of their isolation. Everyone had their own way of dealing with it— partying, working out, overeating, or sleeping for sixteen hours straight. The stress of being on high alert fewer than two miles away from the largest army assembled in human history wheedled its way into one's mind. Knowing that same army was intent on infiltrating the Federation, for reasons unknown, only deepened the anxiety. After his first trip to the border, James understood better the way people react upon returning to normalcy after periods of intense pressure. This time had been unique. James was sound asleep when the pair came back, and he was woken by Deck.

"They're back," Deck said, his voice flat in the darkness.

"Great. I'll talk to them in the morning," James said. He rotated to the other side of his hammock, assuming Deck wanted James to wake up and party.

"We need you, James. They've got some shit to talk about."

The seriousness edging Deck's voice put James on alert. This was real.

They walked to the common area where Stacie, Clint, Jon, and Bob were seated under the open-sided, aluminum roofed area they called their living room. Glass beer bottles glinted in the yellow overhead light, but the atmosphere was far from the jovial party that usually greeted a return.

Stacie's eyes met his when he entered.

"Thanks for waking up," she said, moving on the couch for James.

"Sounded important," he said, accepting the seat. He turned his attention to Jon and Clint who pondered the floor with blank stares.

"Either of you want to start?" he asked. He glanced between the two silent returnees waiting for their reveal with anticipation building in his veins.

Jon looked up first, beginning to speak, but shook his head and went back to focusing on the wood slats. Clint hadn't lifted his eyes to James, but he took a deep swig of beer and spoke. "We found the leader. We also know how serious they are about being here."

James was confused. What the hell was he talking about? They already knew who the leaders were. Confirming it was great news, but serious about being here? They had moved an entire army across the ocean and attacked the only other target left in the world. What does that mean if it's not serious?

"The video's loading from the roaches, but this was too important to wait. From the top, Clint," Stacie said. She nodded at Clint from across the table.

Clint took another swig from his bottle and continued, "Everything was going the same as usual. We identified the individuals we think run the camp. You know the group, Tall-guy-with-beard, Short-woman-with-shoulders, Tall-woman-with-buzz-cut, the same old crew. We were keeping a close eye on them when they received a group of emissaries again. The same big double-blade choppers they fly. This time was special. The whole camp assembled in that meeting area in the center of camp and our three 'leaders' stood at the front. It was incredible. The camp opened even more, as if the structures crawled over night to make space for everyone. Thousands came out to greet the chopper. I mean, *thousands*. No shit, man, it was a sea of people flooding every corner of the camp. This all for one guy with a machete strapped to his back. They gave him a big round of applause and he waved as if he was on a stage, there to entertain the troops. He started talking, waving, and making motions to the crowd. We tried to get his voice on our drones, but the audio blocks were running again. We could only watch and record video with a couple of drones squeezed in for closeups. It seemed like a big celebration until the mood changed.

Clint took another sip of his beer. "Our three people, Shoulders, Buzzcut, and Beard, turned to face the man, locked arms, and got to their knees. Random people from the crowd came forward and tied them together.

"Next, six men were led on stage in a line. We'd never seen them, but they looked like locals. Probably workers from the fields. We couldn't ID them, but one thing was sure, they were scared shitless. Had to be dragged onto the stage. One of them even pissed himself. The machete guy walked behind them speaking towards the ground but intended for the crowd and always motioning at the line of men. It was bizarre."

"What was the crowd doing?" James asked, trying to paint the scene.

"Quiet. Reserved as if they were listening to a teacher in class and not some crazy guy on stage pulling out a machete and waving it at the backs of men shaking in terror," Clint replied, looking James in the eye for the first time.

James nodded and motioned for him to resume.

"Anyway, machete man approached the three on their knees. Without a pause he drew his blade in a slice across Shoulder's throat. She didn't move. Hers was the easiest death. It was freaky, as if she knew her fate, almost wanted it. Dying, bleeding out on a stage in front of her command. After she slumped forward he repeated the process with Beard on the far side of the line. He kept himself upright until his spine gave way and he fell sideways into the Buzzcut. The fall ripped an artery or something because when he toppled over a spray of red erupted in the air, covering Buzzcut's face. The machete guy didn't let that stop him. He cut her throat and let her bleed out, too.

"When Buzzcut stopped convulsing, the man cleaned his blade on his pant leg. Then he lifted a fist in the air and the crowd erupted. He waved, and the crowd rushed the stage pulling the line of locals with them."

Clint paused, staring at the ground as he finished. "We lost track of them in the melee, but blood erupted in a random part of the mob staining a circle of people. More of those circles broke out and finally, the body parts came. Legs, arms, thighs, and heads held in the air, swung about and tossed across the assembly like beach balls at a concert. They tore them to pieces."

James let the horror seep into his mind. Bodies ripped apart by a crowd of frenzied soldiers for what? Sport? Morale?

"One good thing came out of all this," Jon spoke from the other side of the table, holding the neck of his beer bottle. "He's the guy. He's *it*, James. We know the BZ leader."

James nodded his head, "You get a name?"

Clint nodded his head and Bob flipped on his HOLO screen and pulled up a picture of a slender man with a smooth face, dark blue eyes, and short black hair.

"They kept the audio block running, but every lipreading device we have agrees. Commander Raspin."

Sweating in the middle of the jungle Raspin's face floated across his vision. What kind of commander slits the throats of his predecessors? Or has his command tear apart the bodies of prisoners? How'd they even get them in the first place?

James shook his head, his mind's eye wandering to the scene he imagined every morning when he woke. *Stop. Concentrate on what you need to do,* he thought. He stumbled at a slow jog into town and stopped at the plastic cistern of rainwater next to Jose and Selma's front porch. He poured a cool handful of water on the back of his neck enjoying the momentary relief from the heat already mounting in the early morning hours.

"James! James!"

James turned to get bowled into by a pair of bony arms knocking the wind out of him.

"I was going to run with you!" Layla said in a humph.

James held a hand up wheezing for breath.

"Right? You said I could come with you today!" Layla's hands moved to her hips. Even at a young age, she carried a commanding presence.

"Layla! Leave him alone. He can't breathe," Selma said, coming out on the porch. She handed James a glass of water as she turned back to scold the girl.

"He can't do much more to wake you! I heard him yelling in your window telling you to get ready this morning. Dios mío, niña, you can sleep through anything," Selma said, exasperated.

Layla's eyes glanced at the ground, "I thought I had more time."

"Don't worry about it. You can run with me to school this morning, okay?" James said reaching out a hand for a low-five.

"Okay, sorry…" the girl said, embarrassed, hitting his hand with depleted enthusiasm.

James waved it aside. "You needed your sleep. I'll take you one of these mornings. Now get your stuff. I'll wait for you."

Layla shot inside and the door slammed against the concrete as she sped through.

Selma shook her head and picked up a watering can, "That girl. I swear she's her mother all over again." Selma dipped the can in the cistern and watered her peppers.

"Anything new out there this morning?" she asked James over her shoulder.

"Same as always. Me and the monos," James replied, leaning his butt against the low cement wall forming the boundary to the front porch.

"Los trabajadores will be out there soon."

"It's why I go early. They don't need me running by them on their way to work. Also, too hot later."

"Too hot now, but not for these beauties," Selma said. Her hand caressed one of the enormous peppers hanging off a sagging stem held up by a piece of twine tied to a pole.

"Anything new from El Rey?" James asked, nodding at the mansion towering against the deep blue sky across the plaza.

Disgust flashed across Selma's face. "That jackass. I'll shove a pepper up his ass if he comes here again."

James chuckled under his breath. Selma always had colorful ideas for how she would treat the town's millionaire every time James mentioned him.

"So he's up to his old bullshit?"

"Always. Yesterday he was going door to door telling people we should approach those people, La Guerra Blanca. Saying he could make business work with anyone. Idiota." She spat out the last line with venom reserved for the truly hated.

James was surprised at the information. *I wonder if he's already tried,* James thought, renewing his hope that the men Clint and Jon had seen were part of Juan Carlos's contingent and not innocent farmers.

"He come here?"

"He wouldn't dare," Selma responded. Her lethal glare told James how right she was.

SLAM!

A rush of wind brought Layla next to him poking him in the side.

"Let's go!" she said, prancing about with her blue-striped backpack bouncing on her shoulders.

"You got it! See you, Selma. I'll be back in town later, then I'm out for a little, but Kev's gonna take over my classes for me."

"Gracias, James. I'll see you later." She blew him a kiss while her granddaughter dug her toes into the ground and pushed him from behind.

"Vaya! I want to get there before the other kids!"

"Geez, girl, tranquilo," James said, winking at Selma. He flipped his hip around and sprinted to the head of the trail.

"Keep up!" he yelled. He turned to see Layla regain her balance, grit her teeth, and take off after him with every bit of speed she could muster.

"That was cheap!"

"You bet it was."

"Whatever," she said. The girl brushed it off with a much too mature wave of her hand while they settled into a steady jog.

They chatted about the last week. James and the team had taught them how to hide in the woods using the bushcraft techniques they had learned in training. The kids loved going into the jungle, checking the forest floor, and covering themselves with banana leaves while their caretakers searched the ground for them. James asked her questions about the animals she created from the palm fronds. While James might have been better than Bob, Layla was incredible. She had a knack for arts in general. Any medium Paola, Rosa, or Mariel placed in front of her she grasped without a problem. Even musically the girl possessed a rare gift. Some nights James would go to Selma's and listen to Layla play her grandpa's ukulele while Cristina strummed her guitar and sang songs in Spanish on the front porch until it was too dark to see the trail home.

Layla never failed to impress James, and he treated her like a sibling. It was the least he could do for the kindness the whole town had shown during the past months, taking them in as if they were family and sharing their homes with the team. It was over a year since James or anyone on the team had spoken with someone from their own families and the familiarity with the people in town helped fill the growing void. It provided a sense of what they fought for, reinvigorating their desire to take down the BZ with every fiber of their being.

When they reached the compound, smoke rose from the cafeteria's clay chimney and Mariel waved at them.

"¡Buenas!" she yelled. Mariel wiped her hands on her apron and walked out to greet them.

"Buenas, Señora Mariel," Layla chirped. She skipped up to her teacher and wrapped her arms around Mariel's waist, "¿Cómo estás?"

"Bien, bien, gracias. ¿Y tú? You run today with James?" she asked Layla, glancing at James who gave her a thumbs-up. She and Rosa were taking English lessons with James, and she liked to practice when he was around.

"Hola, Mariel," James said, kissing her on the cheek and receiving the same in return. "Where is everyone?"

"No sé. Asleep maybe?"

"Let's go get them!" Layla yelled, taking off into the woods.

James shook his head and grinned at Mariel who smiled in return and nodded her head at the trail. "Go on. Send her back for breakfast."

James took off after the speedy girl until he reached the vines where Layla was waiting for him to enter.

"Can I?"

"Go ahead," James replied. Without another beat, she pulled open the dense wall of vines disguising their camp entrance.

She held it aside for James to enter and he walked through the leafy doorway.

The camp was broken into four arms set up in a cross shape with their living room or common area at the center. Each arm consisted of one designated section. The entrance to the compound went through the equipment and energy section. That was where they stored their battery packs which hooked up to the solar panels hanging in the trees. They powered everything from surveillance cameras to the string of lights in their bathrooms.

The living and bathroom section was the largest part of camp located at the bottom of the cross. It consisted of two rows of four cabinas facing one another. It reminded James of their cots in Croyton's training compound, but with more privacy. In between the rows of houses and backing into the jungle was the bathroom. Four stalls with gray water passing through a sand filtration system back to the river. They had two toilets and a sink with a mirror produced by buffering unused aluminum roofing into a passable reflective surface. It was all designed by Kyle who possessed natural skills for construction and engineering.

The HQ took up another arm of the cross. Personal gear packs were kept in the cabinas. Any remaining armory items were organized in metal carrying cases around the standalone elevated lean-to shelter where the HOLOs lived and the more dangerous items were kept in a hidden locked armory built behind their fridge array. A permanent six-by-six structure with slanted aluminum roofing protected the screens dedicated to providing the most recent images of the BZ border. The rest of the screens were used to analyze data, capture video around their location, and track any BZ data collected during recon missions. One HOLO was always occupied by the code Jon and Stacie were working to decipher. James had been forced to tell Stacie and Jon to take a break more than once and they had all finally agreed to permanently display the code as a compromise so they would rest.

The kitchen was the second largest part of the cross. It held three fridges, picked up from a nearby dump and retrofitted with solar panels Jon had fashioned. One of the fridges was always filled with liquids, another with fruits and vegetables, and the final held any meat, dairy or baked products Kevin created.

Kyle had drawn the plans for the kitchen's layout and had built it using rope, bamboo, and old metal grates scavenged from the same dump as the fridges.

In the middle of everything was a raised square wooden platform. Stairs were on each side and homemade furniture decorated the space. They owned two palm frond couches and four Adirondack chairs made from chopped down trees.

The coolest part of camp was above their living room platform. Similar to their other structures, the platform had open sides under an A-frame roof made of aluminum sheeting, but Kyle had devised it with star gazing in mind. He formed the roof to retract into itself giving anyone under it a perfect view of the sky. At night James loved sitting under the stars watching the inky black sky littered with a wide beach of twinkling white stars. It was his favorite part of camp, and he was grateful to have someone with the building skills to make it happen.

The camp was their home at this point and James loved the feeling of a place where he felt so comfortable, especially after they endured such an extended period on the road.

He took a breath letting the quiet sink in for a second, but it was time to start the day.

"¡Buenos dias, mis amores!" James shouted at the top of his lungs. He shrugged at Layla and said, "Now we wait."

The girl giggled and they watched the cabinas expectantly.

First out was Kevin who poked his head between the sheets hanging in front of his doorway.

"Buenas, jackass," he said, addressing James.

"Buenas, Kevin."

"Buenas, Layla."

"Buenas, Señor Kevin."

"Where is everyone?" James asked.

"Stacie and Clint come back tonight and Jon's camping with Rich. Kyle and Bob left for a run. They came in to get me, but I'm on a rest day. So, thanks for the wake-up."

"Fair enough. Go back to sleep if you want. What about Deck?"

"No clue," Kevin said, shrugging. He squeezed his massive frame through the cabana's doorway to stand in the sunlight stretching his arms high in the air. "Might be asleep still. That guy can snooze through a hurricane."

"Let's get him up, shall we?" James said. He glanced at Layla who smiled with anticipation.

James cut a thick cord of vine hanging next to the camp's doorway and held his finger to his lips. He walked up to Deck's cabana window and tossed in the green rope and yelled, "Snake!"

The result was better than James expected as Deck shot out the door, tearing down the sheet blocking his entrance with the vine hanging on his neck.

"WHAT THE FUCK?!" he screamed, writhing on the floor wrestling with the phantom cobra while Layla and James watched laughing.

Deck, realizing the vine was not a serpent, threw the piece of vegetation away. "Assholes," he muttered, getting to his feet and brushing sand from his pants.

"What the hell, Deck?!" a voice came from the door and James turned to see Cristina, holding a towel around her torso on the threshold of Deck's cabina.

"It was James!" Deck protested.

"It's just a snake," she said, rolling her eyes and heading back inside to gather her clothes.

"They're poisonous here you know," Deck exclaimed, going back through the doorway.

"What's Cristina doing here?" Layla asked, and James realized he may have messed up for a moment when Kevin reappeared with a tray of doughnuts.

"She's getting changed, here, try out one of these," he said.

James mimed wiping sweat off his brow and Kevin grinned, tossing one of the doughy treats in his mouth. He finished it in one bite and held the tray out for James.

James accepted and was rewarded with an explosion of cinnamon and fried dough.

"Goddamn, that's good," he said, licking his fingertips to get the last of the sugar. "You really have a gift."

"I can bake things and blow shit up real good," Kevin said with a shrug.

"What the hell was that all about?" Deck asked. He buttoned his jeans while coming out of his cabina. He looked much more put together and a scowl was etched on his face. He was followed by Cristina who waved for Layla.

"Help me get on my makeup," she said.

Layla ran off and grasped the woman's hand while they walked to the bathroom area swinging their arms together.

"James was messin' with you, Deck. Tranquilo. Have a doughnut," Kevin said. He threw him one of the baked delicacies which Deck ate without looking at it.

"That's incredible, Kevin. Still doesn't excuse you for waking me from… sleep," he said with a coy smile and James waved him off.

"Oh, Jesus, Deck, have some class," James said, walking to the kitchen area.

"What, I didn't say anything?" Deck replied. "Let a guy enjoy his morning rest is all."

"All right, whatever. You can cover for me this week at the daycare, right?"

"Yep, I've got you," Deck said hopping onto one of the countertops.

"Thanks for that. Hopefully last time we need to do this whole shebang, right?" James said, pulling a water from the fridge and finishing it in one go, the cold water dripping onto his chest. He grabbed another bottle from the fridge to sip while he made his breakfast.

"You hungry?" he asked, getting a shake from Deck and a nod from Kevin.

"So, what do you think? We're gonna be able to get in there and just take the guy?" Deck asked casually.

James's head popped up and he looked behind Deck at the bathroom where Layla and Cristina continued applying makeup.

"Relax, they can't hear anything."

"Maybe, I want to hear what Stacie and Clint tell us," James said. He pulled a bag of cut guanabana out of the fridge along with a bowl of precooked oats. Kevin tossed him two metal bowls and a plate. James divvied up the portions while he spoke. "It won't be that easy. Go in there and grab him, but they don't know we're here, right? And this is our best shot at learning more about the BZ," he finished, topping off the bowls with oatmeal and motioned at the spoons for Kevin to grab while he balanced the three plates and walked to the table.

"I know. I'm trying to plan it out in my head. He goes out to meditate, two people keep an eye on the BZ, four people nab him, and another two are perched with sniper lines around the edge of his meditation grotto. That what you're thinking?"

"Something like that," James said. "I'd like three up top and three on the ground. Other than that, yeah, you got it."

"And you don't think he's thought of that?"

"Only shot we have, Deck," James said, getting perturbed at Deck's questioning., "What are you getting at?"

"Nothing, man. Want to think everything through here. I've always got your back." Deck hopped off the counter and clapped James on the shoulder, grabbing a chunk of guanabana on his way to the bathroom.

"I'm gonna head to the school with Cristina and Layla. Time for another day with the chipmunks on cocaine! See you two there?"

James and Kevin grunted into their bowls as Deck gave them a thumbs-up and turned to get the girls.

James was stuck in his head. What the hell were all those questions for? Didn't he know this was their break? They needed to do this before any more people were torn apart in some sort of BZ ritualistic slaying. This was their opportunity. They wouldn't get one as easily in the future. He continued stewing in his mind, muttering under his breath while he finished eating in silence. He stared blankly at the tree line, going over the plan in his mind, step by step. It was how he dreamed at this point. His gaze was broken when Kevin took the plate from in front of him and waved a hand across his eyeline.

"Hey, bud. James!" Kevin yelled and James shook his head, trying to come back to Earth.

"Sorry. Distracted there. Yeah, I'm done, thanks."

"All good, man," Kevin said as he cleared the table and walked to the kitchen sink. "He's right, by the way. To question things. He wouldn't be a good scout if he didn't."

James nodded. Kevin was right. James hated it, but it made him work harder having friends question even the best of intentions.

"I know. I just… I want it to go right," James said.

"It will. Now let's shower and go. You've gotta get your gear together with Kyle and I need to go teach your English class. We have the game tonight too."

James looked at the HOLO hanging under the kitchen's roof—0830. Fourteen hours left.

"I hate these days."

"We all do. Suck it up," Kevin said, pulling his shirt over his head and walking to the showers.

James slapped his cheeks and followed suit, the sound of falling water already inviting him to cool down. *Last one of these for a while,* James thought glumly, turning the faucet with the enthusiasm of a dog going to the vet.

The rest of the day passed in relative calm. He spent his time going over the checklist Stacie had prepared for the team. It covered all the gear they would need and everything on the resupply list requested by the group prior to Clint and Stacie's recon stint. The problem with running a surveillance operation a mile from the most technologically advanced enemy in history was that communications coming from the front lines were non-existent. Early in their strategy sessions, Jon pointed out that they wouldn't be able to speak to those doing recon and would need to plan supply burn two weeks in advance. This meant the team at the border needed to keep an eye on everything in camp and make sure it could last at least another two weeks when they left, otherwise, the new team would have to go without. James knew that wasn't hard to do for things like a malfunctioning battery pack or a low amount of rice. The team could shrink their meals or shore up energy usage, but med supplies, water purifiers, and other necessities were key to survival at the line, especially if something happened. It was the two on recon who were at the mercy of the enemy, and, in the case of a stalemate, James wasn't about to leave anyone resource depleted.

Gear packs had standard issue items for the team—a rifle, sidearm, three hand grenades, three flash-bang grenades, hatchet, bowie knife, thermal poncho, HOLO emitter with a backup battery source, portable solar array, pop-up tent, water pills, med kit, an extra tactical suit, and five packs of MREs. That tallied to about forty-five pounds plus any extra items the team needed to hump through the jungle. Specialized weaponry, like Deck's tactical binoculars or Kevin's light machine gun, weren't on the list but were considered unwritten items of necessity. The team could also bring any other items they wanted, but James made it clear the items had to be carried to and from the camp by the person bringing them and they couldn't be alive. He didn't need Clint bringing one of the jungle pets he switched out every surveillance mission. An escaped tree boa in a five-hundred-square-foot hut was a nightmare James could do without.

Within a few months they were running a well-oiled machine, and everyone had their standard packs and personal items. Stacie and Jon brought extra HOLOs with increased memory to tackle the code-breaking they had been working on for the last few months. Jon also developed programs to track Sentinel locations and Stacie documented the flora surrounding their outpost, listing every plant and its properties in a notebook. Bob carried a HOLO with extra medical books and a simulator Jon had built for him to practice medical procedures using his HOLO and an advanced light dispersion mechanism that gave him haptic feedback and readouts as if he was working on a live person. It freaked James out, but it was great that Bob could get the experience he needed without any actual casualties.

Kyle had a tool set he carried with him everywhere and was constantly fixing things or making improvements to the hut during his stays. It was a little noisier than the others' endeavors but having amenities built by a creative mind made a world of difference when you were stuck in a confined space for a week at a time. Kevin kept notebooks to write down food ideas. He had already filled seven of them and was working on an eighth that James was as excited to try as he had been the first. Clint would carry along a drone and tinker with it during the slow hours. He was working on creating smaller, more powerful engines for the automated machines so the team could use them for longer periods of time without needing to recharge. Deck would turn his HOLO into a keyboard and spend his free time watching videos Cristina had recorded for him teaching him how to play and read music.

James, meanwhile, carried a buck knife he had found in the pile of gear taken from the Federation HQ. He used it to carve animals out of sandalwood that he would bring back for Layla. Most weeks she would deliver one of her palm frond creations and he would do his best to recreate it for her, carving a replica out of the malleable wood. She teased him about his first few creations, but he became better and better as time passed. Selma had even taken him inside her house to show him the carved figurines standing along the girl's bedside.

The items people carried weren't demanding and it relieved James that each person held a sense of independence.

He stood in the doorway to his cabina, checking his gear items off on his HOLO list. He finished the checklist with a flourish, collapsed the screen, and packed his emitter into its slot on his rucksack.

He went outside and stretched his arms above his head walking to the common area where Deck and Cristina sat fiddling with a guitar. Cristina's legs were draped across Deck's lap, and she was teaching him chords again, moving his hands up the stem of the instrument getting him to move smoother in transition between notes.

"There you go," she said and smiled at him.

Deck bit his lip in concentration and accidentally slipped his finger off the chord. She corrected it fluidly moving his hand back in position. James grinned to himself. Deck had mastered those chords months ago, but he had told James he liked Cristina teaching him, so he kept messing up.

James flopped down in one of the Adirondack chairs facing the couch. "You two coming to the game tonight?"

"¡Por supuesto! It's a big one," Cristina replied, swinging her legs off Deck's lap.

"You and Kyle gonna leave after?" Deck asked, leaning the guitar against the side of the couch.

"That's the plan." James kept his answer short, but at this point, there was no way Cristina wasn't aware of their operation. It was decided early on by an unspoken agreement when Cristina and Deck started dating and Rich began visiting Jon that the team's business was the team's business. Rich and Cristina were great people, but the team was doing the most dangerous job known to man and two untrained, inexperienced people getting involved in their operation spelled bad news.

"Cool, man," Deck said, nodding, and the conversation was done.

"You two eating at the game?" James asked, moving to the next topic.

"We weren't sure. Kevin's not going to cook tonight, covering your class and all, so I guess so. You think the empanada guy is there?" he asked Cristina, who shrugged.

"No clue. He's hit-or-miss, but we should go early if you want to eat. Food runs out quickly."

"Good call. Wanna leave with us, James?" Deck asked, standing up.

"Sure. Let me get Kyle and Bob," James replied, pulling himself out of his seat.

Twenty minutes later, they were munching on cheese, chicken, and beef empanadas outside the stadium. Crowds of people crossed in the darkness lit by the dim yellow streetlamps and the brilliant white light from the solar panels Clint had installed for the stadium spilled across the plaza. Vendors were assembled all over the square, selling everything from milkshakes to tacos. It was such a cool experience that James loved about the town. Even in a remote area of the Federation there existed soccer teams—fútbol to the people of Río Negro—with leagues and games held on a regular basis. James always had a great time going to the games, mixing with the locals, and learning more about the area.

Tonight was supposed to be a great match. Layla and her friends had told James that the nearby town of Sanguino was tied with Río Negro for the top position in their division and it would be an intense game. It could be a blowout. James didn't care. He was happy to be distracted for a few moments. *Geez, James, have fun for a minute,* he thought, chastising himself for thinking about the week ahead.

He took a bite out of his third empanada. The cheese burned the corner of his mouth, but it was worth it. Grease burns were standard with food made fresh.

"Thad's increble," he said through a mouthful of crispy dough.

Silent nods around the circle agreed.

"What's up, chaps? And Miss Cristina, how are you love?" Rich said, walking up to them with a plastic sandwich bag filled with homemade ice cream.

"Rich! ¿Como está?" Cristina said, wiping her mouth and kissing him on the cheek.

"Bien, bien. Love coming back here," Rich said, sitting on the bench next to Kyle and tearing a corner of his ice cream packaging off with his teeth. "Nice to get out of the mansions, ya know?" He finished with a wink and got a friendly shove from Kyle.

"Where's Jon?" Kyle asked.

"Grabbing a couple of tacos. He'll meet us here."

"¡Hola, mis amigos!" The team turned to find Juan
Carlos and his team of bodyguards approaching them. The mood
changed instantly. They were on guard, and James suppressed
the urge to clench his fist. Juan Carlos showed up when James
didn't want him around, which, James reasoned, was always.

Juan Carlos was one of the most persistent people James
had encountered in his life. The first three months were a
constant torrent of requests for James and the team to visit his
home for dinner, lunch, drinks, a fiesta, any excuse Juan Carlos
could make to get them inside his compound. Those few months
were spent deftly evading the painfully annoying man, but
finally, Clint had reasoned with the team to get it over with.
They had gone and sat through an awkward dinner where Juan
Carlos had his guards invisible while still having their presence
felt watching every square inch of his pristine grounds. Women
and men from the town who worked on his property carried trays
of appetizers and drinks for the team to sample. Their faces were
masks of cold necessity and James felt like a traitor to the people
of Río Negro every time he took a bite from one of their
outstretched plates. The entire evening had devolved into Juan
Carlos bragging drunkenly about his business successes while
his wife stared sleepily at him and the team nodded with
disinterest hoping the night would end.

James was happy they had avoided future meals so far.

"James and the seven, it's been too long! How are all of
you?" Juan Carlos stood at the edge of the circle with a
serpentine grin painting his lips. He wore a white shirt and light
linen pants. A fedora, cocked to the right, was planted on his
neatly trimmed hair. His wife, twenty years his junior, wore a
tight red dress and her curly hair fell over her shoulders while an
emerald necklace adorned her chest.

"You remember my wife, Carolina?" asked Juan Carlos,
and James nodded at her as she gave a slight bow to James.

"Of course, ¿Como está, señora?" James kept his voice pleasant, but unemotional. He wanted Juan Carlos to leave.

"James, we need to have you all for dinner again. It's scandalous for people like us to not talk," Juan Carlos said. He looked at James with innocent eyes and childish pouting lips.

James was always sick after those requests. "We'll have to one of these days."

"Well, the door's always open. Who's this?" he asked, pointing at Rich and reaching out his hand.

"This is Rich," James said, careful not to reveal more than Rich and Jon would be comfortable sharing.

"I haven't seen him. Are you a part of the team?"

"No, I'm Jon's boyfriend," Rich said, sitting back down.

"Ah," Juan Carlos's eyebrows arched, and he turned around to his closest bodyguard whose face broke into a grin. "I see."

James wanted to kill him. He was ready to snap all their necks. The blood in his head rushed behind his eyes in waves of blind rage. Who the fuck was this guy?

"Heya, boyos and lady!" James heard someone say in the distance, the blood pounding in his ears dimmed the rest of the world as Kevin came from behind clapping him on the shoulder.

James unclenched his jaw and took in a slow breath, making sure Juan Carlos didn't see his reaction.

"Hey, Kevin, we were talking to Juan Carlos over here and introducing him to Rich."

Kevin glanced around the team and noticed the tight lips and uncomfortable expression on Juan Carlos's face.

"Well, okay, I'm gonna get some food, anyone interested?"

The team shook their heads, most of them still glaring at Juan Carlos and his team, but Cristina responded for them. "We all ate, but I'll come with you. Rich's ice cream looks good."

"We should head in and get our seats," Juan Carlos said, conceding he was not welcome, and the short plump man walked away from the team without turning back.

James watched the bodyguards fan out behind their charge, turning around to check that the team was not following.

"Want us to kill him?" Kyle asked Rich, his eyes glued in Juan Carlos's direction.

"Tranquilo, guys. Not the first time that's happened. Won't be the last."

"Fuck them. We can burn that house down, no problem," Deck said, standing to examine the walls of the mansion towering above the plaza.

"All good. Jon and I have thicker skins than that, but I appreciate the support mates."

"Boyfriend, huh?" Kyle said, nudging Rich in the ribs.

"Getting serious, I guess," Deck said, sitting back on his bench.

"Yeah, I guess," Rich said offhandedly, making eye contact with the ground.

"All right, all right. We get it. We'll leave it," James said, clapping Rich on the back.

"Thanks, gents. Now can we head into the game?"

"Let's go!" Deck said, jumping up and bouncing on the balls of his feet. "Cristina and Kevin can meet us in there."

Kyle and Rich led the way while Deck, Bob, and James walked behind them, Bob finishing the last of his empanadas. For a skinny guy, he could pack away more food than anyone, except for Kevin, but it was a close call.

"Goddamn, that's good," Bob said, tossing his garbage in one of the trash cans lining the entrance to the field.

"Did you finish five of those?" Deck asked.

"You betcha. I could have four more honestly."

"I think I'd puke."

"Big surprise."

"Oh, fuck off."

James grinned and handed his ticket to the girls sitting behind the card table managing access to the game.

He felt a tug on his shirt and turned to find Layla standing behind him next to Paola and holding another animal up to him.

"Hey there, kiddo. ¿Como está?" he said, accepting the fragile woven animal with tender hands.

"Bien. My abuela said you're leaving again. Can you make this one?" she asked.

James inspected it carefully. It was an anteater, intricately fashioned with thin strips of palm frond. She had even used the thinner plant fibers to create the stripes along the underside of its belly.

"I'll try," he said, giving her a high five.

"Good! I need another one for my collection!" The little girl slapped his hand and ran into an ongoing game of tag with the effortless friendship known only to the innocent.

"Hola, James," Paola said, kissing him on the cheek.

"¿Como está?" James asked, returning the kiss.

"Bien, gracias. You'll be gone again?" she asked, walking with him under the vivid lights of the field.

"Yes, for a little while. I'll be back though," he said searching the stands for his friends.

"Well, tenga cuidado, okay?" Paola said, patting his arm.

"Always," James said, giving her a smile. "You want to sit with us?"

"I'm going to watch the game with Mariel, Selma, and Rosa, but thank you. We'll see you upon your return."

She kissed him on the cheek again and hugged him, wiping a tear from her eye before joining her friends on the bench behind the home team. Paola and the other women saw the team as their children and James felt a familial connection to them he could not explain. It was nice to be loved like that. James waved at the women who waved back affectionately.

He spotted his friends at the top of the stands and climbed the stairs to meet them. He took a seat next to Bob who pulled a wrapped burrito out of his pocket and munched on it while the ref whistled and the game began.

"You're eating again?" James asked, surprised.

"Don't judge me," Bob said, his glassy eyes focused on the field. "Just enjoy the game."

James grinned turning to watch the field.

Two hours later he tightened the straps on Kyle's back before Kyle returned the favor. The team stood in a line watching the two warriors dressed in their tactical suits, ready for their trip.

"Stay ready out there, boys. See you in a week." Deck said, hugging them first. "You will be missed. And I know you'll miss me, so I sent you both downloadable self-portraits of me to look at while you're gone."

"How would we survive without you?" Kyle said, returning the hug.

With their goodbyes complete, James and Kyle waved at the team one last time and nodded at each other as they sunk into the brush and onto the unlit jungle trail to the front line.

CHAPTER 10

James followed Kyle across the same maze of streams they traversed every trip to the BZ border. He placed his feet strategically around the slippery wet stones underfoot, avoiding a twisted ankle or worse. Kyle would be annoyed if he needed to carry James the last mile and a half to the outpost and James wouldn't blame him.

Intermittent moonlight brightened the jungle casting the brilliant greenery in a bath of silver. Those openings were short-lived though and James looked at a break in the canopy in time to see another rolling bank of clouds cover the luminescent orb hovering over their position. The once still night air was replaced by the patter of water droplets enveloping the air and dripping from the dense treetops in unbroken streams.

"Damn rain," James grumbled wiping the rainwater from his eyes. The whole trip was like that, moonlight for thirty seconds, wet for twenty minutes. Could be more, could be less, but this is where James felt the name rainforest come to life. Even in the rain and depths of the night animals, insects, and even the plants were alive with a steady underlying din competing with raindrops for volume.

"Should we signal yet?" Kyle asked, steadying himself on a wide trunk. He grabbed James's wrist pulling him to safety over the last of the mossy rocks.

"Go for it. We're close enough."

Kyle nodded and set his pack on the ground. He reached into a pocket removing a mirror and penlight. He faced the reflective side southeast and used the light to transmit *"team here"* in Morse Code. He repeated this three times and stopped.

James counted methodically under his breath while they waited for a response. Two minutes passed, nothing happened.

"They could have missed it. Try again," James said.

Kyle repeated the process and James counted to three minutes this time. Nothing.

James was concerned. It was unlike Stacie to miss signals from the approaching team. Something wasn't right.

"Let's move. Hand signals at this point."

"Suppressors?" Kyle asked, returning the flashlight and mirror to their places.

"Definitely," James said, pulling out his rifle attachment and flipping on his night vision scope. "Don't engage unless absolutely necessary."

"Got it, boss," Kyle replied, racking a bullet in his chamber. "Shall we?"

A heightened discomfort bled into Kyle's voice and James sensed the situation was getting to him with Stacie on the other side.

"On me," James said, and he took off into the brush.

Rain dripped in an unbroken lull, masking their footsteps. The air tasted clean. The rain had washed away the death and decay brought on by the sunlight and replenished the forest at night filling its inhabitants with enough life force to survive another day.

James picked his way through the darkness, every movement heightened in the overgrown space. They reached a thousand yards from the hut and James flipped on his infrared. He pointed his scope in the direction of the hut, but the aluminum walls masked his attempt to locate their friends. *Our planning biting us in the ass,* he thought, annoyed at their protective measures, when a branch snapped.

Kyle and James slunk to the ground.

Another snap confirmed their suspicion. Something was wrong. Someone else was out there. He listened for more movement and was rewarded by two more sounds in quick succession coming towards them. He signed at Kyle, forming a plan on the fly:

Move to the other tree; we'll funnel them between us; do not engage.

Kyle nodded in response and darted through the shadows kneeling behind the tree James had indicated.

James waited, the iron in his stomach becoming more pronounced and his heartbeat steadied against his rib cage. The noises grew in frequency and without any pretense a boot appeared, stepping over a log followed by a body clad in a gray suit.

Another leg followed the first and within seconds five BZ soldiers armed with long rifles walked between Kyle and him.

There were two men and three women in the group. They had no clue Kyle and James were watching their every move but pivoted their heads from side to side absorbing every inch of the forest. The woman leading the group held up a hand and the rest of them stopped. She motioned behind her and two of the soldiers spread out, their bodies tense. They inspected the area carefully, practically peeling the bark off the trees to check everything. James inched backward, one foot after the other until he heard a *snap*.

Fuck, he thought, feeling the pieces of the broken branch underfoot. He glanced at the BZ soldiers, each one of their heads facing his way. Their eyes were human but predatory. It was how James must have looked, but it was different when he was the prey. He scooted to the right, hoping to hide in some tall banana leaves when he felt a hand on his shoulder. Clint knelt behind him holding a finger to his lips. He motioned for James to follow him. James signed that Kyle was on the other side of the team, but Clint shook his head and signed back:

Stacie's got him.

James nodded and followed Clint without a sound. When they reached a safe distance, he turned to see the BZ team already scanning James's hiding spot from moments ago.

A few minutes later they crawled up the ladder into the tree hut. They had not spoken yet but upon entering Clint motioned for James to join him at the windowsill. James looked out the pane-less opening and followed Clint's finger pointing in the distance at the BZ team making its way in a circle back to the border.

"They're sending troops out randomly. We've had to be extra careful covering our steps when we head out during the day," he whispered, pulling a blackout curtain over the window and fastening the Velcro edges to keep the hut from emitting light, "Rain will help with that tonight." He sat at the table in the middle of the room with a sigh. "It's been a few nights since they sent out a scouting party. We had a feeling they might try tonight. Good thing we saw your signal. Sorry, we couldn't risk sending anything back."

"No worries. We thought something was up. Where are Stacie and Kyle?" James asked, placing his pack next to one of the hammocks.

"Probably cleaning the tracks. They'll be here any minute."

James was already turning the new information over in his head. Night scouting parties? What was the BZ up to? Why would they need to scout the area? What was happening there?

James inspected his friend under the light of the single bulb casting shadows across his tired face. Clint's skin was slack and the lines around his eyes had deepened. This experience had a way of leaching the life out of all of them.

Even if it was only a week, they all took a serious mental beating, manifesting itself in a type of exhaustion James had trouble describing. For James, tiredness stuck in the gears of his mind and a sluggish response to move overtook him every time he woke in his hammock. It was strange, although he lived with a partner it was more isolating than usual. They were rarely awake together. When they were, the person not analyzing video or setting up drone flight patterns was out managing every other aspect of their recon. This ran the gamut from running inspections, collecting rainwater, working out, or performing some sort of maintenance activity fighting back the ever-encroaching jungle from taking back its property. It left James dealing with a foreboding sense of loneliness.

He started to speak, but Clint held up his hand. "Stacie and Kyle'll be back in a few. She'll want to brief you. Want water?"

James nodded. "Sounds great."

Clint threw him a water bottle from the bucket of refills.

James caught it and took a sip. *Slimy and natural. Gross.* He grimaced scraping a bug from his tongue, not hiding his disgust.

"You'll get used to it again," Clint said, grinning.

"This is my least favorite part of being stuck out here—warm, musky rainwater. Revolting," James said.

"It does suck, huh? Lucky I can leave," Clint said, taking a sip.

"Yeah, yeah. Lucky you."

The door swung open and Kyle entered, embracing Clint from behind with a hug around his neck. "Clint, how you doing buddy?"

"I'm good, man. Don't fuckin' choke me though," he replied, tapping his forearm. "You two clean out there?"

"Yeah, that was a first. Never seen anyone other than Raspin outside the camp."

"It's more frequent than you'd think," Stacie said, her voice flat, shutting the door behind her.

"Good to see you, too, Stace," James said.

Stacie waved at him and took a long chug from the water bottle strapped to her hip.

"This is it, James," she said, breathing in heavily after drinking too fast. "They're starting to explore. We need to move."

"All right, I hear you, but Clint said there's more to tell me. What's up?"

Stacie checked the time on the air gapped HOLO set up opposite the hammocks.

"Don't have a ton of time, so I'll be fast. I left a briefing packet for you two. The BZ soldiers are expanding. I'm not talking about the border, James. I'm talking everything. They're building their presence at the line. More soldiers are coming in every day. We counted fifteen transport ships this week alone. That's more than twenty thousand troops. They're going to move. If we want to nab that motherfucker, we need to do it ASAP."

James nodded. Twenty thousand troops? Where were they all staying? Either way, that was a ton of people to move to the border in a week. Stacie was right. They were planning their move.

"You're right. Anything else?"

"The code. I got the first part of it."

James was surprised. He figured she would have led with that but given her tepid reaction to breaking a code she had been working on for months James was hesitant to sound the celebration.

"And...?"

"It's not ours."

"What do you mean?" Kyle asked.

"I mean, it's BZ code. I was using our standard code-breaking programs, but realized they may not be working because it's not our code."

"So what'd you figure out?" Kyle asked, the same question at the top of James's list.

"That's it."

Silence followed.

"So we know the owner of the code? That's the break?" James said, cautious to avoid insulting her.

Stacie threw her hands in the air, exasperated. "That's pretty big!"

"I thought it'd be a little more… but cool!" Kyle said finishing his sentence and eliciting a hit on the shoulder from Stacie.

"It's plenty cool, assholes," she said, shaking her head and mounting her pack. Clint walked to help situate the straps on her shoulders. "Listen, we might not know the *what* in the code but knowing the *who* is massive. Believe me, Jon will be pumped."

"I'm sure he will, Serial," Kyle said, standing and kissing her. "Sorry, didn't mean to brush it off. Nice work."

"Humph," Stacie replied, returning the kiss and pushing Kyle aside to help Clint with his pack.

"Either way, watch out for patrols and confirm our schedule if you can. I'm going to alert the team. We should move next week."

James nodded. "We're on."

They finished their goodbyes and James turned his back for Kyle to give her a last kiss before the door shut.

It was he and Kyle for the rest of the week. Then they made their move. An anticipatory tingle traveled along James's spine.

James slept first, resting his allotted four hours until Kyle woke him with a nudge.

He did not sleep. His mind was spun, capitulating on how to carry out their plan. He knew the numbers breakdown and where everyone should be during the operation. The person sitting behind at the hut waiting for everyone to return was going to be annoyed, but James figured they would draw straws to decide who stayed. James hoped it wasn't him. He trusted his team to run everything, but he didn't want to be stuck in the hut while everyone else put themselves in danger.

He checked the footage from the returned drone coverage. In place of fixed cameras, the team used twelve drones to record around the clock. The drones were funny little devices about the size of a Roma tomato but shaped like a praying mantis with no legs. They were thin and difficult to see with bare eyes against anything other than a stark white background, especially when they were in flight. Deck had named them the roaches and it stuck. It was also a relatively accurate comparison given their ability to sneak about.

The roaches possessed 360-degree camera views vertically and horizontally, giving them a full sphere of coverage. The cool thing was they used old radio frequencies for control and were able to adjust their flight patterns depending on perceived threats making them nearly undetectable to most equipment. They needed to charge every ten hours, so they were split into two groups of six, monitoring and recording movements along the border twenty-four hours a day with two three-hour periods of overlap when all the drones were in the sky at once. Once a group of roaches returned to the hut, the person on duty would plug them into their solar charging stations and remove their video chips. The chips were fed into a program that Jon designed to combine videos and pick out when they caught sight of people. This way the person watching the feed could speed through their analysis without watching 144 hours of footage from twelve drones.

When they returned to base they fed the files into their network of connected drives and the program did the rest of the legwork. It cataloged every event reviewed by the analyst and more, picking up incidents someone always missed. It deciphered whether the people in the videos were armed, their gender, their body measurements, and a brief description of their activities. It also picked out Sentinels and the various sensors surrounding the BZ border used as defense mechanisms. With the information they received the team designed a map of the entire border that included details on every aspect of each yard stretching for over twenty miles.

To top it off, Jon had it set up to reinspect every image captured after learning something new. It was way over James's head, but so were most of the things Jon did.

The roaches' schedule disrupted the monotony of watching the forest floor. James plugged in the batch that had returned, rewarded by a view of the BZ soldiers patrolling the woods the previous night. He zoomed in to get a better look at the people in the group. They communicated through hand signals and motions, as James and the team did during operations. The same woman led the group throughout their time in the woods and the rest followed her without hesitation.

He played through their whole hike at double speed, slowing when he and Kyle were spotted by the drone, crouching feet away from the soldiers. The air tightened in James's chest reliving the moment.

"That was closer than I thought," he muttered, fast-forwarding to the point where the BZ team re-entered their border.

He paused the shot when the last one crossed the camp's threshold. He found the drone with the widest shot and brightened the image. The border was unremarkable. If a person didn't know it was there, they would walk right through it and end up like the group of men the BZ tore apart weeks ago. James grimaced at the memory. He counted the surveillance mechanisms on screen, three sensors were in plain view and two Sentinels hung fifteen feet above the ground, waiting to do whatever it was they did. James swiped across the screen, opened the control panel, and chose the x-ray filter. He played with the image density controls until he spotted the next layer of security in the trees, four more sensors, another Sentinel. Continuously, James ran down the list of items cataloging as he went.

He wrote everything down in the video logs for his shift before switching to the copious amounts of notes Stacie had kept while watching Raspin.

Their newest target was a creature of habit. Raspin left the BZ at the same time every day. No one accompanied him, the forest was free of any surveillance equipment. The Sentinels were nowhere to be found, floating hundreds of yards away at other parts of the line. Sensors were not installed that far out. He was completely alone. The footage of Raspin didn't help James answer any questions about his intentions. The man sat in the middle of a clearing, his head back looking at the sky. That was it. He stayed completely still, only the movement of his chest gave a hint he was alive. He would remain like that for exactly an hour, then he would get up and return to the border as if nothing happened.

Concerned they were focused on the man too much, James poured over the footage around Raspin examining every piece of the border during the time Raspin sat there, but it was as if he was in camp the whole time. They did not seem to notice their commander went missing for an hour every day.

James couldn't help but come up with questions for the man. Who are you? Why are you all here? Why now? What do you want? How did you assemble your force? Questions kept piling up no matter how hard James tried to stop them. But in a week he'd get his answers.

"Hey, bud, take a break. My turn."

James nodded, surprised that his four hours were over.

"Nothing new on the latest footage. New batch of videos should be back in a bit," James said, picking up his tactical suit and slipping an arm into the familiar camouflage fabric.

"Good stuff. Where you headed?"

"I'll check where we ran into the team. Make sure our tracks are hidden."

"Sounds good," Kyle said. He took a water bottle out of the bucket and tore off the edge of an MRE packet with his teeth. "Stay invisible out there."

"You got it," James said, giving him a thumbs-up and adjusting the suppressor on his rifle. "I'll be back."

James stepped outside and closed the hut's door. He took a deep breath of jungle air, letting the humidity stain his lungs and purge the stale air from the small space he had exited.

"Good stuff," he said to himself, putting the scope of his rifle up to his eye inspecting the grounds. All clear.

He pushed aside the brush used to cover the ladder to the hut and started to the ground. He replaced the brush at the bottom with a rope system Kyle had rigged allowing for one person to operate the whole mechanism alone without needing to wake anyone. It helped solve a lot of initial arguments.

He scanned the immediate area with his scope again for good measure. All clear, good to go.

James made his way east, where they had run into the BZ team the previous night, covering his tracks as he walked. He came to the place where his and the BZ's paths had converged and noted the lack of tracks from either party.

They're covering themselves like we are, James thought, lifting his head and glancing at his surroundings.

He made his way along the path that he had seen them walk via the roach videos. He wound his way around, following the odd turn he had noted from the video until he realized he might be getting too close for comfort to the BZ border.

He stood in the forest, squeezed on all sides by an explosion of overgrown vines and plant life. The BZ border was a few hundred yards ahead. Going any closer would risk alerting a Sentinel. The roaches were the only things that did not trip their security response. Still, he wanted to get closer, get a better look, find out what the hell the BZ was doing. His feet begged to keep walking, but he knew how stupid that would be.

Instead, he decided to check out Raspin's clearing. It was against protocol to add agenda items to a solo walk through the jungle, but it would only be a few minutes. He wanted to create the kidnapping plan tonight and understanding the space beyond the surveillance videos was crucial.

James made his way through the sticky jungle, brushing large fronds from his path and keeping an eye on the sky for Sentinels. He came to a dip in the earth that led to a stream. Raspin's clearing was on the other side of the water and James hopped across it with a nimble foot landing on the far bank. Cloud cover kept light from reaching the forest floor and James walked through a gray-tinted mist. Bugs clung to the netting that covered his face and James brushed them aside to get a better view.

It was wider than it appeared on the video, maybe fifty feet of open space with a plush layer of wispy grass poking up from the black earth. It was unremarkable if anything. James scanned the treetops trying to determine if the roaches had missed anything. Tall, thick-trunked trees with looping branches were interspersed along the edges of the clearing. They were draped in cords of vine hanging to the ground in long arching loops. James remembered from the video that on sunny days the area was lit brilliantly, but today it was unexceptional, a spot of relief from the crushing flora suffocating the ground.

James stayed at the edge of the stream while he turned in a circle, scanning the area and imagining the operation. Three up top would be a definite. It was dangerous to try otherwise. Three approaching—one leading, one glued to Raspin, and a third covering their tracks. Another person would be waiting on the other side of the stream, prepping their path to a hut set up closer to Río Negro where James planned to hold Raspin.

Deck had pointed out early in the planning that they couldn't bring Raspin back to camp. Nor could they keep him in their hut next to the border. Deck quickly solved the problem by scouting out a new location to house their prisoner. He had found a secluded hilltop five miles from the town in a remote section of the jungle. It was perfect for their needs, but the trip would add another layer of complexity to their planning. *Have to do it though,* James reasoned, heading back to his temporary home, done with his assessment.

He covered his tracks and arrived at the hut where Kyle was busy downloading another set of images from the drones.

"What's up, bud? Anything cool out there?" Kyle asked. He was manipulating the drone footage to give him a better view of a Sentinel floating aimlessly along the border.

"Nothing much. Checked out our path from last night," James said, leaning his rifle by the door. "Pretty standard stuff. I also checked out Raspin's clearing," he said. He grabbed a water from the bin, choosing to look at the ceiling rather than at Kyle directly.

"Ha!" Kyle guffawed. "Stacie'd fucking kill you if you pulled that shit with her. Anything the videos aren't picking up?"

James took a sigh of relief. Of course Kyle wouldn't mind him going to see Raspin's clearing. "Same as the roaches show us. Nothing special. A weird feeling is all."

"I get that. Those types of places always give off creepy vibes. That Raspin leaves a stain everywhere."

James nodded. "Yeah, he does. I'm gonna workout and then I can make some food."

"Sounds good, man. Happy push-ups," Kyle said, focused on the footage and taking notes.

James unzipped his suit and peeled it off his shoulders, opting to leave the pants on. He finished his first set of thirty push-ups and breathed in deeply, counting to twenty and repeating the process. It wasn't until the fifth set that he felt a twinge of pain in his triceps. He thought dully about his trip through the woods, and his mind wandered to the village wondering how his class was going that day, but he shook his head dispersing the thoughts.

Too soon to think about home, he thought. He placed his hands back on the ground and lowered his body for another set of thirty refocusing his mind on the upcoming mission.

CHAPTER 11

Wood creaked under the weight of the team shifting their feet in the hut's tight quarters. All eight took up space wherever they could find it. They had finished reviewing the plan as a team, walking through the strategy step-by-step for the thousandth time. James glanced at them, silent and contemplative, reading the playbooks on their HOLOs or fidgeting with gear.

James opened the chamber of his rifle and checked his magazine again. *Both good,* he thought absently. He peeked at the time on the HOLO. Four minutes to go. He closed his eyes and breathed in, clearing his mind and focusing on nothing for a moment. He pushed away his senses choosing to ignore the quiet apprehension building in the hut. He shut out the patter of raindrops and foreboding that invaded his mind. He did not have time to dwell on anything but the mission. James opened his eyes and glanced at the clock—1315. It was time.

James stood and was followed wordlessly by the rest of the team.

Adrenaline coursed through his veins intoxicating his body's natural responses. The thud of his heartbeat rhythmically kept time with each breath of dampened oxygen filling his lungs. The rifle he gripped in his hands was another appendage rather than a metal piece of destruction used to snuff out life. Deck walked next to him, straight-backed and purposeful. This was the biggest undertaking of their young lives. *What wasn't at this point?* James thought, realizing how every operation he took part in overshadowed the last. It was a never-ending escalation of violent confrontations.

They arrived at the stream and the team broke into their groupings. Clint followed Deck. Jon split off in the opposite direction, sticking to the border of the clearing. James and the rest of the team waited for the sign. Intermittent raindrops left warm, wet stains on James's uncovered hands. His tactical suit evaporated the remaining moisture.

A sheen of cloud filtered daylight and gave the forest a drab appearance. Golden columns of light that normally graced these clearings were only a memory.

When they had started prepping in the early hours of the day, James was concerned Raspin might change his mind, and skip a day. It would demolish any plans, certainty, or self-confidence remaining in James and the team, but this was their shot. *It will work,* James thought resolutely. It had to.

He got the signal from Deck up top:

In place; assume positions.

James returned Deck's message with a thumbs-up and motioned for Bob to follow him. Stacie and Kyle slunk wordlessly in the other direction. Bob and James stopped for Bob to settle into his spot. James continued to the northwest corner of the square and, upon reaching his destination, set himself up behind an arrangement of waxy palm fronds.

He assessed his line of sight to the clearing and checked on Deck. He pulled back a piece of greenery that blocked his path to their comms focal point and signed to his friend:

In position.

Deck responded:

Team ready; waiting on target.

James signed his understanding and concentrated on the clearing. He and Bob were set up at the north side of the square. Stacie and Kyle occupied the southern border providing full coverage. In the trees, the team had set themselves up fifteen to twenty yards above ground with Deck perched between Kyle and

Bob. Clint was between Bob and James, and finally, Jon sat high up between Kyle and Stacie.

James had toyed with the idea of bringing Kevin along and saying screw it to the hut. The more people the better was James's rationalization, but in reality, they needed someone hanging back.

Kevin had set up "distractions" throughout the forest that would come in handy if anything went awry. After James explained his reasoning for keeping Kevin on the sidelines, he grunted his frustration but made the team a delicious meal of fried plantains, his way of saying he understood. James didn't mind being spoken to via food, particularly if Kevin was the one cooking.

After determining who was staying back, James's decision for the other positions was easy. Someone big had to be on the ground to take on Raspin if he fought so he chose Kyle, the best grappler on the team. Bob, as their medic, should be on hand for medical emergencies. James wanted to be on the ground for this one and he knew Stacie did, too. Jon, Deck, and Clint would go topside.

The rain let up for a moment and a rare glimpse of the sun's rays traveled through the canopy providing James and the team their first light of the day. Water vapor sparkled in the mid-afternoon sun trickling to the ground like sand thrown into the wind. The earth was silent for a moment and the absence of sound invaded James's mind, giving him a second to appreciate the moment.

SNAP!

A branch broke, and James concentrated on its location. Raspin was here.

The seconds stretched and more branches broke with Raspin's approach. James blew the sweat from his upper lip, tasting salt on the tip of his tongue.

Finally, a shuffle of leaves was followed by a splash of water. James held his breath. His heartbeat jackhammered his sternum with the *rat-a-tat* of a snare drum.

Raspin appeared and for the first time, James witnessed their only named enemy. Consistent with the videos and stills, Raspin was a slender, but athletic man with short, cropped hair. His face was shaved, and he walked with a glide. James could not put his finger on it, but every step Raspin took seemed as if he knew exactly what would happen when his foot touched the ground. He did nothing by accident. Even breathing was something Raspin decided to do.

Like every other time Raspin entered the clearing, he stretched his arms to his sides and over his head in a wide arc. He collected his feet under his butt and sat cross-legged in the wispy strands of grass. He took a deep breath, closed his eyes, and tilted his chin back until he was staring at the sun fighting through the clouds.

He stayed like that for the next two hundred and fifty seconds. James counted in his head, making sure the man hadn't decided to change his routine. He looked at the tree:

Ready?

Deck returned a thumbs-up and put the rifle scope to his eye.

James took a deep breath, flipped off his safety, and stood, training his rifle on Raspin's motionless figure fifteen yards in front of him. He stepped over leaves and branches, careful to place his feet in soft spots on the ground. He glanced at the corners of the clearing. The other team members on the ground walked forward with their weapons trained on the target.

James approached the man sitting with his face toward the heavens and tapped him on the shoulder. He did not move. James tapped him again, jumping back this time and pointing the rifle at Raspin, but received no response.

James glanced at the rest of the team, and they shrugged. *What do we do now?* James thought, wondering if they should pick him up and take off when he caught Deck in the trees mimicking a harder push. James nodded and walked up to Raspin and pushed him off his balance.

Raspin staggered from the sudden force. He shook his head as if he was trying to get something out of his ear and turned to face his assaulter. He stared at James's feet and angled his face to meet James's gaze. James stared into the eyes of the man he intended to kidnap, noting a lack of fear or confusion. It was more of an acceptance. A simple nod was Raspin's first communication with James.

"Well, where am I going?" he asked in a calm voice. James was surprised. Raspin's demeanor was clear and controlled. It struck a nerve in James, and he worked to keep emotion from his face.

"Did you hear me?" Raspin asked. "¿Adonde voy?" he repeated in Spanish. His voice had an edge to it and James was thrown by the confidence. In his current predicament, James would have expected a little more humility.

"Put this on." James pulled a cloth bag out of his back pocket and threw it at Raspin. The slender man inspected it and pulled it over his head.

Kyle and Stacie took Raspin by his arms and pulled him to his feet. The rest of the team was already on the ground and Bob started the exfiltration to their interrogation hut checking the first part of the path and motioning the rest of the team onward. They needed to move fast.

James led the way. Stacie and Kyle followed, holding the prisoner between them, guiding him through the winding forest.

"Is anyone with you?" James asked. He set a quick pace and signed behind him to Jon and Clint to sanitize the capture point and meet them on the trail.

"You already know that answer, I assume." Raspin's voice was matter-of-fact and James glanced back at Stacie who contorted her face.

"Answer the fucking question," James said, fortifying his voice.

Raspin sighed. "No."

"Good. Keep up with the two guiding you. We've got a lot of ground to cover. If you can't walk, we'll carry you. Keep your mouth shut unless we ask you a question and this will go smoothly. That work?" James asked.

"I suppose," Raspin responded. *Something's not right,* James thought pushing his way through the concentrated growth blocking their path. Their prisoner, while cooperative, acted as if this was a walk in the park. As if he expected it.

They arrived at the recon hut and Stacie scrambled to where Kevin was analyzing the drone footage that would have returned moments ago.

James took her position on the other side of Raspin who waited with his shoulders hunched. Jon, Clint, and Deck joined them, emerging from the woods, covering their tracks as they walked.

Deck signed to James:

Are we good?

James replied with a thumbs-up. And Deck started to ask for more information, but James held up his hand. He had to concentrate. Deck returned a scowl, but James ignored him. He would explain later. He wanted Raspin in their interrogation room as soon as possible.

Stacie emerged from the hut and jumped to the ground. Kevin gave them the thumbs-up and James responded in kind. No BZ movement. It was what James had expected, but he didn't like it. *Something is wrong,* he thought and handed guard duty back to Stacie.

He peered at the group getting a series of wordless nods and took off into the woods. The team followed, guiding their best opportunity at learning about the BZ with a black canvas hood covering his face.

CHAPTER 12

The meager light that made it through to the interrogation hut revealed a dull sunset hidden behind a bank of impenetrable clouds. James held waxy leaves aside for Kyle and Stacie guiding Raspin to his new home.

Clint followed, signing to James that Deck, Bob, and Jon were scouting the area. James nodded his understanding and motioned for Kyle and Stacie to lead Raspin to his cell. They took their charge to the hut, closing the aluminum-encased door behind them when they entered.

James and Clint walked forty yards away from the shelter and sat in silence until Kyle and Stacie appeared with an all-clear signal.

"I'd call that trip a success," Clint said, tipping a bottle of water into his mouth, "Nice work, everyone."

"Agreed. That went well. Exactly what we planned," Stacie said, sitting on the ground, exhausted. "What do you think James? Happy?"

James was unsure. The plan had worked. They had their man, but something was off. Where was everyone? The alarm? Why weren't the BZ troops out scouring the countryside for their lost commander? It didn't make sense, but he knew he needed to grin and go with it.

"Yeah, happy as hell everything worked out." James fist-bumped Clint and they took a moment to catch their collective breath. The hike had presented nothing but challenges, more due to the location of their interrogation hut than anything.

When James had decided they needed to scout a location for their holding site, he gave Deck three criteria. It needed to be remote, but close enough for a round trip in a day, and off-putting to deter others from approaching. The last part was key. Remote or not, people in desperate straits saw opportunities when presented. If there was land to grab, it would be gone.

Deck took the job seriously and spent months searching for the right place for their single-cell prison. After weeks of searching, he arrived home one day covered head to toe in scratches with tracks of mud and pieces of leaves stuck to his body.

"I found it," he had said, out of breath. He would not tell James any details about the location. He wanted it to be a surprise. James let him relax for a day or two then insisted Deck show him the prison.

Deck reluctantly geared up, grabbing two machetes and told James to do the same. They walked five miles along a stream until they reached a hillside rife with jungle growth. Deck pointed into the underbrush with his machete and said, "Up there."

Since Deck had stopped, James began to cut in front of him to lead, but Deck caught his arm. "I lead for now. No cuts, it'll let people know we're here."

"Okay, what the hell is going on?" James asked as Deck pushed into the leafy barrier.

"You'll see," Deck said over his shoulder, breaking through the first set of shrubs to reach the canopy-lined hillside. The brush dispersed under the trees' shade and James followed the scout up the hill, confused by Deck's odd behavior. Wet leaves covered the ground and the sunlight was non-existent, so they walked in constant twilight. The air was rich and earthy, vapors from the ground moisture had evaporated and become stuck under the treetop roof creating a natural greenhouse.

Without warning, Deck stopped with a *swoosh* of his machete. The blade gave a loud *thud* when it hit the dirt.

"What the…?" James stopped himself when Deck turned around holding the headless body of a six-foot-long snake.

"Terciopelo, fer de lance, or pit viper. Three languages all meaning deadly as hell," Deck said, tossing the carcass aside and wiping blood from the machete on his pantleg. "They're all over these little hill-mountains. Everyone in Río Negro kept talking about how they won't go anywhere near the mountains because of the terciopelo. No one from town or any farm would dare hike this far into the jungle. It's too dangerous. I hate the legless demons, but this is the definition of isolated."

James looked at the beaming face of Deck, happy with his discovery of the snake-ridden hilltop.

"Well, look at that," James said, his eyes scanning the forest floor. "We need to walk through a death trap every time we visit our guest."

"Exactly! And if he tries to escape, he dies!" Deck said, ignoring James's sarcasm.

James hated that they would regularly have to risk a forest full of poisonous and defensive serpents, but Deck had done exactly what James had wanted him to do—locate a place no one in their right mind would come near.

Returning to the present, James glanced around the immediate area. No snakes in sight didn't mean they weren't there, he reasoned, careful to watch his step whenever he moved. He was on edge. He had not slept well in a week and was verging on fifty hours without rest.

"I'm going to talk to him," James said.

He stood and pulled off his suit's top, changing into a t-shirt from his go-bag. The team members present eyed one another, not sure how to respond.

"Go for it, man. Be careful though. We don't know anything about this guy," Kyle said.

"Other than his knack for slitting the throats of his own soldiers and revving a crowd into such a frenzy that they tear men to pieces. Soooo, we do know a couple of things," Clint added.

"They're both right. Be careful. Most of all don't give anything away about us. No numbers, no 'we've seen this,' or 'we've been around that.' Nothing. Got it?" Stacie eyed him, making sure he replied.

"Of course. I'm not a complete idiot," James said, already walking to the hut. "I've got it. I won't be long."

James reached the door, turned around, and gave a final thumbs-up to soothe their worried looks. Turning the handle he pushed the door open.

The hut was a plain affair, ten feet by ten feet with an elevated cot in the corner. The walls were built with wood from the area and reinforced by leftover sheets of aluminum from their camp. The roof consisted of the same materials and a hole by the door provided ventilation. The floor was covered in rough concrete mixed and poured on the mountain constructing a pseudo foundation rising about a foot and a half off the ground. Kyle intended to guard against snakes and other animals co-opting it for shelter. It was built better than any of their cabinas and as secure as they could make it given their resources. The roof housed two solar panels which fed batteries stationed next to the hut. It had enough energy storage so that whoever was on guard duty could charge their HOLOs and keep in contact with the drones used to monitor the area.

James flicked on the light above the chair where Raspin was strapped with the hood covering his face. The air in the hut was cooler than outside, but the humidity was everywhere. James did his best to disorient the captive by scratching against the walls and stepping heavily every other step on the concrete. He brought a chair propped against the wall and dropped it in a clatter in front of Raspin, letting the legs rattle as it settled on the floor. The goal was to throw Raspin off, make him uneasy. For the last few weeks, James had been trying to recall any of the interrogation techniques Croyton had taught them. The one thing that he knew was an uncomfortable captive made for a more pliable one. At least that was what James thought he remembered. Croyton wouldn't have told him to make a prisoner comfortable. It wasn't in his nature.

Finally, he shut the door with a loud bang and sat in the chair across from their captive. He took a deep breath steeling himself for the moment. He set his face with a blank expression and took off the hood.

Raspin reacted to the light by shaking his head and blinking. James waited, letting him acclimate to his surroundings. Raspin looked at James before turning his attention to the rest of the room. His gaze was spongelike, absorbing every inch of the space. When he finished his inspection, he stared back at James, his eyes revealing more boredom than fear.

"Who are you?" James asked, deciding to get started.

"You don't know?" Raspin replied. His calm voice reinforced the look on his face.

"I have an idea. I want you to tell me though."

"I'm Commander Edgar Raspin of the Republic's military."

"What are you doing here?"

"Now come, come. You know exactly why I'm here. You brought me after all."

James didn't respond. He wouldn't let Raspin play games. His mind was fuzzy and he had not slept in two days, but this was not the time for Raspin to slip around questions.

"What? Don't like the joke? Fine. I was brought in to help lead an assault on the Federation. I think that much is obvious."

"Why?"

"Excellent question, but it would take a long time to explain. Frankly, I'm not sure you would understand. Now, who are *you*? Why are *you* here? Those questions are what interest me most. You see I was meditating peacefully in a forest some hours ago and was taken by a group of at least three people, but I suspect more, to a mystery location. I can answer questions all day, but you… you I know nothing about." Raspin's voice wrapped around the room settling back on James.

Focus, James thought, searching for a better question to ask.

"You say you're the Commander of your army. For how long?"

"About a month, I think."

"Who ran it before you?"

"A small group of loyal soldiers."

"Why'd you take over?"

"Their usefulness ended."

"How so?"

"We all have a time in our lives when we are of no more use to the communal world. My predecessors had reached the end of that useful period. It was my turn to take over. Simple as that."

James let that sink in for later inspection. The throats of three people were slit because they were no longer useful? And they accepted it willingly?

"Why were you in the woods?"

"I was out for a stroll and stopped to collect my thoughts. Very peaceful if you don't get kidnapped."

Interesting, James thought. *He doesn't know we've been watching him.*

"This is your first time out there?"

"Is it yours?" Raspin replied, his eyes angled and his lips turned mischievously.

"How many people do you have in your camp?" James asked, ignoring the question.

"A lot."

"How many is a lot."

"247,000."

James paused, that was far higher than any of their estimates.

"247,000?"

"Give or take, yes. We should have another fifty thousand by next week."

What the hell was going on? How much of a build-up were they planning?

"Okay, now I have a question. Is there any water?" Raspin asked, uninterested in their conversation again.

"In a minute. Why so many?"

"We're planning an invasion of the Federation. Why do you think?"

"From down here? Why not attack from further north?"

"We like the heat. Water?" Raspin was stonewalling him.

"After you answer."

Raspin's eyes turned into slits, and he glared at James with concentrated venom. "We have the space to do what we need here. Half the continent was abandoned after we took out Rio and Lima. Did you think we'd keep trying to hit northern cities? No. We knew what to do. You act as if you're the good guys. As if good and evil have a line down the middle, a yes or a no. They don't. Even black and white are gray in between. Now water."

James's lips tightened and he heard his molars grinding. He envisioned the devastation of Midway, the burning bodies of innocent people and the blinding light that saved his life and killed his mentor. *Keep it together, man,* James reminded himself and he put his hands on his knees to stand. He replaced the hood on Raspin's head and walked out without a word.

He followed the same routine, making as much noise as possible in the echo conducive space, slamming the door for good measure upon his exit.

Goddammit, that was intense, he thought, rubbing his eyes in the dull sunlight. He took a deep breath. He felt the team watching him as he walked toward them. He kept his eyes focused on the ground trying to parse all the relevant information from the conversation.

"What's the word?" Clint asked.

James glanced up from the ground and saw that Jon, Bob, and Deck had joined the group. They were gathered in a semi-circle waiting for his response.

"James, how'd it go?" Stacie's voice was concerned, and she handed him a bottle of water. "You're pale."

"Agreed. You look like crap, man. What happened in there?" Deck added.

"Just the first conversation. Nothing special," James responded, pondering the information in his mind. "Seems like our troop estimates are a bit off."

"How off? What do they have forty? Fifty thousand? I guess fifty might be a little high, but it can't be—" Stacie started to ramble with her numbers, but James interrupted.

"247,000."

The team was silent. That was unexpected.

"We're off by 247,000 or…?" Deck asked.

"That's how many people they have."

"Well, that's a positive note! We were only off by 197,000. Could be worse," Deck said, shrugging.

"Do you think he's lying?" Stacie asked. Her face was concentrated, no doubt readjusting all their assumptions about the BZ.

"No. He didn't act like it anyway. It doesn't seem like he feels the need to hide anything or to lie about the facts. When it comes to the nature of the BZ though, different story."

"How so?" Kyle asked. The athletic soldier stood to stretch an arm over his head.

"He's forthcoming and matter-of-fact about everything large scale—why they're here, who he is, how many people are in camp. Logistical stuff, but personal things he's holding back. He's trying to get me to slip up and admit we've been watching him. It's a minefield of words."

"So poetic of you," Deck chimed in, grinning.

James ignored him. He was trying to figure out what puzzled him about Raspin. He had the constant feeling they were a step behind their captive.

"Now that Raspin's in custody, we need to start our guard rotation," Stacie said. She continued to talk, but James couldn't concentrate on her voice.

What did Raspin gain by hiding his personal activities? James had predicted he wouldn't say anything useful, but Raspin had practically guessed they were watching him. Furthermore, what type of leverage did it give him to tell James about the camp? Why was he so calm? None of it made sense to James and his thoughts swam through a sludge brought on by lack of sleep and dehydration. He drank from his water bottle lost in his conversation with Raspin when a slap on his shoulder jolted him out of his detached state.

"Buddy. Hey. Hey you!" Deck yelled, rousing James's attention.

James shook his head to relieve the grogginess.

"James!" Deck shouted once more, and James looked at him blinking from the harsh sunlight.

"Yeah? What? What's up?" His voice sounded tired even to him.

"When was the last time you slept?" Bob asked, sitting next to James and checking his pulse.

"I dunno. A day or two ago," James said.

"Not good, man," Bob said. The thin medic rummaged through his go-bag. He found the items he was looking for and pressed them into James's palm.

James peered at his hand finding a partially filled pack of cigarettes, a pre-rolled joint, and a lighter.

"What's this?" James asked.

"You've gotta relax, man. That should get you there," Bob said, picking up a bottle of water from the ground. "I'm going to look at our prisoner. He's probably dehydrated and tired. Anyone have an extra MRE?" James remembered Raspin's request for water. He was more tired than he realized.

"Here," Kyle said, tossing a silver packaged meal to Bob's outstretched hand.

"Thanks, and you," Bob said, pointing at James, "get outta here. Go home, smoke that joint, have a couple of beers, have a cigarette. Relax." With that, Bob turned towards the hut and walked to administer care to his new patient.

"I didn't think medical professionals suggested cigarettes and alcohol as relaxation remedies anymore," said Deck, pondering Bob's instructions. "I mean, I agree with everything he said, but he's really taking us back to the days of *Life* magazine."

James grinned and cracked his neck side to side. "I'm gonna stick around until he gets back. Then I'll go."

"James, go home. We've got it," Stacie said, already flipping up the screen of her HOLO, "You're no use to us in this state. Sleep. Don't come back for three days. Don't do *anything* for three days. Deal?"

"Fine, but I can—" James tried to talk, but he was stonewalled by stares. Realizing what he was up against, James lifted his hands in surrender. "All right, all right. I give up. Can someone guide me down the mountain? I don't want to mistake a pit viper for a puppy."

"I got you, man. Happens to me all the time," Deck said, hopping to his feet and pulling a machete from his bag. "Let's go!"

Deck took off into the brush and James followed swinging his bag onto his back. He started into the woods, careful to step in Deck's prints and they made it without any run-ins with the hill-mountain's inhabitants.

When they cleared the brush at the end of the descent, Deck stopped to take a breather and chug his water.

"Oof, even coming down those woods are a bitch. I wish we could cut a trail."

"That was your rule, man," James replied, following his lead and drinking water.

"Fair. Well, I'm gonna get back up there," Deck said. He wiped his mouth on the back of his hand and replaced his bottle in his pack.

"Hey, do one thing for me," James said, "Don't go in there alone. None of you."

"We're professional soldiers, James. We can handle one guy chained to a fucking chair."

"No, I mean it. He's more dangerous than we know. If you're bringing him water or food or whatever, that's fine. But if you want to interrogate or speak with him beyond one-word answers, have two people in there. He's manipulative, Deck. He can twist a conversation with no effort. Two people always, Deck. That's an order," James finished. He added the order piece because of how infrequently he made requests this serious, but he meant it. He had walked into Raspin's hut with a clear head, easily staving off the exhaustion he dealt with on a regular basis. Within the span of fifteen minutes of talking with Raspin, he was wiped. He needed to learn more about the man and didn't want the team risking their own health and safety.

"Jesus, must be serious. Okay, you've got it. Always two of us in there for interrogations."

"Thanks. Watch out for snakes."

Deck shivered. "Don't remind me."

James watched him disappear and turned around making his way to the stream a hundred yards to the south.

The sky had brightened considerably, and the sun was winning its battle against the cloud cover, evaporating any remnants of mist hanging in the air. James set himself on a rock with his feet in the water. He tilted his head back and watched the sky. He wondered where his family was and what they were doing. He thought of his team's families and speculated how often his teammates thought of home.

The shadows on the trees were getting longer and James realized he would need to get going or risk walking through the jungle alone at night. He thought about it for a moment and pulled a cigarette from his pack and lit it. The smoke traveled in wispy clouds before his eyes, and he felt the effects hitting his system.

Screw it, he thought leaning back on his elbows. *I've walked through the jungle alone. Might as well enjoy the moments I get.* He blew out a plume of smoke and watched a pair of macaws fly overhead. He forgot for a second he was sitting at a stream next to a snake infested hill, housing what may be the most dangerous man in the world. *Funny how we get places*, James thought taking another hit and closing his eyes, hanging his head back, and letting the world take care of itself for a little bit.

CHAPTER 13

"How'd you make the shell?" James asked, turning Layla's latest creation over in his hands.

"It was easy! Dámelo, I'll show you." The little girl took three strands of palm fronds and manipulated them, wrapping the fibrous ribbons around one another, explaining the process as she progressed.

She spoke rapidly, mixing Spanish with English for words she couldn't recall quickly enough. Normally James would correct her, but she was so excited to show him her newest techniques that he let her continue without interruption. James watched, in awe of her talents. He loved seeing her bend the long green shoots into any animal she wanted.

"And that's it! See?" she said, handing the delicate artwork to him with an open palm.

"That is really cool, Layla. Gracias," James said.

She smiled in return and blushed. "You could do it. Just need to practice. Like homework!"

James grinned. "Yep, you're probably right. Now it's getting dark. You should be getting home. I'll run with you."

"Last one steps in dog poop!" Layla yelled, laughing as James jogged to catch up to the small body darting onto the trail. When they reached town, Layla turned around and gave him an enthusiastic high five. "Bye, James! Buenas noches!"

"Buenas noches," James called after her. He returned Selma's wave as she stood waiting on the front porch for her granddaughter. James made sure Layla walked safely through the front door and made the long walk back to camp alone.

He loved hanging out after school with the kids. It helped him relax and gave him a moment to laugh. At night though, his mind turned ruefully to the more pressing matters and shifted back to the team's latest events.

The last four weeks with Raspin as their captive had been challenging.

Housing a prisoner was more difficult than James had anticipated. Logistics were their first problem. Two people were at the border for a week and another person guarded Raspin in three-day chunks. They still didn't interrogate him alone, but they couldn't afford to have half of their team away on assignment all the time. Stacie had organized the most complex job board James had seen in his life, but it made sense. Two days was the shortest amount of time anyone spent between recon and guard duty, but Stacie had set it up so everyone usually got a four-day reprieve between each.

The border was mind-numbing, but more interesting somehow with the added knowledge that the BZ was missing their commander. James did not know what to make of the lack of reaction to his absence and Raspin's explanation was not helpful.

"We are not reliant on a person but on the people," he would say and James would grit his teeth. He knew the sentiment might be true but what kind of operation allows their primary leader to disappear and does nothing about it? It made no sense.

In addition, the forays of the BZ soldiers into the forest had stopped. Since Raspin's capture, the border camp was quiet but otherwise continued as if Raspin was still running the show. Transport ships dropped their troop reinforcements at a steady clip, thousands of soldiers at a time, marching in rank off the twin blade behemoths that carried them from wherever the rest of the BZ was stationed.

Raspin, while still their enemy, had proven to be a good house guest. He never tried to escape even when outside the hut and had garnered a friendly rapport with the team. James had played hardball the first week, questioning Raspin only when he was tied up inside the hut and allowing him minimal breaks outside. Kyle eventually intervened telling James the treatment was inhumane.

James had been complaining about Raspin's behavior. "Would you answer questions locked in an unlit cell in eighty-degree heat and 70% humidity all day and night?" Kyle had asked James one night. James realized Kyle was right and gave the go-ahead to allow Raspin more freedom. During the next few rounds of guards, Raspin had made real connections with the group. He showed Stacie some variations of plantlife that existed in the prison camp and even taught Kyle new stretching techniques.

James was the only one not on board with the friendships. He could not rationalize befriending a man he knew murdered nine people in cold blood. Not to mention, James was unconvinced by Raspin's act. He was an expert at changing his facial expressions and behaviors to take advantage of people. He interpreted strengths and weaknesses with skill and used that knowledge to manipulate people for his benefit. Whether it was getting Bob to share his books or Kevin to bring him an extra tamale from dinner. Raspin got what he wanted.

James kept his distance and ignored the requests and ploys Raspin used on him. He hid his thoughts and feelings keeping up a friendly, but impersonal front. This allowed James to question Raspin without revealing anything about himself.

Raspin divulged little knowledge of the BZ and James was starting to wonder if kidnapping him had been a good idea. Originally, it had seemed like their only option. They had needed information and surveilling the BZ for close to a year had reinforced the plan. After they got what they needed, they would either bring him north and hand him to the Federation or leave him in the jungle while they fled. James would have been fine with option two, but he couldn't leave an enemy commander so close to their newly formed family. He wasn't going to abandon these people to protect his own ass. The problem was the rest of the team.

"What would you want to have happen?" Stacie had asked him on more than one occasion. James knew Raspin would want to go back to his people, but it wasn't so simple. They couldn't drop him at the doorstep of the BZ and say, "Hey, we took your leader. Now he's back." But that sentiment was growing throughout the team. Deck was even coming around to the idea of leaving Raspin in the woods and letting him return to his army.

James found himself stuck with a captive who was charming his team and an enemy army that didn't notice their commander was missing, whose reinforcements were arriving at a rapid pace.

The one vital piece of info Raspin had shared came during their first conversation—the 247,000 soldiers camped at the border. The number still shocked James and sent his mind spiraling with questions. Why here? What were a quarter of a million soldiers doing in the middle of the rain forest? He had no answers but knew Raspin did.

Another issue for James was where all the soldiers were housed. A quarter of a million people could not easily fit into the buildings the BZ had erected. Their camp hardly looked as if it could contain hundreds, let alone hundreds of thousands of soldiers and their resources. The whole situation frustrated James to no end, and he wished someone would give him the answers.

He finished his walk back to the school as the pink tinted clouds reflected the last of the sun's light across the well-maintained lawn. Shadows mingled in the oncoming darkness and James stood for a second in the stillness. It was rare to get a moment like this when no one else was on the school grounds. During the day, dozens of kids ran around shouting and laughing. Even on the weekends, the children from town would come play with the toys at the school, a commodity many of them did not have in their own homes.

James breathed in the evening air already tainted by the smell of an oncoming storm. Its approach further evidenced by the dark clouds forming above the mountains in the distance. He stayed there for another moment before uprooting his feet and walking back to camp. For the next two days he would be joined by Stacie, Kyle, Kevin, and Bob. Stacie and Bob would head off to do recon and he was set to relieve Jon of guard duty.

He entered camp, rewarded by the aroma of an already cooked dinner. *Couldn't be Kevin*, he thought. *He's teaching classes tonight and won't be home until late*. Whoever it was, he was grateful. He did not want to cook and a cold meal didn't appeal either. Kyle and Stacie sat on the couch under the aluminum overhang eating rice and beans off the plates in their laps. Kyle waved him over.

"Grab a plate and help yourself, man. Stacie made patacones, too," he said, motioning towards the kitchen.

"Gracias, mis amores," James said, bowing at the couple. He walked to the kitchen and piled rice and beans on his plate and helped himself to three of the thickly cut, deep fried plantain wedges stacked next to the stovetop. He sprinkled salt over his food and went back to the platform in the center of camp. He settled into one of the Adirondack chairs facing the couch and took a bite of the patacones, audibly groaning a sigh of satisfaction.

"Stacie, these are incredible," James said, holding one up, "Don't tell Kevin, but you're better than he is with these little brown beauties."

"Well, thank you, James. And I will absolutely tell Kevin," she said, grinning.

"Works for me. All he's going to do is try to prove me wrong."

"In that case, we should send a runner to the school now."

James smiled and kept chewing. He missed eating with the whole team, but spending time with even a few of them was refreshing.

"What's for dinner?" Bob asked, appearing from his cabina with hazy eyes and tousled hair. He had just returned from a stint on guard duty and was set to head out in a couple of days with Stacie for recon.

"Rice and beans with the best patacones in camp," James said, shoving another forkful in his mouth.

"Don't let Kevin hear you say that," Bob said, walking to the kitchen. He returned with a heaping plate of rice and beans with five patacones stacked in a precarious pile on the edge of the tin plate.

"Get enough?" Kyle asked, eyeing the plate with admiration.

"I like to eat. Sue me," Bob replied, digging in without hesitation.

Even after eating almost every meal with him for over two years, James was shocked at Bob's ability to put food back and watched with fascination as the pile of rice diminished in a series of forkfuls.

"I hope we're not interrupting date night," James said, suddenly self-conscious.

Kyle waved his hand. "Never man, you're good. If we want a date night, we'll find another place to shack up."

"Well say something if you want us to get away," James said, rising from his seat and taking the empty plates sitting on the ground in front of Kyle and Stacie. "I know it can't be easy with seven other people living here and another two frequent overnight guests. Doesn't help to have a small army of children running around the property at all hours."

"Thanks, James. We appreciate it," Stacie said, handing him her fork.

James nodded, ending the conversation. He had been reticent about their relationship at first, how it might affect the group's dynamic. The bigger question, how a breakup might affect the interactions between Stacie and Kyle. After mulling things for a few weeks, James realized he was being absurd. They could figure things out for themselves. Who was James to worry about the end of someone else's relationship? It wasn't fair to them. They were already up against a lot—dating a person involved in the most dangerous job in the world while simultaneously risking their own lives every day. No, they could do whatever the hell they wanted as far as James was concerned.

"Those are some big goddamn storm clouds," Bob said, finishing his third patacone.

"It's pretty calm though. Won't be here for a little while," Kyle said.

James moved to the chair closest to the couch and watched the storm make its way down the mountain range, picking up steam like a skier gathering speed.

From this distance, James couldn't see what was happening on the ground, but given the frequent lightning strikes and increasingly dark clouds, he assumed they were in for an intense couple of hours.

"Anything new with the data batch, Stace?" James asked, leaning back.

"A couple new breaks that Jon found. We're pretty sure it's some massive set of blueprints, but we don't know of what yet. It's all coded. Even the diagrams need to be decomposed then reconfigured and put back together. Either way, we're making some progress."

"Blueprint for what?"

"It's a building. That much we're sure about. The dimensions, the plans, and the basic diagrams we've unlocked all point to that. The thing we're stuck on is this piece we can't decipher. It's present in every part of the diagram but breaking it down is beyond our knowledge. It might be something super technical architecturally, but it has to be easy." Stacie shook her head and added. "Maybe it isn't. Either way, we're making progress now, so it feels good."

"Good for you guys."

"I hope," Stacie said, shrugging.

They sat in silence for a moment, watching the clouds make their way closer to the camp.

"Anyone want a beer?" Kyle asked, pushing to his feet.

"That sounds great," James said, standing up. "I'm gonna get my cigarettes. Anyone need anything?"

"Grab a joint from my cabina. They're on the desk next to my emitter," added Bob.

"You got it. Anyone else?"

"I'm good. I'll take a beer though," Stacie said, tapping Kyle on the butt.

"Me three for the beer," Bob said, doing the same when Kyle walked by him to the kitchen.

"I'm not a frickin' trollop," Kyle said, slapping Bob's hand away.

"Yeah, but you've got a great ass," Bob said, winking at Kyle.

James shook his head, grinned, and walked to the cabinas. When he returned moments later, the four of them sat in a row facing the storm. James handed the joint off to Bob and sat back in the Adirondack chair, careful not to spill the beer Kyle had left for him on one of the armrests.

He lit his cigarette and took a sip of the yeasty liquid. As the cold hit his teeth, a shiver ran through his body, but the second sip reminded him to relax, and his body sunk into the wood-framed chair.

"Anyone else see those reports from the Federation this week?" Kyle asked.

"Reports?" James replied, glancing at Kyle who remained reclined on the couch.

"Factions appearing all over the government. President Braxton's got challengers popping up left and right. They're asking questions about what he's doing and he's not giving great answers."

"Huh, that's surprising," Bob piped up, sipping his beer.

"Is it though?" Stacie asked, glancing up and down the line at them. "Braxton hid a preventable massive attack from the Federation's citizens and pulled all support from the South. He's probably thinking about moving farther north every day. Meanwhile, a massive army is growing on Federation land with no way to spy on it or a plan to do anything about it. The 'answers' he gives are they've got everything under control, but we're going to draft all your kids."

James nodded in silent agreement. As usual, Stacie's breakdown was correct. The Federation leadership bungled everything they touched. James hoped the factions weren't a serious thing, but when war came north, there was no telling what would happen.

They drank beers and chatted until the wind picked up.
Leaves and bits of loose plant material whipping through the air.
When the first drops began, James helped Kyle close the roof
and they all said a rushed good night. James ran to his cabina as
rain pelted the ground, joined ominously by bolts of lightning
illuminating the clouds, adding a violent edge to the winds
tearing through the camp.

James felt safe and secure in his cabina. He pushed aside
his drapes to finish his beer as the storm washed away the day,
preparing for tomorrow with a fresh, cleansed earth.

Rain pounded against his aluminum roof. James's
eyelids drifted shut and when he caught himself sleeping on his
stool, he realized it was time for bed.

When he awoke, the birds in the trees were boisterous.
The rain had a way of flushing out great meals for them
undoubtedly leading to territorial showdowns in many of the best
hunting spots.

James ducked through the low doorway and stretched his
arms above his head. He looked around camp to get a sense of
what the others were up to, but the morning was quiet. A thin
mist hung above the ground disappearing with each passing
second and James glanced at the doorways of the remaining
camp members. Bob's curtain hung over his doorway. Probably
asleep. Kevin's doorway was open, and James wondered if he
had made it home last night or decided to stay in town. He
glanced at Stacie and Kyle's respective cabinas, both open,
probably out for a run or something. *Good for them,* James
thought, actively ignoring the nagging compulsion to work out.

He made his way to the kitchen to prepare a cup of
coffee, pushing the idea of exercise to the back of his mind,
fighting with himself.

*I can take a break. I've worked out every day for the past
three weeks. I deserve the rest.* James let all the platitudes and

excuses pile up in his brain creating a logjam for any other thought. He opened his HOLO and attempted to scroll through the latest log reports from Bob's recent conversations with Raspin when, finally, his guilt beat him into submission. He slammed his coffee cup on the counter grumbling about how even he needed a break sometimes, changed into his running shoes and a pair of shorts, and took off into the jungle.

He found his rhythm after the first three miles, settling into a steady pace. He finished at an old lean-to structure on Paola's property a mile away from camp. It was originally used for farm equipment Paola's husband Hector wanted to keep closer to town. Paola and the school had no need for the building, so the team had converted it into a gym. As homemade gyms went this was impressive. Concrete blocks, milk cartons, and old tractor chains were used as weights. The normal focus for exercise was on using their own body weight to ensure they could exercise anywhere, but sometimes James thought nothing felt better than lifting something heavier than himself.

That day he concentrated on a shoulder and back workout. He ended with a final set of Romanian deadlifts holding a cement block in either hand, dropping the block to the floor with a *bang* upon completion of the last set. The cement bounced on the dense rubber mat, and James stood with his hands on his knees, letting his heartbeat steady and blood flow back to his extremities. His arms were shaking from the exertion and the numbness in his hamstrings told him he'd need a long stretch the next day, but it was worth it.

He splashed water on his face from the crude sink they had set up beside the overhang and took a cold water bottle from the solar powered fridge.

"Hey, bud."

James turned to find Kevin ambling towards him with his backpack slung over a shoulder. He was in the same clothes as the day before and his hair was creased from sleep, but he looked dry.

"Kev, my man, you make it home last night?" James asked, giving him a fist bump as he approached.

"Nah, I crashed at Selma's after class. That storm was wild. Everything stay tied in camp?"

"Nothing out of place when I left for my run."

"Good. I ran into Stacie and Kyle a little while ago walking some kids to school. They said you all ate together."

"That we did. Stacie made the best patacones I've ever had," James said, attempting to get a rise out of their envious chef.

"We'll see about that," Kevin said, grinning, understanding a challenge when he heard one.

"What're you up to now?" James asked, refilling his water.

"Headed back to camp. Might try to nap before I help out at the school this afternoon. Bob's running class tonight."

"I'll see you back there. I'm gonna catch up with Selma. She mentioned something about Juan Carlos the other day but didn't say a whole lot."

"Fucking JC," Kevin said shaking his head.

"Fucking JC is right. What time are you working at the school?"

"I'm done at five. I'll plan on cooking dinner if you want," Kevin said over his shoulder. James heard the gears in Kevin's head turning and wondered how he'd beat the previous night's meal.

"I'm expecting big things," James called after him receiving a calm middle finger in return. "Has to be the best that one," James said to himself, grinning and shaking his head.

He took another bottle of water from the fridge and made his way into town.

During the week Río Negro was busy. Or as busy as a farm-centric village on the edge of the Amazon rainforest could be. The pavilion was a nexus for the community, and it helped James stay informed of the area's activities. James was always stopped for at least one interaction when he passed through. Whether it was BZ transport sightings by a farmer or a mother trying to sell James on the benefits of teaching the bible during their English classes, it was always something.

Today was no different. A group of teenagers hung idly around the stone tabletops under the sparse trees of the plaza. James talked with them, helping them with their English. He was a few years older than any of them, but decades beyond their experiences.

After they left, James sat enjoying the table's cool concrete on his forearms when he spotted Juan Carlos unaccompanied by his normal cadre of bodyguards. James watched him, noticing agitation and distraction clouding his eyes. Something was off and James needed to learn more.

"Hola, Juan Carlos!" James shouted, doing his best Deck impression by waving at the town millionaire inviting him to sit. "I've got some time. Want to hang?"

Juan Carlos's eyes stared right through James. Sweat dripped down his forehead and his normally crisp clean shirt was wet and rumpled accentuating his rolls of fat. He shook his head as if trying to get his vision straight before walking up to James and pulling the front of his shirt over his potbelly.

"Hola, James. ¿Como está?" Juan Carlos's voice was shaky and anxious.

"What are you up to? No buddies today?" James asked, pointing out the lack of security.

"What? Oh no," Juan Carlos said, glancing back and forth between his fortified house and James.

He's waiting for something, James thought and, realizing a lead when he found one, stood from his seat. "You want a drink? I've got nothing but time and you're always bragging about Carolina's mixologist skills."

James kept his tone cheerful and airy. He didn't want Juan Carlos to guess his intentions. James needed to find out why he was acting strangely, and getting inside that mansion was the best way.

"Maybe another time," Juan Carlos said, peeking over his shoulder as James slapped his back good naturedly.

"Come on, no time like the present!" Without waiting for his host to refuse James walked to the front gates of the mansion and waved at the cameras.

"Juan, hurry up. Your guys aren't gonna let me in without you," James said. He did his best to keep things upbeat.

Juan Carlos, unable to dissuade James, shrugged and walked to the gate watching the other side of the square as if waiting for someone.

After waving at the cameras, the doors swung outward and James entered followed closely by Juan Carlos who turned and continued to stare across the pavilion as the doors shut behind them.

Something is seriously wrong, James thought, looking at the grounds inside the fence.

During his single visit to Juan Carlos's estate, the protections and defenses were well hidden, if not invisible, but felt by all. He remembered opulent marble statues, a curated lawn of manicured Bermuda grass, overflowing multicolored gardens, and swarms of butterflies. Juan Carlos and Carolina lived a lifestyle of untouchable perfection, bought with more money than James could imagine.

This time a much less elegant scene welcomed James inside the gates. Guards carrying long rifles and sidearms filled the grounds. The windows of the mansion were shuttered by canvas curtains and James spotted the muzzle of a heavy machine gun poking out above one of the terraced rooftops.

They were at war. James went on high alert, coming here alone had been a mistake.

One of Juan Carlos's guards approached and patted James down in a more invasive search than he had anticipated. The guard quickly found James's boot knife stashed in his waistline. The guard looked at Juan Carlos expectantly who glanced at his guest.

James shrugged at Juan Carlos. "Force of habit. I live in the jungle now. What do you expect?"

Juan Carlos waved at the guard who returned the knife to its spot and continued his search. Search complete the guard guided them to the house. James counted thirty men in full-go battle mode spread from the rooftops to the garden. Something or someone had Juan Carlos scared.

"Expecting trouble, Juan?" James asked casually.

"Always." The reply was curt and offered no chance for a follow-up, so James kept his mouth shut until they entered the back patio where Carolina lounged with a book.

She looked at them from her chair, barely registering their arrival. *Maybe that's how they interact*, James thought, smiling in her direction and getting a limp wave in response.

"So, what can I do for you?" Juan Carlos asked. He was getting agitated and James knew he needed to be cautious.

"Saw you walking and figured I'd say hi. We've been busy with the school and haven't had a chance to talk. How's the farm business going? Anything happening because of La Guerra Blanca?"

At the mention of the BZ Juan Carlos's eyes shifted to the door and his hands tightened in his lap. *That helps narrow things at least,* James thought, pondering his next topic.

"It's all great. We're in the middle of planting season for the piñas. We'll get the banana fields cleared to house more workers in no time," Juan Carlos answered. "How about a mezcal?"

"I'd love one," James replied. Playing his hand carefully James followed up on Juan's first statement. "Clearing the fields for workers? Where are they coming from?" *Why would he need more room for housing?* James wondered. The BZ was miles away and no one new was coming anywhere near the border.

"We run a big operation, James. Can't wait for people to come to us with nowhere to live you know." Juan Carlos relaxed. Pouring himself a drink and the opportunity to deliver a condescending remark seemed to help his mood. He threw a piece of ice at Carolina to get her attention. "Mi amor, ¿quiere una bebida?"

She glared at the ice melting on the white tiled floor and back at him with primal disgust.

"No." She returned to her book without another word.

Juan Carlos made a twirling motion with his finger next to his head and handed James his drink, sitting in a wicker chair on the other side of the table. "Mujeres son locas."

James chuckled trying to keep his host in a good mood, but he could not help noticing Carolina's knuckles turning stark white as she clutched her book.

"We're always looking to expand, James. You see, I'm a businessman. I understand how to make money better than anyone and I have an eye for opportunity. Let's just say I seized an opportunity to make money and did it with gusto," Juan Carlos said with a motion snatching at the air. "There aren't many men like me, James, but you can learn how to be one. Salud." He held his drink out to James and they clinked glasses.

James took a sip of the smoky beverage. Had Juan Carlos made a deal with the BZ? He didn't know how. He didn't know when, but that's what it had to be. It was the only explanation for why he would even think about expanding his operation while a massive military stood miles to the south.

"So the army doesn't bug you?" James asked, probing for more information.

"Not at all," Juan Carlos replied, waving them off as inconsequential. "Everyone's looking to make a deal in this world. And I can deal with anyone." He raised his glass again and clinked James's finishing his drink not waiting to see James's reaction.

That solidified it. He had made some sort of deal with the devil. That's why he had the security running such a tight ship. But it didn't explain his strange behavior as he walked through town.

"So, where were you coming from earlier?" James asked, waving off a refill.

"Here and there. Always something going on. Needed to tie up loose ends as you might say," Juan Carlos replied cagily. He was hiding that part of the story, and James was sure his disheveled appearance wasn't as innocent as Juan Carlos tried to make it.

A loud crashing noise echoed from the front of the house and James's brain shifted to defense. Juan Carlos's eyes snapped to the door and Carolina looked up from her book, showing interest for the first time since James had entered the room.

Yells could be heard and James glanced at his host for an explanation, but Juan Carlos's eyes were fixed on the door.

One of the guards entered the room and Juan Carlos followed him out wordlessly.

James waited in his seat, glancing at Carolina who shrugged her shoulders.

"My husband, he's ambitious," she said and went back to her book.

James stood from his seat. He poked his head through the door and turned back to Carolina who continued to read, uninterested in the dramatics taking place in her home.

James left the room and walked steadily to the front door prepared for someone to jump out at any second. Yells and shouts with increased desperation added to James's confusion and he steeled his stomach for action. Reaching around his back he grabbed the knife from his waistband.

"¡Ayúdame! ¡Ayúdame!" a bodiless voice in severe pain called out, echoing eerily down the hallway.

More shouts followed and James could hear Juan Carlos's voice ordering others above the din. "¡Mudarles ahora!"

James poked his head around the corner and was met by a scene from a battle front's triage center. Watching, he memorized every moment. One bodyguard held a compress to his head while he towered over Juan Carlos watching the rest of the scene over his boss's shoulder. Another sat off to the side, his face a mask of delirious pain, while two other guards were working on a tear traveling down his arm. Something had ripped him from the shoulder to the back of his elbow. Tendons were visible through the shredded skin. James saw white bone shining as the medics dabbed gauze over the wound struggling to hold the blood slicked skin together.

However, most of the action was on the floor where a third bodyguard lay. James could see nothing but the man's feet as a team of men attended to him, his boots convulsed violently while a pool of blood expanded across the floor.

Juan Carlos stared in shock.

James, deciding he had seen enough, crept back to the room where Juan Carlos had left him. Carolina didn't look up when he entered and he sat thinking about what he had seen, wondering what was going on when one of Juan Carlos's men came into the room and motioned for him to follow. James clutched the hilt of his knife as he was guided through the back of the house. Neither of them said a word while he was led out the vehicle entrance.

The guard motioned to the sentry tower on top of the exterior wall and the door opened. James walked across the brick-lain driveway, watched by no fewer than seven of the compound's guards, noticing the long streak of blood covering the ground from Juan Carlos's black SUV to the back door.

When the door closed behind him James walked away in a semi-daze, turning the scene over in his head, committing it to memory.

CHAPTER 14

James took a long walk. He made a wide loop around Río Negro, cutting through tucked away neighborhoods behind the town's main strip. The houses were jumbled together along dusty roads. Bodies of muddy water lay behind the houses where the uneven surface created dips that collected grey runoff and rainwater.

Strolling through the neighborhood while dodging the occasional group of children playing intense games of tag James broke down the scene from Juan Carlos's house. The first bodyguard, barely scathed and standing upright, but terrified. The second seated off to the side, his mangled arm hanging at his side while a team of Juan Carlos's guards attended to its repairs. And finally, the third and hardest one for James to think about, the man on the floor. James did not know the extent of his injuries, but his convulsing legs and the expanding pool of blood led James to believe he would not live to see the night.

The experience kicked James back into mission headspace. For so long he was able to separate the two worlds from one another, BZ in one, Río Negro in the other. However, it looked as if the inevitable was melding them into one. It was only a matter of time until they completely overlapped. James shook his head as he thought about the implications of the BZ making its move to take the rest of the South.

Can't change anything about that, James thought, feeling helpless.

He exited the maze of houses by the pavilion where he had started his walk. He thought about taking a break to talk with Selma and Jose. His mind decompressed and his tongue practically dragged him in the direction of their home, but he

kept on towards the jungle pathway back home. Paths
crisscrossed and curved, breaking, and starting at odd intervals
throughout the wooded area and James, still in a fog, decided to
extend his walk and took a path that would arc around the entire
camp.

He walked through the possible scenarios in his mind,
flipping them inside out and deciphering which ones could be
correct. If it had happened anywhere near their team's section of
the border, Deck or Clint would already be back at camp running
an all-hands-on-deck operation. His emergency radio receiver
hadn't pinged, so that was unlikely. It was also unlikely that Juan
Carlos's guards had found and tried to rescue Raspin as a
bargaining chip with the BZ. If they had been anywhere near the
hill-mountain, Jon would have seen them coming from miles
away and their injuries would have been a bullet through the
temple, not the gaping wounds he had seen.

Juan Carlos could be trying to negotiate business with
cartels or other gangs, but that seemed doubtful. Business for
those criminals was nonexistent in this area. They'd no doubt be
by the border working on establishing new illegal enterprises in
the North.

No one option made sense. Juan Carlos's men had tried
to enter the BZ at a different section of the border and had been
caught. White bone shining through torn skin and legs
convulsing in pools of blood flashed through James's mind,
along with the extreme violence carried out by the BZ on the
men they had slaughtered the day Raspin arrived. If that was it,
Juan Carlos had made a major error in judgment.

James arrived at a flat sandbar where rivulets of water
branched off across a wide swath of the riverbed. The macaws
perched in the trees were screeching and squawking, making
their presence known. James took a second to admire the ever-

moving nature as he watched a lizard sprint across the dry spots in the river and dive into the greenery along the water line.

To be him, James thought with a sigh and turned the river bend where the outline of the clearing that hid their vehicles came into view. He walked under the vines and bunches of Spanish moss used to cover the truck and Jeeps. He checked that no animals were making homes in their vehicles and headed back to camp.

Kevin was sweating over two roaring grills as a steady tunnel of smoke climbed into the night reflecting the sunset. The smell of grilled pork floated through the air and James salivated.

"James, how about a kebab for dinner?" Kevin asked above the crackling flames.

"Sounds good. You have patacones, too?" James asked, grinning.

"Best you'll ever have," Kevin replied, ignoring the jibe. The chef took a swig from the beer bottle sweating on the counter next to him. "Get yourself cleaned up. We eat in twenty."

"Are Kyle and Stacie here?" James asked, already peeling off his shirt walking to the showers.

"They're getting changed now. Why?"

"I had an eventful afternoon. I'll explain over dinner."

An hour later Kevin, Stacie, Kyle, and James sat under the retracted roof watching stars float in and out of sight behind banks of puffy, white clouds. James had finished telling them about his ordeal at Juan Carlos's house and had talked over the different scenarios with them. They all agreed the BZ was to blame for whatever happened to those men, and it was likely the bodyguards had gone too close to the border for comfort. None of them had a clue as to what could have done that kind of damage to the man's arm. James could picture it, like the flesh had been ripped off by someone's hand. Explosions, gunshots, knives, and other weapons could make flesh wounds like that, but this was way more drastic. This was something none of them had ever experienced and the possibilities scared James.

"You said the man on the ground was convulsing?" Stacie asked, her face contorted into its thoughtful stare.

"Yeah, and a pool of blood was growing from near his head. Judging by the look of the other guy's arm, I'm glad I didn't see his injuries."

"The other guy, though, not hurt?"

"Just those two. One was completely fine, but his face was chalk-white. He was scared shitless and covered in someone's blood."

"Do you think the BZ was doing another recon trip?" Kyle speculated, stretching an arm over his head.

"They mostly do those at night," Stacie said, brushing it aside.

"Maybe Clint and Deck did it. If they weren't hurt and didn't want to ruin our surveillance of the BZ recon by breaking radio silence, they could be waiting to tell us," Kyle said, trying again, but the shrugs from the rest of the group answered his hypothesis.

"Fine, I guess it was the BZ. I can't even wrap my head around it though. If they made it through the border's defenses, why would the BZ let them go? Why wouldn't they keep them? Or kill them?" Kyle said, standing and bending over, stretching his legs. "It's not lining up."

"The BZ never does. We'll figure it out though," Kevin said leaning back in his Adirondack chair. "From the ships to the assault to the fucking Sentinel patterns, we always figure it out. We'll do it again."

James nodded. Kevin was right. They would figure it out, but time was of the essence and James worried the BZ was going to move.

"Nothing we can do about it until tomorrow night when I relieve Jon. Let's sleep on it, and if anything else comes up, we'll deal with it then." James stood and clapped his hands together. "I know its early, but I am wiped. It's been a weird day." He waved goodnight and walked to his cabina.

He lay in bed staring at the aluminum ceiling thinking over everything that happened in the past few days when he heard a knock on the siding next to his curtain.

"Come in," he said, propping his pillow against the wall behind his head.

Stacie poked her head in the door. "Got a sec?"

James gestured at the stool next to his desk. "Help yourself, my lady."

"Thank you kindly," Stacie replied with a curtsy, taking a seat. She glanced around the tight space avoiding James's eyes. She wanted to tell him something but didn't know how to say it. James watched her carefully, about to ask what he could do when she broke in.

"I think we should go back."

James was taken aback. Go back? To the North?

"Okay…" James said, allowing Stacie the opportunity to collect her thoughts.

"Taking Raspin was a good idea. Getting more information is why we came here and learning it directly from the source made sense. But he's not giving us anything, James. We know they have a quarter of a million soldiers and counting, probably closer to 400,000 troops by now given the rate of their transports and we don't have any way to stop them. All we can do at this point is reteam with the Federation military and deliver the info we have. It's our only shot. It's the Federation's only shot. And it's the only hope for the people in Río Negro." Stacie went through her reasoning with practiced speed.

She was right. The Raspin scheme was turning out to be an abject failure in gathering any real information. The Federation with all its resources was best positioned to take down the BZ army. The North would need every bit of intel they could get. With their extensive training and experiences since becoming elite soldiers, James and the team were arguably the most capable fighters on the planet when it came to the BZ. But James couldn't trust the Federation. Not after what they had done to the South, their treatment of the team, and Brandt's death. It wasn't a position James was able to justify, but he was willing to hear Stacie out.

"I'm not saying walk back into the Federation like everything's okay, James," Stacie said, reading his mind. "They've done too much to us for me to trust them again. I'm saying we coordinate an evacuation of the town, return Raspin to the border, and hightail it north. When we get close enough to the border, we send an intel packet to them so they know what they're up against and we disappear until the war meets us again. James, we've done all we can here. It's time to realize when a mission's complete even if it doesn't feel that way. This one is done."

James nodded. Her plan made sense but he didn't know if it was the right option.

"So we let Raspin walk back into the BZ? You don't think he'll come after us?" James asked, reviewing her points.

"He's not unreasonable. We'll tell him we're sending him back and leaving the area. We can even say we've got the Federation watching him and if he does anything they'll be blown sky-high."

"Not unreasonable? Huh…" James said, remembering the body parts tossed around the crowd of soldiers. "I think *this* version of Raspin might be reasonable."

"James, it's our only choice."

"Why not bring him with us? Hand him to the Federation when we get north?"

"You don't think the BZ would follow us?"

"They haven't done anything to find him yet. What makes you sure they'd start?"

"They would, James. I don't have anything to back it up, but they would. Your run-in with JC proves that contact has been made between those two groups. He's their eyes and ears here and if we try to move a town and take their commander, we'd be making a mistake."

James mulled this over. She was probably making the right assumption, but it didn't feel like it to James. He was frustrated, disappointed in himself, and annoyed with Stacie. He was sure this wasn't the first time she had talked this over with someone and it wasn't only Kyle. He knew the team must have been thinking about this for a little while if he was hearing about it now. Why hadn't she come to him earlier?

"I would have said something earlier, but this is the longest you and I have been together in weeks and the most time I've been able to think without the goddamn data packet on my mind."

She's reading my mind, James thought. *Witch.*

After a long pause, James said, "I think you're right. I'm going to do my last stint with Raspin and then it's back to the BZ with him. We'll plan to go in twelve days. Gives you and Kyle some time to rest after your stint at the border and us more time to get the town ready to move."

The relief on Stacie's face was evident and she looked him in the eyes. "Thank you, James."

He nodded. "Okay, now get the hell out of here. I need my sleep."

Stacie grinned and walked out closing the curtain behind her. James listened to the sounds of her footsteps fade away in the darkness as he stared at the ceiling, trying to determine where their plan had gone wrong until sleep gave him a merciful respite from his mind.

Chapter 15

The town square was a buzz of activity. It always was on the third Sunday of the month.

Agricultural labor was a brutal, exhausting business and modern conveniences in the North did not exist here. James had even witnessed some farmers hitching themselves to plows alongside their mules and horses. He couldn't imagine what it was like to plow a field in ninety-degree heat and no shade.

The third Sunday was a treat for everyone though. The town held a mini festival attracting even the most remote farmers. The atmosphere was lively with food vendors throughout the square and entertainers juggling, singing songs, and playing instruments. The streets snaking through the village were lined with men and women selling their crafts.

James was impressed by the care each person put into their products. Whether they were oil paintings or beaded necklaces, the detailed precision and love poured into each object were apparent. He had tried to convince Layla to set up a stand with him to sell her animal creations, but she did not see the point.

"I do them because I like to give them to people, dummy." She would say and sprint off. Her ceaseless energy and the purity of her intentions for her artwork impressed and inspired James.

Today he and Bob strolled through the food vendors. Bob held a bowl of ceviche, the tangy smell of the seafood reached James's nose leaving a pleasant, if sour scent, but he hated the stuff.

"I can't believe you like that," James said, glancing morbidly at the bowl's contents.

"There isn't much I don't like," Bob said. "Except raisins. Waste of time, little rabbit turds."

"Raisins? You draw the line at raisins?" James asked, genuinely surprised.

"Hate 'em. By the way, have you seen Paola?" Bob asked, taking another bite of the sour mixture. "I figure she's at Selma's place."

"I was thinking the same, but I wanted to walk here first. I have a feeling she's going to have a lot of questions for me."

Bob nodded. "I would, too, if someone asked me to convince a town full of people to abandon their homes and join a group of eighteen-year-old kids on a trip that may end in war."

"Read my mind," James said, stopping to look at a table with miniature wooden sculptures arranged across the front. The craftsmanship of the figurines was incredible. James picked up an angel and inspected the intricacy of the feathers along its wings.

"Hey, James," Bob whispered, hitting him on the arm. "JC is out. Brought two of his boys with him."

James looked and saw Juan Carlos walking through the crowd, shaking vendors' hands and smiling. Signs of stress or any indication that his bodyguards were severely wounded were not present at all. One of the bodyguards was unscathed, as James remembered, while the other had his arm in a sling. The third was nowhere to be seen.

"Looks like he has some company in the crowd, too," Bob said, pointing out a couple of JC's men hiding in plain sight, watching the vendors, waiting to strike if necessary.

"Let's get out of here," James said, not looking for another conversation with the town's self-proclaimed savior, "Don't need that jackass lying to my face."

"Roger that. I could use some ice cream anyway," Bob said. He picked the last piece of shrimp from the bowl and tossed the soggy cardboard container in the garbage next to the figurine stand.

"Your stomach is remarkable," James said, replacing the angel figurine on the table and smiling at the vendor. He used the exchange as cover to get a sight on the closest JC guards. Recognizing a break in their teams coverage Bob and James made their move.

They weaved through the crowd at a quick pace. James was already nervous to talk with Paola about their plans. On top of it, his level of self-doubt had compounded since Stacie had told him they should leave. He knew it was the right thing to do and that she hadn't intended to make him feel like a failure, but he did. He had pushed hard for this mission and now they were coming away with next to nothing. Saving the town would compensate for the lack of planned success. He needed a little help to push it past the finish line.

They reached Selma and Jose's house. The elderly couple sat on the front porch with Paola who leaned against a support beam. James and Bob received the customary greetings from everyone with kisses from the women and a handshake from Jose.

In all the months he had known their family, James had only heard Jose utter a smattering of words. He reminded James of a rabbit, kind and gentle. He was a gracious host who would offer his seat to anyone who looked in the direction of his home.

With their hellos complete, James and Bob leaned against the low cement wall lining the porch which supported Selma's award-winning peppers on the other side.

"You're gonna have to cut these soon Selma," James remarked, picking one up and testing its weight. "This one's heavier than Layla."

"Claro que sí. I'll sell a bunch of them next month. People have already asked to buy them fresh off the plant." Selma reached out and inspected one of the bright orange growths with pride. "They have time I think."

"Well, they look great to me," James said, shifting his feet as they stood in silence for a few minutes. James wasn't sure how to start, but he knew he needed to get it over with and ask Paola to assist with their idea.

Come on, James, do it, he said in his head as he pinched his arm for good measure and pushed off the cement wall.

"Paola, do you mind if we take a walk? I want to ask you something."

"¡Por supuesto, James! Vamos." She scooped her arm through the crook of his elbow, and they took off through the crowd.

James glanced back at Bob who gave a last-minute thumbs-up, disappearing into Selma's house, no doubt coaxed by one of her recent baking creations.

"¿Cómo puedo ayudarte?" Paola asked, winding her way through the crowd headed nowhere in particular.

"I want to start by saying how much we love it here. I mean, you've taken us into your homes, your families, and made us feel like a part of this place. Everything you've done has been special, from letting us help with the school to organizing English lessons in town. It means the world to us."

Paola smiled and looked at the ground, a blush forming on her cheeks.

"This is more of a home than any of us has had in the past couple of years. We all needed you and can't thank you enough." James said. He steered them towards the empty soccer field. They walked to the bleachers where they were joined by a few teenage couples cozying up higher in the stands.

"You're like family to us, too, James. This year has been… a miracle. You have given this town a hope we have not known in years. You are special to all of us." Paola finished by placing her hands on James's and smiling with tears glistening in the corners of her eyes.

"Thank you. That means a lot." James swallowed. *Get it over with.* "But things are happening that are out of our control, Paola. The Guerra Blanca, they're growing and the Federation military will do nothing to help. My team—us, me and Bob, Stacie, Deck, all of us—we can't fight them on our own. Even with the help of the entire town of Río Negro, the Guerra Blanca is too strong, too big, too advanced. They're beyond our power to stop." James's tongue was dry, and his stomach tightened in agony. He looked Paola in the eyes to finish his statement, refusing to play the coward. "Paola, we need to leave Río Negro and we want all of you to come with us. If you don't, the Guerra Blanca will attack. They will come through here and they will kill everyone.

"I've come to love this place as much as my own home, but I'm afraid that fate won't let us live here happily ever after. We need to leave, and we want you to come with us." James took a deep breath after he finished. Paola looked at the ground tears falling freely down her face.

"I had a feeling this was coming. When you were here after six months I thought there was hope. Hector loved this place more than he loved life, second to his love for me. I know he would fight to the death to save it and do anything to see Río Negro safely through to the end…" She stopped, catching her breath for a second. "But I also know he would say it's the people that make Río Negro, not the place and if you have them, you have everything.

She straightened her back and looked James in the eye. "What can I do?"

James smiled at the woman, impressed once again by her strength.

"You're an influential person in the town, Paola. People listen to you. We need you to start conversations with the families about readying to leave in eleven days."

Her eyes grew wide at the proposition, but James held his hands up to halt her. "I know it's fast. If we want to get north safely though we need to move as quickly as possible. To do it right, we need to go in exactly eleven days." She nodded, her face a mask of internal struggle and deep concentration.

He knew the timeline was hard to digest, but it was the right thing to do. He continued, "Once you've had time to talk to people who want to leave with us, we'll make an announcement in town, maybe at the game on Thursday. Stacie's already developing a plan," James said. Noticing the confused look on Paola's face, he clarified in Spanish, "Las logísticas, entiende?"

She bobbed her head, understanding. "Sí, claro que sí."

"Bueno. Anything else right now? We've got a lot of planning to do, and I have to leave here in a few hours." James stood to go, but Paola stayed rooted to the aluminum bench. She looked out across the field, but her eyes had dried.

"I thought I'd watch my children play here one day. Hector and I both did. We dreamed of our kids waving to us from the field and smiling." Her face held a faraway smile of nostalgia when she looked at James. "I may not have been given my own children, but la gente de Río Negro son mi familia. I do not want to see them destroyed. I want to see them live and grow. I want them to spread what they have learned here to other parts of the world. I hate to leave here, but at least our dreams of growing a family can remain in a new place."

She reached out her hand and James pulled her to her feet. She stood on her toes and kissed him on the cheek. "Vaya,

I'll talk with Selma, Rosa, and Mariel. We'll take care of things here."

James smiled at the woman and left the field at a jog. He needed to relieve Jon.

It was time for Raspin to talk.

CHAPTER 16

The snakes on the mountain left James alone choosing to occupy the sun-pocked shadows in the depths of the jungle. The birds were quiet, no doubt resting after the intense heat of the day. Beads of sweat stung James's eyes, and his shirt was soaked.

He wiped a hand over his face and broke through the vegetation at the top of the mountain where their one-man prison stood.

Jon and Raspin sat at the picnic table peeling the skin off mangoes and cutting strips of the golden flesh.

"So you never left the BZ?" Jon asked, digging around the pit of his mango. "That's pretty wild."

"Why? You have never left the Federation," Raspin said, licking the juices running down the back of his hand. "Same difference. And remember, my area's quite a bit larger than yours.

"That's fair," Jon said, placing his knife on the table. "Want some water?" He stood from the table, wiped his hands on his pants, and nodded at Raspin's thumbs-up.

Jon turned around and jumped. "Goddamn, James! Why the hell you sneak up on us?"

"Good to see you, too, man," James said. Jon's knife lay on the table and James walked over and picked it up placing it out of their prisoner's grasp. James pretended not to notice Raspin's side eye at the move.

"You ready to head back home? I hear Rich is getting in today."

"Yes! We're going out to the falls for a night or two. Should be a lot of fun."

James nodded. Stacie could break the news of their plan when he got back to camp. For now, he needed Raspin in the dark. "Sounds good, man. You need help packing?"

"I think I've got everything," Jon said, picking up his rucksack and rifle from the ground. "See you in a few days." He gave James a casual salute and pointed to Raspin. "I'll see you in a few weeks I guess."

"Have a great time, my friend. Tell Rich I say hi!" Raspin said, waving to his prison guard. James stood next to the table as they watched Jon disappear into the foliage.

James turned to their prisoner and greeted his smile with a blank face. He held out his hand. "Knife."

Raspin looked at him, not breaking his smile, but handing James the knife. "So little trust from you. I'm not going to run away or anything, you know? You people have been nice to me. The least I can do is be a good guest."

"You're not a guest." James said, tucking the knife in the back of his belt.

"Oh? Then am I a prisoner? I see no shackles. I see no cage. I see no striped jumpsuit. If anything, I'm a house guest at a remote getaway in the mountains." Raspin smiled widely and James saw a row of straight, but yellowing teeth.

"Don't care what you think you are. All I know is you're here and can't leave unless we say so. What do you call that?" James stared him in the eyes, challenging Raspin to respond, but he smiled and looked away.

"I don't care as long as you don't think of me as bad or anything."

James shook his head. This conversation was getting him nowhere. He knew he had one shot at the line of questions he wanted to ask. He needed Raspin to be lulled, but it would be a challenge. Ever since their first interaction James had experienced a spine-tingling discomfort when they spoke and it worsened as the rest of the team became more comfortable with Raspin.

For weeks James had struggled with ways to extract more information from Raspin. What would it take to get him to talk? James knew he would not use torture. It wasn't in his DNA. Besides, the research he read did not support it in this kind of situation. He had thought that the team's kindness might glean some information from their captive, but it had created the opposite effect. James sensed Raspin cloaked his true self. Sharing their lives had not gotten Raspin to remove his disguise.

Instead, James had a new plan. The prospect of a willing prisoner voluntarily divulging enemy secrets was gone. James needed something new from their captive and hoped his plan of holding up a mirror for Raspin to get a look at himself would do the trick.

Placate him for a day or two, then make your move, James thought, gritting his teeth. He took a deep breath and tried to be nice.

"Listen, we started off badly again and that's my fault. You want to cook dinner with me?" James felt sick having to pretend with the man.

"That sounds delightful! What are you thinking?"

"How about beans and eggs?"

"Lovely. I'll start the fire if you get the ingredients ready."

"Great." James rationalized he would suck it up as much as he could, meanwhile thinking through the idea in the back of his mind. The time would come soon enough.

The next two days passed with relative ease, calm, and quiet. Aside from watching his step for giant venomous snakes roaming the grass, James liked it on top of the mountain. He would put Raspin in the house after dinner and lay in his hammock looking at the stars.

He spent the first part of his nights reviewing his plan
for Raspin, but after let his mind wander to the rest of the world.
How did Deck, Jon, and Clint take the news that they were
leaving? What was Stacie going to do about the lack of space in
vehicles? How would Paola convince the town to leave? Would
they make it to the North before the BZ attacked again? Every
night more unanswerable questions spun around his head.

Afterwards, he went back to moments at home with his
friends sneaking beers from parents' fridges and drinking them
in the park at night. He recalled the night of his birthday when he
met Kayleigh. He remembered moments in basic training in the
Midwest, two hundred chairs scraping the linoleum floor eager
to eat after a day of grueling work. His mind traced his history to
the present and he thought sadly about how much he had aimed
to accomplish with this trip. How this could have been the
lynchpin to the war.

It still might be, he thought, turning over and closing his
eyes. Thursday was the day.

In the morning, James and Raspin sat at the picnic table
watching a family of birds feed in a tree. Kevin was set to
replace him at some point in the next two hours.

"Love watching nature like this. Very calming, peaceful.
Makes everything okay." Raspin stared at the family's perch
with a dreamy smile.

"It's beautiful for sure," James said. James knew his
moment was coming soon. "So, Raspin, I have a confession to
make," James started. "The day we found you wasn't accidental.
We knew you had been there for weeks. We knew you went
there every day in fact."

Raspin's face remained passive so James continued.

"We actually know a fair bit about you and your people.
We know about your Sentinels, your sensors, your border limits.
We track the transport ships you have coming in every day, and

we were there fighting when your ships hit Midway. Hell, we were some of the first to see how you destroyed Europe and still may be some of the only ones who saw the images of Africa. Wild stuff. Very impressive actually. Turn a fucking continent into a base for your military. Good for you.

"What I can't understand though is why you sit in the woods by yourself? Why week after week you leave the safety of your camp, venture into the trees alone, and sit facing the sky with your eyes closed." James paused to take a sip of water. It was crucial for him to avoid Raspin's eyes and James leveraged his peripheral vision to glimpse at the placid face of their prisoner.

"I think everyone needs a break. Believe me, I certainly do, and I try to reward everyone on the team with the same. What do you do for your team, Edgar? How do you give people time off?"

"I don't really have much say in that," Raspin replied, shifting in his seat.

"No? You have the freedom to leave camp when you like, unaccompanied. How does that work? Why do you do it?"

"Like I've told you many times James, anyone can leave at any time. I'm sure you missed some others walking about outside our camp's boundaries."

"I don't think so. But back to my original questions, how do you blow off steam? What do you do to reward a job well done?"

"A pat on the back and some time off," Raspin said coolly, checking his fingernails, "We're running a military operation here, not some office job. A job well done means you stay alive."

That was it. That was what James needed. He picked up his HOLO emitter and pulled up images from the video footage their drones had grabbed from a distance. The picture wasn't as pristine as it could have been if the shot was closer, but it didn't matter to James. This was his bullet.

"And what about a job poorly done?" James stopped talking and placed the emitter with its screen on the other side of the table. The footage rolled, the same as it had the hundreds of other times James had watched it. Raspin walked to the center of the stage where the three people sat hunched over and bound in front of him. Then he systematically cut their throats and threw the six hostages to the crowd to meet their sadistic deaths.

Raspin's eyes did not blink while he watched the video. When it ended, James started it again. He repeated it four more times while they sat in silence. James shut the screen and turned to Raspin who stared into the distance at the tree line.

"My team, my friends, they think you are an okay guy. They see the person sitting across from me as pleasant, cooperative, even friendly. They believe you won't do anything against us and will stick true to your word. They're convinced you'll even walk back to your army and not come after us.

"Me, I'm different. I don't see that trustworthy exterior. I see the face of the man who slit the throats of his people in that video. A guy who threw six men into a crowd who treated them like chicken bones in a dog pound. I see a murderer. I see pure evil. In our first talk, you said good and evil aren't polar opposites, and you're right. I know who you are." James's voice cut through the still air with a sharpened edge. "The gray area does not exist in you, Edgar Raspin and no amount of bullshit will convince me it does."

James expected a look of shock from their prisoner but was taken aback when Raspin turned to look at him. The stony features that greeted him from across the table emanated a hatred James had never experienced.

"What now?" asked Raspin. His tone resembled the calculating timbre of a cold-blooded killer. "Will you keep me here forever? You think you know so much about me? You overplayed your hand, James. You showed me what you know."

"I showed you what I wanted you to know," James said coolly.

Raspin nodded his understanding, his stare boring holes in James's skull. "My question remains. What now?"

"Against my better judgment," James continued, "we're going to release you back to your people."

Raspin's eyebrows arched into a question.

James held his hands up, "We're leaving. We're going back north. We'll drop you at the clearing and we're gone. I want assurances from you though that we get four days before you come after us."

Raspin gave a gruff laugh. "Why would we chase you? What do you have to do with our mission?"

"My thoughts exactly. So why not give me your word? We get to leave, unharmed by your army, with a four-day head start. That is, if they let you live long enough to make the call." James glowered at Raspin.

Raspin remained silent and the two of them froze in the moment. The air held a charge of an unseen force and James experienced a deep seated, pure hatred for the man that would be with him forever.

"You have a deal," Raspin said, nodding.

James nodded. "Good. You'll be home in eight days."

"I look forward to it," Raspin replied, and he continued to stare at James until they were interrupted by a shout from the bushes.

"Hey!" a voice called out.

James turned around in a flash, his sidearm already in his hand when the greenery parted and Kevin broke through into the clearing.

He held his hands up seeing James's gun. "Whoa, easy, man."

James replaced the pistol in its holster. "Sorry, Kev. Spooked me is all."

"No worries. This kind of isolation can get to you," Kevin said. He patted James on the shoulder and placed his pack on the ground next to the table. "What're you two doing?"

"Just chatting," James replied. "I was telling Edgar about our plan to drop him back home."

"Yes, excited to get back to camp," Raspin said, the honey-layered tone restored.

"All right. I'm gonna get my hammock strung up and then I'm cooking dinner. Brought us some tilapia for the night, Raspin. You like fish?"

"Love it!" he said, rubbing his hands together. "Quite a treat."

"Good. James, you can head out whenever you want."

James looked across the table at Raspin one last time, catching a flash of the vile creature living behind his forced exterior.

"Okay, I'll get my stuff." He reached across the table and shook Raspin's hand, meeting his eyes. "Good talk."

"Good talk," Raspin replied, and they both let go.

James let the hatred he had for Raspin solidify itself into a cold stone in his stomach.

"Goodbye, James," Raspin said as James turned to get his rucksack.

"For now," James replied.

He went to Kevin who was still setting up his hammock. On his first stay, Deck had cleared a nice grassy area of any vegetation, reasoning that he liked to see the snakes before he stepped on their heads. James always appreciated that kind of thoughtfulness from a team member.

"The town ready?" James asked Kevin.

"Ready as it can be. Paola's talked to all the families she believes will join. At the soccer game tonight, she and Selma are going to present the town with their options."

"Good. Any of our people going to be there?"

"Stacie wanted to help out with the presentation, but she's on recon duty. Besides, it might be better if it doesn't look as if we're meddling in their affairs," Kevin replied, handing James a nylon string.

"Makes sense to me. Anyone else going to be there in the bleachers though?" James wrapped the plastic sheathed cord around the screw dug in the tree.

"Deck, Jon, Clint, and Bob are probably already saving their seats. Not to mention Rich and Cristina. They've got it handled, man."

James nodded. He knew they'd do everything he wanted. He wished he could be there for the announcement. Gauge the reaction of the crowd for himself.

"I better get going." James shouldered his pack and took his machete out along with a pair of infrared goggles. It was getting dark and even cold-blooded serpents couldn't hide from their gaze.

"You two have a good few days. Bob'll be around to relieve you soon enough," James said, giving Kevin a fist bump.

"Right on. Safe travels," Kevin replied, finishing what would be his home for the next few days.

James glanced at the table where Raspin sat staring into the woods and prayed silently that the enemy commander would keep his word.

After a tense trip down the mountain and the standard five-mile hike back to camp, James arrived home. Pulling back the vines to their headquarters, he found his team plus their significant others in the rest area.

He approached them, expecting lively conversation and thoughtful planning for the next stage of their journey, but emotions were subdued. The atmosphere was tense, not the normal relaxed mood on nights like these. The faces of Cristina and Rich flipped back and forth between each other and the members of the team sitting in silence.

Cristina waved him over. "Hi, James. How was the trip?" She stood and kissed him on the cheek and Rich greeted him with a handshake.

"Not bad. Doesn't seem like everything's okay here though. Did something happen?" James caught the worried glance between Rich and Cristina.

"Well, mate, things were… ahhh, a little bit off tonight," Rich started, tripping over his words as he continued. "You see… umm, Paola was doing great, really, *really* great. She made her appeal, and the town was all behind her. It was awesome to see, really." Rich stopped at that point and looked at the team whose jaws tightened at once.

"Rich, what happened after that?" James asked, the pit in his stomach grew by the second.

"Well, there were some other people in the crowd and they…. ummm…" Rich stopped and nudged Jon on the shoulder who shook his head, the line in his jaw getting tighter.

Cristina rapidly spit out the rest. "Juan Carlos was there. He trashed the idea and called you all silly fake mercenaries who don't know anything and should stop interfering in things they don't understand," She sat back in her chair and crossed her arms, pushing deep into her seat to avoid the reactions.

James was shocked. Juan Carlos was calling *them* out for trying to rescue the town? What the hell was happening?

"He did what?" James asked, trying to wrap his head around what Cristina had said.

"He said, yo—" Cristina started but Deck interrupted.

"He fucked us, James. Someone tipped him off about our plan and he fucked us. He's making his move to take the town and doesn't care if everyone fucking dies because of it." Deck was fuming.

"What was the response?" James asked, trying to imagine the scene.

"Paola tried to speak again, but he pushed her off stage, encouraged by boos from his supporters," Clint said, speaking for the first time, "Then he talked shit about us for the next hour. He finished telling everyone the cowards who wanted to flee could do so, but he was staying and would make anyone who remained a millionaire like him."

"Yeah, the greasy potbellied shit for brains spent ten minutes spouting off about knowing people in the BZ. How he would help make everyone wealthy beyond their wildest dreams. Leaving would be an exercise in stupidity and those sticking with him were set for life while those abandoning the town were condemned to failure. He kept going on and on after we left."

James nodded, acknowledging he had heard them, but was having trouble putting the pieces together in his head. Juan Carlos had made a deal with the BZ and was trying to keep the town captive. He needed workers for something and promising wealth to the desperately poor was his way of getting them.

James's fists tightened. "What's the damage? How many people will come with us?"

"No sé," Cristina said, shrugging. "Maybe a few dozen."

Hearing this knocked the wind out of James. He was stunned! A few dozen? That was barely the families in houses surrounding the pavilion. That meant there were hundreds who weren't joining them. Hundreds of families who would be crushed by the BZ because of an egotistical little man who had the power to say and do whatever he wanted with no repercussions.

The fury built in James's throat, and he ground his teeth.

"What do we do now?" Jon asked, finally relinquishing the hold on his Adirondack chair to sip his beer.

"Nothing else we can do. We guide the families who want to come, and the rest will stay here," James replied. Visions of charred bodies from the last BlankZone attack floated through his mind.

"This is when you need a Brandt, someone who takes it completely into their own hands," Deck said, his head hung between his arms. "There's something beautiful in sacrificing everything like he did."

James nodded, but they had their answer. They had done what they could.

"We're not going to do anything. We gave the people the option to leave and that offer stands. The ones that don't… I hope they know what they're doing." James stood from his Adirondack chair. All of a sudden he felt sick from the night air and wanted to lie down to forget everything about the past few hours.

"I'm going to get some sleep." He waved goodnight to his team and walked to his cabina, beaten in mind, body, and spirit and in need of a blackout sleep.

CHAPTER 17

Deck led, padding silently along the familiar path to the BZ border. Mossy stones lining the streambed looked different in the daylight and James was surprised at the amount of wildlife they encountered.

When they reached the maze of streams James helped Kevin guide a hooded Raspin across the slippery rocks scattered throughout the shallow water. He was surprised at the muscle tone Raspin had maintained during captivity.

James's foot slipped in the pebble lined streambed, and he inadvertently splashed water on Raspin.

"Hey, no splashing!" Raspin said good-naturedly to which James responded in silence. He had no interest in talking to the man.

They finished their hike and arrived at the hut. Kyle waited for them at the base of the tree, his gear leaned against the trunk. He gave a thumbs-up to the group as they approached. James responded in kind, and the team sat Raspin on the ground under a palm tree in the clearing.

James tied Raspin's hands behind his back and secured the rope around the tree. With a tug on the knot, he whispered to Raspin, "Wait here. We're coming back."

"Oh, goody." The humor in Raspin's voice had disappeared.

James pointed to a spot on the path for the team to convene out of Raspin's earshot.

Silently finishing their water bottles under a bamboo patch, the team mentally prepared for the final part of their mission.

He had chosen Jon, Kevin, Kyle, and Deck to accompany him on the trip. The others were pissed, but James had explained to each one his reasoning for needing them to stay behind. Clint, their mechanic, had to ensure every vehicle was ready to go. He also needed to check over the other vehicles joining their caravan. The tight timeline meant he couldn't join them and finish his inspections in time.

Bob was responsible for doing health checks on everyone joining the trip. He also needed a good understanding of everyone's dietary needs. Another set of time consuming tasks.

Stacie was the hardest to convince that she was needed in camp. He had half expected to turn around and find her following them at a distance, but she was the most vital part of their travels north. Stacie understood the logistics of their plan more than any of them. She needed to concentrate.

None of the three liked the exclusion from the Goodbye to Raspin Tour, a name dubbed by Deck, but their skillsets and the needs of the townspeople were too important to compromise.

James's heart thudded in smooth rhythm against his sternum. His breath was even, and his hands were steady.

"Everyone know the game plan?" James asked, surveying the group. The question was rhetorical, but the nods were good to see. They all knew what was happening. This was the easy part. Next, they would be guiding more than seventy inexperienced travelers a few thousand miles through mountainous jungle, across dangerous rapids, and God only knew what else to reach the North. That was the hard part. Dropping Raspin, that was nothing.

"Deck, you're in the lead. Get up high and secure the area. Jon and Kyle, when Deck gives you the signal, do a sweep of the perimeter and establish yourselves on the far side of the clearing. When you're done, signal back to us. Kev and I will come in with Raspin. At that time, Deck, I want you heading back to the ground. Once Kevin releases him, we leave in retreat formation with Deck leading us out. Jon and Kyle, you two have rear guard. When we lose sight of the clearing, speed it up." James glanced at the camouflaged faces of his friends. Unflinching eyes returned his gaze.

"Let's go."

Without hesitation, the team broke formation and retrieved Raspin. With the prisoner standing between Kevin and him, James nodded at Deck, and they were off.

The walk to the clearing took minutes, and James's stomach tightened with every step.

Deck sped ahead of the team and within a minute had located his perch. He signaled for Kyle and Jon to get in position. James waited with his hand on Raspin's arm. With his other hand, James flexed his fingers ready to get this over with. He hated the vulnerability of the area.

The brush was so thick that James couldn't see more than a few yards beyond the edge of the clearing. That bugged him, anything could be lurking out of his sightline. Luckily Deck was outfitted with an infrared scanner on his tactical binoculars which would reveal any problems.

After what seemed like an hour, James got the signal from Kyle. Time to move.

He nodded to Kevin, and they pulled Raspin into the center of the clearing. James pushed Raspin to his knees while Kevin bent to untie the rope binding his wrists.

James glanced at the azure sky peeking through the hole in the treetops. It really was a peaceful location. The silence and seclusion of the spot increased James's understanding of why Raspin chose this as his personal grotto. James took a deep breath, glad the hardest part was over when he sensed the silence. It wasn't normal. Why was it this quiet?

Spooked, he looked at the trees. Something was not okay. Kevin was packing the rope in his rucksack when James looked above his head. He spotted dull grey metal hidden behind the brush below the tree line.

"Kevin, get down!" James shouted and the world erupted in violence.

Dark gray figures sprang from bushes. James felt a jolt of pain in his hip, as he was lifted from his feet, and slammed into the ground. In a split second, he rolled in time to avoid the hazy outline of an arm from crashing on his neck.

"They're HOLOs!" Kevin shouted as he grabbed one of the semi-transparent humanoid figures and snapped its arm off.

The result was unexpected. Rather than dissipate with its broken arm, the HOLO shook off the stump and reproduced the limb. It sprinted at Kevin who was busy fending off an attack from another HOLO and jumped on his back.

What the fuck? James thought, flipping onto his back and pushing off the ground in time to dodge a kick in the jaw from the translucent outline of a foot.

James whipped out his sidearm and took three quick shots at the HOLO's chest, but there was no reaction from the blank faced creature.

This was something James had never experienced. He tossed his gun to the ground, and reached for his knife, unsure of what to try next.

All around him sounds of carnage, silenced rifle shots, and grunts filled the air.

He waited on the balls of his feet for the HOLO to make a move, but James was tackled again from the side. Falling to the ground, he shifted his body weight and jammed his knife into the HOLO's head. Nothing.

How the hell do you kill these things? James thought, hooking an arm under his attacker and launching from a squat, slamming it into a tree.

The other HOLO was running at James again, and realizing he needed an escape, James jumped to the closest branch and pulled up, swinging clear of the HOLO's grasp. He spotted a Sentinel hovering on the other side of the tree and grabbed it, smashing the disc into the wood. It shattered in his hands and James dropped it to the ground. At the same time, he looked to see that the HOLO crawling up the slippery bark had vanished.

The HOLOs and the Sentinels are connected? James thought. He scanned the area for other gunmetal discs. One flew next to a tree across the clearing, and he dispatched it with a throwing knife, demolishing the HOLO Jon had been grappling with seconds earlier.

"The Sentinels! Get the Sentinels!" James shouted from his perch, searching for more missiles to throw when a hand wrapped around his ankle and yanked him from the tree.

James smashed his head against the trunk as he fell, and his world faded to black in a sea of chaos and fear.

PART III

CHAPTER 18

Darkness was the easy part. Holding onto the perception of reality was more difficult.

His world was a mirage of fantastic figures swirling in a space devoid of color or brightness. Dim light allowed him the benefit of shapes, but he could not shake the feeling he was imagining it all.

The drab intensity of his surroundings made it seem as if someone or something was there with him. How could they throw him inside such an unassuming cell after the brazen attack in the middle of the woods? It didn't make sense and he could not dig deep enough to determine the source of his mental discomfort. Whatever it was, James could not shake the feeling that his mind was sloughing its acuity by the second.

He slapped the ground with his open palms listening to the sound echo off the walls, and bounce off the steel before settling on the floor.

There was no way to tell how long he had been incarcerated, but he guessed a week or longer judging by the stubbly growth on his cheeks and chin. He had become well acquainted with his room. The cot where he sat was his anchor. It was where he slept, ate, thought, stared, and forced away the anxiety circling his psyche.

He rested on the thinly stuffed cot facing the room. To his right was the slot where his captors delivered food on a schedule. James assumed the deliveries were made every twelve hours, but it was purely a guess. Across the room was a hole that James, once again, assumed was his toilet. At least that's what

James had used it for. *If it's not, then they are in for an interesting discovery at the bottom*, James thought wryly.

Directly across from James, in a corner sat his stack of trays, or as James thought of them, his calendar. Fifteen food trays stacked neatly on top of one another. James wasn't sure if anyone would come to get them, but for the moment, the platters were his only reference to time.

The prison's routine was easy to follow. Twice a day, as far as James could tell, a tray would fall to the ground through the slot. Every time it opened, James hoped to see brighter light come through, but to his disappointment, the outside room was kept as dark as his. The sound of the slot's sliding door was all that reminded James that a world existed outside of his isolated box.

He could not place the food's origins, but it was unimpressive. A mushy grain and some tasteless protein to accompany it. The first few times he received the platter James thought he might be eating human meat, but after a few tortured thoughts about eating a friend, he decided to go with it, realizing how ridiculous that sounded. He was concerned a little at how easily he had accepted the act of cannibalism.

The familiar clatter rang in the room, and the slot closed again in a rush. He pawed the ground to locate his food. He picked up the tray and shuffled to his cot, careful not to spill the contents of his meal.

He gummed the squeaky grains and let his mind drift.

He closed his eyes trying to forget the solitude and thought back to the time before all this. Before he woke in the room, face down on the rough concrete floor with a banging headache and sore back.

The HOLOs had thrown them for a loop. James was shocked at the sophisticated tech in the advanced defensive tools. Impervious to bullets, knives, and everything James had in his arsenal. The thing that worked was knocking out their actual power source. He saw the flash of static air in his mind's eye, reliving the moment he had figured out the secret to eliminating their attackers.

Then he was hit on the head and *poof*, the world disappeared.

James had thought back to that moment countless times. Trying to figure out how the Sentinels and the HOLOs worked. He had determined that the Sentinels were really emitters. That was as far as he made it with any degree of certitude. However, it did not explain the impervious nature of the HOLOs.

More than anything, James wanted to know what happened to the rest of his team. Maybe the battle shifted? Maybe they were safe and sound heading north with the people of Río Negro? In this scenario, James realized, he was presumed dead, but at least they were continuing the mission. Thinking that way gave him a deeper sense of seclusion than he already felt. The fact that he was here, sitting in a cell, getting fed through a slot in the wall, counting his days by stacking metal trays, and pooping in a hole, convinced him that something else had happened. Right now, his team was planning a way to get him out. They wouldn't leave without absolute confirmation that he was dead. It wasn't their way.

Maybe the rest of the team sat alone in dark rooms thinking the same as James. Maybe one or all of his team were watching the unlit space in their cell, staring in the direction of their trays stacked in a corner, thinking about each other waiting for something to happen.

He convinced himself that his friends and teammates were not dead. They had made it out or they were in here with him. That was it.

"Quit it," James said out loud, sensing a spiral of depression well up from the depths.

James chewed the tasteless meat with his molars, focusing on the food while he tried to ignore the carousel playing across his vision of the faces of his friends as dead.

When he finished, he placed his tray carefully on top of the others. He counted them for what must have been the twentieth time since his last meal. Sixteen metal platters stacked one on top of the other. Their sides perfectly uniform, fitting together with precision and James felt some sense of calm knowing he could always check the trays to regain his sanity.

He crawled to his cot and lay on his back, looking at the ceiling. He hummed under his breath, trying to stimulate his mind with something other than thoughts he could not control. After what might have been five hours or two minutes, James rolled off the mattress. He lay face down breathing in deeply, placing his palms parallel to his shoulders. He tensed his muscles and started his push-ups.

He did a set of thirty, lowered himself to the ground, counted to twenty in his head and did another thirty. He repeated this time and time again until his shoulders were giving out and his chest became a burning mass of lactic acid. Then he rolled himself back onto the cot and drifted into an exhausted sleep.

The rats scurrying in the pitch-black woke James as their sharp claws scraped and scrambled on the other side of the steel walls. When James opened his eyes, he tilted his head back and took a deep breath, ready to face another wait for his next meal.

He went through his routine. Toilet. Push-ups until exhaustion. Stare at the emptiness, trying desperately not to think about the rest of his team. Toilet again. Lie in bed. Planks, counting heartbeats to denote seconds until he couldn't feel his abs. Back to bed. Food. Push-ups. Sleep again.

As if on cue the scratch of little claws moving near his space woke James. He assumed there were vents overhead or behind the metal walls. Which meant he must be housed in a larger facility. Strangely, the rats were comforting in the absolute loneliness of his environment, and he came to rely on them as disease-ridden alarm clocks.

Time dragged by with each segment of wakefulness. James was past the point of caring if anyone came to see him. He would continue his routine until they stopped feeding him. He knew he had to keep some routine to maintain a semblance of life. Otherwise, they would have won before he even knew what had started.

When standing, the trays in the corner now reached past his knees. James had counted thirty-six platters after his first meal during that wake phase.

If his guesses were correct, that would mean he had been in there for eighteen days. This estimate was on the higher end, but there was nothing he could do about it so why bother? To help erase the thought of time from his head he began another round of push-ups until his triceps turned to jelly and he was using his lower back to throw himself into the air to finish a set.

James's torso collapsed to the floor, and he lay there for a few moments, enjoying the fatigue seeping through his limbs. In his current state, he felt a renewed sense of the world righting itself even if he was stuck alone in a cell with rats as a source of comfort.

The familiar sound of the slot opening interrupted the monotony, but James didn't bother to lift his head. He waited the standard five seconds to hear the tray drop to the floor, but nothing happened.

That's strange, he thought, turning his head toward the slot. A fluorescent bulb shined through the opening casting a dusky white glow into his cell. For James, it was the sun.

He was dumbfounded. Certain that someone had mistakenly kept the light on, he sprang to his knees and crawled to the wall. He put his back against the entrance and looked at his cell.

It was disgusting.

The trays were molding on top of each other and for the first time in weeks, James could smell the odor in the room. The light somehow delivered a more visceral perspective and James was revolted.

I guess trays of weeks-old food and an open hole in the ground for a toilet don't make for healthy living conditions, James thought, wrinkling his nose at the stench.

Wanting to see the world outside his cell, he turned towards the door as the cover slammed shut. James dejectedly returned to his half-lit life.

Without warning the door opened with a *clang* and the light James had found intriguing moments earlier became a nightmare. He held his hands to his eyes and curled over in agony. His retinas were seared by the sudden illumination and, after essentially zero exposure to external stimuli for weeks, had to be permanently damaged.

While he rolled on the floor stifling the screams in his throat, two pairs of strong hands picked him up off the ground. James kept his eyes closed while they wrenched his arms behind his back and yanked him through his cell door.

They dragged James along a maze of twists and turns until they stopped and placed him against a wall. The squeak of a spigot got James's attention and a blast of tepid water hit him square in the face. He struggled to breathe while the hose concentrated on other parts of his body.

He stood drenched and cold while a pair of hands grabbed his arms and another cut off his clothes. The material fell from his body. Before he knew it, they were hosing him down again while he stood naked and partially blind. He shook uncontrollably with ice in his veins unable to process his emotions as a frigid bite settled in his bones. He stood, exposed, with his eyes shut tight waiting for what would happen next.

A rough towel scoured his body followed by a pair of light fabric pants pulled up around his waist. Finally, his captors regained control of his arms and led him from the room, barefoot and shirtless, but at least cleaner.

Gaining confidence in himself, James took a stab at opening his eyes. A dimly lit concrete floor welcomed him. He mustered more bravery and cautiously opened his lids further, not daring to lift his head.

His captors wore combat boots and their pants matched the uniforms James had seen the BZ army personnel wear during their excursions in the jungle. The floor was poured concrete but looked hastily made, not smooth like a long-term facility. The corridor was no more than six feet wide, and they had made no turns.

The people dragging him stopped. James hung his head lower and closed his eyes, careful to hide his state of consciousness.

A door opened and he was carried inside a room and propped in a chair. His arms were released and secured to his seat. The combat boots stomped as they walked out the door.

The door swung shut. James waited in silence with his chin drooped to his chest. He waited, counting his breaths between heartbeats. He sensed another body nearby but was not going to move. He could be patient. It was all he had left.

"Welcome, James." The voice of Raspin chilled the air and entered James's brain with a noise, not unlike a car crash. It was a voice James knew he would hear again one day. He had hoped it would be long into the future after the BZ had failed their mission. Now, there it was. Sitting across from him, in a power dynamic that favored his enemy.

James gritted his teeth and looked at Raspin hiding his ire and managing to hold an almost bored look.

"Hello, Edgar," James said, careful to mask the emotion in his voice.

"Role reversal, huh?" Raspin said, smiling a sickly grin.

"I don't remember locking you in darkness for extended periods of time."

"That was your mistake then."

"Agreed."

"Oh, James. There is a lot you need to learn. Maybe not for your future, but at least to understand all that you don't know as your career ends." Raspin put his hands on his knees and pushed to his full height.

"I've been waiting for this moment for a long time. Ever since we spotted you and your team by the border with that woman from the town. What's her name? Paola? You had such a determined look on your face. Ready to take on the world. To take us down. If I had not known better, I might have been nervous." He looked at James and grinned, "Good thing I knew better.

"My predecessors were positive we needed to do something about you and your team. They were convinced you were going to attack, but I had a hunch that wasn't the case. At least that wasn't your primary mission. I couldn't prove it, but I was the one calling the shots. I got my way in the end. I knew I needed to get close to you. To find out who you were. It was easy to do once I had your attention, but it took a lot of planning and work to get here."

James kept his face stoic and listened, feigning nonchalance. Internally, he was unraveling. *Raspin had planned all of this?* James thought, reeling at the idea that all this time he and his team had been manipulated.

"Ohhh, yes. I know what you're thinking right now. How did I do it? Why? Well, the why is the easy part. You're the ones. Your team is the sole reason the Federation is standing right now. You figured out our plan, and against your own government's best efforts made us pay for not torching that fucking city from afar. You were right when you said that you knew us better than most. You do, but I know you, too, James. I know your team. You listen to them. I mean, you took their advice to let me come back here. That part was easy. Hell, I thought I almost had you convinced for a second, but you proved impervious to my charms." Raspin paced the room with his hands clasped behind his back.

"Once I made the decision to take you as a hostage, I had to map out my plans carefully. You had to truly be captured. Make no doubt about it, I could have strong-armed the entire thing, but you would have died. I have no doubt about your willingness to sacrifice yourself to save your friends. It's who you are, James. I needed to show you a piece of myself to lure you. Killing my lieutenants was easy. They were the cake topper. I knew that would set you off, and, boy, was I right. It was a matter of time until you ran your kidnapping scheme, which was a complete guess on my part, but I figured you were watching carefully for a reason, and voilà, here we are now." Raspin stopped and spread his arms as if to show off how his grand plan had worked. His face held a smile his eyes did not match, and the lethal glare that Raspin held in check for those weeks as a captive shone with a fire James understood lay at the core of the man's soul.

"You slit the throats of your own leaders and had men torn apart to lure me as bait?" James asked.

"The leaders to an extent, yes, but they were proving less useful with each passing day and the slaughter of the men was a necessary evil helping to instill the instincts required in my soldiers. War is not a game for those without the stomach for its vicious proclivities. I prefer to keep those who serve under me prepared for the violence and ferocity that a battlefield demands."

Raspin stopped for a moment to take a sip of water, giving James a chance to get a better look at the room. The decorations were austere, the cement walls all but bare. A flag with three intersecting triangles hung behind Raspin's desk which was even less impressive, a plastic card table with foldable chairs on either side. It did not seem like a room used for anything other than informal conversations like these and James began to wonder what Raspin really wanted.

As if reading his mind again, Raspin continued. "You see, James, you have the edge on my army in battle. You have the ground experience, the intuitive sense of movement getting you from one step to the next. You walk towards enemy fire flying around your head and survive from heartbeat to heartbeat. My people, they have not experienced that part of a battle. The cities we took in the South rolled over and we walked through their front doors. We've only been dominant. They've only experienced the aftereffects of an attack but have no clue what it feels like to participate in something as visceral as combat.

"But that's not what interests me, James. I don't care about your experience. I don't need you training my men or helping me create a ruthless effective war machine. As long as I have people like your little Mayor man bringing his people by, we'll always have plenty of practice with the odd spat of senseless violence. What I need to understand is how you tick. What makes James move in the morning? Do you understand?" Raspin's brow furrowed when he looked at James. He was sincere in his questioning and James was taken aback by the way in which Raspin bared his soul to explain his intents.

"That I can't figure out. How you stayed strong. Even after being locked in a room clueless regarding any aspects of your incarceration. Your mental state after weeks of limited rations, no human interaction, and total darkness is unchanged. Meanwhile, hardened men have broken under the same conditions in mere days. You have something else driving you, James. I intend to find out what it is."

Raspin stopped and sat behind his desk. At the same time, the door behind James swung open hitting the wall. Two guards entered.

"We'll talk again tomorrow."

As the guards removed his restraints, James gritted his teeth and thought through what could be the last ninety seconds of his life. If he clipped one of the guard's knees from behind he might topple into the other one long enough for James to dive across the table and smash Raspin's head into the cement until nothing remained but pulp on the floor. James held his breath, considering the possibility with every fiber of his being as he lifted his leg to locate the knee of his attacker, then placed it back on the floor.

His team would come, and when they did, he'd be ready for them.

"Have a good night," James said, mustering a pleasant voice to mock his captor, but Raspin's eyes never left the HOLO on his desk and James was dragged from the room with questions swirling through his mind.

CHAPTER 19

Three trays later, James was still going over his first conversation with Raspin. One thing was clear. JC had been messing around the border's edge. The vicious wounds and horrible death suffered by his man on the oil-stained floor of his compound's garage told James everything he needed to know. They had run into the Sentinels. How much more JC was responsible for, James had no way of telling. All he knew was JC was playing a dangerous game with an enemy he did not understand.

"Typical," James muttered shaking his head.

A clatter from the door knocked James from his thoughts. Seconds later the guards removed him from his cell. They led him through the corridors shirtless and barefoot with his captor's hands gripping his biceps. During his initial trip, James was only able to see the floor and leather boots of the BZ military. This time he made an effort to familiarize himself with the rest of the base.

He walked, tripping once when he stopped to glance through a rare, open doorway, but the interior of the room was too dark to see anything. His misstep caused the guards to drag the tops of his bare feet across the rough pavement scraping off a layer of skin. The pain shocked James system, but his captors seemed not to notice. They were not stopping for anything.

The walls were hewn stone and interspersed with gnarled tree roots. The ceilings consisted of hard packed dirt and large rock formations with spindly roots dangling at random intervals. Fixed to the ceiling was an unbroken halogen light that switched off when they left an area turning the vacated space behind them an inky black.

So, we're underground, James thought looking at a tendril of skinny roots that had snuck through the rock. *Now we know where those 300,000 soldiers are hiding*, he reasoned, remembering the idyllic scene above ground.

The guards maneuvered their way through the labyrinthine complex with ease passing other soldiers frequently. James assumed there must not be a ton of space, but then again he had no idea how far they had dug. *Could be miles*, he supposed, recalling the retired nuclear silos people in the Federation had converted to homes.

They stopped outside an unmarked door and James was greeted by Raspin intently reading a HOLO propped on his desk.

The guards sat James in the chair opposite Raspin and secured him to the seat before they left the room swinging the door shut.

James waited in silence while Raspin swiped across his screen, his face contorted in thought. Instead of staring at his captor James took another look around the room. It was all the same. A cement floor and walls with a single desk across from the door. *Not very entertaining*, James thought, deciding to try and make Raspin uncomfortable by staring at him until he acknowledged James's presence.

He counted heartbeats in his head and had reached nearly ten minutes' worth when Raspin put down his HOLO.

"How is everything?"

"Pretty shitty, I'd say," James replied, choosing to remain the aloof hostage.

"I figured. I'm sure you have a ton of questions today. Hadn't realized we were underground I bet. Also, wouldn't be surprised if you thought I might have switched your quarters, now that you've seen daylight, but I figured you might enjoy being back in your cell. Homier."

Raspin made no attempt to smile after his last statement confirming James's guess. He was put back in his cell as a method to break him.

"Let's take a walk," Raspin said. He rose from his chair and picked up a long metallic strap from the table. He walked behind James and placed it under James's Adam's apple. The piece of metal curled around his neck and secured itself, sticking to his skin and fitting tightly around his windpipe.

"This is what we call a HOLO collar. Different from what you might think of when it comes to traditional holograph tech. Like our telecoms and the Sentinels, it borrows from the same building blocks. The collar is linked to the base's system, but it runs off its own power source." Raspin unfastened one of the arm restraints from James's seat, but before undoing the other, Raspin stopped and looked James in the eye. "Remember, if you make one false move, this thing will clip your head off."

He unclasped the other arm and left James sitting in the chair, the collar snugly around his neck.

He tried to tug at it, getting some elasticity on his first attempt, but the device never got bigger than his chin.

"Come on, there's a lot to talk about." Raspin waved for James to follow, and they walked out the door as the lights dimmed behind them, to a familiar darkness.

"Our whole base is powered by fission energy, not a new tech by any means, but we are more advanced than the Federation in harnessing it. Those HOLOs you saw with our Sentinels, genius, huh?" Raspin looked at James and smiled, but James kept his eyes focused on the hallway.

"I'm guessing you saw our Sentinels from your satellite imaging of the border when your intelligence managed to break through our defenses. No bother though. You never saw them in action. Those who did, well, we did our best to take care of them." James thought back to the compound with Croyton and the team. Their HOLOS were like those running here. The difference was Croyton's version hadn't needed an emitter nearby, at least as far as James knew.

"Years ago when the Federation managed to steal our data we knew you would replicate everything we'd already done. Hell, you're probably used to seeing those kinds of HOLOS, but most likely didn't expect them to be running off human movements behind the scenes."

James turned his head in Raspin's direction, temporarily dropping the passive expression he worked hard to maintain.

Did he say human operators?

"I guessed right?" Raspin said, glancing at James. "I expected someone in the Federation would have replicated that by now, but looks like the whole code hasn't been cracked yet."

James's mind churned. HOLOs run by humans via Sentinels, data stolen years ago, and Raspin knew about their attempts to break through the BZ's defensive satellite dome. What didn't he know?

"These operations are very tricky. Sentinel HOLOs require a lot of power. I mean, think of trying to keep a static electric current running through a field of undefined matter long enough to create a human shape. Then have it physically interact with the world around it, mimic movement, and do everything but think for itself. Remarkable really."

"Is that why you didn't use them in your attacks? Too much power?" James asked, wondering why Raspin was telling him all this and hoping to glean some helpful information.

"One reason, yes. In reality, machines can't do something so natural, so primal for humans. Domination is built into our DNA. We're a connected species, James. I believe attacking without a human element negates the effect of a war. Don't you? If we had sent a bunch of Sentinels in there with their respective human charge, we could have done some damage. But humans can be much more… creative in their destruction." He grinned at James and stopped in front of a door. He opened it and waved for James to enter first.

On the other side of the threshold was a room full of men and women wearing combat suits and unfamiliar masks. They each stood in pods with transparent walls ensconcing them like cocoons.

"This is our operations room," Raspin said walking down one of the rows. "All two hundred people in here are tied directly to a Sentinel in the field."

Two hundred? James was shocked. They had never seen that many Sentinels and James wondered about his team's appreciation for the scope—or extent—of the BZ's presence at the border.

"Granted, that's two hundred at a time. There are six hundred Sentinels in operation in eight-hour shifts throughout the day."

"How do they work?" James asked, stopping in front of a pod. A woman stood stock still wearing a BZ military uniform and a mask that stretched back to fit behind her ears. The front of the mask was flat and black covering everything but her mouth and chin. James walked around the woman to get a 360-degree look at the rest of the setup.

"The walls of each pod are holographic sensors taking continuous images of her body. The mask and helmet are capturing her brain waves and the Sentinel on the outside is operated by her thoughts." He walked to the front of the room where rows of masks sat on stainless steel shelves. He picked one up and pointed at a serial number with a QR code emblazoned on the back of its neck protector. "Each one of these is hardwired to a Sentinel operator. There can only be one operator for each Sentinel. The space between operator and Sentinel is somewhat limited, but as you and your friends found out, they make excellent guards."

James's mind rushed to his friends, thinking of what it must have been like to take on two hundred of those unbreakable HOLOs at once while one of your teammates lay unconscious. He shook his head and concentrated on the present. *Listen to what he has to say. Don't get distracted by his attempts to get under your skin*, James thought. He kept his eyes focused on the tech, not letting Raspin glimpse into his psyche.

"The Sentinels give us the ability to protect our borders and save our assets for battle. It's a win-win situation," Raspin finished, but James had turned his attention back to another one of the operators. The man James watched did not move, same as the woman. He touched the walls of the pod. They were similar to his HOLO and stretched when he pushed like flexible glass. *What hope do we have against something like this?* James thought, his mind spinning with new questions about the BZ.

"Let's go. More to see," Raspin said, leaving the room abruptly.

James caught up in the hallway bumping into a BZ soldier on his way through the door. James put his hands up as a silent act of pardon, but the BZ soldier did not acknowledge his existence. She kept walking without giving him a glance.

Weird, James thought, jogging to catch up to the quick pace of Raspin's long strides.

"The key to every successful military is the balance between good and evil in your objectives. War is inherently evil by its nature. Philosophers can wax on about the moral certitude of engaging in combat for the greater good, but everyone who enters a war is in it for their own good. The villain or the truly evil side is the one that sees no end to a conflict unless everyone else is dead or agrees with them. It's a paradox to success."

"What does that make you?" James asked, wondering through what lens his captor viewed himself.

"I'm okay with being evil. I believe in my mission enough to ensure it survives even if it paints me as one of the most infamous leaders in history. If I win, I write that history in my own words. I plan on winning."

Raspin pushed open a set of swinging doors revealing another large room, with tables stacked front to back filled with BZ soldiers seated shoulder to shoulder. Aside from some muted sounds, the eerie quiet of the room was unsettling. So much so that James inched closer to his captor for safety. *Great, my protector is a man who throws innocent people into the arms of his soldiers to tear limb from limb*, James thought ruefully.

Raspin winded his way through the tables until they came to a dais at the front of the room. He stepped up and stood on the platform opening his arms wide. The shuffling in the room stopped and James turned to see every soldier staring at their leader.

Silence echoed off the stone walls, creating a pit in James's stomach and he worried that Raspin was about to make him one of the ritual sacrifices that kept his soldiers familiar with gore. Instead, he raised his arms and the soldiers in the room stood as one pushing seats and benches behind them.

Raspin held his pose scanning the room as if seeking imperfection. With a slight nod, he lowered his arms again and the soldiers returned to their activities, eating, or continuing some other silent task, focused on anything but each other.

James was thrown by the display of subservience. Hundreds following orders blindly was not something he was used to seeing and the command Raspin had over the people in his army was alarming.

"We are obedient to the cause," Raspin said speaking to him from the platform. "Nothing else matters. There is one objective and that is to spread the Republic to all parts of the earth.

"Our governments are monoliths but it is the Federation that has done a disservice to its people. Why is it that an entire continent gets left in the dust at the first sign of trouble? How is it that a government lets its people die for its own causes? Politics are the ultimate evil here and our approach changes the world in a truly honest way. We believe in an existence of complete openness. A place where we share pure thought. Where we adhere to the fundamentals of our beliefs so deeply that when our mission is completed all are striving for the same goals. Autonomy in your Federation is an illusion. We understand the cost of freedom, which right now means the lack of it. Everyone must fully invest their lives and beings to create a uniform world to reset the balance and make things right again.

"The belief that the world can continue to flourish while everyone is free and able to choose their own paths in life is nonsense. Structuring the world around honesty and truth becomes the forefront of life and is of the utmost importance. Those are the building blocks of our world and why we are here." Raspin finished his monologue with a flourish, stepping from his stage and clapping James on the shoulder.

"You think people discovering their own version of the world and creating individual paths is wrong?" James asked, trying to follow Raspin's line of thinking.

"I think the current path leads to a dead world. A place where humanity is stripped of its basic function to create and find happiness."

"And you accomplish that by controlling your population? By waging war on the part of the world that disagrees with your message?" James was working to grasp the theory behind Raspin's beliefs.

"For now, yes. This won't work unless the whole world is on the same page. Otherwise, we are doomed to fail as a species. The key is transparency here, James."

"There's no room for different countries, cultures, beliefs, or disagreements with one another? Isn't that inherently human? It seems that you've chosen your belief in domination as central to humanity's ethos."

"What countries, James? Only the two of us remain. You'll understand," Raspin said with a grin and walked away, waving for James to follow. "One more thing to show you."

James followed glancing at the blank-faced, muted soldiers reading their HOLOs or eating. He could not get over the lack of humanity the BZ military displayed. He shook his head and felt an odd relief that he would have hours alone in the darkness to mull over everything. He made a mental note to commit what he saw to memory and stepped out of the room, taking one last sweeping look at the soldiers, unaware of their own oddities.

Raspin's heels clicked on the cement floor and James struggled to keep up as he rounded corner after corner avoiding the fast-moving BZ soldiers. James seemed to run into every one of them.

Finally, Raspin stopped outside another door and opened it, standing to the side. He ushered James through and shut it behind them. They stood in complete darkness until an unknown signal turned on the halogen bulbs flooding the space with light.

James stared at the sight in front of him. Thousands of bunks were laid out in endless rows stretching hundreds of yards into the distance and fading into darkness.

"I wanted you to see this so that you understand what you're up against. We built this as if it were nothing and we'll fill it as easily when we begin to try," Raspin spoke. His eyes glinted in the artificial light while he gazed at the rows and rows of empty bunks. "They're empty for now, but soon they'll house thousands. And this is the beginning. This is stage one, James. We will bring the Federation crashing to the fiery pits of hell and we'll do it with you watching. These bunks, these barracks, this base is less than a slice of what the Republic of World Order intends to achieve. We will use millions, tens of millions of soldiers to win this war. We will be successful. You will lose."

He looked at James with resolute eyes.

"Remember this place when you think you have won, when you think we have given up. We are starting. We will take the Federation land by pure force and there is nothing you and your people can do to stop it."

James stared at the cavernous room, breathless at the amount of work such an enormous undertaking required and in such a short amount of time with plans to fill each one of those cots with soldiers. If true, the numbers were staggering. Hope drained from his body.

"Come on, time to head back to your quarters."

As was his habit, Raspin left the room without waiting for James. The lights shut off and James stood in the doorway casting a reverse shadow against the enveloping darkness, wondering what chance the Federation had against an enemy as vast, powerful, and motivated as the BlankZone.

Chapter 20

James sat in Raspin's office again staring at the wall behind his captor's head with the collar attached under his Adam's apple.

Raspin had yet to look up from his HOLO and James waited, pretending to be bored. In reality, the anxiety from his tour had caused a spiral into hopelessness. What was the point of fighting an enemy like the BZ? Why did the Federation bother at this point? Millions would die and James knew the BZ would not rest until everyone was under the control of the BZ's Republic of World Order or whatever Raspin had called them.

He was lost in his thoughts when Raspin placed his HOLO on the table.

"So, how have your last couple of days been?" Raspin asked. His hands were clasped on the table, and he looked at James without concern or care on his face. It was remarkable how reptilian Raspin's attitude was towards other human beings. His commanding presence, high intellect, and penchant for guessing the future were incredible, but his humanity did not exist. James never felt any connection to Raspin. He only harbored mistrust, fear, and loathing when in his presence.

"Fine, I guess. Not great being thrown in a dark shithole and released every few days to talk with a sociopath who hides underground like some sort of mole person. But fine." James tried to imitate Deck as best he could. If he couldn't have his friends with him physically, he could at least channel their best traits.

The smile on Raspin's face was out of place. It was a grin of malice and impatience. Alarm bells rang in James's mind with growing intensity.

James stared across the slim desk and maintained his passive expression. Internally he tumbled through the possibilities of what could happen.

"For one of the first times in my life, I am stumped, James," Raspin said, returning James's gaze. "I detach you from all other beings. I limit your social interactions to zero. I regulate your light, your water, your food, and your life. It's been weeks and you've spent more time in darkness than in light and you continue to trudge on. Remarkable is the word that comes to mind."

Explains why no one says a word around here, James thought, and he kept listening to his jailer's diatribe.

"I told you during our first meeting in this room that I wanted to find out what makes you tick, what drives you to chase us so relentlessly. When even your own Federation has abandoned its people. You still try to help." He said the last words with contempt, mocking him. "I suppose it's commendable." Raspin stood from his seat and paced the room behind James while his heels clicked on the cement. James focused on the wall as the sound echoed around the barren room. His stomach had tightened to the point that James thought his intestines were in actual knots.

Raspin continued, "I cannot figure it out, so we are going to try two experiments. We will see how you respond."

The hairs on the back of James's neck rose. Whatever this was, he knew he wouldn't like it.

"How advanced are the Federation's defenses? Where are their heavy modifications and where should we expect resistance?"

James was shocked. *Does he think I'm still with the Federation?* he thought quickly, trying to decide the best way to answer, and shrugged.

"No clue. Left the Federation months ago. Thought you knew everything, Edgar," James goaded.

Raspin came back into view and leaned against the edge of the desk. His expression showed he had expected resistance, but James had nothing to give him. Eventually, Raspin would see that, and then what would he do? James didn't want to think about that scenario.

"You expect me to believe that a team as well equipped, highly trained, and motivated as yours came here without Federation resources? You monitored us for close to a year with no Federation support?" Raspin shook his head and chuckled to himself. "I am not surprised you're reticent to share information with us, James, but I can assure you there are no other options. So, let's try an easier question, where are the primary Federation defenses?"

James chuckled. "I'm telling you, Edgar, you're talking to the wrong guy."

"Hmmm. Well, a bit of persuasion might help."

James's eyes narrowed and Raspin's grin turned into a genuine smile. He walked around to the other side of his desk and flicked a screen up from its surface. The back of a HOLO greeted James and he watched while Raspin toyed with the display for a moment before stepping back from the desk.

"Last chance."

"Got nothing for you, pal."

Raspin shrugged and swiped one more time across the screen. James glanced around the tight space waiting for a HOLO to emerge from the wall or a group of BZ soldiers to come from behind carrying a Medieval torture rack, but there was nothing.

The fuck is going on? James thought, readying himself for something dramatic to happen, but nothing did.

What is this? James thought, taking a deep breath when he felt his windpipe fight against him. *What the hell?* James tried to breathe again, but his body would not respond. He stared at Raspin confused. His lungs burned and his chest heaved as it tried to suck in air. Terror swelled in James's mind and the all-consuming need to breathe took over. The lights in the room lowered. A black spot popped at the corner of his eye and a stream of stars swept past his vision.

Raspin watched with delight. The lights flickered and the world swam. *The collar*, James thought. He tried to raise his hands to tear off the metallic band, but his arms were strapped to the chair. Even still, it did not feel like he was choking, but rather drowning in the air.

The fear and adrenaline coursing through his veins reached a fever pitch and all he could think of was his next breath.

Darkness enveloped his vision, cold water drenched his face, and he took a deep breath. His lungs had regained their function. He lifted his face to Raspin standing with an empty cup.

"Ahh, there we are. Lost you for a second. Nothing cold water can't fix." His voice and demeanor were casual, but the horror from the incident remained cemented in James's brain, stuck in his memory like a hot coal searing his every thought.

"What the fu—" James started, but Raspin cut him off, holding up a palm.

"Please, can I explain?" His smile returned. "It's my favorite part."

He leaned back against the plastic table with his arms folded across his chest.

"That little necklace we gave you can constrict your airway to cut off your breathing or take your head off, but that's messy. Why damage the throat of the person I want information from? It makes no sense. The beauty of this device is its unseen implementation of interrogation tactics. Rather than destroy your neck by causing physical damage and making it difficult to understand you, I decided to focus on the mental aspect of our exercise." He leaned over and tapped the band fastened around James's neck.

"This thing answered all my prayers. I don't need to harm anything to instill the fear necessary to extract information. Our HOLO tech can do that job. You see, the band can deploy an invisible mesh through your throat that suspends a kind of ball in your windpipe. I control the size of the ball as I wish, allowing you to breathe or not breathe as much as I please. Brilliant, huh?"

He beamed with pride, but James's mind was swirling with the memory of being choked to unconsciousness.

"It's a funny thing, fear. It can be a great motivator and, unfortunately for you, it will be. Now that you understand exactly what is going to happen when I do not get what I want, shall we continue?"

He peered at James, his eyes snakelike and unflinching. A cold dread mushroomed through James's nervous system, flooding him with a kind of terror he had never experienced in his life.

"Where are the Federation's defenses set up?" Raspin asked, and James shook his head again.

"I don't know."

"Wrong answer, James," Raspin said with calm delight as he swiped his finger across the HOLO propped on the desk. The reaction came on slow again. The panic set into James faster this time as the strangling effects of the collar took over.

Raspin bent and whispered in James's ear, "Truth is, James, I like this part of our discussions the most. We can do this as long as you want."

He stood back up and swiped his finger all the way to the right this time and James's lungs collapsed. James could do nothing to stop the world from disappearing.

Icy water ran down his face again and James's vision returned, offering him a glimpse of his tormentor's smiling face.

"And we're back. Care to try again?"

James looked at his captor with a mixture of seething hatred and bottomless fear. *The second I get the chance, I'll kill him,* James vowed.

Raspin tilted his head like a puppy. "Nothing yet? Suit yourself."

The airflow stopped once again and James gripped the arms of his chair, bracing for the pain.

They spent hours in Raspin's office. Round after round of James passing out, waking to a face full of water, and choking again, never-ending torture.

Finally, Raspin relented for the day and the guards retrieved James. James had never been so happy to lie in the dark on his cold, unwashed cot.

Staring blankly into the darkness, he listened as the rats scurried in their tunnels around him. Air passed through his mouth and James relished every second, never realizing how he had taken a simple breath for granted. He reviewed the events of the day in his head. His memory was blank at the times he lost consciousness when unable to answer Raspin's questions. The significance of those gaps was what James held onto the most. Not because of the fear that lodged a burning pit of anger firmly in his gut, but because it gave him hope. For the first time since taking Raspin back to the clearing, James understood something that Raspin did not.

He was no longer a part of the Federation. James's lack of knowledge about the Federation was the sole reason he was alive.

CHAPTER 21

Torment was James's existence.

James always struggled when the guards came to return him to his torture chamber. The first time he fought back, he managed to incapacitate the soldiers who entered his cell. While they were unconscious, he crouched on the far side of his dingy living space, waiting for more. He lashed out violently with his hands and feet through three waves of soldiers. Eventually, ten men rushed in at once and draped a weighted net over him. In an effort to free himself, he ended up becoming tangled in the tight squares and the soldiers were able to drag him across the rough cement to Raspin's office. There he was treated to another session with the collar while the scrapes on his body bled and the bruises from the guard's batons blossomed into a tapestry of reds, blues, and purples.

The experience did nothing to deter him. Each day when they came to retrieve him, he pushed back, but more jailers always waited in the wings. Raspin took nothing for granted. He understood the danger posed by James, even in his torture-weakened state, James was a threat to his kidnappers.

He lay on his thin, damp cot breathing deeply, reminding himself he was alive and the outside world existed. Remembering he had a team, friends, family, and no one would desert him. Believing himself became more difficult with each passing meal. He had all but stopped his workout routines and existed in mute silence, punishing himself with thoughts of the next series of questions from Raspin, even taking a twisted solace in the injuries he sustained fighting the guards.

James spent his time replaying scenarios in his head about Raspin finally believing that James wasn't withholding information; that he actually knew nothing. Would he kill him immediately? Would he stop the torture and release him? Or would he never believe anything James said until Raspin got something out of him, true or not?

James played these scenes over and over, deciding all he could do at this point was keep his mouth shut. *It's the only thing I have,* James reasoned.

He was stuck in a terrifying cycle and had no idea how to break it.

A squeaking hinge alerted James to their presence. He never acknowledged the soldiers who entered his room or the rough hands that reached to pick him up. Instead, he grabbed a foot planted next to his head and ripped it towards his cot. Then lashed out with a leg making satisfying contact with another guard's kneecap as a baton crushed his stomach knocking the air from his lungs.

James doubled over, rolling off his cot onto the floor coughing while more guards entered the room and lifted him, thrashing and screaming, in their grips.

He was carried through the hallways past listless BZ soldiers not caring to notice the captive yelling obscenities and struggling to break free from their comrades' grips.

Raspin stood in his regular spot, beaming at the sight of James's anguish. The guards strapped his arms and legs to the chair and left without uttering a word.

"Feisty!" Raspin exclaimed, walking over to James. He attached the HOLO collar to its familiar spot. The raw skin on James's neck stung at its touch.

"How do you want to do this today James? Shall we start where we finished yesterday?"

"You tell me, Edgar," James replied. As broken as he was, he had to show some fight.

"I thought we could try something different today. What do you say?"

James glanced at Raspin who smiled walking to the door and pushing it open. He returned to his desk and leaned against the dense plastic.

"Do you know how many times you have been here, James?"

James shrugged.

"Eleven times. Feels like a lot fewer to me though. Not every day of course. That'd be crazy, but time flies when you're having fun." Raspin smirked. "Your misplaced loyalty is limiting your ability to stop all this. It also has me wondering if I made the right move from the beginning of this whole exercise. When I began to question you, I told you there were two methods I could try. Now I realize the second might be my best hope."

James watched his captor. *What is he saying?* Raspin waved his hand and James sensed more people enter the room.

From the corner of his eye, James saw two guards appear and place a chair to the side along the far wall. Then the guards turned James to face the other chair. When they left, two more soldiers entered carrying a large body with its head hanging listlessly and its face hidden behind long scraggly hair.

After the person's arms were strapped to the chair, the head lifted.

Kyle.

James's heart lurched and the strange combination of relief and panic flooded through him.

How long had he been here? Were the others here, too? What was happening?

James stared at his friend in muted amazement. Kyle shook his head, peering around the room in confusion until he caught sight of James sitting across from him.

"James, what the…? What are you…? How long?" the shock in Kyle's voice matched the expression on his face. James tried to form words but could not string anything together.

"I love reunions," Raspin said mockingly. He approached Kyle and attached a HOLO collar around his neck. "Old friends, pals, brothers-in-arms getting back together. Feels like ages, I'll bet!"

Raspin's voice sounded in the background, but James was so blown away by the presence of his friend in this hellhole that he could not pretend to pay attention to their abductor. One of his friends was alive. That was all that mattered to James. He took a breath, letting the thought sink in for a second, enjoying something for the first time in who knew how long.

We can work with this, James thought. He nodded at Kyle who gave a slight grin and nodded in return focusing his attention on Raspin's speech.

"As I was telling, James, I have two methods to get information from you. The first is not working. I do not have what I need, so let's make this simple. You will take turns watching each other suffer. I will stop when you tell me something. Sound good?"

James's gaze was intense as he worked hard to maintain eye contact with Raspin whenever he looked in his direction.

"I told you, Edgar, we don't know," James said, finishing his sentence firmly.

"Yeah, how many times are you going to suffocate me before you realize that I'm telling you the truth? I don't know anything. Neither does James," Kyle added, his voice belaying the same frustration and fear James had experienced.

Raspin gave each of them his sickly smile. "Yes, of course. We will see."

He returned to his desk and shifted the toggle on his HOLO while he made eye contact with James.

"Where is the Federation mounting its defenses?"

"I don't know."

"Wrong answer," Raspin said, and James glanced at his friend whose mouth gasped for air.

Enduring his own experience of drowning had been a living nightmare. The helplessness of being unable to breathe coupled with his inability to stop the torture by giving answers drilled into his psyche. This was completely different. His own torture was one thing, but watching a person who was like a brother suffer the same treatment was unbearable. The agony of complete powerlessness destroyed James and he fought with every fiber of his being to keep from breaking his arms while attempting to escape his bonds. All he wanted was to jump across the table and tear Raspin's trachea out with his bare hands.

But he could do nothing but watch in terror as Kyle's eyes swam with fear until he passed out. Raspin dipped his cup into the bucket behind his desk and splashed it on Kyle's face.

Kyle shook his head groggily, blinking his eyes through rivulets of water falling from his hairline. Raspin returned to his spot behind the desk. His finger was already poised above the HOLO screen.

"Again?"

James and Kyle peeked at each other from the corners of their eyes. *This was their life*, James realized, *at least until Raspin believed them.*

"Come on, Edgar. Can you at least warm the water next time?" Kyle said. The shaggy-haired soldier gritted his teeth, visibly shaking as oxygen flooded his system.

"Hmmm, able to make jokes still. I guess it's your friend's turn." Raspin's smile was gone, and he flicked his finger again. The breath vanished from James's lungs.

This experience repeated itself ten more times for each of them. By the end of the session, blank spots popped up in

James's vision and the walls lining the path back to his cell shuttered in and out of focus.

They left him on the ground without a word and James heard the clatter of a tray falling to the cement floor.

James pushed himself to sit. He picked up the tray, inspecting the edges of the food for any mold he could remove.

Unable to distinguish between the levels of rot he choked down the vile food while he reviewed the day's events.

Kyle is alive. He basked in relief for a second. He had at least one friend living in this world and that bit of hope was enough motivation for James to stomach the rest of his meal. He didn't know why, but he started doing push-ups again for the first time since Raspin's interrogations began.

Between sets, James thought about Raspin's position. He sensed their tormentor was scrambling. Why else would he reveal them to each other? It gave James hope and a reason to keep going. Maybe there was more Raspin would disclose— other people or events that neither of them knew about—but that was unlikely. Raspin had told him this was his plan the whole time, and the fact that he didn't know that James and Kyle were no longer a part of the Federation cemented it as his last option.

I guess that's a good thing, James thought, pushing off the floor and stretching his calves in a bridge at the end of his set.

He needed rest. He took a deep breath and slumped against the wall.

James inferred from Kyle's appearance that he had received the same treatment as James. Maybe a little different, but deprived of light, freedom, edible food, and interaction with anyone other than Raspin. He wondered if they were the only ones here.

As far as I know, James thought, struggling to figure out a reason Raspin might keep another one of the team a prisoner at this point. He had two, no need for more.

Eventually, James lost track of his thoughts. When he closed his eyes James knew there was a reason to keep going every day. Someone else needed him as much as he needed them.

It was enough for him to fight.

Chapter 22

Cold water clung to James's thickening facial hair, and he struggled to gasp for breath upon another rude awakening at the end of Raspin's glass.

He lifted his head to find Kyle's tortured eyes. James felt as if he looked into a mirror after every one of these engagements. Kyle's head dripping water from his greasy locks. Each one straining to keep from cracking a tooth while they watched their friend fight for breath. It was all the same. Painful realization always sunk in destroying him anew each time Raspin swiped his finger across the HOLO screen.

"Enough for today." Raspin's normally gleeful voice had been replaced this session with a gruffer tone. He was curt, giving less time for each of them to answer his questions. He even went so far as to suck the air out of James's lungs one time, showcasing another terror-inducing function of the collar. The whole time James thought his rib cage was going to collapse as the tissue in his lungs pinched like a deflated balloon.

The guards collected Kyle first, and James waited patiently for his turn.

Raspin hunkered in his chair, not interacting with James. Usually he took the downtime to goad and prod his prisoner with veiled hints at the state of the world and the weaknesses of the Federation. Something was off this time. He barely recognized James's presence in the room, instead swiping through his HOLO, not spending enough time between screen changes to do anything.

James shrugged. *Not my problem*, he thought. He stared at the blank concrete, a sight he much preferred to his torturer.

Back in his cell, the familiar clatter of a food tray hitting the ground reminded James that he needed to work out.

He picked up the tray and placed it on his bed, careful not to spill the water when he put it down. Before he could talk himself out of it, James started his push-ups and went over that day's session.

He and Kyle had been interrogated together ten times and the questions remained the same. Where was the Federation starting its attack? Where were its defenses? How was the Federation fortifying its borders?

James knew Raspin was trying to learn about the Federation's defenses from them. That much was obvious. But why? Hadn't he seen their war machine up close and personal? Didn't he know the Federation could devote enough resources to only one front at a time, especially against the BZ's firepower? But Raspin didn't know that. He thought James and Kyle had inside information that they could relay to the BZ military. They were asking the wrong people though, and James wondered how long until Raspin figured that out.

He spent more and more time in between sessions gaming out the situation in his mind. One thing was certain. Raspin would kill them if he found out they didn't know what he was asking for. James was already certain his execution would happen in the next few sessions. Raspin's demeanor soured by the day and if today's reaction to their answers was any indication of the future, then James knew his fortune.

James finished his push-ups and fought down the rancid food, forcing it past his tongue and chewing with the outside of his molars. The quality of his meals had degraded significantly during his stay. James thought it was related to his performance during the interrogations, but hoped it meant that things were devolving on the BZ base at large. It had been at least a month and a half since Raspin had taken him and Kyle captive.

He finished his meal, washed it down with a glass of gritty water, and placed his tray on the growing pile. Kyle's nervous tick of stretching during periods of prolonged thought and concentration had inspired him to try the same and he began a stretching routine. He found it helped to clear his head by focusing on one thought during a single pose. It was nice.

Clint's going to hate this, James thought sitting with his legs apart touching the ground in front of him, and reaching out as far as he could while counting thirty heartbeats.

He was about to switch positions when a flood of light surprised him as the door swung open. His hands darted to his eyes and he was bowled over by a rush of bodies. Hands grappled at his arms and legs to hold him still. The abruptness of the attack startled James but he regained his composure and lashed out with a fist, making solid contact with an ear. A grunt from one of the BZ soldiers gave James some satisfaction as they held him on the ground mercilessly pounding his ribs to a pulp. James fought violence with violence, clawing, kicking, punching, and biting until their advantage in numbers won out. They cuffed his arms behind his back and wrapped his legs together with cords.

James lay hog-tied while four guards stood by the doorway. The guards who had subdued James were visible beyond the edge of the room and James wiggled around so he could see the entrance to his cell.

A shadow cast across the center of the entryway, and Raspin entered with a stool in his hands. James watched him with suspicion. Raspin had never visited his cell. What was happening? Raspin placed his stool in front of James and held a hand to his mouth.

"My word, you have quite the aroma in here, James." As Raspin spoke he pulled his shirt over his nose and mouth, but his eyes remained fixed on James, unflinching and cruel, "Also, is it really necessary to go through this every time we come for you? It's exhausting."

"I thought you didn't like to hurt your prisoners."

"My soldiers think otherwise, besides this..behvior."

"Treat me like an animal and I'll act like one."

"We've noticed," Raspin said, shifting his eyes to the hole in the corner of the room and back to James. "Even a dog can train itself sometimes.

"What do you want?" James spat the words out, self-conscious of his filthy state but unwilling to relent.

"Well, James, I will not lie to you, things are not going to plan. I had expected you and Kyle to cave quickly, but you did the opposite. You got stronger somehow. You two have bounced back remarkably since I brought you together. Not at all what I thought would happen, but that's okay." Raspin stood and used his toe to lift the edge of James's mattress revealing the creeping mold that had grown under it over the past weeks.

"You are a lot less predictable than I had anticipated," he said, not masking his disgust as the bed fell back to the floor. "I figured we get you and your friend in a room, you think your friend's going to die, and voilà! You tell me everything I need to know.

"However, that has not been the case. No. You two have been obstinate. But I think I figured out what's wrong."

Raspin reached out a hand and lifted James's chin, forcing eye contact. James's skin prickled at the touch of Raspin's disturbingly warm, soft skin. His serpentine eyes remained fixed on James and his wide smile revealed a set of even teeth.

"How dumb was I to keep it going? Right? I mean, you came in expecting the same treatment every time. You were prepared to deal with the torture and leave. But what if there was no coming back? What if I never released the valve in your friend's throat?" He stood and stared at James. The blood rushed to the back of James's eyes, and he glared at Raspin whose shadow cast his imposing presence in the room.

"The next time I ask my questions, James, you should answer because if I do not get what I want, I am going to kill your friend. Or maybe I'll kill him for fun. Either way, come prepared to decide how much you value that man's life."

"We've told you all we know," James said, breathing sharply through the pain in his ribs.

"Suit yourself. We will hear your answer tomorrow."

Without another word, Raspin turned on his heel and left James alone in the darkness.

It was too soon before James sat in the chair across from Raspin, his arms tied firmly to the armrests. He had not slept since Raspin's visit to his cell. His stomach flipped over and over while his mind raced through the ramifications of Raspin's words. James needed to tell his captor something and fast. But what? He had nothing to give him. All he could say was what he knew and that was absolutely nothing.

Raspin's frenzied demeanor from the previous day was on display, but there was an undercurrent of sadistic delight emanating from his presence. James sensed that Raspin wanted this to end one way or another. His patience was spent and he needed answers. If he didn't get them it was done for James and Kyle.

The guards entered dragging Kyle into the room, knocking James back to the present. They tied him to his chair, secured the collar around his neck, and left without a glance in their commander's direction.

James looked at Kyle out of the corner of his eye. A trail of blood flowed freely to his chin, but he gave James a nod. He was fighting.

I wonder if Raspin visited him, too, James thought. *It's possible,* he reasoned. Raspin had a fondness for pitting people against one another. He hoped Kyle had come up with an amazing plan to free them. He was still following those lines of thought when Raspin's voice broke through his concentration.

"And here we are again, gentleman. We will start the same as we do every day. Kyle, you're first. Where is the Federation planning its defenses?" Raspin's finger was poised above the screen, waiting for Kyle to answer, almost bored.

"Edgar, I told you, we don't know anything."

"I see." Raspin trailed his pointer finger across the screen and the wind vanished from James's lungs. The searing pain and fear of drowning crashed into James. No matter how many times it happened, there was no getting used to the terror.

Before he knew it, James was waking up with water dripping in a steady stream onto his chest.

"Come on, Raspin. I told you we don't know anything!" Kyle's voice was faltering for the first time, and James, more dizzy than usual, looked at his friend.

"We'll see about that," Raspin said, ignoring his prisoner's pleading, "James, don't forget, there's no time left." Raspin's eyes glinted in the harsh ceiling light. Pure evil and a desperate mania flooded the room. Raspin was serious. He was going to kill Kyle if James didn't do something.

"Good luck," Raspin said, looking at Kyle. A bony index finger swept with finality across the HOLO screen.

Kyle looked at James, confused, as the collar took effect. James could tell his friend sensed something was different.

James was in a panic. Raspin was going to kill Kyle and there was nothing he could say to stop him. Raspin would not believe the truth.

"Edgar, we're not lying. We don't know anything."

Raspin's eyes remained fixed on the man dying in the other chair and toyed with the collar's toggle keeping Kyle at the edge of consciousness, but James knew his friend didn't have long.

"When I brought you to our camp, I knew I was taking a risk, James, but this has gone on long enough. Tell me what you know."

"I don't know anything!"

"Liar!" Raspin screamed at him, losing his composure. The man's hysteria had taken over. He had snapped. He would kill Kyle. James watched his friend's head slump forward and he cursed under his breath. *I have to do it.* He took a deep breath and looked at Raspin.

"We're AWOL, Edgar. We deserted the Federation over eleven months ago to come after you. The BZ attack in the North was allowed to happen. The government was sacrificing the city to get the war effort on its side. My team wanted no part of it, so we left."

Raspin's eyes calmed momentarily, and he glanced at the HOLO monitor looking back at James. "That doesn't explain the gear."

"They were abandoning weapon caches all over the fucking place. We stumbled into one, took what we could, and got out before their drones destroyed the rest of the stockpile. I swear, Raspin, we don't know anything else. Please. Stop." James knew he had potentially erased their usefulness, but it was worth it. His friend's life was worth more than the leverage it would take to stay alive. And despite the circumstances, a weight lifted from his shoulders. Whatever happened now would be up to Raspin. It was the first time their captor was learning information he had not known, and James hoped he was rattled enough to rethink his decisions.

Raspin's finger hovered over the screen, but his eyes remained unwavering on James.

"Please. I'm begging you, Edgar," James pleaded with every piece of his being and hoped any possible shred of humanity in Raspin would listen.

Raspin looked at the desk and James's head slumped in exhaustion as their warden's finger trailed across the screen. James whipped his head up and Kyle's chest stayed completely still for three seconds before a vicious heave kicked off a violent coughing attack. James had never been happier.

With a faraway voice, Raspin spoke, "We will talk tomorrow." The guards returned, removed James's arm restraints, and carried him from the room. On his way out he twisted his head around and saw Kyle's eyes twitch to life as guards lifted his limp body from the chair.

That eye flutter was all he cared about. Kyle was alive. They'd figure out the rest together.

CHAPTER 23

Raspin's manic stare flipped between his prisoners. James did his best to maintain sporadic eye contact with their tormentor while waiting for him to speak.

James and Kyle sat next to one another in their familiar chairs with HOLO collars wrapped around their necks. It was as if they had been summoned to the principal's office. *Strange time to remember that*, James thought as Raspin stood from his seat.

Raspin's shoes clicked as he paced the small room. The sound of his hard rubber soles reverberated in James's ears, eliciting an increased sense of foreboding with each step.

The clicks stopped and Raspin's presence hovered behind him.

"So you left? You left the Federation and they did nothing to track you down and drag you back?"

"That's right," James said glancing at Kyle out of the corner of his eye. He was unsure of what to do but tell their story. "They may have been on our tail, but they had bigger things to worry about than eight kids on the lam."

"Hmm. Maybe. And you stumbled upon supplies? Pretty lucky, don't you think?"

"Even a blind squirrel, right?" James said, gaming out where Raspin's questions were headed.

"Ha! Yes, I think that's accurate for everything your people do. And how did you get here? How'd you manage to find us? Know where to look?

"We met a woman farther north who needed a ride home. The same one you spotted all those months ago when we took our first look here. She was worried about La Guerra Blanca." James emphasized the language change to underscore their embedded nature in the community. "You all made quite the impression when you moved in if you didn't know."

"I'm sure." Raspin was quiet for a moment then the clicks of his heels resumed.

James peeked at Kyle who made eye contact with him and shrugged.

After longer than necessary Raspin returned to his seat and stared at both of them in turn while he spoke.

"I've decided I believe you. Oddly enough, your story makes sense. The fact that you chose to relinquish your leverage in this situation shows you are the stupidest person in the world and too controlled by sincere care that I must believe." Raspin's eyes had taken on an exhausted red haze. *He's struggling*, James realized, noticing the indicators of stress eating away at their captor.

"The Republic and I believe that your decision to give up your position to save your friend illustrates how weak you are, James. If he had died, you would have been able to continue living while I found new ways to get information from you, maybe even diving into some of our newer… techniques of persuasion." Raspin gave a smile as he continued that pinched a nerve in James's spine. "We could have brought the rest of your friends on board. But, alas, we won't be able to work together any longer.

"Instead," Raspin said, waving a hand over the HOLO screen on his desk, "I'll keep the one who at least seems… malleable." Raspin's smile induced a fresh wave of nausea that seeped into James's brain. What was happening?

"What're you doing, Raspin?" Kyle asked, his eyes unwavering from the HOLO under Raspin's fingertips.

"Saying goodbye to our dear friend. It'll be us from now on, Kyle."

"Wh—" Kyle shouted, but his voice was cut off and James saw Kyle opening his mouth in a silent scream of pain.

"Electricity is such a basic but useful tool when used effectively." Raspin smirked at the agony masking Kyle's features turning his attention back to James.

"You should have let him die. I don't tolerate weakness from anyone, even a prisoner," He flicked his finger across the screen and his lip curled into a sneer. "Goodbye, James."

The wind vanished from James's lungs replacing the familiar sensation of absolute panic. James knew this would be the end. There was no stopping Raspin's intentions with a last-ditch confession.

The world swirled and James lost focus on Raspin's desk. His head became difficult to hold up. The pain in his lungs ate away at his chest as he gasped for air. He struggled against the restraints on his arms and legs willing to do whatever it took to escape from his tortured, asphyxiated state, whatever it took to survive.

James concentrated for a moment, forcing his mind to a calmer space as he attempted a breath. Black spots and stars popped before his eyes. This was his death. James looked at his friend screaming imperceptibly in emotional and physical agony.

The room grew into a swirl of spots. James's mind drifted. How had he come to this point? He had never imagined ending up in an underground prison cell thousands of miles from home tied to a chair choking to death.

James lost vision in his right eye. His left eye focused on Raspin's cruel smile as he struggled to keep his grip on reality for another moment.

At least Kyle's going to live.

James knew the end was near when an unexpected shift hit the room. James thought it was his mind processing death throws, but somehow he took a breath. For whatever reason the collar jolted in place and disrupted the invisible mesh blocking his airway.

What's happening? James thought as reoxygenated blood returned his sight for a moment.

Raspin's face looked surprised, confused, and then angry.

Another shake of the chair and the collar's strangling effect faltered once more giving James the opportunity for another breath.

He glanced at Kyle, who looked back in confusion. He mouthed to James, "What the fuck?"

James did his best to return a shrug when Raspin stood and walked behind them to the door.

James watched Kyle crane his neck to get a look at their captor, but the chair limited his ability to peek at the back of the room and he turned around shrugging his shoulders.

The collar's choking effect had returned, but was much weaker, allowing James to fight through the HOLO tech blocking his trachea. Slowly he pulled in breaths.

The room shook again, lasting longer this time, and the lights flickered. James wondered if this was what an earthquake felt like. *That'd be poetic justice*, James thought, *Raspin buried a alive and suffocating with his captives.*

Raspin returned to his place behind the desk and fiddled with the HOLO screen. His face was a mask of concentration. He didn't bother checking on the prisoners seated in his office.

He doesn't know I'm still alive, James realized, glancing at Kyle who was tapping his foot on the ground to get his attention.

Another rumble shook the room and James glanced at his friend, noticing that Kyle was signing to him. He had gotten an arm free. It dawned on James, the tremors were messing with the energy source for the BZ. The same power that held everything together, including their restraints.

Hope leaped into James's mind while he waited for another strike from the mysterious ground sways. Another thunderous movement of the earth. James breathed, lifted his arms, and broke the weakened bindings with ease.

We have a shot, James thought looking at Kyle who had all his limbs free now. The slack restraints hung limply across his forearms.

Raspin's face was transfixed on his HOLO screen and his brow furrowed with concern. Something was very wrong in the BZ's underground base and James knew this was their shot to escape.

After another shake, James was completely free of his restraints. All that remained were their collars.

The earth's growls were more pronounced. James glanced at Kyle who counted down on his fingers.

Three, two, one.

Simultaneously they pulled their collars off. A wave of relief washed over him. They had a chance.

All at once the door burst open and five guards rushed into the room.

Raspin's face flipped up for the first time since the rumblings began. His eyes flew to the restraints lying on the ground and the collar in James's hands.

"Kill them!" Raspin shouted, swiping a finger across his HOLO, setting off an ear-piercing alarm that tore through the compact space.

James and Kyle reacted in unison whipping around to meet the guards.

The first guard's jaw met James's fist. James grabbed the front of his shirt and pivoted, throwing the man's head into the path of the baton swinging toward Kyle's face. Blood sprayed into James's eyes as he dropped to the floor with the limp body clutched in his hands.

Kyle dispatched the baton wielding guard with a quick jab to the throat while James ripped the legs out from under the next guard in line. Throwing himself forward with all his weight, he slammed the woman's head into the wall. A crunch greeted the back of her skull and her body slid to the ground propped next to the open doorway at an awkward angle. James snatched the baton out of the female guard's belt and smashed it into the kneecap of another. Screeching in pain, the guard lay doubled over clutching his leg as James stood and crushed his knee into the side of the man's head.

He looked around for the final attacker and saw Kyle holding the guard's windpipe with one of the restraints before twisting and snapping his neck.

The body went slack. Kyle and James heaved for breath, looking around the room filled with disfigured lifeless bodies.

"Raspin," James said. He had lost track of their primary tormentor in the melee and turned to an empty desk with a HOLO light illuminating the cement wall.

"Motherfucker," Kyle growled, pushing the guard's dead body off his legs and jumping to the door. "He's down the hall!" Without waiting for James, Kyle sprinted from the room and James tore off after him.

In the corridor, James caught sight of Raspin's legs disappearing around a corner.

"Right!" he shouted to Kyle who raised a thumb in the air and took a wide turn, wary of Raspin possibly waiting on the other side.

James raced on, using the leverage from his arm to swing around the corner and maintain his speed.

He caught sight of Raspin at the end of the hall with Kyle closing in on him when a door opened and BZ soldiers poured out, blocking Raspin's path.

"Federation prisoners escaped! Kill them!" Raspin shouted, pointing at James and Kyle.

Kyle looked back at James. As much as James wanted to catch Raspin and tear his larynx out with his bare hands, this was not the time. They needed to get out of there. The shaking of the hallways worsened by the moment, and patches of dirt fell from the ceiling with alarming rapidity. Whatever was happening above ground was certain to cause the BZ underneath it to cave in. They needed to leave or risk being buried alive.

"Leave him!" James shouted, waving for Kyle to follow and he sprinted back down the hall towards Raspin's office. He ran inside trailed closely by his friend who slammed the door shut and barricaded the entrance with the chairs and two of the stiffening bodies. Jamming the back of a chair under the handle he gave James a thumbs-up.

"That oughta give us a few minutes."

"That's all we have," James replied, picking up Raspin's HOLO, grateful the device was open.

James swiped a finger across the screen and pulled up a menu laid out in an unfamiliar display and unknown language.

Goddammit, James thought, searching for anything he could use when he spotted a camera icon. He tapped the symbol, and a slew of live video feeds sprang to life. What James saw took his breath away.

Drones dropped from the clouds in waves, releasing charges and returning to the air. Their packages destroyed the BZ's infrastructure in torrents of flame. James flipped through the shots. Chaos reigned supreme. BZ soldiers ran wildly, desperate to shield themselves against the onslaught of firepower, but it was too much to handle. Scores of drones rained explosives on the BZ troop positions rendering chances of defense useless.

"What's up? What do you see?" Kyle asked, and James waved him over.

"Cavalry arrived in time."

"Holy shit looks like the Federation changed their minds."

"Maybe," James replied, still in shock. The timing was impeccable. The attack must have knocked out the connections to the entire base. James could not believe their luck.

"We've gotta get out of here," James said, remembering they were underground. Survival meant navigating a minefield of BZ soldiers and friendly bombers.

"Damn straight. I thought that thing was hardwired. How the hell is it working?" Kyle asked, inspecting the emitter.

"Independent battery pack," James replied, tapping the thin rectangle attached to the device. He turned his attention back to the map. " We need to find an exit and I have no idea what any of this shit means."

"Hit that map."

James saw the square sitting alone in the top right corner. He tapped the box and the scene switched to a 2D map of the base.

Attempting a maneuver they used on their own HOLOs James pinched the screen and lifted. A 3D model of the base sprang to life with active cameras providing a live feed of everything happening in the vicinity. The map key delivered a health check of the buildings. James watched a section of the BZ base crumble over a live feed as a wave of drones struck one of the red areas.

Glad we're not there, James thought, focusing his attention back on an exit route.

"Here." James pointed at the map and with his finger snaked a path through several areas untouched by the bombing. "We'll follow this corridor to the left. Might be our way out of here."

"How the fuck are we supposed to get through all those BZ soldiers?"

"Throw on a uniform," James said, pointing at the blood-slicked cement.

Kyle lifted one of the bodies least affected by the crimson liquid pooling on the ground. He removed the top of the suit, carefully avoiding the back of the man's crushed skull.

James followed his lead and within seconds they had transformed into BZ soldiers.

They studied each other making sure they checked out. It was odd seeing Kyle wearing the enemy's clothes as much as it was for James to be in them. He hoped the hectic scene outside would distract anyone from noticing the large swaths of blood marking their uniforms. Another rumble shook the room and James lost his balance. He steadied himself on the desk as the lights flickered again.

He grabbed the HOLO from the desk and shoved it into the front of his open shirt.

"We gotta move."

Kyle nodded and yanked the chair away from the door handle.

James steeled himself for a frenzied rush of soldiers on the other side, but no one was there. The base was in a panic. Soldiers sprinted by without even noticing their prisoners or the five bodies lying on the ground. Everyone was in survival mode.

"We're invisible," Kyle said, and James shrugged.

"All the better for us."

Without waiting to be apprehended by anyone, James took off at a sprint with Kyle on his heels.

He pulled the HOLO out of his shirt while they moved and planned out their course.

Soldiers ran with and against them. Randomly, James and Kyle switched sides of the corridor to avoid getting snagged in the hordes of scrambling bodies blocking the narrow halls. Dust from the ceiling floated in clouds and soot saturated the air.

Chunks of rock and dirt piled haphazardly on the ground, and the shaking became more violent by the moment.

The vibrations underfoot were almost out of control. James's body ping-ponged around the corridor. He pushed off escaping soldiers, and cracking walls and hoped the explosions would dissipate as they neared the surface. *That'd be wishful thinking*, James thought, *if the Federation's plan was to decimate the front and prevent a BZ attack, that's what they would do.*

The same survival instinct gnawing at his gut was reflected in the eyes of the BZ soldiers. Their faces were no longer blank and emotionless. Eyes that had submissively followed orders and ignored his suffering were focused on living to the next moment. He could not help but feel a pang of empathy for the people stuck underground trying to escape death. James pulled and yanked his way through the crowd. These were not the automatons he had seen in Midway or during his fights with the guards. These were terrified human beings striving to survive, same as he. After endless hours spent listening to Raspin wax on about his control over those in his command, he wondered again how many of these people were here of their own volition. How many would follow given the choice? How many believed in the BZ's war? These thoughts crashed into James's mind as he stumbled his way amongst the crowd, choking on the air, hoping his last breath wouldn't be under a pile of rubble.

Finally, they reached the end of the corridor where a wide sloping hallway showed them the way out. BZ soldiers packed the mouth of the exit and more poured from the honeycombed tunnels that converged at the base of the incline.

It's like an ant hill, James thought as BZ soldiers struggled to escape.

"Come on, push through," Kyle shouted, and James's friend muscled his way beside him. Together they forced their way uphill until their bodies squeezed out of the opening to the cave.

Relief flooded James's mind as blue sky shone through clouds of thick black smoke wafting in the air. James was lost in a dream, admitting to himself for the first time since the beginning of his incarceration that he had given up on seeing the outside world.

"Get to the edge of the camp!" Kyle shouted and tugged James's arm as he pointed to a fresh wave of drones aimed at the entrance where they stood.

James followed Kyle's lead through the tangle of bodies. Smoke and flying debris ruled the air. James's vision became blurry. He did everything he could to keep his friend's blood and soot covered back in his sight.

He heard a *swoosh* overhead and spotted the drones a mere fifty feet above him. He turned around in time to see them drop their explosives on the mouth of the base.

Flames erupted as screams of agony filled the air. Soldiers who had been battling to break through the masses were just smoldering bodies. Even those twenty yards from the entrance were not far enough to avoid the fires and fell as burned husks of human flesh. Unable to cry out, they crawled across the ground as their skin sloughed off their burning limbs.

Amidst the horror, the concrete structure groaned. James and Kyle ran for shelter behind a burnt-out building. They watched, mouths agape, as the top of the building broke in half and caved in on itself. The collapse was nothing spectacular, but the implications ate at James's insides.

Thousands were trapped under the rubble, bound to suffocate or die of injuries sustained in the explosion and there was nothing anyone could do to help.

"They're regrouping." Kyle's voice broke into James's thoughts. He followed his friend's gaze to the teams of BZ soldiers convening in small groups throughout the compound.

Powerless to execute their original plans, they were setting up new defensive measures. James watched as a team of BZ soldiers erected air defense guns and took out a wave of drones headed farther into the camp.

"We need to get out of this place," James said, realizing it wouldn't be long until the BZ regained control of the situation. He searched their location, getting a sense of their bearings. Heavy brush stuck out fifty yards from their position and he grabbed Kyle's shoulder.

He pointed for his friend to see. "There. We can hide in there while we search for a way out."

Kyle nodded and, glancing around to make sure no one was watching, took off at a sprint for the shrubs. James followed seconds later but was left in the dust by his friend.

I forgot how fast he is, James thought, watching Kyle jump acrobatically into the bushes and disappear under a sea of green.

James dove into the brush and rolled to a sitting position. He put a hand against a tree and stayed low to the ground.

"Kyle," he whispered, hoping to find his friend without needing to stand and give away their position. He waited for an answer. The smoke washed over him, but he was removed from the chaos and shielded in the forest. The explosions were background noise in the dense foliage, and the drones flew silently above him, lethal figures against an azure backdrop.

"Kyle," James repeated a bit louder this time.

He cautiously pushed through the thick undergrowth, unwilling to pop his head up to look for his friend.

Where was he? James asked himself as worry settled in his gut. He hadn't been that far ahead of me.

"Ky—" A hand covered his mouth. A pair of green eyes smiled above a dark camo mask.

"We've got him with us, buddy. Let's get you home," Deck said, pulling down his face cover and putting a hand under

James's arm. "Keep it quiet. They could have those fucking Sentinels running around."

James knew that wasn't possible, but was too happy to respond. All the terror, panic, confusion, and loneliness from those weeks locked in the darkness collided in his head. The moment he had dreamed of and clung to throughout his isolation had finally come true.

"Good to see you, man," James said, exhaustion overcoming his body and mind.

"Always, brother," Deck replied, grinning. "Now let's get out of here."

Deck pointed the way and motioned for James to lead. He pushed through the underbrush unable to keep track of the questions swirling around in his mind.

All he knew was his friends had come to get him.

CHAPTER 24

Water tasted better. Clean water.

Who knew this was all I needed in life? James thought, swishing the lukewarm liquid in his mouth. He spit out his mouthful, realizing it consisted mostly of his saliva. He took another refreshing swig from the canteen and downed it faster this time.

Leaves blocked his vision in every direction. James was beginning to think they were going in circles when they broke into a pocket of minimal vegetation. Seeing who it was, Kevin and Bob relaxed their defensive stances and smiled at James. Putting a finger to his lips, Kevin waved James over and wrapped his arms around his neck in a tight hug. Bob did the same and pushed James back for a cursory examination. James signed he was okay. Bob nodded, but James knew the medic in him wouldn't be satisfied until he had a chance to inspect James head to toe.

James turned around, but Deck was gone. He glanced at Kevin and Bob and signed:

Where'd he go?

Kevin replied:

He's covering your tracks. He'll be back in a minute.

James nodded, but had more questions. He signed:

Where's Kyle? What's going on?

Kevin grinned, and signed:

Jon's got Kyle. We'll catch you up at camp.

Leaves rustled behind James, and he turned to find Jon and Deck leading Kyle through the undergrowth.

"What the fu—" Kyle began to speak, but Deck wrapped his hand around from behind, muffling his voice.

Kyle nodded as Deck whispered in his ear and signed to the group:

They're focused on defenses. Kevin, you lead. Bob, stay in the middle of the pack with Kyle and James. Jon and I will take rear guard.

The group nodded at their scout and James waited for Kevin's wide frame to create a path through the brush.

James followed Kyle while they trekked through the woods. Kevin moved with deliberation and speed, breaking trail while Jon and Deck ensured they did not leave one. They walked in silence. Echoes of explosions became fainter with each footstep.

The familiar smell of plant debris, mulching soil, and fresh rain replaced the scent of smoke. James's legs were wobbly. He hadn't walked that far in weeks, maybe months for all he knew. He was surprised at how good he felt though. Deprived of freedom to move or experience sunlight, his routine of push-ups and sit-ups must have kept his body sharp.

Working out helped, he thought, running into a low branch and cursing under his breath. *Sharp enough, I guess*, he thought, rubbing the scratch on his forehead.

His main concern was his eyesight. So much time deprived of natural light in almost complete darkness must have lifetime effects. James did not know what to expect, but he was not accustomed to the uncharacteristic loss of depth perception.

I'll get it back. Time's a hell of a drug, he thought, ducking under a thick branch.

He took a sip of water from his canteen and nearly ran into Kyle. They were stopped at a random point in the woods and James glanced around the area, wondering what was special about this plot of land.

Kevin dropped the pack from his shoulders and Bob did the same, putting his hands on his hips. Shaking his head, he looked back and forth between Kyle and James, as if he couldn't believe it.

"Goddamn, it's good to see you two," Bob said, smiling.

James chugged more water, savoring the taste of the untainted liquid.

"You have no id—*OOF*!" James spat out the water as a pair of arms wrapped him in a hug.

Deck's arms coiled around Kyle and James in a suffocating embrace.

"You two had us worried *sick*!" Deck said, the relief in his voice evoking the same emotion expressed in the strength of his hug. "We didn't know what to do."

"Easy, buddy. And thank you," Kyle said, patting Deck's back. "We're okay. We're here, right?"

"Yeah, we made it out," James said, gently prying Deck's arm loose. "Now can you all tell us what's going on?"

"Love to," a voice spoke from beyond the surrounding greenery as Stacie, Clint, Rich, and Cristina walked into view.

Clint, Cristina, and Rich made their way to James as Kyle and Stacie united in a long kiss.

Allowing the couple a moment of privacy, the team turned their backs to continue their reunion.

James was overcome again by emotion. Here they were—his team, his friends, his family. They had rescued him. He had no idea how, but they had.

Stacie's arm hung over his shoulder, and he turned to hug her.

"Glad you're back," she whispered in his ear.

"Glad to be back."

She let go, smiling, and Kyle wrapped an arm around her waist.

The team stood, quiet for a moment. Over the next few hours, James knew he would learn everything that had happened, but for now, he felt complete.

"Anyone hungry?" Cristina asked, holding a basket in her arms.

"Starving," Bob said, peering into the woven wicker container. "What've you got?" Bob reached his hand in but was slapped on the wrist by Cristina.

"Bob!" she said, shaking her head and holding the basket out to James and Kyle.

"Oh, right. Yeah, you two go first," Bob said sheepishly, peeking over Cristina's arm.

James grinned and pulled out a tamale. He unwrapped the palm leaves from the densely packed parcel. He took a bite, savoring the taste of corn, pork, and spice on his tongue. It was the best thing he had tasted in his life.

"Okay, who should go first?" Deck asked, handing fresh canteens to James and Kyle.

James took a swig of water and nodded at the group. "You all can start. Kyle and I can fill you in after. One question first. How long has it been?"

Deck glanced at the team. James realized they were only now understanding the nature of James and Kyle's time at the BZ base. *Unfortunately for them, it's going to get worse*, he thought, searching the team's faces.

"It's been three months, James," Stacie said, her voice soft and careful when she spoke.

James knew the number would not be low, but he was surprised. Three months. A quarter of a year gone. Three months spent underground enduring repeated torture.

Nothing we can do about it, James thought, doing his best to stomach the first hard truth of the day. He knew there would be more. He needed to be ready to accept them.

"I can't say I'm surprised," James said, looking at Kyle who shrugged and looked at the ground with a blank stare. "So, what happened?"

"Well, after you two were knocked out, those Sentinels kept coming," Deck spoke, not waiting for anyone else to volunteer. "There were dozens of them, and it was all I could do to keep from being ripped out of the tree. I kept firing until I was on my last magazine when I realized they were gone. It was us three in the woods—Kevin, Jon, and me. You two were nowhere to be found.

"We discussed whether to head back to camp or rush the BZ base right then to get you out, but decided we needed to regroup."

"Cooler heads prevailed," Jon interrupted.

"Either way," Deck said, brushing off the comment, "we went back and the convoy was ready to go. We had to decide: delay or go. Our decision is obvious."

"No one left?"

Deck shook his head. "Paola and Selma weren't going anywhere without us. We knew we had to stay close to the BZ compound. We moved what we needed from camp and set up a few new surveillance huts. We've been here since."

"What about camp?" James asked, wondering what they had done with all their gear.

"Transported a bunch to our new huts, but otherwise we left it there. As I said, proximity to the BZ base was key. We've been running a constant surveillance operation since you were captured. Cristina and Rich even moved in with us. It's been a slog.

"We kept running into brick walls, too. Nothing from the BZ. They were quiet. Transport ships stopped. Jungle reconnaissance was non-existent. The Sentinels didn't even cross the border. They went dormant. That's when we caught a lucky break." Deck's eyes shifted to Stacie.

She looked at James and spoke in a low tone. "After you had been gone for two months, we were running out of options. There was no sign of life at the base. The same shit over and over every day. Raspin had vanished and time was not on our side. I made a call."

For some reason, a pit formed in James's stomach as he waited for Stacie to continue.

"We contacted the Federation. I sent them an upload of all our data about the BZ base and told them two of us had been taken hostage."

James's mind spun. She reached out to the Federation? The same Federation they had run from? The Federation who had allowed millions of its own citizens to be killed? The thoughts and emotions flying through James's head were struggling against one another for supremacy. He knew they had been in a tough spot, but by contacting the Federation they lost their anonymity. They gave up their trump card. The Federation had all they needed to drag them home.

"James, we didn't have a choice."

James nodded. He was not sure how to respond yet. He needed to learn the whole story.

"I understand. What next?"

Stacie eyed the rest of the group with apprehension as she continued, "We waited to hear something in return but got nothing. They never responded. We sent that same data packet again a week later, three days later, then every day. We were giving up hope. Then, we got a reply."

Stacie nodded at Jon who flicked on a HOLO screen and held it out for James and Kyle to read:

Attacking tomorrow.

"We couldn't find a signature or sender, but we regrouped and got ready. It wasn't long before the drones appeared and now here we are." Stacie spread out her hands and smiled at James. The muscles in her jaw clenched. "I know you wouldn't have wanted us to ask them for help, but we didn't know what to do. We had to. I…" Stacie's voice broke.

"You made the right call, Stace," James said. He hated giving anything to the Federation, even something that saved his life, but he would have done the same in her situation. Whatever the fallout, they would figure it out.

"Nice work, Serial," Kyle added, receiving a push.

"Now how about you two?" Stacie asked, regaining her composure.

"Care to start?" James asked, gesturing at Kyle.

"I do not," Kyle replied, looking at the forest floor.

James didn't want to talk about it either. He had questions about what had happened outside his prison cell. He didn't want to go back there, even for a brief explanation of his time, but he knew he would have to tell them.

No time like the present, he thought.

"I don't want to go into a ton of detail, so I'll give you the basics. How things happened. That okay?"

"Whatever you want to do, man," Deck said. "We're happy you're back."

James gritted his teeth and took a deep breath.

"I woke in a dark cell. I don't know how long I was out or how long I went before seeing anyone else." James relived the experience while Kyle interjected with the minor differences between their incarcerations. It felt like he talked for hours. He described the Sentinels and the rooms underneath the base. The cavernous space the BZ had prepared for its forces and the ethos behind their fight.

He described how the guards relished fighting, his forced isolation, and the fleeting looks he got in the mess hall from the BZ soldiers. He described the sadism of Raspin, the forced conformity of the people in the military, and his understanding of the BZ's manipulation.

Finally, he talked about the torture. The silence was acute during the moments when he told them about the device that repeatedly strangled him unconscious. How he woke up with cold water dripping down his chin. How he had watched his friend suffocate on a loop. How they broke out as the attack started and watched the drones bury the BZ army under a pile of cement and steel.

The group listened in rapt attention, but it would not have appeared so to the casual observer. James caught their eyes focused on anything but James. They could not look at him. Hearing James explain his and Kyle's horrific experiences seemed to send them on a journey he could not follow. For the last three months, they had been as powerless as he. When he finished, the group sat in stunned silence until Kevin stood and patted James on the shoulder.

"Glad you're out of there."

"We all are," Clint added.

"Thanks. I'm pretty happy about it, too," James said with a wry grin. He was exhausted. Detailing his imprisonment, drinking clean water, and eating more than moldy scraps had wiped out his remaining strength. He stood and stretched his arms above his head. "I know we have a ton to talk over, and, Bob, I know you want to take a look at me, but can I get some sleep?"

"You got it, bud. I'll show you the hammocks." Deck stood and took James by the shoulder.

James waved a silent goodnight to everyone as Stacie gripped Kyle's wrist. "You should sleep, too."

"Mm-hmm," Kyle said, his eyes glassy. "That sounds nice."

James clapped Kyle's shoulder as he walked by. He followed Deck to a stand of trees hosting a circle of hammocks.

"Pick your poison! Well, not really. That one's yours," Deck said, pointing at a hammock in the middle. "Feel free to move it anywhere you want, but we figured you might want us around your first night out."

"Appreciate it," James said, resting his weight on the hammock and testing its strength, "This will do, thanks."

He had not realized how strange it would feel to sleep outside his cell. He sat on the edge of the elastic fabric and swung for a moment.

"I'll let you get some sleep, but happy you're here, James." Deck patted him on the back and left.

"Thanks, bud," James said to which Deck responded with a wave over his head as he disappeared into the foliage.

James removed Raspin's HOLO, carefully placing it on his bed for the evening. He peeled off the BZ suit, dropped it to the ground, and stared at it. The white material had turned a dusty gray. The chest and neck areas showed splotches of the guard's blood and it was ripped on the arms and knees from his falls while escaping the underground fortress. The soiled uniform pulled on his thoughts. For a moment he was underground again, the collar locked around his neck as Raspin's coal black eyes stared across his desk. James gripped the hammock and returned to reality.

"I'm here," James whispered out loud.

He lay on the stretched cloth, swaying side to side as a cool breeze brushed his face. He took deep breaths and stared at the gold-tinged treetops.

Twelve hours ago, he had been locked in a dark cell waiting to be beaten and dragged to his death. He was able to describe the moments to his friends, the day-to-day facts of his incarceration. What he could not do was explain the piece of him that lived in that cell. The part of his brain forever morphed by the darkness.

CHAPTER 25

James was up early the next morning. He lay prone, scared to open his eyes, terrified yesterday had been an impossible dream. As if the world understood his need for a reminder, Kevin's snores drifted in the stillness and dew-laden air bathed his face in a dense layer of vapor. He blinked.

Rays of sunlight poked through the tree canopy. Moisture twinkled in the light and James breathed in the fresh jungle scent of life.

Gone was the stench of his cell. Gone were the rats scurrying in the walls. No more tray clattering to tell him the time. The cues that served as reminders of his life in prison had vanished and were replaced by something indescribable.

Perfect. That's what this is. Perfect, he thought, stretching out on his hammock. With his hands clasped behind his head, he dangled his foot off the side of his suspended bed and pushed. The nudge was all he needed to swing while he watched the forest wake.

They'd head back to town today and leave in the next week. Or at least that's what James assumed. He was excited to see everyone. Selma, Paola, Layla, Mariel, and Rosa were probably worried sick. He was worried about them in return. He would even be happy to see JC again. *Well, maybe wouldn't go that far*, James reasoned, hoping the potbellied tyrant would keep out of his way until they were gone. He had no interest in having further conversations with the self-proclaimed king of Río Negro. They would pack up and leave before he meddled further in their business.

"Psst, James."

James turned to see Cristina and Deck waving. Deck held a plate of cut avocadoes and the basket of the remaining tamales sat at Cristina's feet.

"Hungry?" Deck asked in a bad whisper.

James gave him a thumbs-up and slid off his hammock. He was famished.

"Come on, we're going to eat over there," Deck continued, whispering in a low voice while pointing over his shoulder.

"Yeah, I got that," James said, already walking towards them.

"I wanted to make sure you understood what was happening."

"I understand," James said, standing next to Deck. "You are horrible at whispering."

"I'm a great whisperer," Deck replied, affronted.

"Shut up and go eat," Kevin growled from his hammock.

"See," Deck said, turning around flippantly.

"That just proved my point," James replied.

"Psshh."

Deck waved him off and James shook his head, grinning.

"How the hell do you put up with him?" James asked Cristina.

"Patience is a virtue, James," she replied, taking his arm and walking through the woods behind Deck whose loud footsteps were making James doubt the prowess of their so-called scout. "That and we play the quiet game a lot."

"That makes sense."

"Would you two be quiet? People are trying to sleep." Deck turned around, scolding them.

Cristina and James glanced at each other and continued walking behind Deck, the loudest person in the forest.

They eventually came to a clearing Deck deemed far enough from the rest of the group to talk at normal volume.

"Tamale or avocado?" Deck asked James, holding them out for his selection.

"Both an option?" James asked.

"Geez, fat ass, I guess so."

James grinned and took a slice of the avocado from the plate and bit into it. He was rewarded by the greasy fruit melting as soon as it hit his tongue. He had dearly missed food.

Sitting on tree stumps they ate together laughing and talking, forgetting their situation entirely. Slowly, the rest of the team joined them until all ten sat in a ring, sipping their canteens, and watching the sun rise higher in the sky. For the moment, it was a group of friends eating breakfast.

"That was amazing," Kyle said, stretching out and lying on the forest floor. "I haven't eaten like that in forever."

"Wait until tonight," Kevin said, throwing an avocado pit into the woods, listening as it crashed through the leafy walls. "I'm going to grill everything we have in camp."

"I'm salivating," Bob said, taking out his weed and packing a bowl.

"Not yet, Bob. Let's get back to camp first," Stacie said. "We've got work to do."

"Fair enough. Speaking of in the clear, anything pop up on the sensors, Jon?" Bob asked repacking his smoking supplies.

"Nothing alarming. I checked our cameras this morning. But you all should take a look at this."

Jon flipped up a screen and the preloaded display bathed their faces in light.

"Holy shit." James was not sure who said it, but it was the only thing going through his mind.

The jungle utopia that had been built into the natural beauty of the rainforest was demolished. The groves of small trees that had housed the homes and offices of the BZ soldiers were reduced to burnt trunks. Gargantuan trees, centuries in the making that had ringed the base in shade and secrecy were toppled over, broken at the base like discarded candle sticks. The entrance where James and Kyle had escaped was a cracked heap of rubble with bits of rebar poking through the wreckage. Black soot and charred surfaces covered everything. The flames had created a scorched earth, an unhealable scar. Even the defenses the BZ military had hurriedly set up were melted pieces of metal.

The Federation must have put something extra in those charges, James thought, his stomach churning at the temperature needed to melt that steel.

Brooks and streams that intersected the property were filled with ash and dirt-laden water. Pieces of debris and smoldering shards of buildings traveled in their neatly cut pathways bobbing in the gently flowing water until they sunk or ran into a body crisscrossing the path.

That was what James noticed the most. The bodies. Thousands of bodies and body parts strewn across the ground. Burnt corpses or mutilated torsos and limbs flung from their owners during an explosion. Blood pooled in the small craters staining the ground and in some areas corpses were stacked one on top of the other as if symbolizing unity at the last moment of their lives.

It was a scene out of a nightmare and the visuals gave James flashbacks to Midway.

James was struck by a confusing buildup of sympathy for the dead and deep sorrow over the loss. This was the enemy who had beaten, tortured, and nearly killed him and Kyle, but he could not shake the feeling that the scene was wrong.

Nightmarish memories from his time in the BZ prison, the terrified stares of the people trying to escape, and the looks of helplessness on the faces of the BZ people during his time underground filled his mind.

James's commanders had drafted him at seventeen and turned him into a perfect tool of war. They had tricked him into looking at the world as black and white, but the gray area was far more prevalent than anyone realized.

He watched as Jon flipped between the various camera angles until he had had enough. James backed away from the group and noticed Kyle doing the same. They nodded at each other and stood behind their friends. They were forever bonded in horror, inheriting a unique understanding of their enemy.

We're ahead of them, James thought. From their shared experience he and Kyle had learned there isn't good and bad. There's always a spectrum.

The rest of the team stepped back from the screen in a state of shock, oblivious to Kyle and James's reactions. James preferred that. *They'll have their own things to deal with one day*, James thought.

"I guess they left," Deck said. The scout sat on the ground with his face scrunched in concentration.

"Federation didn't give 'em much to stay for," Clint said, following his lead and sitting. "What's the move now?"

"I say continue with our plans to go north. I'm sure we'll have willing travelers in Río Negro now," Stacie said, glancing at James. "Other ideas?"

"Stick to the plan. How much crap do we need to bring back to camp?" James asked. He was looking forward to his reunion in town, wondering what new creation Layla had for him.

"We've got three bases spread out around here. It'll take most of the day to gather everything, but should be home by nightfall," Kevin said, cleaning the remnants from breakfast.

"Let's get going. I'd love to sleep in my hut tonight," Deck said, standing in a rush and making his way back to the hammocks.

"Yes, you were the one we were concerned about getting back home," Stacie replied, rolling her eyes.

Deck flipped a middle finger in the air and kept walking.

After five hours of cleanup and packing the team was ready to go. James had what felt like an entire kitchen strapped to his back and he wanted to get moving as fast as possible. He was dressed in a combat suit, the only extra clothes the team had packed, and his legs blended into the woods while he waited.

"Come on, people," James urged.

"I'm coming, I'm coming. There's a lot of good shit on this HOLO, James. Hard to put down," Jon said. He closed the screen and packed Raspin's HOLO safely with his own.

James had given him the stolen device before ritualistically burning his BZ clothes.

Rather than wait until they were back in camp though, Jon had opened it and found a treasure trove of information. He proceeded to spend most of the packing time pouring through the data packets while copying and transferring everything to a separate blank HOLO emitter he carried for just such an occasion. Or at least that's what he'd said, and James believed him. Who else but Jon would carry around a blank, completely unconnected HOLO to copy data onto?

James was happy to be shouldering the extra burden of packing so Jon could work on the HOLO, but Rich and Kevin weren't as understanding. They watched their techy flip between his screens with mounting frustration while they sweated. The fact that a four-hour hike back to town through dense rainforest lay ahead did not help. Jon had not noticed.

"You done with that shit yet?" Rich asked in a haughty voice.

"Oh, please. You'd do the same if you could," Jon replied with a snobbish grin. He walked away with his packs fastened on his back, following Deck and Cristina through the freshly cut trail.

"I'm gonna fuckin' trip him when we cross the streams," Rich whispered to Kevin.

"I'll help," Kevin replied.

James grinned and walked behind them. He hadn't realized how much he missed this.

They hiked for hours in the humid jungle air, not pausing for anything. The team was focused on their mission to leave. This job was complete. Getting the people of Río Negro to safety was their objective now. James sensed they were close and wiped a band of sweat from his forehead.

Salt stung his eyes and blurred his vision as he stepped over a log and ran into Kevin's back.

"Again," he said, shaking his head to clear his eyesight. "You have to give some warning when you stop."

"Hey, not my fault. Jon and Deck gave the signal to stop."

"That's weird."

James made his way to the front. Clint, Jon, and Deck huddled around a HOLO. Their brows were identical, furrowed in deep concentration as they watched the screen.

"What's up?" Stacie asked over his shoulder.

"No clue. I just got here," James replied, shrugging. "Deck, what's going on?"

"It's our cameras. Something's off."

A familiar stone formed in James's stomach.

"What do you mean?" Stacie asked, concerned.

"The cameras, they're not live. They're on a loop," Jon spoke up, pointing at the screen, "I've been checking them the entire walk and that bird gave it away. At first, I thought I was imagining things or it was a different bird, but then I looked closer. The bird hops right, hops left, stops, then does it again five minutes later."

James watched the HOLO as the bird did exactly as Jon described. It stood still on the branch while Jon sped the video forward five minutes and the bird repeated its dance. What was happening?

"Someone hacked our cameras."

"Can you get us a live look?" James asked, his mind spinning into battle mode.

"Give me a few minutes."

"Hurry. Everybody, get your gear together. This could be the BZ. Could be the Federation or something else entirely, but whatever it is, we've got a problem," James said. He took the pack off his shoulders and accepted a rifle from Deck. An unspoken understanding circled the team and while Jon took control back from their hackers' the team readied themselves.

James's stomach was tight. This couldn't be the BZ. They had already left, right? Who else could be causing them problems? Who else could take their camp?

"Done."

Jon flipped around his HOLO screen and showed a split image of four snipers sitting in their camp's trees.

Jon zoomed in on one of the camouflaged marksmen. James was relieved to see it was not the BZ, but it wasn't Federation either. There were no discernible markings on the soldier.

"It's fucking JC," Stacie growled. "He must have figured we'd be coming back after the attack."

"So he decided to spring a trap when we returned. What an asshole," Deck muttered under his breath.

"You think he took hostages?" Bob asked, checking the contents of his med kit.

"Assume yes. Deck, how far until we can take out those snipers?" asked James.

"About a mile."

"You all know the drill. Deck, Kevin, Bob you're with me. Stacie leads Kyle, Jon, and Clint. Cristina, Rich we'll need you two after we clear the area so pull together every First Aid thing you can find. Everyone ready?"

The faces staring back at him didn't flinch.

"Move."

CHAPTER 26

Vegetation hid their approach.

James scanned the tree line through the gaps between leafy branches and mossy tree trunks. The fading sun illuminated the team walking a yard apart, their weapons at the ready. James looked at Jon who kept one eye on his HOLO monitor.

"Jon, how much farther?" he asked.

"Another hundred yards, then we can set up counter snipers."

"Hold up, everyone," James said, putting a hand in the air. The team crowded around him, their faces reflecting sheens of sweat. "Deck and Bob, when we hit a hundred yards, I want you two in the canopy. Kevin, we'll make our way straight at them. Stay low."

Stacie chimed in directing her charges, "Kyle and I'll split left. Clint, Jon, you two have the right flank. We'll come at them in a pincer if we have to."

"Sounds good. Let's move."

The team broke. They thought as one, seamless, automatic, and connected from countless hours of practice.

James and Kevin kept to the ground and moved with precision through the undergrowth. Damp soil and lengthening shadows rendered them invisible. James looked behind and found Deck peering through his tactical binoculars in his sniper nest.

Deck signed:

Bob to my right; eyes on target; stay there.

James glanced at Kevin who bobbed his head assuring James he had received the same message.

They waited for a signal.

A crash sounded from the camp, echoed by two more. He waited for the last to fall but heard nothing.

He glanced at the trees and Deck signaled peering down his rifle:

Three down; fourth took off.

"Shit," Kevin muttered, bringing his rifle scope to his eye and standing to his full height.

James held his breath.

Kevin's finger twitched three times.

"Got him."

Wind exited James's lungs in a rush. *Thank God*, he thought, and gave Deck a thumbs-up.

James followed Kevin's trail through the dense greenery. Only after crossing the camp's threshold, he realized it would have been smart to check for booby traps. *Got lucky, I guess*, he thought, inspecting the ground.

He dipped under the vines and saw the soldier Kevin had shot lying face down with his arms splayed at awkward angles.

The man wore semi-camouflaged clothing, a simple pair of dark pants, and a ripped faded green t-shirt. Blood blossomed from the puncture wounds to the heart inflicted by Kevin's bullet. James turned him over with a toe wondering why Juan Carlos would send such an unprepared soldier to do this job while providing no way to communicate with the compound.

What the hell is going on? he thought, shaking his head while he looked to see if he recognized the man. He got no clues from the gaping blank eyes and stubble on his chin. James walked away, leaving the limp body for the jungle to recycle.

He met Stacie carrying the key to the armory.

"Never found this. Couldn't have been here long," Stacie said, inserting the key into the slot. The door swung open releasing a rush of stale air.

"Glad they didn't," Jon said, flipping up his HOLO screen and displaying a map of the town.

Kevin held the doors open and Stacie stepped in. She handed parcels of varying sizes to Clint for further distribution as Bob and Deck entered the camp.

"That's my bad, guys. I had him. He got behind that goddamn tree line too fast," Deck said, shaking his head. "Should have been the first one I took out."

"No sweat. Kevin took care of it," James said, accepting a silencer from Clint. "Finish getting your gear people then we'll take a look at the map. Jon?" James glanced at their tech expert who held up a finger.

"About done here." He swiped his finger across the screen and a 3D image of the town spun up in the middle of the team.

"What's our route?" Kevin asked. His newly donned suit rendered him almost indistinguishable from the foliage.

"They'll be expecting a battle, but I doubt they want one," James said, pondering the words as he spoke and gazing at the map. "They want to take us out quickly. We're not part of their plan and could unravel everything for JC. We also know there are about thirty guys in town."

"Twenty-six now," Deck said. "Thanks to this fella." He emphasized his words, slapping Kevin on the shoulder.

"Jon, anyone at the school?"

"Nada. These were the four left outside of town on the cameras I have. JC's expecting us."

"Right. If we had time, we could come up with a detailed approach. Since we don't, we keep things quiet for as long as we can. Pick off as many soldiers as possible and when they return fire go full-on assault. Clint, do we have those .50 cals on the Jeep's roofs?"

"Sorry, took 'em off for the trip," Clint said shaking his head.

"No worries. It was a long shot. In that case, Kevin, we'll need you to bring a light machine gun to act as a base of fire." James reached over Jon's shoulder to the HOLO display, lowering it to the ground and spinning it so the compound was facing forward while they looked at it from above. The team crowded around and listened in silence as James mapped out his plan. "Stacie and Kyle, float by the school and post up by Selma and Jose's house. Make sure they're okay and meet us at the compound.

"Deck, you, Clint, and Bob need to get over the walls on the right." James pointed at the entrance to town. "You'll have to cross the road, but I think you can manage.

"Jon, Kevin, and I will go through on the far side of town here." James pulled the map to the left showing streets and houses snaking their way to the concrete walls of the compound. "I'm sure that area is heavily protected, but we'll make some noise to distract them. Should give you three enough time to move in on the right side of the compound and give you two," he said, nodding at Kyle and Stacie, "a chance to secure our friends."

"We're on it, man," Kyle said, his leg pulled into a stretch.

"Deck, once you three are inside, take the walls and clear the courtyard. I have no idea what's back there, but if you move quietly, you should have few problems. When you're done, open the garage. We'll meet you there. Who has the earbuds?"

"Right here, boss," Clint said, tossing him one.

"Good. Keep your channels open, everyone. We're working on three fronts, so if you run into trouble speak up. Got it?"

Nodding heads greeted his statement.

"Jon, can we access any live cameras in town?"

"Nope. Didn't want to spy on our neighbors and all that."

"Fair. Guess we're entering blind. Assume the place is armed to the teeth and keep an eye out for booby traps. We move fast and take them out with all manner of force. Any questions?"

Another show of determined faces met his gaze.

"Good. Let's get this over with."

James donned a headset and heard the click in his ear as it turned on.

"Testing, testing," Deck said. "Everyone heard that?"

"Got it," Stacie said turning to address James. "See you on the other side."

She led Kyle through the brush. Her head floated above the leaves as it disappeared into the sea of overgrown flora.

"Same here," Deck said. He melted into the vegetation headed in the direction of town trailed by Clint and Bob.

"Then there were three," Kevin said. He slung a rifle over his shoulder and lifted a light machine gun off the ground.

"Come on, I'll lead," Jon said. James and Kevin followed him into the brush.

The golden rays, so prevalent when they had approached camp, were absent as they hiked towards the town. The sounds of animals usually at a fever pitch in the early evening were nonexistent. It was as if the violence of the last two days had sent nature into a state of shock.

James reviewed the situation as they walked. JC had thirty soldiers defending the town. *Twenty-six*, he thought, correcting himself.

James didn't know what weapons Juan Carlos's militia kept in their compound, but regardless they had the advantage. Trained militia defending from a place of strength, nestled amongst a sea of friendlies. Jon's hand interrupted the thoughts spinning around in his head. The dull yellow glow from the streetlamps interrupted the darkness, casting mottled light across Jon's face. James turned left taking the lead around the corner of town. He stepped over one of the streams that snaked through the forest and stopped holding a hand in the air. Jon and Kevin settled in the forest on either side of him. Their shallow breaths told James they too wrangled the nerves tumbling through their guts.

The calming aura of the town had been replaced. A palpable energy flowed like that of a crowd watching a tightrope walker. Unsettled and uneasy.

James glanced in the direction of the other team members' positions and hoped they were in place.

Jon eased over to him and whispered in his ear, "On your mark."

The sweet-smelling night air floated in the darkness. The world stopped and James was alone sitting in a rainforest.

He lifted his eye to his rifle scope and examined their target.

He had been right. The streets were heavily guarded, even this far out on the edge of town.

Soldiers milled about with rifles. Their movements were jilted and stiff.

Jumpy group, James thought. Checking the rest of their path, James lifted his scope above the tops of the aluminum roofs and focused on the compound. Silhouettes of further militia members walked the walls' ramparts and scanned the aluminum rooftops.

There are a lot more than thirty out there, James thought, counting at least thirty ground troops covering the entrances to town. Where did they get all these people?

His mind spun. Was this the BZ? Where did they come from? What was JC up to?

Realization trickled through his mind as the picture cleared. Nervous soldiers, four snipers at the camp, hastily thrown together uniforms, no comms equipment, no booby traps. JC wanted this. He hadn't stopped the people from leaving. He had created an army.

James gritted his teeth. His team was walking into a bloodbath. Juan Carlos intended for them to cut through the townspeople.

"What an asshole," James muttered under his breath.

He waved for Jon and Kevin to get a look at the town while he contacted the rest of the team.

"Juan Carlos is using locals as his new army."

"I was wondering where all these new recruits came from. What do you want to do?" Deck responded.

James was stuck. He had never intended to kill people who had no real choice in all this. He needed to find Selma, Paola, Layla, and everyone else who wanted to leave. What could he do?

"Stacie, any eyes on our people?"

"Negative. The plaza's pretty busy though. Looks like JC's pros. Wait—"

Shots erupted. The heads of the newly recruited soldiers in the streets whipped around to the jarring ricochet of bullets in the distance.

"Stacie, Kyle!"

James waited. *What happened there?*

"Deck, can you see them?"

"Sending Clint to help."

"I'm on it."

James's eyes searched the moonlit town full of amateur soldiers reacting to the bursts of gunfire echoing through the thin streets. They stumbled in the darkness, disoriented and uncertain, bumping into one another and following conflicting orders. James was caught in a blur of confusion, anger, and fear.

"Jon, why can't we get in touch with Kyle and Stacie?" James asked over his shoulder.

"No clue," Jon whispered back. "JC could have a comms jammer set up in front of the compound, but we won't know unless I take out my HOLO and I can't do that here."

Multiple shots rang out from Stacie and Kyle's position while explosions became more frequent by the second.

Deck's voice came over the headset. "James, you gotta make a call."

"Go, now."

"Roger."

James held his breath and shoved down the wave of nausea rippling through his stomach.

He picked his shot and held his breath.

James fired. The head of his target whipped back as did the one next to him. James moved towards the town as Kevin's light machine gun roared to life.

Jon and James's silenced rifles picked off men in quick succession while Kevin's constant round of bullets kept any chance of a counterattack at bay. James focused forward, trying not to think about Stacie and Kyle's radio silence.

Confused soldiers filled the path to the compound standing at the wrong time or moving with indecision. James stifled the mounting guilt as he carved his way through town. His focus was on his team and his friends, the people who had become his family over the past year. He clenched his jaw and continued until they reached their destination.

Jon and Kevin stopped moving and posted against a concrete barrier. They had made it to the wall of the compound.

He motioned for them to hang in the shadow of the fortifications.

The three of them stood panting, less from exhaustion than adrenaline, while they reloaded.

James's mind swam with an urgent fear he had not experienced during other battles. What was happening with Kyle and Stacie? He wanted to radio them but needed to wait for Deck and Bob. Until then all he could do was count on the firefight raging in front of the compound to provide him a small piece of hope that they were alive.

He glanced at the top of the wall. No one there. What was taking so long? Deck should have been there by now. They needed to go.

He tapped Kevin's chest and signed:

Door breach.

Kevin nodded in response and pointed at the pack slung over his shoulder. James gave him a thumbs-up, and Kevin swept over to the aluminum sheathed entrance. James counted under his breath as he waited for Kevin to finish his work when he heard a gurgle from above.

He leaned out from the shadows and jumped back as a soldier's body dropped inches from his face, landing with a *thud*.

He glanced up at the ramparts and saw a wave from a nearly invisible arm.

Within seconds the garage door creaked open, and Deck's face popped into view.

"Never fear, Deck's right here," he said with a wink.

"Took long enough," James replied with a grumble.

"I took the right amount of time. There were like thirty guys inside this goddamn place, and you said do it quietly."

"Yeah, yeah. Let me in," James said, pushing him aside and rolling under the low opening.

"This is the last time I secure a whole compound for you. Ungrateful," Deck muttered, pulling James to his feet.

"You're right. Good work," James said, relenting.

"Thank you. Now let's find this motherfucker," Deck said, turning towards the mansion.

"You see how Clint, Stacie, and Kyle are doing?"

"No, but judging by the scene in here they'll be fine. Let's finish the job," Deck replied, his eyes scanning around the corner.

Deck was right. Their job was to clear out the compound, find Juan Carlos and any of the townspeople he had taken hostage. A pang of anxiety washed over James as he thought of Layla and Paola trapped somewhere. The image steeled a sense of resolve and fury within him.

"Kevin, switch out for the silencer. You can leave the machine gun here. Everyone, follow my lead. We clear anyone remaining in the courtyard and make our approach to the house."

James took off without looking to see the reactions on his team's faces.

Deck had made a good point. The grounds were littered with bodies. Some had fallen from the walls and others had pulled themselves back inside from the front to die on the manicured grass. Moonlight reflected in flickering pools of blood. It was as if he was staring at dozens of glistening ponds that had sprouted at random across the grassy floor. He suppressed his sudden revulsion at the scene.

Guess the team out front took care of a lot more than we knew, James thought, listening for the gunfire echoing intermittently over the walls.

Deck broke in front and walked to a body propped against the compound's front wall.

Grasping it from behind, he dragged the corpse across the ground towards James and the team.

What the hell is he doing? James wondered when he noticed the soldier's hand twitch as he tried to shake out of Deck's grip.

Deck put the man down when he reached the rest of the team.

"Diga."

James recognized him as one of the pros in JC's employ. Despite the man's training and experience, his eyes were terror-stricken as blood drained around a piece of shrapnel lodged in his neck.

"Por fa, ayudame."

James crouched to look him in the eye. "Primero hable, entonces podemos ayudar."

The man searched the faces around him for some sort of mercy, but the grim stares that greeted him destroyed any hope in his eyes.

"Roof."

James nodded at Bob. "Give him some gauze."

James walked away followed by Deck. He was about to enter the front door when a silhouette shifted in the dark interior. The glass door shattered, and James dove out of the way pulling Deck to the ground.

Bullets flew overhead until the unmistakable *chink* of a jammed rifle echoed down the hall. James popped up in a heartbeat and ran after the shadow.

He twisted and turned through the dark mansion following the labored, panicked breathing of the man he knew was Juan Carlos.

"Pare! Stop!" he shouted, but to no avail, as he heard a door swing shut with a *slam*. He approached the heavy wood slab testing the handle, locked.

James drew his side arm and shot the bolt. He sprinted up the thin staircase on the other side when an echoing shot rang out. Searing pain engulfed his arm. Blood flowed through a hole in the fabric of the suit covering his shoulder.

Goddammit, he thought gritting his teeth through the pain and continuing up the stairs. He made it to the top and checked both hallways. He held his breath, listening to his heartbeat, waiting for JC to make a move.

The pain increased in the darkness grinding through his nervous system and taking over his thoughts. Hearing a scratch down the hall James didn't hesitate. He let loose a salvo of shots that were met with a grunt and a crash of glass.

James walked steadily to the end of the hall and found Juan Carlos crawling on his hands and knees with a trail of liquid staining the floor in his wake.

"Don't move, Juan," James ordered. He turned in a circle and yelled, "Bob? Where's Bob?!"

"Right here, man," Bob said, appearing at James's elbow.

"Check him and keep him alive. We need answers."

Bob nodded his head and flipped Juan Carlos over inspecting the wheezing man as he held a hand under his back. Standing up, he shook his head and returned to James.

"You hit his lung a few times. Without surgery, he's got an hour."

James's mind went blank. He hadn't been face-to-face with someone he had killed since the first life he took.

"Can he talk?" James asked, swallowing the confusing emotions swirling in his mind.

"Should be able to but go quick."

James patted Bob on the shoulder and walked to Juan Carlos. He grabbed the smaller man's lapel and hauled him to a sitting position against the wall. James crouched on his heels facing his enemy.

Juan Carlos's cocky demeanor and confident stance had changed. His face was covered in sweat, smeared streaks of blood and dirt with a tangle of wet curls plastered to his forehead. His eyes swung between lucidity and terror while his teeth clenched and unclenched in obvious pain.

"I hit your lung, Juan Carlos. You're going to die in under an hour. Before you do, I want you to tell me where the townspeople are."

"You have the supplies. Fix me," Juan Carlos replied, desperation in his voice.

"We can't. Tell me, where is everyone?" James's tone was cold. Juan Carlos's eyes twitched with fear whenever he looked at the team members circling James.

"Juan, it's over. Tell me where they are." Dread filled James's stomach as he watched the excuse for a man ponder his next words, staring at the ground.

"Juan."

Juan Carlos kept his eyes low and finally looked at James. His glassy pupils were losing life by the second.

"I never accept those who have wronged me, James," Juan Carlos whispered, and his hand darted to his pocket. Before James could react bullets popped behind James's head and Juan Carlos's limp body slid to the ground with three red spots adorning his chest.

"What did he mean? Those who have wronged me?" Deck asked, lowering his weapon in unison with Bob.

James's mind spun. Something was not right. Where was everyone in the town?

"Spread out. They can't be far."

James's heart was hammering as he stood and swayed.

"Easy, buddy. Let me look at that arm," Bob said, holding James upright.

"I'm fine. We need to find Paola."

"Jesus Christ!" Kevin exclaimed from the hallway. Bob slung James's arm over his shoulders and led him into another room. Juan Carlos's wife was draped across a loveseat, her throat slit. Blood covered her body, masking her torso in a sea of red.

"Is this what he meant?" Jon asked, walking to look at the body up close.

"That's self-inflicted," Bob said, leaning James against the door jamb and stepping up to examine the wound. "The knife's next to her hand and the cut trails off at the end."

"Who was he talking about?"

The fear seeping through James's veins took on more urgency. Where was everyone? What was going on with Stacie, Clint, and Kyle? He realized the gunshots had stopped and he turned to the stairs.

"Slow down, man. I need to look at the exit wound," Bob said, firmly holding James in place.

"The gunshots. They're done."

"Goddammit," Deck said, and James heard him rack a magazine in his rifle, "Kyle, Stacie, Clint! One of you fucking answer!" he yelled out.

The silence was maddening, and James turned to their techie.

"Jon get—"

"Already on it," Jon said, the HOLO's display illuminating his sweat covered face.

Every second that ticked by was unbearable. Bob cut the sleeve off James's arm and wrapped a bandage around the bleeding wound.

"We're up again. Jammers, like I thought."

Bob finished tying the knot on his arm and James turned towards the stairs. His head was light as he barked into the mic, "Clint, Stacie, Kyle! One of you, answer!"

His stomach twisted with anxiety as the earpieces crackled until finally an answer.

"We're okay. We're out here. We found… we found them." Clint's voice trailed at the end.

James scrambled down the stairs, his good arm clinging to Bob's neck while he ran to his friends.

"What's happening, Clint?" James spoke, the fear in his voice was clearer than the thoughts churning through his mind.

"James… we…. we were… I…" Clint's voice went silent and a rush of air came through the headphones.

"Clint? Clint!"

The earbuds went silent as James let go of Bob at the bottom of the stairs. He sprinted across the blood-soaked courtyard through the open door of the compound.

Dull yellow lights illuminated the plaza at random and a full moon lit up the scene casting shadows across the desolate surroundings. Kyle and Stacie sat on the ground hugging each other, and Clint stood with his hands on his hips staring into Selma and Jose's house.

James approached the three of them with his mind turning numb. He was in a dream. A nightmare. This was not real.

He approached Clint and touched him on the shoulder, but sensed what was coming.

When the rest of the team arrived, he turned and looked at the entrance to the house and saw the pool of blood trickling out from inside. His mind went blank.

He dropped to the ground and closed his eyes as hot tears rolled down his cheeks.

He watched Bob sprint to the door followed by Deck and Kevin, but they emerged moments later, pain etched on their faces.

James sat looking at the house. The once proud garden marred with bullet holes and trampled pepper stalks. The home that had welcomed them like family, ruined.

Bob stood with his hands on his hips staring into the house.

"No Paola or Layla in there."

Hope. That was all James needed.

"They're around somewhere. Let's start treating—" The words tumbled out of his mouth and his knees gave out.

Bob grabbed James under his shoulders and lowered him to the ground.

"You're doing nothing, James. We'll come get you the second we find anything, but you need to rest. You've lost a lot of blood and are still recovering from your escape from prison two days ago."

James's vision swam and he nodded, realizing an argument was pointless.

"For a minute or two…"

"Rest, buddy. We got this."

James closed his eyes, holding onto the sliver of hope that they would find Paola and Layla hiding safely as he pushed the deaths of his adopted grandparents from his mind.

CHAPTER 27

James awoke with hope burning the next morning. Layla and Paola were safe out there. He had to believe that. He had tried to dream away the violence of the night, wishing the scenes flashing through his nightmares were figments of his imagination, but the reality was undeniable.

James lay under a tree, half of its trunk missing from a grenade blast. He shook his head and grains of sandy dirt from the plaza's ground fell from his hair. His arm was sore, but the pain was bearable due to the heavy dose of clot-safe painkillers Bob had prescribed. Those would wear off soon though. He peeled back the tape and gauze to examine his injury. With a sense of detachment, he inspected the bullet wound and damaged skin poking at the bullet's exit and entrance wounds with curiosity. He replaced the bandage, taping it back over his skin.

The pockmarked walls of the compound rose in front of him. Reality settled in and sensations from the previous night flooded his brain. His memory elicited images of silhouettes tripping over themselves in the dark and firing sporadically as he raced through town mowing down his opposition. He recalled his uncertainty in hearing the intense gunfire with no answers from Kyle, Stacie, and Clint. Then JC's final words and Selma's bloody mausoleum of a home.

James shook his head to rid himself of the visions, but they were permanent fixtures.

A bank of mist floated above the treetops and James stood, balancing against the demolished wood. He sniffed the air, detecting a hint of wood smoke, and followed the charred scent to a house bordering the square.

He ducked through the concrete doorway where he found Kevin hard at work.

Broken eggshells were piled high in the kitchen sink while Kevin stirred their contents in a metal bowl assisted by one of the women from town. The oversized chef stopped his task to dip a finger in the batter from another bowl for a taste. Satisfied, he handed the eggs off to his sous chef and flipped on the stovetop's gas burners. The flames licked the bottom of a cast iron pan while Kevin turned his attention to the bread toasting on a flat skillet. James watched, impressed, until Kevin's head popped up for a second and nodded at James.

"Coffee's on the counter," he said, pointing at the collection of coffee makers brewing the dark liquid.

"Thanks," James said, filling a cup. Outside, people moved bodies in wheelbarrows covered in bed sheets. He turned away from the scene.

"Where is everyone?"

"Clint, Rich, and Jon are bringing a bunch of our solar panels here to town. Theirs were damaged in the fighting. Stacie, Deck, and Cristina are helping Bob attend to the injured. We wanted to give you and Kyle some more rest."

"Where's Kyle?"

"He was posted up by you in the plaza."

"Thanks," James said. "Do you need help…?" James asked, realizing he should offer to stay.

"Get out of here, man. How often do you get held hostage, escape while explosives are dropping all around you, and run a rescue mission in less than seventy-two hours? Enjoy the break for a minute. I'll get you when it's time to clean the dishes. Can't let you sit around and do nothing forever," Kevin replied with a grin.

"Shout if you need me," James said, pouring another cup of coffee, uncomfortable without a task.

"Leave."

James did so without another word, smiling at the woman who buttered pieces of bread as Kevin threw them to her from across the kitchen. She smiled in return before turning her attention back to the giant man in the small kitchen tossing hot bread in her direction.

James took a sip of the acrid liquid, enjoying the slight burn on the tip of his tongue. He searched the plaza until he spotted Kyle sitting on a bench at one of the stone tabletops. His legs were stretched out in front of him, his fingers gripping the soles of his feet.

"He's too flexible," James muttered, shaking his head.

James walked towards Kyle holding the steaming mugs in the air. "I come bearing gifts."

"Savior!" Kyle said, accepting the cup and blowing steam off the top. He took a sip and let out a sigh. "I never thought I'd experience something like this again."

"You mean drinking coffee in the middle of a spent battlefield?"

"You know what I mean."

"Yeah, I do."

The two were quiet for a moment, relishing the thoughts of freedom shared between former prisoners.

"You see anyone else yet?" James asked, sitting on the opposite bench and resting an elbow on the table.

"Stacie stopped by to say good morning. This whole thing is fucked, man."

"How so?" James asked. He had his own thoughts about the situation. He suspected most of the town hated him right now for killing their family members, and rightfully so.

"Turns out we came at the right time."

"Oh?"

"Those amateurs JC hired weren't even from Río Negro."

"What?" The update caused James to sit up straight.

"They were hired guns he found around the countryside. His bodyguards were recruiting all over the place. Wasn't just the BZ they approached. Small farm owners and their workers could serve in his militia for a promise of future leniency or some bullshit. None of them knew what they were getting into either. JC was intent on keeping us out and killing anyone willing to follow us north. He had imprisoned a bunch of the men and boys in town to keep families in line. We already saw what he did with Selma and Jose."

James pushed the thought from his mind.

"Any word on Paola or Layla?"

"Nothing yet. A lot of the kids are missing, too, but Stacie's on it."

"I'm sure she is," James said, but the pit in his stomach continued to grow. *No news is good news*, he reasoned.

"We'll find 'em, man."

"I know," James said, wishing the horrible images of various possibilities circling through his brain would stop.

James glanced at the crews of men and women transporting bodies in wheelbarrows from the alleyways and streets. Now knowing more about the soldiers he had killed somewhat helped him rationalize his actions, but he was still haunted each time he thought about the shadowy figures dropping to the ground and the role he played in it. Dozens dead in a manner of minutes. He couldn't control the vivid scenes that flashed in front of his eyes.

Get a grip, he thought. He clenched and unclenched his fist. His fingernails made grooves in his palm and blood rushed into his fingertips upon release.

"Food's up, boys!" Kevin called from the front step of the house, distracting James from his tortured self-reflection.

"Let's eat," Kyle said. He swung his legs off the porch and jogged to the house where Kevin had set up a large table.

Five minutes later, James was seated with a plate of food. Kyle and Kevin sat hunkered on either side of him eating like it was their last meal on death row. James scarfed down his food with reckless abandon. It helped wash away the guilt pummeling his psyche. Taking a break from his meal, he glanced at the sky and saw a pattern of clouds skipping across the expansive blue backdrop.

"Hey, look who's up!" A hand clapped James's on the shoulder and he craned his neck around to see Clint's smiling face. The beefy mechanic did the same to Kyle sitting on the other side of the table.

"How you doing, man? Heard you're donating a few of our solar panels," James said, taking a break from shoveling food into his mouth.

Clint shrugged. "Figure we won't need 'em much longer, right?"

"Sure," James agreed, realizing that their time here was at an end. *What's next?* he thought for a second, refocusing. "Any word from Bob or the others?"

"Nothing yet. Saw Bob running around earlier though. He's a man possessed. He hasn't done anything but treat patients since last night."

"I'm sure," James replied, recalling the worry on Bob's face when he tried to get James to take a break.

Jon and Rich walked to the table with their plates piled high with eggs, flour cakes, beans, and toast.

"James, Kyle, glad you two are finally up," Jon said with a grin.

He sat with a clatter next to Clint while Rich took the space Kevin made for him on his bench.

Rich shook his head. "Don't listen to him, James. He tried to sleep in too, but I made his lazy ass get moving."

"I was up and at 'em."

"Sure you were," Rich replied, rolling his eyes.

James chuckled into his eggs and took another bite of food. He would have to deal with last night's horror and the pure sadness eventually, but for the moment he was happy to sit with his friends eating breakfast.

They hung at the table, talking about preparations they wanted to make for those staying behind. That evolved into the logistics of preparing to travel with all the people who wanted to join them. Clint was explaining the finer mechanics of setting up long-term solar options when Cristina walked up to the table.

"Hey, guys." Cristina sounded depleted. Her eyes were ringed with exhaustion, and her bouncy hair was tied back in a tight ponytail exposing a sharp widow's peak. Her sleeves were rolled up to the elbows and her hands had been scrubbed raw. *She's been busy*, James thought, preparing for an update.

"Hey, Cristina. Get something to eat," Clint said, opening a space next to him on the bench.

"Later. Maybe later. Uhh… James. I… you…" Cristina's stumbled over her words.

"Where is she Cristina?" James knew.

"We found them in the school."

Hope. The one thing he had left evaporated. In an instant, James was on his feet.

The forest's path whipped by him in a frenzy as vines and leaves tore at his face. Finally, he saw the school around the bend.

A group of kids sat on the ground, shellshocked, staring straight ahead with glazed eyes, their faces covered in dried dirt, and leaves stuck in their hair. Deck and Stacie handed out plates of food.

They glanced at each other as James emerged from the trailhead.

Deck looked at James. His eyes were red, and James couldn't tell if he had been crying or was outright drained.

"Inside," Deck said.

James nodded and made his way through the open doorway to the cafeteria.

Bob was on his hands and knees attending to two bodies stretched out on the floor.

James walked over. Mariel and Rosa looked back at him, beaten, bruised, and grimacing in pain, but alive.

Rosa's swollen eyelids parted, and she smiled at James through cracked, blood stained lips.

Bob turned around, noticing the look on his patient's face.

"How're you feeling?" he asked James.

"Where is she?"

"James, I should really get a look at that arm of you-."

"Where is she, Bob?" James interrupted. He needed to know. He needed to get through this.

Bob sighed. "They're in back."

"They?" The pit in James's stomach grew and seeped outwards from his body in a cold sweat. Tremors ran in hot coils up and down his arms and his vision blurred. "Who's 'they,' Bob?" It was not a question.

Bob's head drooped to his chest, and he patted Rosa's shoulder. Tears ran from the corners of her eyes as she stared blankly at the ceiling.

"Come with me."

Bob walked to a large enclosure that had been partitioned off with bedsheets. He held them aside beckoning for James to follow.

James's feet were lead. Embers of fear and the agony of loss already ripped through his thoughts. His legs moved instinctively. When he reached the opening, the wind rushed out of his lungs and the earth fell from under him.

The wood table Rosa and Mariel had used to serve food from had been repurposed. On it lay two mounds covered with white sheets. James didn't need to pull back the covers to know the faces he would find. He walked to the table and put a hand on the cool wood. The surface was covered in cuts and scratches, worn from years of use and love. He stared at the bodies of the two people who mattered most to him in this town, lifeless and still.

"How?" James asked.

"Rosa was able to give me some of the details so far, but maybe we should go outside, James."

"Here's fine." He didn't want to move. He wanted to stay near them for as long as he could.

Bob sighed and leaned against the sink, pulling off his latex gloves and tossing them into the metal basin.

"When Juan Carlos took the town, the kids were all at school. The town must have flipped pretty fast because Rosa made it sound as if they heard gunfire and then, *poof*, the soldiers arrived. Paola made everyone hide in the woods, but she stayed. They took her inside and tortured her for information. Rosa didn't hear much, but from the sounds of it they were asking about us."

A pang of guilt jolted through James's gut.

"Anyway, when they finished with Paola, they searched the grounds. They were chopping through the brush with machetes looking for everyone when Layla made a run for it. Rosa says they shot her in the back while she was running through the jungle. The rest of the kids screamed and that was the end of it. They corralled them and beat Rosa and Mariel to within inches of their lives. The rest of the guards headed back to town. They must not have cared about keeping the kids because those snipers were the same ones guarding the school. After the soldiers left them, Rosa told the kids to run back into the woods where they hid. Stacie and Kyle never would have seen them passing by."

James's mind spun, but he did his best to grasp all the facts. "How are they?" He nodded in the direction of the women laying on the floor beyond the sheets.

"I think they'll be okay, but they're in rough shape right now."

James was numb to the world. Why did she run? What was she thinking? The anger and simmering hatred he felt towards the men who murdered that innocent girl were compounded by his feelings of overwhelming grief.

"Why'd she run?"

"Rosa and Mariel didn't know. They tried to get her to stop, but they said she kept saying, 'James will know.'"

His fists clenched and he bent over the table. His emotions from the last twenty-four hours crashed into him at once. The people he had meant to protect. The family who had adopted him as their own. All of them. Gone forever.

He was broken.

Chapter 28

The row of graves stretched the length of the buildings in the schoolyard. The size of the burial plots ranged from three feet to six feet, interspersed at random. Wooden crosses and jungle orchids adorned the dirt mounds with individual pieces decorating the grave heads.

James crouched next to one of the smaller mounds. His hands clenched and unclenched as he struggled to control his emotions. It had been like this for days. Unable to process or come to terms with anything that had happened here. The stain on the earth was forever etched with this graveyard and the violence it represented. Once a place of peace and love for the children was ruined for eternity.

He put a hand in his pocket and pulled out the woven turtle he had found on Layla's bedside table. Looking at it, his vision clouded and his mind filled with a torrent of emotions.

He gazed at the white, purple, and blue petals of the orchids on the tiny grave and placed his hand where her head would be.

"I hope you don't mind if I keep this," he whispered. "I think you'd like that."

He half expected the wind to shift or a bird to fly overhead telling him she loved the idea, but there was nothing. Just a memory of a hand slapping his and sprinting off to dinner.

"I'll see you around I guess," he said, patting the dirt one last time and standing.

A smattering of mourners walked the grounds holding flowers and plastic containers filled with water.

James stepped silently through the crowd making his way to the trail in the forest back to their camp.

The jungle was quiet. Even after four days, nature was cautious to deem the world safe again. *It may never be,* James thought, pained at the reality of the destroyed paradise.

He wound his way over tree trunks, around soldier ants collecting their meals, and under banana leaves blocking the path. When he reached the camp, he pulled back the vines and entered. It was deserted except for Stacie who sat alone with a HOLO emitter on her lap.

Her face was pinched in thought as she examined the display. From his angle, James could not make out the images and, judging by her confusion, neither could Stacie.

"Any luck?" he asked, sidling up to her chair.

"More questions, but at least all the folders are unlocked," she replied, her gaze focused on the screen. "I think it's blueprints of the ships though."

James was surprised. That was a big break.

"The ships? Like *the* ships?"

"Yeah, *the* ships. There's also a ton on here about electromagnetic field manipulation and new fission power reactors. Raspin's HOLO had the key we needed to decrypt the rest of the data packet. If we can give this much information to the Federation," Stacie shook her head, "we may be set."

A glimmer of hope fluttered in James's stomach. *Something to hang onto*, he thought as his mind faintly connected this moment to one in the future where their plans worked.

"Hey, come take a look at this, you two." Kyle waved at them through the vines to the path out of the jungle.

They glanced at each other, and James felt the familiar stone in his stomach drop.

He dipped under the vines holding them aside for Stacie to make her way through. The team huddled around a HOLO floating against the edge of the loaded canvas-topped truck.

James's breath stopped when he saw the screen.

The cities of Los Angeles and San Diego were awash in flames. One of the ships he and Stacie had discussed sat miles off the coast and hundreds of the gunships they had defended against in Midway were cruising through the water. The scene switched and panic struck James's heart as he witnessed a line of transport ships miles long, already beached with hordes of BZ soldiers entering the cities, taking over the ruined infrastructure.

"Holy hell," Stacie whispered.

"That's not all," Jon said, and he flipped to another screen.

A file appeared at the top and James's eyes widened. "OPERATION DROP ZONE" was printed across the screen. It was a copy of the document Croyton had leaked to him admitting the Federation had orchestrated the attacks on Midway and the South for political reasons.

"The Federation's sinking. They ordered martial law, but cities all over the country are revolting. New Orleans, Chicago, Philly, Detroit, Kansas City, Jacksonville… the list goes on and on. They're disavowing the Federation and making pledges to form regional coalitions against the BlankZone. Meanwhile, the West Coast is under siege and two other ships have been spotted making their way farther up the coast. Evacuations of San Francisco and Portland along with every other major coastal city are underway.

"The Federation is defunct. The BlankZone is going to walk right in."

James's heart hammered. Was this real? Or could it be a fake video being pumped over the airwaves by the BlankZone? A sick vision of what they wanted. He could not believe it, but in a strange way, he understood it. The Federation and the

BlankZone wanted the same things—power and strength through war and a controlled population. The Federation had manipulated its people one too many times and now the kingdom was crashing to the ground. The hegemony it held, the absolute control it had seized all those years ago and squandered by leaders who abused it for selfish purposes.

He thought back to President Braxton. How flippantly he had behaved when guarded by the black suits flanking his every move. It was always arrogant men who destroyed the world. Rage and determination crystallized in James's brain.

The people in the Federation did not deserve this. Nor did those living in the BlankZone. Leaders like Juan Carlos, Braxton, and Raspin decided the fates of their countries or communities without consideration for the people living in them. Abusing the strength and power they were given and taking more regardless of how many millions died in the process.

James turned from the screen and walked back through the vines to the camp.

He needed to think. Clear his head and get away from everything for a moment.

The fridge was plugged into one of the last solar panels in camp. The rest had been moved to town for those staying in Río Negro.

He opened the door and took out a bottle of cold water.

When he stood back up, Deck was leaning against the side of the fridge. Startled, James jumped at the sight of him.

"I swear to God I'm putting a tracker on you," James said, grinning and shaking his head.

"Do it. It'll be fun trying to beat Jon's tech." Deck winked. He opened the fridge and pulled out a bottle for himself. "Want to walk to town?"

"You bet."

The two left on a side route avoiding the ongoing burials, mourning, funerals, and sadness that hung over the graveyard nestled in the jungle. When they passed a line of people carrying a casket, James and Deck stepped off the path.

Their faces remained passive as the group moved swiftly by, nodding their thanks before disappearing beyond the bend in the trail.

Deck made sure they were out of sight as he motioned for James to keep walking.

"I hate this shit," Deck said, shaking his head.

"Me too," James replied, ducking under an overgrown banana leaf blocking the trail, "The problem is there will be no victors here to tell the story in the future. We all lost."

"Ain't that the truth."

After what seemed like thirty seconds, James and Deck were walking over the bridge and under the lights announcing the entrance to town.

The trees still standing in the plaza were clinging to life. Charred marks showed where explosives had landed nearby during the firefight. James glanced at the trunk he had slept next to after the battle, its side torn out from a grenade. What used to be an oasis of nature in the middle of town was now a shocking reminder of the violence everyone had endured.

"They're troopers, huh?" Deck said, nodding at Rosa and Mariel organizing the children's cargo into the vans headed north.

The two women were directing the children and some adults in last minute packing activities. The scene was a jumble of confusion, but the steady demeanor of the two women held the process together with practiced ease. Rosa hobbled on her crutch calmly pointing at the next items the children would need to pack. Meanwhile, Mariel, her arm in a sling and white linen bandages on the back of her head assisted in picking out the items they would need from the houses.

"They really are. We'll need to help them out a lot on the road."

"No shit. Speaking of the road, what do you know about leading thirty kids and over a hundred adults through half a continent?"

"Fair point."

They waved at the women who returned their hellos with quick gestures as they continued to chatter in Spanish with the children in the maelstrom of packing. James smiled. He was happy they'd be along for the ride.

Deck and James continued their walk, winding along the streets in no particular direction. James enjoyed the exercise knowing this would be the last time for a while they would be able to stroll aimlessly with any safety. Soon, they would have to watch their every step. If the Federation devolved even more, it might not be the BlankZone they had to worry about.

Can't dwell on what you can't change, James thought, forcing his brain to drop it. There had been enough negativity over the last couple of days and he needed to focus on things he could control. At least that's what Bob told him.

The town ended in the deep thicket of brush at the place Jon, Kevin, and James had entered four nights ago. Flashbacks to flashing muzzles and bumbling soldiers flooded his senses. James gritted his teeth to bring himself back to the present. He looked past the greenery to the point where the river came into town. At other points along its path, the water raged with a force that could break a person's bones. When it passed Río Negro, however, it was lazy, almost asleep, curling around the edges of town in a sweeping motion. Its banks were deep but gentle. Centuries of erosion balanced the speed and direction of the clear liquid as it lent both its name and calming presence to the settlement.

Deck paused, looking up and James stopped, following his gaze.

A flurry of macaws graced the branches of a tree. Their colors swirled in a brilliant pattern of greens, reds, blues, and yellows. Their chatter was almost deafening.

"It's wild, isn't it? Two years ago we started out and now look where we are. Made it through two of the biggest battles of the war, traveled thousands of miles across a damn continent, met some awesome people, grew our family, all of this." Deck took a deep breath. "It's remarkable but…"

"But…?" James asked, looking at his friend.

"But was it worth it?" Deck asked, walking to the edge of the water snaking its way around the trees.

James followed him and posted up on an old stump while Deck jumped to the river's sloping beach. He picked up a stone and threw it in the water. The pebble disappeared with a plop and fell to the sandy bottom. James wondered where and when the pebble might resurface. What would the world look like when it eventually broke into a thousand tiny pieces of sand? He was lost in thoughts of the future when Deck's voice brought him back to the present.

"Cristina tells me how amazing this place was. How it healed her, saved her life, and made her feel like she was worth something. She insists that everything we did was worth it, but I… I don't know."

"Yeah, like if we never came here?"

"Exactly! Would it have happened at all? I dunno. Sometimes I think Brandt made the right move. Go out with the enemy. One big bang and you win."

James nodded. "Problem is he didn't win."

"In a way he did."

The two were silent for a moment, reflecting on their old commander. James admired Brandt's bravery and dedication, his willingness to leave his family for a greater good, and setting in motion a series of events that no one could have expected. James knew he did not have that in him and was surprised to hear his friend so reverent of Brandt's final decision.

Deck pulled out a crumpled cigarette and lit it, letting the smoke fly away over the gentle water. He handed it to James.

"Don't you start planning that kinda stunt, Deck," James said, taking a pull and handing it back.

"Ahh, don't worry. Cristina'd kill me before I tried it," Deck said, winking at him. "Besides, who would keep an eye on you? Someone needs to tell you to get out of your own head sometimes."

"I'll get through it," James said, trying to focus on the world around him rather than look his friend in the eye. He clenched and unclenched his fist unconsciously before noticing it and putting a hand in his pocket.

"You made the right call, James. If we hadn't moved when we did that night, who knows what would have happened? Those kids would be a part of Juan Carlos's regime, dead, or in some sort of sick servitude. We had to move."

"Yeah."

"No. Not yeah. This is your job. You're the one who got it, and it sucks, I know, but you made the right decision."

James glanced at his friend whose eyes bore a hole right through him. He knew Deck was right, but he couldn't forget those soldiers fumbling to hold their rifles straight, bodies falling in the shadows, marking the path to the compound. Some of the kids he killed were no more than sixteen, following the orders of a man who promised them riches and freedom he would never deliver. He worried he would become a man who handled moments like those without a problem. Men who look evil in the eye and nod in recognition. If James could go back and find a way to avoid amateur soldiers slipping in the blood of their friends, he would. There was never taking back something like that, but he tried to rationalize it all. Those men had witnessed Juan Carlos murder his friends and his soldiers kill a young girl.

They may not have all been guilty of the death, but they were responsible for it in some way.

"It'll take some time."

"It should. If it didn't you'd be the nutbag who tried to take over a town, right?"

James nodded.

"Good. Now I have a question for you."

James's eyebrows arched.

"Why do you think Croyton never told us about the Sentinels? He had the HOLOs, right? Why not come out and tell us what the Sentinels were? Hell, Stacie said the drive looks like it has tomes on the tech and how to neutralize the threat. Or at least lessen it."

Deck never ceased to impress James. That thought hadn't occurred to him, but it was a good question.

"I don't know, but I'm guessing you have a theory."

"I think Croyton knows more about the BlankZone than anyone." Deck's thoughts were prepped and ready. "I think Croyton told us all he could, anticipating we would want more. I think that he orchestrated that cargo drop we stumbled upon and the evacuation. He meant for us to find that data packet. He expected us to make it to the edge of the BZ and come away with something. I think that motherfucker planned the whole goddamn thing."

Deck's eye twinkled in the afternoon sunlight and James looked at his friend with slow realization. Maybe Deck was right. Maybe Croyton had predicted all this would happen. Maybe it had to happen so the team would crawl back to the Federation and hand deliver the dagger that would destroy the BZ. Maybe Croyton knew they needed to find a new edge of darkness to become the warriors he required. The ones who would deliver his final blow.

"Too bad he won't get the end of his plan," James said, throwing a pebble into the stream.

"True, but it'd be pretty remarkable if that was the case. The plan still on?"

"You bet. After what's happened to the Federation, it makes more and more sense. Do you know how many Río Negros there will be? How many small-time assholes will try to take over their districts, horde food, supplies, weapons, and even water? We're the only people suited to fight that. We've seen a lot and experienced the war from different sides, Deck. We know the dangers of a power vacuum. It's our job to look after the people."

"I like the move. We ever going back to the Federation? You know, fight at the macro level and all that?"

James shrugged. "We're better used elsewhere. When the dust settles, we'll see. One day it might be worth taking a better look at those blueprints Stacie found."

"I like it. Stick to the shadows."

"That's the plan. Help people."

"Sounds too simple."

"Probably is." James sighed, and he reached out his hand to pull Deck up the bank. Deck offered him the end of the cigarette and James pulled on it one last time before stubbing it out and putting the butt in his pocket to throw out later.

The last thing this place needs is me tossing garbage everywhere, he thought.

"Come on, we've got a long trip."

"It's so nice here though," Deck whined. "It's cold there, and the government's under revolt, the land is in danger of being taken by the BZ, and it's *cold*."

"All that'll be here in a matter of weeks, too."

"It's warm though."

"Come on," James said over his shoulder. Deck walked behind grumbling about how he'd never eat another banana until he came back. "They're stupid up there."

When they arrived at camp, the team was throwing their personal belongings into the Jeeps. Clint ran around checking that the solar panels were connected correctly to the car batteries and Kevin was putting out the fire on the grill for the final time. The hulking chef poured a bucket of water over the coals sending steam billowing into the green treetops with a *hiss*.

"All packed for you man," Jon said as James went to check on his Jeep.

"Who's driving with me?"

"That'd be me, pal." Bob's hand slapped him on the shoulder as the medic threw his gear bag into the trunk. "Figured we'd let the couples drive together."

"They'll have fun with Deck," James said, sad to lose his driving partner, but happy to be with Bob. He could use a little rest and relaxation.

"All right, let's get this show on the road!" James yelled and the team nodded to him as one. "Stacie, Kyle, you two have point in the Hummer. Clint and Kevin follow them in the truck. Couples take third. Bob and I will finish the convoy. When we get to town, we'll place the vans in between and take off. Questions?"

The same silence that greeted James almost every time he asked that question welcomed him again.

"Let's head to town then, people."

"You want to drive?" Bob asked.

"Sure. I'm guessing you'll have more to do in town than I will."

"Got that right. These kids never change their damn wound dressings."

"Can't we do that at our first stop?"

"Sure, if you're okay taking a bunch of staph infections north with us," Bob replied, pulling a bag from the trunk and inspecting a glass vial in the sunlight.

"Fair enough. Can we try to move out from there within an hour?"

"Deal," Bob said as he tossed the bag on the floor in front of him and shut his door. Stacie honked the horn announcing her exit as she pulled away in the Hummer. The canvas topped truck did the same and James began to follow suit when he abruptly jumped out of his seat. Bob looked at him quizzically as James opened the trunk. His rucksack was on top of a pile of medical supplies. He rummaged in the side pocket until he found what he was looking for, the letter from his father and Layla's turtle, both there. He retied the pack and jumped back up front.

All the vehicles had exited the camp. Their tire tracks left deep impressions in the damp jungle soil.

James rolled down the window and looked around at the paradise they were leaving. Golden light burst randomly through the canopy while howler monkeys called in the distance and macaws cried out from the treetops.

James breathed in the dense, humid air letting it out of his lungs in a rush. He steeled himself. He hated leaving and wanted more than anything to live in this place for the rest of his life, happy and content with his friends. But that was not the lot he had pulled. He turned on the ignition, and the engine roared to life.

"Time to find out what's next."

Glossary

Asian Republic – otherwise known as the BlankZone (BZ). The part of the world East of Europe that stopped responding to any interaction with the rest of the world after the Melt.

Combat Suit – tactical uniform that is designed for use in battlefield situations. Multiple versions of combat suits exist with the newest versions containing highly elaborate camouflaging technology.

Emitter – a device used to support the display of a HOLO.

Federation of the Americas – the continental government organization comprised of every nation state in North and South America. Formed as a response to the Melt.

Forgotten World - an independent, pseudo-terrorist organization that is believed to have taken over the BlankZone.

HOLO – an acronym standing for Highly Operable Light Object. HOLOs have a wide range of capabilities and are used in telecommunications, visual representations, and have uses far beyond their current known abilities.

Ion Shield – defensive devices that utilize ionic charges to protect military units in the field.

The Melt – an event of unknown origin that separated the world and created a rift between the East and the West during a heightened period of global interaction.

Midway – newly formed city after the Melt that can be found along the East Coast of the Northern Federation in the Mid-Atlantic region.

Río Negro – town in the Southern Federation near the Blankzone border.

Roach – a small, automated video drone used for surveillance activities.

Sentinel – a defensive tool used by the BlankZone to protect its borders.

ACKNOWLEDGEMENTS

Writing a book is supposed to be the loneliest thing you can do. From sitting down at a computer, notepad, typewriter, or with a stack of napkins, a writer is supposed to be reclusive, almost vampiric in their pursuit. It's a solitary endeavor, or at least that's what I always imagined when I started my first book. I could not have been more wrong. For ten years I toiled away in that isolation trying to finish a book that was not headed anywhere and it was not until I finally started talking about it more that it came to fruition.

Nearly two years after its release I find myself going through that same process in (at least in my opinion) record setting pace. All I needed was people there to help me. From my publishing team to encouraging readers like yourselves (and even some very unencouraging readers), having people involved along the way is the best method to get this out of my head, onto paper, and into your heads to deal with.

My first thanks go to my editors and designers. My cover and graphics designer Daniel put together another awesome cover that encapsulated exactly what I wanted for the book and started us down a great path for the series. I love that he can take what I say and visually represent it with such creative precision, I'm so excited to continue working with him.

Same as the last time I got an incredible amount of feedback and assistance from my copy editor Hannah who took my work and shaped it into a place where everyone else could follow what I was trying to say. I cannot say enough about the job she did for me yet again. However, Hannah was not my only editor this time around. I have immense gratitude for my Mother. She was my first editor for this book. Her meticulous attention to detail and constant research on the right way to set up a story put this book into a place where it started to make sense. She started the same as I did when I wrote the first book, unsure of what to do and how to do it, and figured it out with a level of professionalism that I never expected in my three decades of being familiar with her.

The second group of people I want to thank are those who took place in our launch team activities and my marketing director, also known as my wife, Alexa. The people on the launch team were so great at both reading the book and posting their reviews all over Goodreads and Amazon. Those reviews are crucial to us getting the book out there and were a massive reason why I was able to push myself through the process of writing a second book. I cannot wait to work with more people in the future to help us get the word out!

Alexa, as always this is quite literally impossible to do without you involved. I do not have the patience or mind to deal with most things marketing related and count myself very lucky to be married to such a talented and supportive spouse who can help me work towards a dream. Thank you for everything.

Finally, I want to thank the readers from the first book. If you find yourself at the end of this book and are reading the acknowledgements wondering what the hell I'm talking about second book then you are in luck! There is another book that you can read right this second. In all seriousness, without people reading this, and without some of the incredibly kind and supportive comments I got both online and in-person I probably would not have wanted to keep writing. I write these stories not just because I want to add an extra few hours onto my work day after dinner, but because I want to tell these stories and I want them to connect with people. I am so excited to keep working through this series and hope that all of you continue on the journey with me.